The Hedge

The Hedge

Judy,
with great affection,
Anne McPherson

a novel by
Anne McPherson

Inanna poetry & fiction series

INANNA PUBLICATIONS AND EDUCATION INC.
TORONTO, CANADA

We gratefully acknowledge the support of the Canada Council for the Arts and the Ontario Arts Council for our publishing program.

We are also grateful for the support received from an Anonymous Fund at The Calgary Foundation.

Note from the publisher: Care has been taken to trace the ownership of copyright material used in this book. The author and the publisher welcome any information enabling them to rectify any references or credits in subsequent editions.

Cover artwork: Nella Marchesini, "Self-Portrait with Book," 1923-25. Private collection, Turin. Reprinted with permission.

Library and Archives Canada Cataloguing in Publication

McPherson, Anne, author
    The hedge / Anne McPherson.

(Inanna poetry and fiction series)
Issued in print and electronic formats.
ISBN 978-1-77133-092-3 (pbk.).— ISBN 978-1-77133-095-4 (pdf)

    I. Title. II. Series: Inanna poetry and fiction series

PS8625.P525H44 2013   C813'.6   C2013-905395-6
                                               C2013-905396-4

Printed and bound in Canada.

Inanna Publications and Education Inc.
210 Founders, York University, 4700 Keele Street, Toronto, on, Canada M3J 1P3
Telephone: (416) 736-5356 Fax: (416) 736-5765
Email: inanna.publications@inanna.ca   Website: www.inanna.ca

for Sarah
best woman

Contents

Much Madness is divinest Sense –
To a discerning Eye –
Much Sense – the starkest Madness –
'Tis the Majority
In this, as all, prevail –
Assent – and you are sane –
Demur – you're straightway dangerous –
And handled with a Chain –

—Emily Dickinson

mr Hopkins the Gouernor of Hartford vpon Conectecott, came to Boston, & brought his wife with him, (a godly younge woman & of speciall partes) who was fallne into a sadd infirmytye, the losse of her vnderstandinge & reason, which had been growinge vpon her diverse yeares, by occasion of her givinge her selfe wholly to readinge & writinge, & had written many bookes: her husbande beinge very lovinge & tender of her, was lothe to greive her, but he sawe his error when it was too late: for if she had attended her househould affaires, & suche thinges as belonge to women, & not gone out of her waye & callinge, to meddle in suche thinges as are proper for men, whose mindes are stronger &c: she had kept her wittes, & might have improved them vsefully & honorably in the place God had sett her. he brought her to Boston, & lefte her with her brother one mr Yale a merchant, to trye what means might be had heer for her. but no helpe could be had.

—*from* Governor John Winthrop's Journal, April 13, 1645

I
The Voyage Out, 1637

1.

WHOEVER SAID THAT IT WAS MADNESS to attempt an ocean crossing at the tag end of winter has never sailed on the *Hector*. She has been to Boston many times, and, like her namesake, she is used to fighting her way robustly through whatever onslaughts the ocean can devise. Before we left Portsmouth the master gathered us all together to assure us that we would come to no harm on his ship.

So far, there has been no hint of trouble from the great Atlantic. I have heard people say over and over that we are under the Lord's special providence. They repeat this like a refrain, as if they do not wholeheartedly believe it, that it most surely is his will that we go forth to plant this new colony in his name, and so, we will arrive safely. Inwardly, I think the hearts of these homeless travelers are quivering with anxiety. Still, even the most hardened sailors, whose religion is the sea, agree that this voyage is particularly well-favoured.

What slight uncertainty I feel comes in little prickly tremors blown in on the salty wind, which only add to the excitement of this great adventure. There is nothing to worry about today, however, with the sea as smooth as a slate, only a light wind ruffling its grey-green surface. I have been leaning against the ship's rail as I do every day that I can, trying to take in everything around me, the sights and sounds both old and astonishingly new. On this grey morning the deck is crowded with people. With the heavily clouded sky suggesting rain later in the day, we have all burst from our tight quarters to stretch our legs before being driven inside again. It is comical to see everyone swell their chests to swallow as much fresh air as they can, hoping to blow out the nasty infectious odours that have settled in lower decks, and are now nesting inside our bodies and saturating our clothing. Some of us have already been gripped by sicknesses and carried off. Last Tuesday an elderly woman of fifty died of consumption and was sent to her rest in the ocean. I watched the sailors sewing her body cautiously into a linen shroud with two sacks of lead shot at her feet to weigh the body down. We had a brief funeral, but still it gave me a peculiar feeling, as I imagined being tossed away like a heap of last winter's mouldy potatoes. I would hate to die at sea. Also, a child born prematurely to a sweet, delicate mother died a week after we set out. Rumour has it that the mother will probably be the next to go, despite all our fervent prayers to spare her.

I am standing on the after-deck, which is the preserve of the planters and their families, who have paid dearly for the privilege of being here. There is just room enough for us to exercise, to take short turns around the deck, and to allow the children a little space to run about playing a not very satisfactory version of blind man's buff. They are not so full of bounce as when we set out, poor dears. I hope no more get sick.

On the foredeck all the other passengers are gathered — herded together, you might say. They are the labourers, servants, artisans and farm workers—mostly young people headed to the colonies for profit or piety, or both. We have no need of slaves, thank goodness. Indentured servants will work harder, thinking about their eventual release. I suppose they are not bothered by the lack of room on their deck, as they are used to crowded tenements and streets back home. They may be thinking of all the living space they will have wherever they are going.

Even by stretching over the salt-scoured rail as far as I dare, I cannot see past the huge square-rigged sails to the foredeck, but I can hear plenty. How the water carries the sound! I had never thought about that before. The invisible people in the bow seem as near as the person standing beside me. I can hear babies crying, hungry and colicky. Occasionally, a burst of laughter floats back, or voices mingle together, but the sound dies away as quickly as it arises. What can there be to amuse them, I wonder: a tall story perhaps, or a silly mistake like someone falling over a rope and landing in a stranger's lap? It must not be much fun spending all this time stuffed like herring in a barrel. A slow sad tune drifts back, one I have heard many times before in Wales, here sung by an old man whose voice is cracked with age. It brings tears to my eyes, but I refuse to let them fall. I do not want reminders of what cannot be regained to spoil this voyage. Mostly though, all I can hear is the low constant murmur of voices speaking of everyday things in unaccented tones. I am going to try to remember it all, the ordinary as well as the peculiar. My journal will fill up quickly with all my new discoveries.

Right from the moment we left the harbour, I knew my whole life was about to change. To begin with, I have never set foot on a ship before. In my memory, I keep some little glimpses of a time long ago, when I was sitting in a boat being rowed by a big curly-haired man, my father I think, the boat smacking the waves, and I laughing as the spray hit my arms and legs like a shower in the sun. I remember the sound of the boat's hull grating on to the pebbled beach, and being scolded for jumping over the side too soon. I did not mind at all getting wet. You dried off quickly running along the warm sand with the breeze blowing in your face.

That is what children do, if they are lucky — give themselves up to the smiling elements. But on this voyage that by now shows no landmarks, no welcoming beach or protective bay, the elements are shifty, and have the reputation of being cruelly indifferent to human fate, an idea I would never have countenanced as a child. No matter that our Puritan leaders remind us that the frequent sea-borne tragedies are demonstrations of God's considerate plan, still it seems to the rest of us that it is the ocean, the winds and the skies that govern lives out here. Today's fair sailing might become tomorrow's tempestuous rout. As hard as I try to assent to what the ministers are saying, there is that huge implacable ocean in front of me that I know will have its own way. Does it contend with God? Or does God allow it to follow its own nature? These are impertinent questions I do not dare ask aloud. Despite my belief that the elements do not care about humans (even if God should care about them), at times the dreamer in me thinks they are speaking to me. It is as though the mystery and the possibilities of this great adventure are being revealed in water and sky. The shiftiness and the cruelty? I do not think about that.

Who am I, and what will I become in this New World? If anyone asks, I can only say, with happy pride, "I am Anne Yale Hopkins, wife of Edward Hopkins, trader, and soon to be planter in Hartford upon Connecticut. Wherever that is," I would add, for I don't have the faintest idea about my destination. Edward tells me that the Connecticut is a long and stately river beside which the tiny new plantation of Hartford is nicely situated for farming and transport. It pleases him, both as planter and trader. About the colony itself he has no information. We have no friends there to send us letters, so apart from these skimpy facts, I know nothing. It will all be a great surprise.

There have been so many abrupt changes in my life, ever since I was a small child. Will this one, at the ripe age of twenty-two, be any better? It is bound to be! I should not be so naïve as to think the future will be spread out as merrily as a field of buttercups. It is going to be hard work adjusting to the colony, I am sure. I must expect some disappointments, some shocks perhaps, and I will certainly miss my old friends, especially my cousin Jane. Leaving everyone behind was a high price to pay. But when I weigh it against the misery I felt so much of the time in London, and the grim prospect for the whole country, the departure was worth it. Standing here, now with a lusty breeze blowing, and the vast mystery of the ocean all around me, I have the feeling that the whole world is opening up for me at last. The empty horizon tells me that nothing in the future is predictable, nothing fixed forever by the circumstances of the past. I may shed anything I choose — bad memories, unhappy thoughts, mean people with strict rules of conduct — I may even get rid of my stays! What matters most is that I have Edward. Together we will make a fine beginning in this New England.

And it certainly is a beginning, for up until now I can hardly say that we have enjoyed the usual felicity of newlyweds. Although we have been married for a whole year, we have had little time to get to know each other's wishes and ways, with all the flurry and haste of preparing for our departure. Edward, who understands the political current well, made sure that all our plans were kept secret until the last possible minute, for fear that we would not be allowed to leave England. So neither of us was at ease until we were on board and saw the coastline disappear into the night.

I see him now, on the other side of the ship talking to one of the planters, and suddenly from the deep place inside me that is my treasure house of pure joy, my love pours out to him. I want to rush over and wrap my arms around him, but I hold back. That must wait. I can hardly believe that this handsomely formed man, with his gleaming black hair and smooth skin, who walks so straight and tall, is my husband. He is fifteen years older than I am, the oak to my — what shall I be? An aspen? A willow perhaps. I bend in the wind, but I do not break — at least I have not so far. Edward has the dignity and self-possession of the oak that no wind brings down. Who would think from his carefree manner now that he is taking two lives into his hands as we venture across an immense body of water into a land scarcely known to anyone except for some savages?

There is a mighty turbulence in the water not far from the ship, which makes me turn away from contemplating my husband, but not for long. I turn back quickly and call, "Edward, come and see! Here are whales!"

I can see the look of relief on his face, as he extricates himself from what must be a tedious conversation, and walks to me with a light spring in his step, his arms swinging easily. I say, "Look, they are breathing water! Have you ever seen such a thing in your life?"

He peers over the rail. "I have seen a whale before, but never a school like this. How many do you see? I count five."

"At least five. Oh, I think I see another. Look at them all spouting together like a palace fountain! Do you think they are singing a melody that we can't hear?"

Edward shakes his head, amused. "What an imagination you have! These are only giant swimming fish. Isn't it strange enough just to see them as they are?"

I say, "You're right, but I wonder what Jonah learned about them when he was lodged inside the belly of the whale. The Bible doesn't say." I cannot take my eyes off these marvelous creatures.

"That's probably because it isn't important to the story. It was his repentance and his prayer to God that mattered." A sobering reply, too sober for me at that moment.

"Well, I would love to know more about them. If I get swallowed, will you be sure to rescue me?" The whales are swimming away from the ship now, their gray humps almost one with the waves. I reach for his hand.

Edward straightens up. "Anne, when you say things like that it sounds as if you are poking fun at Scripture for not answering your questions. I know you are just being merry, but it could be taken the wrong way if you were overheard. You should be careful."

He looks at me so gravely, I am surprised. "Don't worry so much, Edward. I'm really trying to behave like a proper married woman. It's just that sometimes I can't help seeing things differently." I link my arm through his, squeezing a little.

"Yes, well, perhaps I'm being too cautious. You remember how we had to guard our tongues in London for fear of informers. It's a hard habit to get rid of. Anyway," he reaches over to pat my hand fondly, "I married you because you are different. I didn't want to have an ordinary wife, and I certainly haven't got one."

"Do I annoy you sometimes with my silliness?"

"Of course not. You are my enchanting beloved wife. Ever since we married you have brought sunlight into my pedestrian life, and I know you will be even more of a comfort in the days ahead." The frown is gone, the wrinkles smoothed out. "Will you be describing the whales in your journal?"

"Yes, but I can leave out the part about Jonah, if you like."

"Perhaps you should, if you are intending to circulate your book. There are too many reformers who are much more severe than we are who would attack you for those comments, if they should get hold of a copy."

I am not easily admonished. "There you go, worrying again. I was only intending to send it to Jane as usual, and she will copy it and pass it along to our friends. We all think pretty much alike."

"Then of course, do as you wish," he says mildly, drawing his arm away reluctantly but firmly. "Now I must go back and finish my conversation with Mr. Cheever or he will think me rude. He's trying to instruct me in the best way to salt pork." His eyes are twinkling mischievously. As if he did not already know all about pork.

I laugh at this, and give him another squeeze as he turns away. These little gestures are new to him. He told me that his family had never been demonstrative, and so he is only slowly learning to accept having his hand stroked, or his arm squeezed in company. I tried once to kiss him on the street outside our London house, and was quickly rebuffed. Later, he mentioned gently that extreme public demonstrations of affection such as kissing were frowned upon by the saints, and that we would have to be more circumspect. I could see that it made him unhappy to tell me this. He loathes making me unhappy, and besides he is coming to enjoy it, I know. Now in private, that is quite another matter.

The whales are frolicking in the distance, tossing themselves in the air, capering like children after lessons. Someone on the foredeck has started to play on a pennywhistle, and for a few moments I think the whales are leaping to the tune. I start tapping my foot, and jigging from side to side, but my antics do not keep time with the whales'. Why should they be tamed by anyone, these great leviathans? They have their own music, I believe, despite what Edward says about my fanciful ideas.

2.

IF ANYONE HAD PREDICTED a few years ago that I would marry a rich gentleman merchant, I would have laughed outright—and cried inside. Living as I was in my stepfather's bleak house in London, I could not imagine ever being married at all, for anyone Mr. Eaton would consider suitable for me, I was sure I would have refused. Of all the men who had visited the house, including traders, bankers, advocates, and ministers, not one could have made me happy. I lumped them all together, these serious Puritans, as gloomy blackbirds, with eyes that darted about looking to fasten on sins, and beaks to mutter about guilt. The air of that house was dense with darkest piety. Even my mother had absorbed it like a heavy scent that you rubbed on to cover up worse odours around you.

The only people in the house who tried to evade this atmosphere were my two brothers and myself. Little Thomas was so cheerfully unaware of others' moods that he wandered through the household thinking his own young thoughts and keeping out of trouble. My older brother David was, and remains, the opposite, with his sharp intelligence, and a rousing temper (like mine), which he brought into play whenever he disapproved of something of consequence. He said to me one day, "I am determined to do well in business, so I can leave this house and go far, far away. I have had enough of our stepfather and his heavy-hearted kind."

"I don't blame you for wanting to go. If only it were possible for a girl to get away! It's so unfair that you can leave and I cannot."

How I hated that house and all the Eatons in it! I prayed: "Dear God, take me out of here. I will do anything, even suffer fools gladly, if only I can escape."

I told this to David, who said, "Don't make rash promises. The Lord might hold you to them, and then see what a pickle you'd be in." Still, I thought, could anything be worse than here?

When the names of certain burghers came up in conversation—one stolid, red-faced, perspiring old coot was mentioned over and over, with significant glances in my direction—I knew they were going to try and marry me off. I realized then what David meant about rash promises. So I changed my prayer to: "Dear God, I take back my former promise. If I do get away from this house, let it not be worse, wherever I go."

David tried to cheer me up, "Don't lose hope, Anne. I am always on the lookout for a good husband for you, because I know you can't bear it here either. I will find someone to please you. You might even fall in love with him," he teased.

"How ridiculous! You are making it even worse than it is, saying that. I don't even dream of a fine husband any more. It makes me too miserable."

That conversation took place three months before the day that David came into the house announcing that he wished to bring a friend of his to meet the family. "He is a merchant like yourself, stepfather, and very successful. He has been doing a lot of trading with the Bay Colony and the West Indies. I think you have many interests in common. May I invite him to dinner?"

So David brought him to meet us all. "Mr. Hopkins, my sister Anne."

"An honour, Mistress Yale."

I had heard of people being blinded by the striking presence of a stranger so that they could not turn their eyes away, that they then felt as though their heart would pound its way through their skin, that their voice got stuck in their throat, so they could not speak—well, that was the way it was when I first saw Edward.

Seated at the dining table I tried surreptitiously to watch his every move: how his fingers, long and firm, handled the cutlery; how he ate, soundlessly and without speaking through a mouthful as many do; the way he turned his fine head or his shoulders, smoothly, as a man comfortable with himself; how he bent easily to listen to my horrid step-grandmother, and then responded with courtesy to her nonsense.

In between all this politeness I caught him glancing slyly at me. So, he was not the stiff model Puritan. There was blood flowing here, and across the table I could almost feel its warm pulse. My own was racing as never before, and I felt my face turning red as I fought to hide what was erupting in me — desire. Yes, for the first time, I was drawn, nay pulled, towards a man, whom I had scarcely met.

Then I stole another look and saw that he was sitting forward in his chair, not so much at ease as I had thought, inclined in my direction. I caught his eye and felt something fly between us — a spark of lightning, it seemed like. And still we had barely said a word to each other. He does say, "An honour, Mistress Yale."

After dinner, David, the cunning matchmaker, asked Mr. Hopkins if he would like to come into the hall and view the invention he had almost completed. "It is a machine for adding numbers," he said. "You come too, Anne. It will interest you."

The three of us left the room. None of the others followed, not caring a whit about David's ingenuity.

It was an intricate device, I could see, but when he began to explain it, I found it hard to grasp the idea of how it worked, my mind being occupied elsewhere. Standing beside Mr. Hopkins, I sensed the warmth of his body, and a delicious clean odour I associated then with clover and rosemary, but now with sweet-smelling sheets and pillows.

He was saying, "I see," and "How clever," and "So that's how it works," but I could tell that his attention was also divided. I looked at him trying to be interested, and thought, I love this man. Was it possible that he...?

David said abruptly, "There's something I forgot to bring out. I'll go and fetch it. I won't be long." He dashed out of the room.

What to say, and who to begin? Dear Edward, he was the brave one. "Mistress Yale, I know we have hardly spoken, but I wonder if you would let me visit you again? I would dearly like to know you better."

Quickly I said, "And I you. Oh!" Realizing how brazen I sounded, I tried to recover, looking down at my feet. My cheeks were burning, but I could not stay like that forever, so I just looked back up at him and said, "Please come and visit whenever you can. I am at home most of the time."

"Do you like to walk in the afternoon?" He had such lovely wrinkles around his mouth when he smiled. There was something about his eyes too. They were such a dark grey, and their gaze seemed to come from a long way back, as though all his thoughts had gathered there.

"Oh yes, that is the best time for a walk." I must have sounded so eager. Any timid man — or one who was not a little besotted — would have backed away then. But Edward only smiled more widely.

We both looked a little guilty when David sauntered back, holding a small piece of metal, his excuse for leaving us alone. The smug look on his face showed that he knew what had happened. Well, good for him. He had done what he had promised. I could hardly begrudge him his triumph.

It did not take long for my discarded dream of a happy marriage to be brought to life again. Mr. Eaton and Mr. Hopkins — my Edward now — found that they did indeed have many business interests in common, which they discussed amicably for hours on end. I could not remember a time when my stepfather had been so agreeable. My mother looked upon the possibility of a marriage for her eldest daughter as a way of ridding herself of one of her troubles. She was not one of those women who had a gift for childrearing, and had treated it as a burden ever since her first husband, my father, had died when she was quite young, and I was only four.

So Edward and I walked, talked, strolled in the park. We also visited the New Exchange in the Strand where I pored over the books for sale, and he stood near, a less curious browser. It was odd, though, how often we would reach for the same book and our hands would touch. Once we laughed aloud, admitting our little game. One afternoon when I was telling him for the second or third time how I loved to read, and how I had tried my hand at writing, he said how much he admired that ability in me, but that even before that he was struck by my beauty. My beauty!

I protested. He said, "Do not belittle yourself, Mistress Yale. You have the most appealing features, your eyes especially ... no, please let me go on. I must tell you that the first time I saw you I couldn't stop looking at you. Do you know that one's eyes give away one's character, and yours are so unguarded, so direct in their gaze. It makes me believe that you could not do a mean thing in your life."

"Wait and see!" I said, and then stopped myself. What was I saying to this almost stranger?

"I shall indeed, but I know I will not change my opinion," he said disarmingly. I wanted to kiss him then and there. Fortunately, I did not, or I might have sent him away in a fright. Forthright though I am, I knew there was a limit to a woman's boldness. Instead I said, "Well, I do enjoy your company so much. I won't be having any mean thoughts when I'm with you. This is the most wonderful springtime I have known in years — ever," I amended.

He said, "That's true for me, too. London will never look the same to me again, now that I have seen it with you." I looked in his eyes. So intense was their yearning, it almost made a sound.

I thought he was going to continue, but then we both became aware of all the shoppers and strollers that surrounded us. Edward controlled himself, became the proper gentleman, and suggested we move along. The hour for supper was near, so I knew there would be no more intimacies shared that day.

On another fine afternoon we were walking along the Strand, and up ahead I saw a flurry of carriages about to set out from the gates of Denmark House. I ran ahead, then stopped to wait for Edward to catch up, took hold of his hand and tried to pull him along, saying "Quickly, please! We mustn't miss her!"

Edward said, "Hold on now, not so fast. Anyway, how do you know it is the Queen?"

"I just know. It must be. Please come on, I've never seen her." He let himself be moved along even faster than his usual brisk pace.

Luckily for both of us the carriages came out of the gate travelling in our direction. I stopped and stared into them, quite rudely I was sure. In the second carriage was a woman with masses of brown ringlets spilling out from her wide black velvet hat. She looked over at me, and her sweet, finely sculpted face broke into a little smile. I curtsied as low as I could, though I felt almost paralyzed and I was sure I would faint. "It is Henrietta Maria," I whispered as the carriage dashed away. "I don't care if she's a papist, she's beautiful."

Edward, who of course had bowed at the carriage, said, "Yes she is, but she's not doing the King's cause much good with her religion."

"Do you think she might be sent away?"

"If it comes to a war, she will probably go back to France, rather than risk being imprisoned here."

"Oh dear, she looks so fine and happy. I'd hate to lose her so soon after I've just seen her."

"For her sake and everyone else's, let's pray that there is no war," Edward said fervently.

One day, he brought me to see his own town house. It sits in a quiet street, as clean as any in London. (He keeps it still, which makes me think he will one day want to return to England.) It was not too small, with eight rooms, and very well-appointed, especially considering that it was a single man's house. I could tell that from the absence of anything beyond the strictly useful — no curtains, no table scarves, only one painting, of an ancestor, he said — it needed a woman's touch. I longed to be the one. Even so, I admired everything about it, including the furnishings of such good quality, and said so, while trying my best not to give away what I was thinking: why would he take me here, if not to ask me...? Is he truly serious? It turned out that he was, because right there in the parlour he said: "I am almost past my prime, but do you think that you could make your life here with me, because I wish very much to take you as my wife?"

"With all my heart!" I said, so eagerly that I surprised even myself. "I have been hoping for ages that you would ask me. Yes! Yes!" I did not know which of us smiled the more broadly.

Then I took a deep breath. "Are you sure you want me? I'm not the least bit prepared to be a trader's wife. I know nothing about keeping house or entertaining or whatever else it is that matrons do. Do you think you could bear to live with someone who loves books and queens and — all that sort of thing?"

"I can do more than bear it," said Edward. "I will love it. As for the life of a trader's family, I am sure you will take to it with your usual high spirits. It's not so difficult to learn, you know. You can do anything you choose, but mostly I hope you will choose to be my dearest girl and wife."

For a second the question hung delicately between us. I thought to myself, perhaps I can do better than my mother did. Out loud I said, "Then I am entirely, devotedly yours, from this day on, dear Edward."

At that, with great courtesy, Edward kissed my hand. Breaking with the courtship tradition, I took his face between my hands and kissed him soundly on the lips. Surprised, then with a surge of pleasure, he kissed me back. We clung together for longer than respectability permits—but who would see us? — and finally let go. As we left the house, we dropped the other's hand as we reentered the world of proprieties understood and followed.

The rest can be told briefly, because brief it was. We were married quietly by a minister known to Mr. Eaton and Edward, a soft-spoken courteous man who seemed pleased at our union. My mother, who had decided she was fond of Edward, asked Mr. Eaton for some money, so I could have a gown of rose-coloured London silk for the occasion. Edward thought it suited me wonderfully, with my dark brown hair and hazel eyes. The wedding supper was simple, without even a bridecake, so Edward and I had to delay our first kiss until we left the Eaton house and entered ours. Then we made up for our restraint, not lustily, but with the eager delight that builds up when you have had to wait so long for your pleasure. On my first night in bed with a man — my husband! — I slept after our coupling as I had never done before, like one of those Italian frescoed angels resting on a cloud, with my beloved beside me.

3.

MY HAPPY RECOLLECTIONS are interrupted by a terrified shriek, followed by the sounds of something smacking the water, and a flurry of cries: "Help! Man overboard!" "Fetch a pole!" "Throw a rope!" and, "He can't swim, he's going under!" I look around for Edward, to see if he is going to help, but he must have gone below the deck.

I peer over the rail as far as I dare, but at first I can see nothing below except churning water. Then comes another mighty splash, and people are shouting, "Over there, see he's come up!" "Oh, mercy, can you reach him? Here's the rope!" Finally, the master calls, "Good man, Jed ... now don't lose him ... hold tight ... easy, get his hands on the ladder ... that's it ... good work, come on!"

I see two men floundering in the water. One head keeps going under and bursting to the surface again, like someone desperately bobbing for apples. From where I stand, I would not give them a chance of surviving. Then, miraculously, one man is grasping the rope ladder weakly, and being supported and shoved up from behind by the other one. More sailors reach over the side to haul them up, one by one. As the second man, Jed, is heaved over the rail, a loud cheer goes up. "Bravo Jed, you did it!" The rescued sailor has collapsed on the deck, a shivering heap of sodden rags. Jed looks no better.

Later, I learn that the unhappy sailor had been standing lookout at the masthead. He saw something peculiar in the water approaching the ship in a rush. Alarmed, he began to call and waved excitedly with one arm when he lost his grip on the ropes and fell into the ocean. According to seamen's gossip, this sort of accident is none too rare, and many who fall do not live to tell the tale. This young man should be thankful that Jed is such a strong swimmer. Most of the crew would not dare to risk their lives in the water. They cannot swim, and see no need to learn, for, as one of them told me, "We'll only drown in the end anyway, so why bother?"

This afternoon the Reverend Mr. Stone, who is returning to New England on the *Hector*, calls a special meeting to give thanks to God for saving a life, thereby confirming once again his special providence towards this voyage and these planters. I find out after the meeting that the young sailor, now recovered but sorely shaken, had asked Mr. Stone if he would write a note for him to his mother in Devon, to tell her about his frightening experience and amazing rescue. He was refused. The minister's time is fully taken up with weightier matters, he said.

I ask myself, why did the minister act so uncharitably? Surely he would have known that the story would get back to England, embroidered and falsified as they always are. His poor mother might have thought he had drowned. A letter to reassure her would have taken little time to write. Was it so important to acknowledge God's protective arm over this great venture, and so petty to care for the protection of one frightened creature?

Later, Edward tells me that Mr. Stone is to be the assistant minister in Hartford. I say with a sharp edge to my voice that I hope this afternoon's uncaring response to the sailor is not a hint of things to come. He is quite surprised to see how angry I am about it, but does not say anything. Then, still riled up about the minister's refusal, I speak to the master, and offer to write the letter to the sailor's mother. He thanks me, and says that he will be doing it himself. From the way he speaks, I do not think he thinks much of Mr. Stone's attitude either.

All of this I note in my journal. This is a practice I have followed ever since my youth, when I lived in Wales with my Grandfather Yale after my father died. It was Grandfather who gave me my first journal, and taught me to record whatever I saw and thought about, even if it seemed commonplace at the time. He said I would come to value these thoughts later on.

On this voyage, I write in my journal every day without fail. I record all that is new to me, which means just about everything that happens. For instance there was the day they caught a porpoise and we ate it. I did not like the look of it, but the sailor who had served it to us said it was excellent meat, so I tried it. It was just as horrible as it looked, like bacon gone bad. I decided to stick to bonito, a fine and plentiful fish that seemed eager to be caught. The seamen say that the sight of many porpoises playing in the sea is a sign that the weather will turn bad. To me, it is a sign of foul meals ahead.

The greatest wonder of the voyage so far, apart from the schools of whales, is the ice mountain we encountered off the banks of Newfoundland. It looked to me at first like one of those huge cliffs we had seen along another shore, but when we came closer we could feel the chill of it, and were astonished to hear that it was made of ice. One person among us, who has a scientific frame of mind, said that it was standing on the bottom of the sea. Another, disputing this, said that it would move and go further south, melting as it reached the warmer climates. I had hopes that it would travel with us, but I was told that it moved much more slowly than we do, which I could easily believe, as it looked to be a hundred times bigger than our ship.

The breeze has risen to a brisk wind, blowing my hair around so it covers my eyes and catches in my teeth, as I stand at the rail with my mind occupied elsewhere. The salt from the spray sticks to my hair, and I spit out the sea water. Watching the colours move in the ocean with the hurl and roll of the waves, I try to peer into its depths. What is down there? A world of creatures who never see the light of day, so many fathoms below me they are. It is strange to think that they live apart from us, unaware of the beings who believe they are masters of the universe. Just as it is with ourselves and God, I guess. But at least we know God is there and has us in mind. Do these sea creatures know about us?

I am reflecting that all in all, the voyage so far has been even more thrilling than I had hoped. These marvels of the ocean are worth every bit of hardship you have to put up with to see them. True, I have not been sick for a day. I am in good health to begin with, I have drunk my daily portion of lemon juice to prevent scurvy, and I take a dozen turns of the deck twice daily. This latter routine was prescribed by my stepfather, who can be seen regularly on the after-deck practising what he preaches.

4.

I T MAY SEEM ODD that Edward and I are travelling to New England on the same ship as my mother and stepfather, when I could hardly wait to leave their company before I was married. Actually, our final destinations are different, as the Eatons are stopping in New Haven colony, and we are going on eventually to Hartford. We will have a short stay with them until preparations are completed for us in Hartford. It cannot be helped, and, with Edward beside me, I am sure I can put up a good front, and try to mask my dislike of the situation.

It was at my stepfather's suggestion that Edward took up the notion of coming to New England. For some time he had been disturbed by conditions in England, both political and spiritual. Edward is a quietly moderate Puritan, who wishes only for good government and the freedom to worship as one chooses. We talked about this often before deciding to leave the country.

"I am loyal to King Charles, despite what Archbishop Laud tries to tell him about Puritans, but I do not think the country has been well served under the King's personal rule. We need a parliament that will govern the country wisely and fairly, but the King seems to be persuaded by his favourites and his own appetites to do whatever he pleases."

I said, "Do you think we will have a civil war if matters get worse?"

"It seems likely. Look what a disastrous situation we have now, with the King up north fighting the Scots. Did I tell you that my brother Jonathan has gone to join the King's forces? The silly young fool!"

"Oh, Edward, he is a farmer, not a soldier. He doesn't know how to fight!"

"I know. I tried to talk him out of it, but he would not listen. He's such a strong royalist, and a stubborn person to boot. We must pray for his safety. I fear for him."

Another day, Edward came home for dinner after visiting my stepfather. He ate silently, cutting and chewing his food without giving it any attention. He was so serious, I decided it was wise to wait for him to speak, rather than probe. At last, after we had finished, he told me what was on his mind. "Mr. Eaton has decided to leave England for the new colonies. He says that God's wrath is coming down on this country for her faithlessness, and that the longer we stay the more likely it is that we will become corrupted like the rest."

"Surely not, Edward," I countered. "You for one are never going to change, and I hope to heaven I am not either. My stepfather would never believe you would lose your integrity and your honour, no matter the circumstances."

"Perhaps not, Anne, but I think Theophilus has a point. The country is going through disastrous spiritual times linked to this overwhelming political upheaval. He says that we who have not turned away from the Lord's path must collect the faithful remnants and go to a place where there is no religious animosity and no threat of war."

"Could there ever be such a place? I wonder," I said.

Edward continued. "He says that the new colonies we establish will be communities of faith and good will. They will become, if we are true to our beliefs, a new Jerusalem, and a light for the world. What do you think of that?"

I said, "It sounds almost impossible to me. Many people are so mean, so narrow and grasping, and they make others miserable. How could they change that just by going to another land?"

"People like that will not be joining us. We will only take those of like mind and morals. Besides, this new order we will bring in will ensure that no one has reason to be envious or to want to steal from anyone else. There will be plenty of land for everyone, freedom to worship, and the opportunity to improve one's situation in every way."

"And yet man is born to sin," I countered.

"Quite true, but with a well-regulated community and the help of God, we can rid ourselves of the opportunities for sin — many of them, anyway."

"You sound as if you believe in Sir Thomas More's utopia, my dear ," I said, teasing him a little.

"No, I'm not so deluded, but at least in the New World we have the opportunity to leave behind what is worst in our society, and to make a fresh start."

"Well … yes." I was beginning to allow his vision to persuade me.

"On the practical side, there will be some new commercial possibilities. Theophilus says that he can see us developing a good shipbuilding enterprise there together. I would love to do that. Fancy having our own ships crossing the seas, carrying goods from there to England, the West Indies, perhaps even the Far East one day." His eyes were sparkling now. Here was the Edward I loved, full of eagerness for the future. His manner showed quite a change from the last few months, when every discouraging day made him quieter, and his expression more sober and unmoving.

He went on to say, "I cannot see any reason not to leave — apart from leaving any good friends who decide to stay behind, that is."

I considered this, my mind whirling. The idea of leaving England had never occurred to me when I married Edward, even though I knew he was a trader. Yet his arguments for leaving were so cogent, his plans for a new colony so reasonable. Edward always looked cautiously before he leapt.

"Have you spoken to David? What does he say?"

"He says he will go to Boston and set up his headquarters there. He has already been trading with the Bay Colony, and is doing very well. He says he remains a royalist, but is afraid of what will happen if Charles remains obdurate and the most rabid nonconformists force him to do what they want."

"Thomas will go too, then."

"Yes, if he wants to continue to apprentice with David, which we all think he should. He will make a good trader himself one day."

I groaned. "Oh what a choice to have to make. If we go, I must say goodbye to my friends here and in Wales, and to every good thing I have known all my life. I might never see the lovely old house in Wales again. Plâs Grono is my favourite place on earth. You know how I feel about it."

He nodded.

I went on. "But if we stay, I lose all my family, and sit here in this miserable city that is breaking out in all sorts of violence everywhere."

Edward stood up and walked over to the window. Turning, he said, "I agree, it won't be easy to decide. London has been my home for more than thirty years, and I love her. Let us take time to think and pray about it, then, so that we will know what is best."

So we left it for a few more weeks. Neither of us was happy. To decide was too difficult. We talked about it in the evenings sitting at the supper table, and afterwards we prayed together, asking God to guide us in making a choice. On Sundays we attended a quiet meeting of other likeminded people, all praying to discern the Lord's will. Then we walked, sometimes all the way to Tower Bridge, thinking of nothing else. Not even a break in the winter weather cheered us up. We turned the idea of leaving over and over. Were we foolish to be pinning all our hopes on settling in a land we hardly knew? Edward had been there for a visit, and said it was beautiful, but entirely uncultivated. In the towns there were no shops, no businesses, no streets to speak of, and the houses were not as comfortable as ours. He thought this would change quickly with all the new colonists coming in.

Edward assured me that the planters who were already there, and their families, would be very agreeable, and would soon make up for the loss of my old friends here. I was not convinced about that, but I tried to believe him. Finally, after realizing that we had no other good choice, we took the momentous step and said we would go.

One day, a month or so later, Edward came home very early for dinner, an anxious frown on his face. "Anne, we must leave. Now. There are stories everywhere about a plague of smallpox, and many people are dying. I must take you away from here before it moves to our part of the city."

"How did it happen?" I asked. I must say that the thought of succumbing to the smallpox sent a chill right through me. What a horrible way to die.

"No one knows, but our ministers are saying that it is God's punishment against the church and the Archbishop for the flagrant way in which they have introduced popish customs, and silenced those ministers who would not conform."

"Oh! So the corruption of the flesh is the sign of the corrupt soul. Oh dear! Will anyone be spared, do you think?"

Edward looked at me curiously, as if wondering whether I was speaking out of the other side of my mouth. I was not sure myself if I was being honest, or ironically skeptical.

"We don't know, but what we do know is that if we do not leave here right away, the chances of catching the smallpox are great. I have ordered a coach to take you back to Plâs Grono for a little while, until I find us a ship and arrange for our belongings to be sent on board. It is a good thing we have been considering this for some time, since I have made many preparations, and we can set out quickly. As soon as everything is ready, I will come for you."

So that was how it was that we finally decided to cross the ocean and plant ourselves in Hartford upon Connecticut.

5.

TO GET BACK TO MY STEPFATHER — and I can hardly avoid that, for here he comes now, advancing with his usual military stride in my direction — he is not a mean or cruel man, or even an unpleasant one most of the time. When he married my mother, an impoverished widow with three children, everyone thought him a most generous man, which indeed he is. Generosity to the weak and the poor is part of the treasury of Puritan virtues. However, full-blown, undisguised affection is not required. He could not show it, even if she wished for it. Although she never said so — she did not confide in me — I think that what she wanted was comfort and a life where she could be more than an indigent relation. Besides, after eight years of widowhood, Ann Yale, though daughter of a bishop, and widow of a well-lettered husband, must have come to realize that others' sympathy for her lonely state was wearing thin. She had few friends then. While handsomely provided for on his Welsh estate by her father-in-law — my beloved grandfather was a noted advocate — she probably could see that the elderly gentleman would be glad if she were to find another mate and depart. I remember that he showed her every courtesy, but his patience was strained often by her constant self-pitying attitude. So when Theophilus Eaton, a wealthy London widower, came along to court her, she was ready and willing to marry again. Of the rigidity of Mr. Eaton's Puritan views she either knew nothing, or if she did, she had decided that the game was worth the candle. We young Yales were to discover those views together, when we moved into his London house, and found it chillingly decorated all over with righteousness.

Needless to say my mother's and stepfather's presence on board the *Hector* is an irritant only superseded by the indigestible meals, and some of the twice-weekly sermons. What is worse is that the only two other members of the Eaton family that I truly dislike are, of course, travelling with them: Mr. Eaton's aged mother, whose sour disposition worsens with time, and my young half-sister, Hannah, aged five, who is the product of my mother's late desire to indulge a child rather than ignore her. By marrying Edward I had thought I would escape from this household. Nearly ten years under Mr. Eaton's formidable rule was beginning to wear down my spirit. I needed a year of marriage to get back the vitality and curiosity that I was told I had had in such abundance when I was young.

Now, here we all are together again, but it will not be forever, I keep telling myself. That makes it bearable — except for when I meet the old woman, that is.

My stepfather approaches. I am trapped.

"Good afternoon to you, stepdaughter. And what has been attracting your eyes? I saw you looking over the ship's side quite intently." His tone is moderate, hoping to receive a courteous response. I comply.

"I was watching the young sailor who fell into the water being rescued by another, and then I suppose I just kept on looking at the sea."

"Ah yes, the sailor who did not drown. There is an example of the mysterious nature of the Lord's mercy, as the man is not even a churchgoer, let alone one of the saints."

"And the man who rescued him?" I ask. I know I am leading him towards some lofty moralizing, but I cannot help myself.

"He also is not one of the visible saints. We must look to *Job* for the explanation, namely that the rain falls upon the just as well as the unjust. Similarly the ocean may support all sinners, both the declared and the undeclared. The Lord has his own reasons for this." He pauses, as if turning the page for the next point in the sermon. "Let us hope that this encounter with the saving hand of God will bring both men to repentance, and some of the passengers too. There are many on this voyage who have no idea of the love of God, and do not care to hear of it." Mr. Eaton nods sagely, convinced of his own words.

"I wonder how you have discovered who are among the saints?" I decide to pursue this matter, to see how far my stepfather will go. He of course has no idea that I want anything more than to be instructed, as is to be expected. Mr. Eaton is a man of sound education and enunciates his principles clearly.

"Why, by inquiring of them individually where they stand in relation to the laws of God. Mr. Stone and I have spoken to each and every man, and some women too, and where we have not been satisfied with their answers, Mr. Stone has held a second interview. Some of the men are very hazy about their faith, and he has taken the opportunity of this voyage to instruct them. I think that by the time we arrive in port we will have added several to our number."

Poor souls, they cannot escape you on this little ship, I think. Aloud I say, "You must be spending a great deal of time helping Mr. Stone with his ministry."

My stepfather cuts in quickly. "It is important for the sake of the colony I am building. My aim is to make New Haven a community composed entirely of visible saints. I wish to avoid controversy, and keep out all manner of evil and danger. It can be done, but we will all need to be firm and clear in our resolve."

To be fair, I must acknowledge that Mr. Eaton's paternal approach to New Haven is not entirely a matter of overwhelming self-assurance. Before he left England it had been decided by the colonists in his party that he would be the governor. Such a clear-headed, devoted, and wealthy Puritan was just what they would need. They did not know he would want to take on the minister's job as well.

I look at this huge man with his heavy brows and deeply rutted face. He must have been an impressive figure in his youth, and I can imagine how he could have persuaded a new colony to follow his example in earlier days. Today, though, his body grows flabby, and his stomach distends, perhaps from spending so much time sitting with his head bent over to pray. Below his greying rusty beard is a wrinkled and wobbly neck. When he blows his nose, as he does just now, the sound is more like a goose's honking than a trumpet. Time has not improved his appearance, but I admit that he still has tremendous presence — a presence that shows more concern for good order than for the people whom the order serves. Thank goodness Edward and I will not be living with him for long.

"It is a pity that you and Edward will not be staying on in New Haven," Mr. Eaton says. "You would find it a true beacon of the faith, I believe." *Honk, honk.*

I say, truthfully, "I am sure you will achieve your aim excellently, Mr. Eaton. I hope you and my mother will be happy there. But Edward and I have another place to fill."

He blows his nose again, and turns a little as if he intends to leave. He has made his statement. "Yes, I suppose Hartford has need of your husband. I must go inside. I think this wind is not good for my lungs. I will send your mother out to you."

He disappears into his cabin. He is torn, between his duty towards me, and the urge to finish a conversation that has not gone exactly as he wished it to. I think he senses my criticism without knowing what it is, which gives me a wicked sort of pleasure. As for his obligation to me, I know he does not like to see me standing here alone, so he will fetch my mother. An unaccompanied woman could get into trouble, even on this crowded ship with almost no privacy! How old-fashioned he is. Does he not realize that many women today go out alone to visit each other without even a servant to accompany them? That in London some perfectly decent women visit the shops on their own? He would call them "hussies," I am sure, but they are not. And I have been told that among the saints there are women who journey to other towns, not to preach, but to hold prayer meetings and to interpret Scripture to groups of women. But Mr. Eaton accompanies his widowed mother everywhere. I suppose it is she who taught him to be so protective. She is still the matriarch, the horrid old woman. He is outwardly strong, but beside her he is a timid hare. The picture of Mr. Eaton hopping behind his mother is too much for me. I start to giggle.

6.

WHILE WE WERE TALKING, clouds heavy with rain have gathered over our heads, The sea has become greyer and grumpier, but I am still in no hurry to go below. I grip the rail tightly as I walk along searching for sea-fowl, which do not appear. I am wearing a green flannel gown, which was warm enough when I first came outside, but offers little protection now. I do not feel the cold very much, though, as I am still thinking of my little victory over my stepfather, foolish though it was.

The wind has grown more boisterous now, the sea has risen high, and I am starting to fear for my footing. I turn around to look for help in case I should fall. Seamen have begun to reef the sails, calling to one another to pull on the ropes. Just at this moment my mother appears at the open hatch. "Anne, come in!" she shouts over the roaring. "We are going to have a terrible storm."

I need no urging now. Without thinking about my safety, I stagger towards the hatch just in time. A seaman comes out from nowhere, and closes it down firmly. My mother escorts me to my cabin. Inside, where the lamps are lit, it seems so hospitable after the turmoil without.

My mother says quickly, "I will go and find your husband, who is probably with Mr. Eaton now. You'll be better off with him." She obviously prefers her own husband's company to mine at such a time, and I cannot say I blame her. She leaves in a hurry. The wind by this time is truly forbidding, insisting on having things its own way. I sit on my bunk and listen to its demonic howling. I have never heard anything like it in my life. I wonder if what they say about demons is true. How they spend all of eternity howling in the dark, bereft of the light of heaven. How their only reprieve from the ghastly perpetual night of hell is when they are sent to earth to torment us.

The sea, partnered with the wind, heaves and sets, heaves and sets, as the wind exhales, draws back, and disgorges its loud breath again and again. For some time it keeps up this regimen, making my stomach a little queasy, but it is nothing serious. I am thrown about on my bunk, but do not fall off. I know that the tossing ship is keeping Edward in his sheltered place, wherever that is. I wish he were here, but I tell myself I am not afraid. The storm will be over soon.

There is an ominous lull, the ship rights itself, the wind slackens, and then with one piercing shriek it attacks again. The ship lurches heavily causing loose objects to crash and swirl around on the floor of the cabin. Then both the lamps go out. Everything goes black. I cannot see. Panic-stricken, I scream. Suddenly, I do not know where I am. I am in a no-place, an abyss, a haunt of death. After that I remember nothing.

People told me later that I screamed on and on as if I were being pursued. That was not how it was: terror had enveloped me like a dense black blanket, and I truly thought I was going to be extinguished just like the lamps. I must have fainted at the end. The next thing I know, Edward is standing beside me, holding my hand and stroking it over and over. My body is so limp and weak, as if all the blood has drained out of me, that I turn my head to the wall and sleep.

Edward insists that I stay in bed until I am fully recovered. He sees me start to tremble every once in a while, and says he thinks I might be getting the ague. I know that he is secretly worried that I will take another fit — I cannot think what else to call it. It came on so suddenly there was nothing I could do about it. I have been in dark places before, but never like this, without warning. So I lie in bed, wondering and fretting.

Outside the cabin I dimly hear him ask someone, "Has this ever happened to her before?" and a voice that sounds like my mother, says, "No. Yes. Well, perhaps. I have a vague recollection of something like this, but I cannot recall the circumstances. She was just a little girl, so you can't expect me to remember something so far back. Of course, she has forgotten it too, no doubt."

She was right; I had forgotten, if anything like it had truly ever taken place. But why in heaven's name did this happen? I fear the dark now even though I know it is foolish. I am not superstitious by nature, although perhaps I should be. The great storm arose on the Ides of March.

II
Hartford, 1639

1.

THE LAST TWO YEARS have passed so rapidly that I have been delinquent in writing my cousin. I know she will be wondering whether I am pregnant yet, but I do not think I will tell her just yet how hard we have tried for a child, and how unsuccessfully. No need to worry her.

April 25, 1639

Dear Jane,

Please, please forgive me for keeping you waiting so long for a letter. I know you are dying to hear all about it, but I must tell you that I have never been so much occupied in my life since we arrived here, and happily so, too. It is all quite different from what I expected, and, thank God that it is so, entirely opposite to the horrible year we've come through in New Haven, staying with the Eatons. (Although I've told you something about that, I had to be discreet in case my letter fell into the wrong hands. One day, my dear, I shall give you the real story.) This has been the only time when I have been angry at Edward for letting my stepfather persuade him to linger in New Haven for so long, in the hope that we would change our minds and join that community instead of going to Hartford. Edward admires Mr. Eaton for his high principles, but finally he saw how strictly the community would be run, and he said that we would leave. Perhaps my anger had something to do with it too: I was so furious that I threatened to return to England and live all by myself at Plâs Grono. He was shocked at the suggestion, and immediately told my stepfather that we were leaving. So all's well that end's well.

How shall I begin to tell you about my new home? Hartford is beautiful in its own primitive way. It is strange and familiar at the same time: strange because of the land which is a green and abundant wilderness, utterly untamed, with a little patch carved out of it where we are building a town; and, familiar because the houses and roads that are being built remind me of a small Welsh village as it might have been at the beginning. All in all, what this colony and the others are making is a new England, and in the end it will not be like old England at all, but a new creation. So our ministers tell us, and so I believe too.

What does it look like? I can hear you asking. Give me the heft and the feel of it, this Hartford, you say. I shall try to recall my first sensations when we arrived. It has been so hectic that I have not written in my journal for weeks, so I will have to rely on my imperfect memory.

We left the Eatons in New Haven on the 2nd of April, and not a moment too soon for me. They were both polite and amiable when we parted. My mother gave me a kiss and an old cutwork cap she had grown tired of which was, she said, still perfectly good. My stepfather presented me proudly with a book of Psalms newly translated by a New Haven clerk. Mr. Eaton says the young man will be a strong and godly minister one day, mark his words. I am sure they were as glad to get rid of us (me, really, not Edward, who is still Mr. Eaton's friend), as I was to leave. Even Edward declared after we left that the air in their house was "frequently stifling for lack of free discussion." For all his good nature, Edward does not like to be preached to by anyone except those whose vocation it is. I do not think we will see very much of them, not over once a year.

We travelled along the coast and up the river on a good sturdy pinnace manned by four sailors and and a young crewman who did everything but row or tend to the sails, including preparing some rather dirty meals for us. We did not mind much, as we were so happy to be on our way to "our town," as we began to call it. Even sleeping on bare planks covered with clothes and blankets was not such a great hardship. The boat rocked pleasantly, the stars came out brilliantly (I hadn't seen a sky like this since our ocean voyage), and we kept each other warm. In the morning birds sang to us; they sounded like thrushes, so melodic and flutelike, but they hid in the trees and I could not see them.

The Connecticut is a lovely river, deep and broad. In some narrower places, willow trees came right to the edge, and waved over the water. There were sections where the current was so strong, the oarsmen had a hard time making any distance. Mainly, though it was not too much work for them, and they sang as they rowed, keeping the rhythm steady. Their voices were so well-matched that I told them we would make them into a real choir by the time the trip was over. I had forgotten for a moment that choirs are no longer permitted in meeting-houses. The men would have to keep to their boats.

I think the river has a voice, too, full and spirited, but what it sings I have not yet translated. When it murmured sweetly, it seemed to say, "Welcome strange travelers." But when the mood turned sour and the rhythm raged, then I wondered if it was telling us, "Go home, you are not wanted here."

Along the shores were great stands of oak and maple that spread as far as the eye can see. This would be our dowry, Edward said, for we will soon be selling timber all over the world. We saw a number of curious sights: an inlet where the river seemed swollen with fish that neither of us had ever seen before. The crewman threw in a line and in a few minutes caught enough fish, which they called "bass," for our dinner. They were delicious. Further along where a little stream joins the river, we saw a beaver dam, but no beaver. The sailors said they were not much to look at, even though the hats made from their pelts were so handsome.

The strangest places were the Indian villages. At one point in our journey, as we moved along, almost in shadow from the thick forest that covered both banks of the river, the trees thinned out and daylight sparkled through, and suddenly we came upon a great cleared space where an assembly of little brown huts was gathered. They were not like any huts we would see at home. They were pointed at the top with a wooden chimney for the smoke from their fires to escape. The poles that formed the frame were covered with the dried hides of animals or thatch, and these peculiar shelters were said to be very warm in winter. I could not imagine what it would be like to live in one with the smell of meat cooking and wood smoke spiralling into the sky all day long. One of the seamen told me that they often burn down, and then the Indians just build another one the same way.

As we went by one village, some Indians were fishing. They stood up and looked at us, still as statues. We bowed to them, but they did not return our greeting. I suppose we looked as peculiar to them as they did to us. I am hoping to learn a lot about them, which I will send on. Edward says I must be careful, though. It could be dangerous if my curiosity ran away with me. He worries about me too much, I think.

Closer to our townsite the forest ended, and we saw a lush and beautiful meadowland. All its grasses bristled in the sun, and lead right up to the jetty where we landed. And oh, Jane, such a greeting we had! There must have been sixty people waiting for us — almost half the town. Someone must have sent word that we were coming this day, because there they stood all smiling and waving to us, not like the dour Puritans I am used to. Many of them knew Edward from his visit last year and saluted him warmly, and, I thought, very respectfully. They were just as gracious to me, and a little curious about me from the looks and exchanges I saw among the women. I suppose they were wondering why an upstanding and prosperous citizen would marry such a young and probably foolish wife.

There was such a hustle and bustle on the landing that I can hardly remember anything that was said, or the names of the people who were introduced to me. What I do remember is the gaiety and brightness of the crowd. All the women's clothing was in wonderfully soft and cheerful colours, reds and greens and blues of all tones. I found out afterwards that they use dyes made from trees and plants grown near the town. The Indians showed them what to use. The men, too, wore little touches of colour in their neckerchiefs or hose. That was one of the first surprises here. Did I tell you before that in New Haven everyone wears black, or grey or dull blue every day, not just on Sunday?

After this cheerful but rather bewildering welcome, servants took our trunks and boxes, and we were to set off with a few of the citizens to accompany us to our house. Then the sailors who had brought us from New Haven came up to say goodbye. I wanted to give them something for their trouble, and Edward said he thought that was a kind thing to do. So I took out the purse he had given me before we left England, and handed each one a sixpence. It was the first time I had spent money myself for anything at all, and it made me feel like a free person instead of a needy dependant.

They all thanked me heartily, and one of them tried to kiss my hand, which I would not allow. "Save that kiss for a young New England beauty," I said.

"Aw, mistress, you are a beauty yourself. Not many could hold a candle to you," he said with a big friendly smile.

"Cheeky man, you'd better be off now," I said, but he could see how merry I was and did not take offence.

Edward was getting ready to reprimand him, but changed his mind and smiled too. He is learning that not everything someone says is meant to be taken seriously. I think he must have had little laughter in his young life. Then, the second time it happened, when someone tried to pay me a compliment about my appearance, he did not reprove the speaker, but later myself, for being what he called "free" with another man. I cannot tell you how much his words hurt, even though he spoke gently. Of course I contradicted him vehemently. But that was several weeks later — much too far along for this letter. Edward can get quite upset about little things sometimes. I think it happens when some weightier matter is bothering him, because it is not going well.

Well, the sailors wished us Godspeed, and took off into town to find the ordinary. I was surprised that Hartford had built one so soon, but travellers, and citizens too, do not want to be deprived of their draughts of ale, friendly conversation and, most likely, rollicking bawdy songs. The sailors would get beds there for the night before going back to Boston, this time under sail.

Then we walked through the town to our house, and I was so tired when I got there from the long river trip and the excitement of the arrival that I hardly noticed where I was. There were a few people in the house, servants probably, standing in the large hall. I remember a fire burning and cooking smells, roast meat of some sort. But I could not keep awake, and asked if I might go to bed right away or else my head might be worn off from nodding so much. I fell asleep with all my clothes on, and did not notice until I woke up next morning that I had been undressed. It must have been my new maidservant Nellie who did it.

My hand is aching from writing so long. I have been at it for over two hours, and I must stop here from utter weariness. A messenger is leaving soon with letters to England from Edward, so I will send this along too. You will have to wait for my next letter to hear about the house and the town, and what we are doing. I will write again tomorrow.

I miss you sorely, dear Jane.

Your affectionate cousin,

Anne Hopkins

2.

W E WERE NOT THE FIRST people to live in our house. By a stroke of luck, or the will of the Lord, we did not have to build a new one, which would have taken months, and would have kept us in New Haven even longer. A year was more than enough for me.

If it were not a sin to be so, I would be proud of this property, which I consider the fairest in town. One day, after Edward and I had been settled in New Haven for several months, and had already decided to leave, word came from Hartford that Mr. Debenham and his family were returning to England, and would be selling their house and land. Edward went quickly to Hartford to see the place, and decided immediately to buy it.

"Mr. Debenham and I have made a satisfactory arrangement," he told me, sounding rather pleased with himself. "It is a well-built solid house, and the land is excellent. We can move there in the spring. I'm sure you will like it."

"Why can't we go there right away?" I said, so eagerly it almost took his breath away. "Let's just pack our goods and go!"

Edward was torn between smiling and frowning. "We cannot, Anne, not until the present owners have left. Now, don't look so downcast. Spring will come sooner than you think. And we'll go just as soon as the weather is mild enough."

Another thought struck me, and I brightened a little at the idea. "If only we could be there for Christmas! Do you think the owners might leave by then?"

"No, I am quite sure they will not travel to England in the middle of winter. It would be utter folly."

"Oh, of course not. That means we will have no Christmas at all then," I said forlornly. "I just heard Mr. Eaton telling one of his assistants that they were going to levy a fine of five shillings on anyone who celebrated the festival. It is to be a working day just like any other day. I hate this town."

"Well, I don't think you will find any of the other colonies celebrating Christmas either, even if there are no fines." He was trying to cheer me up, but it was cold comfort. "There will be other special feasts to celebrate other events that come up, and other days that are important to us here. Wait and see. Soon you will forget you ever cared about Christmas."

"I've heard people say it is pagan and popish. How stupid! How can it be both?" I was working myself up to a proper rant. I knew it was not just about Christmas, but about living with the Eatons, the severe New Haven saints, and the frustration of not being free to be ourselves in our own house. Edward looked upset, and so he should be, as he was not the real target. I calmed down a bit and said, "Well, I will wish you a blessed Christmas all the same, and you must do the same for me."

"I will certainly do that, in private, if it will make you happy," he said, kissing my cheek. You could see the relief written all over his face, that I was not going to storm about. After that the subject of Christmas was never mentioned between us.

All winter I pestered Edward for details of the house and the setting. All I knew was that Hartford was laid out at the junction of the Connecticut River and a tiny riveret they call the Little River that runs through the town. "Draw me a plan, and show me exactly where the buildings are."

He did so. "Here is the road going through the town on the south side of the river, and our house sits just here beside it." The street was not named yet, but soon after we moved there it began to be called Governor's Row, which stuck. "Along this side of the house are the stables, and behind are the dairy and the cowshed together. It's a short walk from the house to the dairy but for safety the cattle must be near the house. That's why I am having a high stone wall built around the house and stables and barns for protection. See, here it is." He drew it in for her.

"Can there be so many predators around the town?" I asked.

"Some, but, from what I have been told, the human predators are the worst. Quite a few cattle have disappeared without a trace. If wild beasts had killed them, the bones would have been found at least. We are going to be an easy target for thieves, from both the road and the river sides."

"And I thought this was such an upright community we were going to," I said wryly.

"It is, but there are always a few bad apples in every peck." Edward matched my tone.

I laughed. "Or wolves in every pack."

Edward said, "Seriously, though, there are always the Indians to think about. It is very quiet there now, but after the horrendous Pequot battles, we must be prepared."

I could understand that, even if I was not happy about it. We arrived here just after the fighting had finished, and all the Indians to a tribesman had been killed. Indeed, the stories of their vile attacks were being repeated so vividly that it did seem essential to have a wall around one's property, to safeguard people as well as livestock. They said that the other tribes who lived around Hartford seemed peaceable enough, but that one never knew.

"Show me again where I will have my garden." I turned back to Edward's plan.

He pointed. "Here, on the private side of the house."

A picture of the garden-to-be formed in my head. "That's where I will have a small orchard, and roses growing up the walls, and all sorts of flowers below them. And a pond. And herbs, too, especially rosemary and thyme, and sweet marjoram, and camomile for tea!" I ended with a flourish. Throwing my arms around him I said, "It's going to be simply beautiful!"

"It's all yours to decide," Edward said, rubbing his head on my arm. "We can order seeds and cuttings from England. Choose whatever you like, but it would be better to concentrate on edible plants. There is so much work to do, and so few hands to go around. I don't think anyone can be spared to look after something that has no useful purpose."

I digested this idea. It had not occurred to me that a radiant garden would not be wanted, to soften our harsh and strenuous lives. My quick rejoinder was, "That's so. But I shall look after it myself. I've never had a garden. I will love it." I looked at him to see whether he approved. It was a suitable work for a gentlewoman, gardening. He must agree.

He did, with reservation. "I am sure you will, if you can find the time to care for it. I expect that you will want to give it up after a while, when your days are filled with other activities."

I had the feeling that there was something he was not telling me, but no matter, I would not press him. I would find out soon enough. So I said, "Oh no, I would never do that!" My head was already full of colours: I would have carnations and pinks and anemones and daisies. I would also have lilies for purity and bergamot for richness. There would be tulips in all the new colours, pale daffodils, and royal purple irises. And lilacs! We must have lilacs. "Edward, do you think we could get a lilac bush, a whole one, so we wouldn't have to wait too long for it to flower? At Plâs Grono we had lilacs everywhere!"

By this time Edward had turned away and seemed to be concentrating on a paper he had received. He just nodded, peering over his spectacles, and said, "That sounds like a good idea." I went on planning my garden, wishing I did not have to go through another winter before starting on it, and with no Christmas!

The only thing that made life bearable over that long period of incarceration in New Haven was planning how to arrange the new house. It was that infamous winter when the ground froze so early that the seeds did not germinate. All the people were afraid they would starve, and many did, and died. The Eatons, however, had brought over enough grain to see us through, and even had some to share with those most endangered. Still, I have never experienced such a cold winter as that winter, before or since.

I spent ages deciding on furnishings, seeking out carpenters in town and in Boston who could make the pieces I urgently required. Besides the bed, which we had commissioned in Boston, there would have to be a bookshelf and writing desks for both of us. Since Edward would do all his business in his counting house, he would only have a desk box for the few letters he would write at home. Mine was to be the larger one, fitted with a good stand.

We needed chests and cupboards for pewter, linens, and clothing. In London, I had seen a pattern for a chest, its panels carved with flowing leaves and flowers. I fell in love with it, and even though it supposedly bordered on ostentation, Edward agreed that we should have it. I asked him to write to England for it, as local workmanship was not up to such detailed and refined decoration. The day he wrote, I ran upstairs humming a tune I made up as I went. Sure enough, was not old lady Eaton standing in the corridor, frowning. She was so disapproving of my levity she would not even speak. My tune faded right away. Whenever I was truly excited about something she cast a spell of gloom over me.

At the same time that we ordered the chest, we commissioned two mahogany drop-leaf tables, one for each parlour. These new designs were far more practical for our needs, I told him, than the old trestle tables the Eatons still used. I thought they were much more handsome, too, but I didn't say so. Edward was not difficult to persuade, but one must go slowly. If this is what housekeeping was going to be like, I thought I might enjoy it.

I might have known that my spending so much time on the purchases of household goods would not be popular with my stepfather. His house had fine furnishings, but he acted as if he did not even notice their existence, his mind being on loftier matters. Why such a pretense should be so important to him, I failed to see. One day, he found me in the hall, rubbing my hand over the surface of my writing-desk, which had just been delivered. Silky as a cat's fur it was. That must have been the last straw. He asked Edward for a word in private in his study.

Edward came out of the room with his lips pressed together, his head down and leading like a battering ram. He was so annoyed by Mr. Eaton's remarks about my acquisitiveness that he could not help telling me. "I don't like to repeat others' criticisms, but this time Theophilus has gone too far, even for me." Then he told me how the conversation had gone:

"He said, 'Your wife certainly seems to be looking forward to being mistress of her own house.'

"I said, 'Indeed she is. I am so glad she is taking hold this way. It has helped her get through the hardship of this winter.'

"Eaton said, 'Don't you worry about her enthusiasm for all these new furnishings she is forever talking about? I would not like to see her become too proud of the house, which is to be vain, in the broadest sense of the word. Or even too gluttonous—I believe one might use that word to apply to belongings.'

"I said, 'I don't look at it that way, sir. She is exuberant, and wants to make our home respectable and welcoming. I think that aim is perfectly suited to our position in the community where we will be living.'

"'Of course I do not intend to intrude, or to correct you in your dealings with her,' he said. 'Yet I must warn you that she can stretch that exuberance too far sometimes, as perhaps you yourself may have noticed. There is a time for high spirits and a time for restraint, which she has not always understood very well.'

"I saw that the veins in Theophilus's neck were bulging, as they often do when he senses that his views are being challenged. All the same, I said, 'I thank you for pointing this out. However, in the short while that we have been married, I have had nothing of that sort to complain of. And I know she is anything but vain or greedy." I wanted to end this conversation, which would only get more irksome, but I wasn't going to play into his hands by conceding even a little bit. So I changed the subject. I said, 'We are both keen to get on with our work in Hartford, as soon as this heavy winter is over.'

"'Of course you would be,' he said. I was glad he could take the hint, and we began to discuss matters of business where we are in agreement."

Edward finished his account of the conversation and looked at me apologetically. "I am sorry, Anne, to tell you this, as I know what you think of your stepfather already. I am a pretty mild-mannered person most of the time, I think, but sometimes Theophilus does irritate me thoroughly, no matter how hard I try not to let it show."

I said gloomily "Nothing changes. Mr. Eaton's righteous attitude slaps me down every time I speak out about anything. I remember once when I brought a boy home who had some beautiful fresh white mushrooms to sell, and he saw us and was downright nasty to the boy and sent him away. He told me I should control my exuberance, as if it was a swear word. I remember I said, 'Don't you like surprises, even nice ones like mushrooms?' He just stiffened right up and turned away.

"I've always been amazed that you two get along as well as you do. Let's forget about this, we'll soon be away, and free of all this condemnation." I wrapped my arms around him, and he stayed there letting me do so, until he remembered that the men were delivering the new, wonderfully decorated chest at any moment. I was out of the room ahead of him, headed for the door.

One afternoon, I decided to try and ask my mother for some advice about the new house. When I went to look for her, I found her sitting idly in the hall, absent-mindedly tapping her foot, as if she did not know why she was there. It seemed like a good moment to ask for help. I wanted to know, for instance, how should I keep the linens to prevent them getting mildewed in the dampness? Nothing ever dried completely in this climate. When I asked her this, the reply was, "How should I possibly know? It is trouble enough just to keep things clean. You will just have to put up with whatever you have there."

This answer did not satisfy me, of course. She did not have her mind on my problems. She made it quite clear almost daily that she had enough trouble of her own with a six-year-old girl to supervise, and another child on the way. Still I persisted; I had nowhere else to turn. "But should I have the workmen build me a drying closet close to a chimney? Do you remember, I think we had such a thing at Plâs Grono?"

Her exasperation was evident in her tone. "No, I don't remember, it had nothing to do with me. The servants took care of everything there. For goodness' sake, why don't you ask someone else — some goodwife with nothing else to think about? Oh, here you are, darling. Did you sleep well?" She turned away from me to lift Hannah, still rubbing her eyes, into her lap. "I won't be able to do this much longer, my lap has almost disappeared. Anne, would you bring a bowl of milk for Hannah? She's thirsty, aren't you child?"

Hannah nodded, eyeing me suspiciously. Why did she always look at me like that? You would think she was afraid I would carry her off somewhere horrible. Not a chance. If Mother did not stop fawning over her, she was going to grow into such a nasty, whining girl they would have to pay some young man a fortune to take her off their hands.

Acting like a dutiful daughter I went off to find the milk, resenting every step, and with no more inkling than before as to how to dry clothes.

I had noticed, over the course of my time in New Haven, that my mother was acting peculiarly. In Wales, she had been overwrought with grief, self-pitying and often just miserable. But then there were times when she would lighten up, the silly merriment of the young wife would peek through, and she would forget herself for a while. Her marriage to Mr. Eaton appeared to have squelched all that for good, even though it had swept away the misery too. She seemed to live on a smooth plane in London; rule-bound and sober though it was, it must have suited her in a city where everything was fearfully mercurial. But ever since we arrived in New England, and particularly since her most recent pregnancy began, she was starting to change again. There were outbursts of anger and impatience, like the one I just described. Like the rest of us, life in London had not prepared her for New England, nor was having her fifth child at the age of forty-five an event to look forward to. She had already lost two infants in childbirth. I heard her complaining once to Mr. Eaton that this was not what she had bargained for at all. His rejoinder was that God's will was to be followed and rejoiced in at all times. It was he alone who knew what was for our good. The next child was to be considered a special blessing, coming to her in her middle years, and after her other losses. "If it doesn't drive me crazy, my being so old," she countered. They had moved out of earshot, so I was spared from hearing Mr. Eaton's reply.

I did not know how she could bear being there, with that harridan of a mother-in-law always looking over her shoulder, and Mr. Stick-in-the-mud Eaton, and that child. I was glad to be leaving, but there were times when I felt so sorry for her that I thought I should stay. She needed someone, even if she did not care that much for me. Perish the thought! I was on my way.

3.

NOW, HERE I AM at last in a new house in a new town with an almost brand-new husband, and the prospect of making many interesting new friends. Anyone who has come this far and put up with such difficulties must have extraordinary vision, and some thrilling stories to tell. I can hardly wait to meet them.

This first morning I walk around our spacious house, stepping carefully around the last of the workmen who are finishing off some new moldings in the hall, and peeking into the parlour and the small private parlour beyond it. I must look like an idiot to them, darting in and out with an enormous grin on my face, but I cannot help myself and I do not care what they think really as I am enjoying my new mistress-ship so much. I go over and look out of each of the large windows in the front. They are the best part of the house so far, with twelve panes in each so the sun can pour in all day long. No one can complain of gloomy surroundings here. Apparently we are such an important family that these grand leaded glass windows are considered quite suitable for us, as they were for the Debenhams, also a trading family, or so Edward told me when he was sketching the house for me last winter. It seems that the sun, whose rays are free to all, is limited by our laws only to the most deserving. The Lord's largesse is graded according to rank.

I am thinking about what houses can do for one's life, my own at least. Are they really the outward sign of the people who live in them? Like Plâs Grono, for instance; it suited my grandfather so well. Like him, it was a strong, alert house, shabbily self-satisfied, breathing an air of comfort and kindness. How can a house be kind, I wonder. By allowing one the room to grow, play, wander, muse, laugh, and cry. A house like that does not reprove one for showing emotions of any sort.

That was not the situation when I lived in the Eaton establishment in Bullard's Lane in London. It was more like a jail than a home, with its cold bare walls. The furniture was sparse, even though it was handsome. Such a grey house, its formidable look was the very mirror of its owner. The light coming through the heavy windows always seemed thin, the wood burned weakly in the huge fireplaces, and the vast stone floors echoed every step you took. Cowed by the aloofness of the place, I was never at ease. There were no sheltering corners for me to hide in with a book. Books were read at a table, whilst sitting on hard leather chairs intended to keep one's back as upright as one's mind. And they were read aloud.

"It is Anne's turn to read tonight," Mr. Eaton would say. "You can continue with Chauncy's sermon where we left, on page 314 where it is marked, and go to the end which is…" he turned the pages, "on page 323."

Then, sitting in the parlour between my mother and stepfather, with old Mistress Eaton glowering in her corner, I would begin, trying to give some inflection to this turgid material (the Reverend Mr. Chauncy was a terrible windbag), to make it bearable for myself, even if none of the listeners cared. They were obliged to ingest this matter, whether they admired it or not. Rhetorical estimations hardly came into it: Mr. Eaton would have none of them, and my mother's thoughts were never engaged by reading of any sort. As for my brothers, their minds could be counted on to be as far away as possible, just as mine would have been, given the chance.

There was no fury in this house, except what I held inside my stomach, and which gave me cramps. Sometimes, after I had finished reading, and Mr. Eaton had concluded the evening's prayers, my anger would start to rise, ready to burst out of my body, and I would fly to my room. Then I would let it loose.

"What's wrong with them?" I would cry. "How can they stand to read this horrible pedantic stuff night after night? It's like living with statues here. Even my mother has lost her desire to weep and rage the way she used to. Where has the spark gone? Will I lose it too?" Anger always led to tears, and I would press my head into my pillow and cry till I was worn out.

No one ever came to ask what was wrong, and, of course, there was no one to answer my questions. I realized that the perpetual sitting still, and that sombre, doom-centred house were telling on me. I needed to get away, run, shout, wave my arms, jump over fences — something, anything, to prevent an explosion, which was sure to come if I were restrained much longer. If Edward had not come, I do not know what I would have done. So that was home for me in London — a place I wanted to escape from.

It was not the sitting still that bothered me the most, it was the reason for it. I can sit quietly when I want to. I love to spend time alone, outside on a bench in a park perhaps, or in my own chamber tucked into a chair, letting my mind travel along any path it chooses. Sometimes it will start racing ahead with an idea that just comes to me. At other times, it just meanders wherever it pleases, like a bee nuzzling for nectar. But, in Bullard's Lane, the mind was not free to roam. It was this horrid waste of time and thought that I hated. It was like living in a dreary cell, a prison of the mind that shut out the fresh air of discourse, the light on the path of the intellectual quest, and even the cloud-capped towers of dreams.

Now, in Hartford is a house empty of old complaints, a tabula rasa for a freshly minted loving couple. This is going to be different from those other houses I have known. It will be neither creaky and contentedly settled, like Plâs Grono, nor chilly with regulated disapproval like Bullard's Lane. It needs character, and Edward and I will give it that. In my mind's eye I see the house of my dreams realized, a place where happiness reigns and the mind is free.

On this, my first morning in Hartford, I am on my own. Edward has gone out to see about the delivery of some grain to his mill. The mill was the second purchase he made last year, after buying the house. The mill's previous owner had become rheumatic after living for two years above his business, and was eager to sell and attempt something drier by way of a trade. Edward bought him out, and then hired him to stay on until he could train another manager. A man he brought over on the *Hector* will take it on shortly, but in the meantime, Edward has his hands full. "I'm sorry to have to leave you so early on your first day, but I will be home for dinner. I know you and the servants will get along splendidly." He kissed me goodbye, and was off.

So here I am, mistress of this whole, vast, wonderful house. There are seven servants to help, but, although I have lived in houses with many servants almost all my life, I have never had to supervise them, or decide what their duties should be. Edward said he would be leaving all that to me. I tell myself I can handle everything, even though I am ignorant of what that is.

First, I think, the obvious task to complete is the unpacking. There is this great pile of our belongings in boxes and trunks cluttering up the hall. It cannot stay there one minute longer. Everything else can wait. Two young men are hovering in the back of the hall, looking me over, I suppose, so I tell them to take the trunks that hold our clothing upstairs to our chamber. I am so excited about seeing our own things again that I forget to say thank you. I will apologize for that later. Then I ask them to find Nellie to help me.

Nellie is the only servant I have met, the only one who has a name attached to her. Nellie had brought me up a cup of broth while I was still in bed, gingerly set it down beside me, and bade me a whispery "Good morning, Mistress." I hardly saw the back of her before she disappeared. Now I will have a chance to find out what having my own personal maid is like.

We set to work, opening the trunks and laying all their contents on the bed, the chair, even the carpet, before deciding where everything should go. I work alongside this stranger, and am amazed at her energy. She is bony thin, half a head shorter than I am, and yet she can fly around the room like a squirrel on a fence. At first she says nothing, keeping her head down and her eyes fixed on the task. But gradually I melt her nervousness — it is my famous exuberance that does it — and she grows as chatty as I am.

"Oh, look here," I say. "Here's my second-best costume. It hasn't been out of the trunk since we left England. It survived the trip very well. What do you think?"

Nellie's eyes open wide. The gown is the palest blue with little sparkling bits in them. "It's so lovely, I've never seen anything so beautiful in my life. It will come out just perfect after it's hung out."

"But this old wool gown is a mess. Do you think you can rescue it?"

Nellie examines it carefully. "I can try, Mistress. It will take some cleaning, but I think it will surprise you when it's done."

When she smiles she is quite pretty, and her skin is as soft as goose down. She is not the pathetic waif I took her for in the first place.

As the morning goes on, the two of us unwrap all my gloves, neckcloths, handkerchiefs, collars, caps, and aprons, laughing and exclaiming over each item. In a matter of hours, Nellie's manner changes from that of a stiffly polite maidservant to the somewhat deferential companion. We are just about the same age, I guess. She is like a young cousin come in from the farm to visit the wealthier city relative. At the same time, I am beginning to treat her almost as a friend. I did not realize until now how much I miss having someone to talk to about girlish things.

After an hour or so, Nellie, upon going downstairs for a needle and thread, hears a buzz of disgruntled conversation coming from the kitchen. She comes back to me looking worried. "I don't want to upset you, Mistress, but some of the other servants seem to be a bit unhappy right now. I wasn't sure I should tell you, but I thought you should know before matters got worse."

"Oh dear, do you know what it is about?" I ask.

"Well, it seems they haven't been given any orders, as the master has gone off to the mill, and you" — she hesitates for a minute and then laughs — "are 'upstairs giggling with that silly wench Nellie, who we don't know at all.'"

I laugh too, but then decide it is not all that funny. Most of the servants came with the house. They are all indentured, most of them for seven years, and Edward purchased their papers. Nellie is a new arrival, found by Mistress Hooker, our minister's wife, who had written to Edward suggesting her for my maid. He thought the girl could have no better reference and promptly hired her. This was supposed to be a nice surprise for me. Silly Edward, it did not occur to him that I might rather choose my own maidservant. As it turns out, Nellie is exactly the sort of person I would have chosen myself. It dawns on me that the other servants would be understandably irked that I am spending my time with her before speaking to them.

I say, "What else are they saying?"

"'What about the meals? I don't even know how many I am to cook for, let alone what she would like me to serve. She probably doesn't know how long it takes to prepare a meal. What if she doesn't come downstairs until almost dinner time?'" Nellie rumbles, in what I discover later is a fair imitation of Cook's voice at her testiest. I learn soon enough that Cook's temper is never smooth. From the sounds of Nellie's hilarious copycat voice, she is almost at the boil.

"Then Henry said — he's the one in charge of the household, after you, that is — that they must just carry on as before, and if the mistress doesn't like it, he will have to tell the master that they had no instructions, and did what they could."

"And then Cook said —" Nellie looks at me naughtily and lowers her voice to a man's bass, "'Well, I will have to make do with what is in the larder and the garden. No one has given me any money for purchases,' and she went off to the kitchen, muttering under her breath, along with Ardyth, who helps her.

"The rest were standing about waiting for orders, so Henry sent them off to do the sweeping and dusting and washing the corridor. I'm sure they will all be perfectly satisfactory, once you get to know them." She puts her hand to her mouth, wondering if she has gone too far.

On my very first day and? I have put my foot in it. How was I to have known? Who could have instructed me? My mother never ran her own household. She tried occasionally when we lived with Grandfather Yale, but she was in such a state that the housekeeper more or less ignored her and kept on as she had always done. After she became Mistress Eaton the younger, old Mistress Eaton ruled the roost. She grudgingly allowed Mother to arrange a few things, but she certainly did not want me around at all, underfoot, acting silly, so she said. Whenever she saw me hovering around the kitchen observing, she sent me away, with "Don't bother Cook, she might make a mistake," or "Don't look in that pot, your hair will fall in and ruin the soup," or "Go and tidy your room." All I was good for, in her books, was sweeping the dust from under the bed. The old bat would even check to be sure I had done it just right.

If I had been a seasoned housewife I would not have started on my unpacking before making arrangements for the household. At least I should have called in all the servants first thing in the morning, and introduced myself to them. Well, never mind, it is too late for that. We have almost finished unpacking by this time, so I come downstairs to meet everyone, wherever they can be found. By noon I have met them all, and done my utmost to mollify everyone, particularly Cook. When Edward comes home, she serves us an excellent dinner of cod, clams, beans, corn bread, and some dried fruits, and we compliment her on it warmly. Nellie is having her dinner in the kitchen when Cook comes out looking as pleased as Cook can be, and says, as Nellie reports: "She just ain't had the experience, that's all. I don't know how she's going to manage." I have to agree with her, but I will manage all the same.

After dinner Edward asks Henry how the household is getting along, and Henry assures him, without a hint of the doubt he feels, that all is well.

I tell myself that in the days to come I will start the morning by consulting with Cook, with Henry and with Zachary the gardener, but I am sure I will almost always agree to anything they suggest. They know much better about these things than I do, so I will tell them to decide, and let me know. I will learn, but it will take time.

4.

OUR FIRST VISITOR ARRIVES today, just after breakfast. Nellie rushes to answer the knock on the door, and Edward follows her quickly to see who it is.

"Welcome to Hartford, Mr. Hopkins." I hear a strong voice, mellow and impressive, used to public speaking I expect.

Edward says, "Reverend sir, please come in. How kind of you to call."

I know who it must be: the town's respected spiritual leader, the Reverend Thomas Hooker himself. What an honour this is.

He is no stranger to Edward, though I know him only by reputation. The most celebrated of all the "silenced" preachers in England, Mr. Hooker's compelling sermons are still passed along the Puritan underground even after his escape from detention by leaving the country and his arrival here. His zeal for founding a community of gathered Christians was catching. On meeting him for the first time, Edward was instantly persuaded to link his fortunes with Mr. Hooker's in Hartford rather than go to New Haven or Boston. I hear Edward's heartfelt greeting and discern his deferential manner.

"I wanted to be the first to call on you and your good wife, and to inquire about your journey," the older man replies, standing in the hall as he removes his wide-brimmed hat and cloak.

Edward ushers him into the room, and presents me as proudly as if I were a duchess.

"Mr. Hooker, here is my dear wife, Anne Yale Hopkins."

Mr. Hooker bows, then straightens. He looks at me as if trying to take in the whole of my character in the manner of someone who needs to understand in order to love; and, it is only when such understanding has taken place that he can love unconditionally.

He says, "I am heartily pleased that you have come, Mistress Hopkins. Hartford will be all the richer for the presence of your husband and yourself. The congregation particularly welcomes you. We are already preparing to accept you both as members." He turns to Edward. "The report of your faith has preceded you."

I stand in the same spot, fascinated. This dignified person with the beguiling smile is the man about whom I had heard so much in England. The man of great learning and understanding, the preacher whom even Archbishop Laud was afraid to touch for fear of an uprising. I know all that, but no one has prepared me for his appearance.

He is tall and of slim build, not just the result of fasting, but of good bones and healthy flesh. Although I know he is older than Edward by a few years, he looks younger, sprightlier. His pitch-black hair curves in soft waves around his lean face with its high smooth forehead and long but unobtrusive nose. His lips — and here I catch myself staring — tell of friendly warmth, gentle seriousness, and, yes, a fondness that has nothing to do with the desires of the spirit. This latter notion comes into my mind and is then pushed away in a flash. I could be mistaken. Above all, the Reverend Mr. Hooker looks every inch a patrician, which is surprising, as he comes from yeoman stock. I ask myself, could anyone be as handsome as he is and still be church worthy? I am smitten. Whatever you tell me, I am ready to believe, I swear.

I sit down now, and listen, probably with a benighted expression on my face, to the two men discussing the affairs of the town, the new families who have arrived, the building that must start in order to house them properly, and the need for a governor and full council now that the town had grown so much.

Turning to me, Mr. Hooker says, "The women of the congregation are eager to greet you, Mistress Hopkins. There are not nearly enough of them yet, but we have hope that many more will be joining us, with their husbands. Even with all the farm work and household chores they have to do, they insist on gathering once a week, to help one another and to be sociable. You must come as soon as you are settled in."

I say right away, "Oh yes, I'll come next week for certain."

He pauses for a moment. "You will find life much simpler here than it was in London. It may take a while to get used to it."

"Oh, but I am already accustomed to that after a year in New Haven. Nothing could have been plainer," I say, and then bite my tongue. "I mean, I have no reason to regret being in Hartford instead of London, where everything is topsy-turvy and noisy and vicious. Here it is Eden compared to that city."

Hooker smiles knowingly. "Yes, London has become intolerable, for Puritans especially. But don't expect Connecticut to be a pure delight, either. We are in the midst of a vast wilderness here, in which we are struggling to make a garden. There are lots of dangers around us, threats to both body and soul." He looks at me intently. "You appear to be plucky enough to handle the remoteness and austerities of living here. I think you will get on very well."

Edward asks, "What about the Indian problems? Are the attacks truly over?"

"For the time being, but there is always the fear that there will be another uprising. Their numbers have dwindled, though, and those who are left are struggling to survive after this fierce winter."

I ask, "Are there no Indian peoples who are friendly to us?"

"Yes, indeed. The neighbouring tribes are friendly enough. They helped us a great deal with food and planting when we first arrived two years ago. We couldn't have endured without them."

I say, perhaps too eagerly, "Oh good. I hope to meet some of them, and see how they live."

Edward and Mr. Hooker exchange looks. Edward says, "Perhaps you shall, Anne, but remember, they are savages. They don't understand our ways, nor we theirs. You will have to be on your guard all the time."

Mr. Hooker adds, "There are plenty of other good folk to meet first, before you go troubling yourself about the Indians. If I were you, I would take one step at a time. Learn what others can tell you about the Indians before you go to see for yourself. That's my advice, although you haven't asked for it."

I say, "It is good advice, thank you. I won't rush in like a fool, I promise." I beam at him. He may say whatever he pleases and I will pay attention.

Right now, he says his farewells. The day after next being Sunday, he will see us again soon. I catch myself wishing it were tomorrow.

What a man! So unlike the pious ministers I have met who dare not look to right or left for fear of corrupting themselves. There must be more like Mr. Hooker, but where they are hiding I do not know. He reminds me of David in a way; he has the same vitality and assured manner. But David does not have this full-blooded saintliness that draws me to Mr. Hooker like a deer to birchbark. I must put this down in my journal. I dare not admit it to anyone else, not even Jane. And also that I would love to meet a real savage.

5.

TODAY BEING SATURDAY, Edward rushes out early, saying that he has to complete his accounts and look over his bills of lading before the day's end. I ask, "Could I come and see the mill with you?"

"I am sorry, my dearest, but there is so much to do I wouldn't have time to show you around. Another time."

"Come home early," I say, "I'm feeling a little strange all alone here."

"Of course I will, since tomorrow is the Sabbath. But you aren't alone. There are all the servants if there is an emergency of any sort, which I am sure there won't be."

"Oh no, it's not that —" but then I wonder what it could be that bothers me. The servants are respectful, Nellie is a dear, Mr. Hooker is gracious and not overpowering. The people who brought us home the night before last were as near to rowdy as I have ever seen Puritans, and effusively friendly. I guess they had been preparing their welcome in the tavern.

So why am I so anxious, I wonder. After Edward kisses me tenderly and goes off hastily to his counting house at the mill, I stay in the small parlour pursuing the question. Edward is the only person I know in this whole place. That is an odd feeling, new to me, because wherever I have lived I have been surrounded by familiar people. Even if some were not so pleasant, at least you knew how they would behave towards you, it was something you could count on. I am the stranger among people who know each other. Will this new land have changed them, and will I change too? Will I find new friends who will become as dear as the ones I left behind?

There is so much to discover it almost overwhelms me.

I try to talk sense to myself: do not borrow trouble; stop sitting here fretting and do something. So I decide to go for a walk, to have my first look at the town. By skipping out the door on the private side of the house, away from the stables and the servants' eyes, I feel the guilty excitement of a schoolgirl who has avoided the teacher's baleful reprimand. I pass through the whole town, walking on both sides of the Little River, from end to end, trying to capture the essence of this settlement I am to be part of.

I have already made up my mind that I will be the colony's first historian, writing down whatever I can learn about Hartford and its surroundings, including the church, the first planters, and everything to do with daily life. My first journal, which I am going to call *A Connecticut Spring*, will be written for the small intimate circle of which Jane is a part. So this is what I write after my first excursion:

April 12, 1639

"The first thing that takes my breath away, literally, is the air. Spring comes later here than in England, so there is a bit of a chill left, and at the same time the damp smell of the earth reawakening, its feet soaked, its skin opening its pores to allow the little green shoots to emerge. The only perfumes come from this reborn earth and from the forests of pines that protect the outer limits of the town. The sharp intensity of the pine scent fades the further I go along the road towards the Little River, and by the time I come to the ford it is the smells of building that reach me. My nose is filled with the insistent stuffiness of fresh lumber being sawn and hammered into new houses; but then, it is liberated by the enticement of cooking fires and their simmering stewpots. And everywhere, tossed into the air by carts, cattle and people, is the dust. You cannot avoid building without leavings, but the sawdust is so thick in places that one wonders whether, if you could gather it all together again, you could build a second town!

"The town is in two parts, divided north and south by the Little River, and joined by a ford. Both parts lie also along the west side of the big river, the Connecticut, and so each part has a large meadow and a good stretch of salt marsh for the cattle, protected by a long fence, which everyone may use. Edward has another piece of meadowland further up the river, so he does not share in the common ground. To my untrained eye, his land looks even more lush than the other. We shall have to see how well our cattle fare. Mr. Hooker calls this a struggling garden in a violent wilderness, but to me it is already a rich and flourishing land.

"As I walk the length of the town as far as the upper meadow and back, I am amazed to find the place so empty. Where are the merry folk who met us when we arrived? I expect to find crowds in the street going shopping. How unlike Wrexham, our Welsh county seat, where on a Saturday you could meet everyone you knew hustling to market, stopping for a quick chat to pass on the week's news, and then going home with their baskets full of fresh fruit and vegetables. I remember the tinkers and the actors at the market most days, their air of light devilry, their teasing antics. I even miss the drunkards spilling out of the ordinary at all hours, calling out nonsensical greetings. Here it is like a graveyard. There is not a soul walking along the road, except a single man with a cartload of rocks, who eyes me curiously. I try my best well-wisher's smile but it brings no warm response. I fear there are no convivial Welshmen here. Maybe my first impression was an illusion caused by fatigue.

"Eventually I determine that most of the men are at work in their fields — those who are not building houses — and the women are inside preparing meals for today and tomorrow. On the Sabbath, one does not fuss with food. If the day goes the way it did in New Haven, by the time you have dressed and walked to the meeting house, sat there the whole morning, greeted people after the service, walked home, eaten dinner, walked back, taken in the second service, walked home again, swallowed a little supper, said prayers and got ready for bed — it turns out to have been the heaviest day of the week. The servants, who are supposed to be able to rest from their work, hardly have time for visiting their parents, or for courting, or whatever they please. And they call the Sabbath a day of rest!"

This first real night in our own house (last night does not count, as I can hardly remember falling asleep, curled up in the curve of Edward's body, a convex pair if ever there was one), the walls are so thin we whisper our tendernesses, giggling once or twice at the thought of being heard by the servants. Then we lose all discretion, linking our bodies in the best man-to-woman way, not caring at all when, as the wondrous moment comes, our sighs ring out in that silent night.

6.

ON THIS, OUR FIRST SUNDAY, Edward and I set out in good time, with the servants keeping a solid line close behind us walking in order of importance: Cook first with Henry, Nellie with Jenny the housemaid, Zachary the gardener shepherding Peter the youngest hand, and finally Ardyth the scullery maid with Seth, the other hand. It appears that no one is to be in doubt as to who their master is. I take Edward's arm, as usually happens. I do most of the talking as we walk, pointing out curiosities that strike me and asking questions about the church, and more importantly, its ministers.

"Look at that quaint house, Edward. It's half in the ground. It reminds me of a Welsh miner's hut."

"It's made in the same way, actually, with rushes for the sides and roof. You can see how digging it into the hillside gives it support and warmth. Huts like these are just temporary, though, until the new people can afford to build better. They are dangerous, so I think they will be disallowed."

"Why is that? Oh, I see, there is no chimney, and those rushes would flame up in a minute. Do you think Mr. Hooker will preach this morning?"

"Almost certainly. He speaks in the morning, and Mr. Stone speaks in the afternoon. Don't make such a face, dear. I know you were unhappy about Mr. Stone's behaviour on the ship, but perhaps he has changed since then. He's been here over a year now. Maybe Mr. Hooker has softened him."

"If he can't, no one can. Mr. Hooker could persuade anyone to be kind," I say fervently.

"Now you're jumping to conclusions again. You've only met Mr. Hooker once, and already you are praising him to the skies," he teases. "Of course you're right about Mr. Hooker. Let's hope you are wrong about his associate."

"He can't be all that bad if Mr. Hooker admires him."

"I believe he does, yes, even though they don't seem much alike," Edward says.

We have come to the ford, and across the riveret I catch sight of a tall white clapboard house with a wooden slat fence across the front. "See that house, Edward. I passed it yesterday and wondered who its owner was. It's so handsome."

"It belongs to our worthy Mr. Hooker," says Edward." I know you will agree that he deserves it, though I'm not sure that you'll feel the same about Mr. Stone's next door."

I look to my left at another house, somewhat smaller but just as well built as Mr. Hooker's. "As to that, I will hold back my opinion until I know more of the man." I am laughing now, mostly at myself.

We chat this way until we are almost at the meeting-house grounds, when in unison our expressions become serious and we stop talking, as befits the occasion, our first entrance into this congregation.

Anyone seeing a New England meeting house for the first time would not call it a striking building — anything but. Its sole purpose is to supply the primary needs of the congregation in the form of prayer and instruction, for, in order to become a visible saint, attention to God's word, penitence, and faith, are required. Such trivialities as ornate buildings, gilt vestments, exotic odours, and elaborate music, are not only unnecessary but downright hindrances. The worst that can be said of them is that they are popery, which is kith and kin to devilry, which means the death of the spirit. Of course I disagree with all such condemnation, having been raised to love the beauteous worship of our handsome parish church in Wrexham. Still, I would have to say that the modesty of this little meeting house — a plain, square, wooden box, without steeple, altar, pews or ornament of any sort — suits our simplified lives, as well as the directness of the spiritual vision encouraged here.

I came to loathe going to the meeting house in New Haven, dreading every service. I know I am a sinner — is not everyone? — but to be made to feel like an unrepentant worm three times a week, to be coerced into a relentless examination of one's guilt, made my skin crawl and my stomach turn over. Of course, the preachers would say that was what was supposed to happen on your way to salvation. But, truth be told, I could not see how the pastures of the blessed fit into the picture of gloomy, grovelling creatures that the New Haven preachers painted.

This meeting house is different. For one thing, it is ours, in the centre of town, where the whole community comes together. For another, there is Mr. Hooker. Enough said. Edward and I take the places we are assigned on the front benches, on opposite sides of the room, both of us facing the end of the table where the two ministers will sit. It occurs to me that for all that the saints abhor symbolism, they have not got rid of it. This arrangement of benches on three sides of the square shows all of us to each other, and lets us feel what it is like to be gathered together. Like a large family.

I look around as circumspectly as I can, and find that everyone is looking at me, at least, it seems like everyone. You are not supposed to acknowledge anyone during this solemn time, and it makes me feel a bit uneasy, being stared at, and not being able to respond. They all pretend they are not staring at me, just into space, but I know better. I try the same trick, but wherever I glance sideways I find someone's eyes on me, so I stop, and consider first, the walls, then the floor, and finally my lap. It would not have hurt them to paint the walls or stain the benches. And it is hard to see very well in here without any windows. I suppose it helps to keep the room warmer. It is chilly today without any heat. I can imagine what it is going to be like in winter. Maybe Edward can ask to put in a stove. There is no point in dying of pneumonia indoors if we do not have to. We will have trouble enough outside.

At this moment everyone stands up. The ministers are arriving. Here is Mr. Hooker with Mistress Hooker beside him; she is a large flowery woman, whose imposing chest, wide shoulders and solid torso fill out her long wool cloak handsomely. She carries herself comfortably erect, her expression serene. She is used to being the centre of attention. Behind them come Mr. and Mistress Stone. Beside the minister's long angular frame, as bristly as a bulrush, his wife doubles her steps to keep up, as she barely reaches his shoulder. She is a drab little reedlike thing, swallowed up in her clothes. I cannot decipher anything about her from her face; it is as bland as butter. She stares straight ahead of her, concentrating on her entrance.

After we are all seated again and bend our heads for a moment of silent prayer, Mr. Hooker stands and immediately begins his sermon.

"My text for this morning is *Matthew* 11, verses 28 and 29: 'Come unto me, all ye that are weary and laden, and I will ease you. Take my yoke upon you, and learn of me that I am meek and lowly in heart, and ye shall find rest unto your souls'."

His voice fills the room, rich and fluid. He reads Scripture as if he is totally immersed in it, as he probably is. He pauses. No one makes a sound.

"My dear friends, this is the heart of Christ's message for us, for today and every day. We come here, as we do over and over again, to learn what that promise is, for we keep forgetting. We come to find out what it means to take Christ's yoke upon us, for we have been unwilling to do so. And we come to learn of him who is meek and lowly of heart, for we are proud and think wrongly that we are great."

Mr. Hooker leans forward intensely, his eyes moving through the room to engage every single person's attention. He need not have worried: all eyes are fixed on him. I am reminded of the great eagle, symbol of John the Evangelist.

"We have been singularly blessed, to be gathered here in New England. Back in our former home, we have seen and understood how God has shown his displeasure towards his people, those he had chosen for a new Israel. They have disputed, disobeyed, warred among themselves, and falsely treated the gospel. They have angered God and now he is withdrawing from England. He is packing up his gospel because none will buy his wares. But he has continued merciful, and has not withdrawn his protection and his love from everyone. He has sent out his Noahs from their homeland before he disappears from it completely. We are among those fortunate few who have taken part in his little fleet of arks. We have travelled on the high seas, enduring dangers to body and soul, and were always supported and preserved through God's providential care.

"Now we have come here, and God has given us New England as a refuge, a rock, and a shelter for his righteous ones, and for those who desire to be saved. We have undertaken the voyage together, we have landed safely, and now we must lay hold on God and his promises."

I feel the solemn warmth of his words filling my whole being. I have never been stirred like this before. Other preachers whom I have heard had been mostly harsh and chilling, as if they were sentencing you to hard labour or to death. Some others had voices so dusty dry they might as well have been reciting a rule book. Then there were the florid ones, the smug old Laudians, who had not realized that times had changed, and more was demanded of them than self-congratulation. Here now is a man who is living with great devotion in the present time, and is encouraging, persuading, insisting that everyone join him with all their hearts. I try to take in and remember every word.

Mr. Hooker reaches the core of his sermon. "And how shall we be brought to the knowledge and love of God? Why, by undertaking another journey, far more rigorous and far more rewarding than the one we have recently undergone. This is a journey each one of us must take on his own, although we have others for guides and comfort along the way. Each person must set out on the perilous waters of life in order to save his soul; but be assured, the boat you take is neither leaky nor unstable. The promise of Scripture is the boat with which to carry a perishing sinner over to the Lord Jesus Christ.

"Learn of the Lord Christ, for his word is faithful, and his promise sure, and there you shall find rest as strong as Mount Sion. It is by that word that you shall be judged on the last day.

"Be not afraid. Launch your boat, praying fervently every moment of every day to the Lord our God to carry you carefully and guide you across the turbulent sea. Only trust in him and in the promises he has given in his Holy Scripture and you will arrive safely at the other shore."

I am captivated, both by his words and by the thrilling sound of his voice. This is the mission we have been sent on, and here is the man who can lead us. If any one can bring this little group to its safe haven, he can. I, who have never known what it is to be a visible saint, will try to learn. This is the first time I have ever wanted to.

I must admit that up until now I have been a reluctant Puritan. I was raised by a bishop's daughter in the house of my Grandfather Yale, a loyal servant of the King and, therefore, an Anglican. I knew no Puritans until my mother made her strange alliance with Theophilus Eaton. The strait-laced side of Puritan life was all I learned in my stepfather's house — joyless, humourless, colourless. When I married Edward, I told myself that in time I would take on his beliefs and customs as my own. Edward is no tunnel-visioned firebrand. He is a Christian whose thoughtful conversion to become a visible saint has led him to do his duty, and to seek salvation in his own quiet way. I love that about him. The faith of the saints would grow in me somehow, too, I believed. Now I can see how it might happen, with Mr. Hooker's guidance.

After the prayers, in which I join wholeheartedly, the ministers and congregation stand up and move outside to greet each other. I can scarcely get to my feet, I am so stiff. It is only now that I realize I have been sitting for an hour and a half without even noticing the time passing. I hope the meetings are always like this.

The scene outside is a disappointment after the stimulating experience indoors. On the bare brown plot of ground surrounding the meeting house, which even the weeds have vacated, small groups of people in uniformly black costume are standing. Why must serious purposes be so unattractively draped? Why is the only colour today to be found in the words of the preacher? How I would love to praise the Lord in scarlet and blue, as we used to. At least the conversations seem genial and animated.

Mr. Hooker has a word for everyone as he or she comes out the door. To us he says, "What a fine day for your first Sabbath. I will take it as a sign of God's favour towards you and all of the Hartford saints."

Edward agrees that it bodes well for everyone. Despite my wish to believe everything Mr. Hooker says, I think that the timing of good weather with our arrival is just a pleasant happenstance, though I certainly do not say so. As I move along to let others speak to Mr. Hooker, I come face to face with Mr. Stone, who is standing beside him. His smile of recognition looks forced and faint to me, but he bows politely, and introduces his wife. "I trust that you have settled properly into your new house," she says in a fluttery but unmusical voice.

"Yes, indeed, although I still have plenty to learn about it. Everything is so different here," I say.

"I shall call on you this week, and give you some help," Mistress Stone says. "Everyone needs advice when they first arrive."

I am flabbergasted. This little person, who seems so flimsy and dim, is going to give me advice! I keep myself from laughing, and instead manage to say, "That is very kind of you." I can see that Mr. Stone is looking me up and down, assessing my costume. A little frown suggests that he does not approve of it. Too grand? Too poor? Too heavy? Too thin? How could I know, and I do not care. It is a lovely day.

Edward, meanwhile has been speaking to Mistress Hooker. As I turn to join them, I notice that Mistress Stone is also examining me from head to toe, as if I am some strange creature from the antipodes.

Mistress Hooker is refreshing after this cool survey. "So this is Mistress Hopkins! I have been longing to meet you after Mr. Hooker came home and spoke so warmly about you. How are you getting on? Can I do anything for you? When will you come and visit me? Well, perhaps you don't have much time yet. Are you planting a garden? Do you like bees?"

I answer as best I can, but the questions fly out so fast I do not have time to get to them all. It does not matter too much, apparently; Mistress Hooker does not seem to care whether I reply or not. I am a bit mystified by this exchange. Is my interlocutor genuinely interested in everything about me, or is she just a feather-brained well-wisher? As wife to the brilliant Mr. Hooker, surely she has to be an intelligent woman. Time will tell.

The people mingling outside the meeting house seem to have made us the centre of attention. I am introduced all round. Most of the men are gravely solicitous, the women about as cheery as Mistress Hooker, and my anxiety about being on display vanishes. What a happy community this is. For the first time in my life, I feel I could become a part of some place, make a home of my own. The day is warming up, the breeze is gentle, and even the plain meeting house on its flat unrelieved ground seems, to me, to be even better suited to our community's honest, forthright nature.

Feeling so euphoric about everything and everyone, it takes me a while to notice a little knot of women who are clustered around Mr. Stone, talking earnestly. Every so often one of them looks over in my direction, but whether I am the focus of attention or not, I cannot decide. I am too busy exchanging pleasantries with many other strangers to give it much thought.

Only after I come home I start to wonder why none of the group came over to be introduced. They must have had something important to discuss with Mr. Stone, I reckon. Would I recognize any of the women if I met them somewhere? I am not sure. There was a tall bony person with a chicken's neck, about as old as my mother. I would know her again. As for the rest, it is hard to distinguish people who are dowdy and solid and all dressed in black. I put them out of my mind.

The rest of the day passes as Sabbaths usually do, with a hearty dinner, a walk through the town, the second lecture at the meeting house, and a quiet evening afterwards. Mr. Stone preaches an interminable sermon, to which I pay irregular attention. He cannot help it, I tell myself; he just does not have the gift. Anyone would have a hard time speaking after Mr. Hooker, but Mr. Stone's lack of oratorical skill makes it worse. I must try to make allowances, and think more kindly of him. What a difficult thing it is, sometimes, to do one's Christian duty.

7.

A DELEGATION OF PLANTERS has come to the house today to see Edward. I am not aware of their arrival, as I have gone down by the river to watch over the planting of the oak saplings. Edward tells me that I have a good eye for what people are coming to call the "prospect of a place." I observe the two husky men who are digging — such a beastly job in the heavy mud bank. Every so often one will stop, lean on his spade, push his cap back on his head and look at me as if to say, are you absolutely certain this is where you want this tree? Once, he says it aloud, "I hope you don't change your mind, Mistress, because these are mighty big holes to have to dig twice." I say, "Well if I do, it won't be until they are at least twenty years old, so you don't have to worry." They both laugh at this, and get back to work, throwing the dirt out of fresh holes with new gusto. Laughter lightens loads. I do not change my mind about any of the locations, and the results of their heavy labour, the lines of sturdy saplings, are well situated, I think.

Back at the house, with a basket full of violets I found along the bank, I discover we have visitors. I lay the purple blooms on the hall floor and go into the parlour. Four men are standing there, eyes fixed steadily on Edward, as rigid as the stone figures at Hampton Court. I realize immediately that I have interrupted something important, and start to withdraw, but Edward calls me over to him.

"I think you should stay and hear what these men have to say, Anne. It will affect you too." He introduces me to the group, who are, from what

I can discover, all well-to-do planters and visible saints. It strikes me that Edward has some inkling of why they have come.

Without further pleasantries they come to the point, each man speaking in turn as if he has a particular part to play, and has learned all his lines well. Mr. Smithurst speaks of the need for a governor, as the colony is now so large that it requires the services of a council, a court, and regulations to cover everything from fire watching and prevention, to the docking and delivery of goods. To ensure that all these decisions are made agreeably and in a timely manner, a governor is necessary, and an assistant too, in case the governor should be absent or otherwise unable to serve.

Having delivered the general speech, the rest of the men elaborate on each particular. Mr. Talbot speaks next. "You have already had administrative experience and know many government officials. No doubt you have learned to discriminate between honest and deceitful practice."

"We know you are upright in your dealings with other merchants," Mr. Goodwin adds. "You have had to establish rules of conduct and propose laws regarding shipping and the handling of goods."

Mr. Lowe speaks last. "We know that you have many enterprises in hand, but we are sure you are capable of taking on many more. It seems to us that you are one of those who is most contented the more he does." He looks at the others, who nod seriously.

Mr. Smithurst concludes for them all. "We think that your good will and understanding are the qualities most needed in a governor. There is no one else who could fill the position better." He gives a great sigh, as if the weight of his delivery has been lifted off his chest, and he can breathe again.

Edward sighs too, but it must be for a different reason. I reach out to take his hand, and then pull back quickly. This is too intimate for the circumstances. I realize that I am holding my breath, waiting to hear what he will say.

I look at the four men standing uneasily in a row, watching Edward, looking for clues to his reply. Apparently his decision means a great deal to them.

Edward says, "I am certainly not the only person you should consider.

I know I am somewhat older than the others I am thinking of, including all of you (they shake their heads), but age isn't the only quality required."

Mr. Lowe says, "Your greatest gifts are your sense of fairness, and your trust in the old standards we brought over with us."

Edward interrupts, no doubt to prevent them from having to say their piece all over again. "Thank you for all you have said, and for the honour you are doing me in inviting me to take this position. I cannot give you an answer today. I must first discuss this with my wife, and spend some time in prayer to discern the Lord's will in this." The men seem astonished that Edward would consult with me, his wife, on such matters.

Mr. Talbot breaks in. "We have all prayed about it, and believe that it is the Lord's will."

Edward responds firmly, "It may be his will for you to ask me, but I must find out if he wants me to accept." The rebuke hurts. Edward reaches over to Mr. Talbot and grips his shoulder. "You have done your duty well, friend, now I must do mine." A wan smile lights Mr. Talbot's face, and vanishes just as quickly.

"Thank you, good people, for coming. I will give you my answer as soon as I know it."

They troop out slowly, one after the other, after saying goodbye to me, not sure whether they have been given a good sign or the opposite. We watch them marching stolidly down the road, worrying about what to say to those who have sent them.

Edward turns to me. "Well!" I say, and sit down with a thump. He takes the chair beside me. "You could have knocked me over with a mere breath. Why didn't you tell me they were coming?"

"I didn't know."

"But you knew they would be coming some time, didn't you?" I persist.

Edward looks sheepish. "Yes." I stare hard at him. "In fact there was some talk of this before we left England."

I gasp. "Edward!"

"I'm sorry, Anne. I didn't want to tell you in case it didn't happen, and have you worrying for no reason."

"Me worry? What an idea! Me as governor's wife? All that entertaining, visiting, being treated as a senior woman in the colony, like Mistress Hooker herself? Why should I worry about that, me the renowned hostess and mature leader of women?" I am playing the injured party for all it is worth, but, in truth, the only thing I am really angry about is Edward's secretiveness.

Edward looks astonished at my outburst. He is hesitating, not knowing whether to be angry or to apologize. Instead he says nothing, and waits.

I begin to take in the implications of this proposal. Here I go again, about to enter another new phase of my life — because of course Edward must accept, and I must encourage him to do so. It is as if I am climbing up a steep hill, bristling with thick woods so I cannot see the way, nor what waits for me at the top. I suppose no one's life is any different, but mine seems to shift so rapidly and without any warning, and above all, so drastically.

I sit there drumming my fingers on my lap, taking stock. What shall I say now? I have disturbed him enough with my irony. I will have to make up for that, but the only way to do it is to say what I really think, not just put on a fair face and pretend that all is well.

I look up at him. His forehead is wrinkled and his mouth tight as a string. I give him a little smile. "I think you are absolutely the best person to be governor of Hartford, and that you should accept. I'll be very disappointed if you don't."

He looks hard at me. "Do you mean that?"

"I do. It will be a difficult job, for you especially, but in the end we will be happy that you took it on. You must seek the Lord's will, of course, if you are still in doubt, but I am certainly not."

Edward lays his hand over both of mine. "But for you, Anne, do you think it won't be too much of a strain? You won't have to entertain except occasionally. This colony is too small for that."

I say, "No, we aren't like London society. Truthfully, it frightens me some. This isn't what I expected my life to be like when I came here. But I suppose I will find out what's required of me, probably by attending to the way Mistress Hooker acts." I start to laugh. "I don't think I can fire off as many questions as quickly as she can, though."

Edward says, "She's not always like that, but yes, she is a woman you can learn from. She understands as well as her husband the true ways of the saints. And you have such a quick mind, you will pick them up just like that." He snaps his fingers.

I have not the heart to tell him it takes more than a ready mind to do these things. I will need an extra dose of that pluck Mr. Hooker saw in me. Instead I say, "Well, then, why don't you say yes, and see what follows?" I kiss him with a good loud smack. He promptly does the same.

Edward goes away to pray in private, and I return to the garden.

9.

DESPITE WHAT EDWARD SAYS about the lack of entertainment here, I seem to be holding open house every day. People are coming, to pay their respects they say, although I think it is curiosity that drives most of them especially after they heard who is to be the colony's governor. The only happy exception is Mistress Goodwin, who lives four houses away. She and her husband were among the first group to plant in Hartford, three years ago, and there is a sort of understanding here that the earliest citizens should do what they can for the new. I have already heard her praised for her godliness and warm-heartedness.

I am quite taken aback by her appearance, however. She is short and stout, and has a red shiny face that is spoiled by a few dull patches. That is not what upsets me, as she laughs a lot, and when she does, her whole body joins in with much jiggling up and down. It is her way of walking that is worrisome. Her legs are so stiff that it seems she has no joints in her knees. She has to place one foot carefully in front of the other when she walks. I see her grimace, though she tries to hide it by looking down at the ground. It is obvious that she is in pain. When I invite her to take a seat in the parlour, she has to hold on to the sides of the chair, and let herself into it slowly, but she cannot help flopping down with a bit of a thump.

This room is much too cold for a woman of her age. She must be well over forty — and with such weakness. Yet I cannot ask her to come back to the kitchen where there is a good fire blazing. Perhaps when I know her better, but not on a first visit. I pull the bell cord for Jenny the house maid, and when she comes in, I ask her to lay a fire in here.

Mistress Goodwin protests immediately. "Goodness, no, Mistress Hopkins, don't go to this trouble and expense for me. What with all the wood needed for building, there is little enough left for our cooking fires."

"Oh, but we have a good enough supply of wood so we can spoil ourselves once in a while," I say. "Besides, I am going to spend some more time in here later, as I have some things to do." Before Mistress Goodwin can inquire what I might be doing in the parlour in the middle of the day, I change the subject. Perhaps I do not need to worry: Mistress Goodwin does not look like the nosey sort. She seems like an even-tempered, cheerful person.

I shiver and say, "Here it is, the middle of April, and still frost on the ground. What are the winters like in Hartford, Mistress? We had such a cruel one in New Haven last year. I hope they don't get any worse here."

"No, the winter here isn't dreadful, but it does take some getting used to. We have been through three winters now, so I suppose we are as prepared as can be. That first one was challenging, I can tell you. We were not prepared for it at all. We had no idea it could be so cold, and we had never seen snow like that, three feet deep at times. It buried the whole town. The bay and the rivers froze over, so the men couldn't fish, and even the deer were scarce. I thought we would die of cold or starvation, or both. Of course, we hadn't had a good harvest to begin with, so there was hardly any grain."

Even though the fire is now sending out some warmth now, we both shiver at the thought of that ordeal, and then laugh at ourselves.

"What a horrible time. How did you ever survive?"

"Some of us did not. There was so little food to go around that some people towards the end lived on nothing but acorns and purslane. Even though we shared what food and fuel we had, a few people didn't have the good health to come through. It was mostly children we lost, and three old people."

"How sad that must have been, especially for a colony just starting out," I interject.

"It was indeed," Mistress Goodwin nods her head slowly, remembering. "We survived for two reasons, really. One was the kindness of the Indians who gave us corn and the occasional side of venison. And above all, it was because of the Lord's special providence. After everything we had been through to get here, I am sure he wanted us to live, to light our faithful candle, and carry out his will in the new country. If he had not wanted it, our candle would have gone out for certain." She smiles at her own words.

I nod my agreement, thinking how difficult it would be to blow out her steady candle. Yet she does speak truly. These poor helpless first planters would have died without such faith in the Lord's sustaining power. "Then I won't be so anxious about the winter. It cannot be nearly as bad as that one was."

Mistress Goodwin shakes her head. "Nothing like it! Look at our houses today, so snug and warm. Our first houses — well, they were cellars and shacks at best, and some people even had to stay in the tents they brought with them, on those terrible cold nights. The next day they were so stiff they had to be thawed out by the fire before they could move around. They were as white as the sheets that froze on our clotheslines!" She chuckles at her own exaggeration.

She is the soul of amiableness, this good woman. Fancy calling our houses "snug," when even on this spring day the draughts whirl around my ankles, and climb up my back, no matter how many layers of clothes I put on. I shall never complain about our handsome and spacious house, but on cold days like this I think a small well-caulked cabin would be so much cozier.

Reminiscing about those early days in the colony keeps us going on until almost noon. "Goodness, how late it is. My husband will wonder if he's to have any dinner today," Mistress Goodwin says, starting to rise. I take hold of her elbow to help her out of her chair, and we walk arm in arm to the door. I wish her a fervent good day.

This is one of the pleasantest times I have had since I arrived. I intend to see a lot of Mistress Goodwin. I need a good friend here, and I think she likes me too.

9.

GRADUALLY, MY LIFE IS BEGINNING to take some shape as I am coming to know the routines of the town. Now I can find my way around for any errands I have to do, and as I go about I meet people on the street — not too many, never a crowd — who tell me the local news, both fair and foul. Every day there seems to be a fresh disaster, such as death by misadventure or the will of God, depending upon your point of view. And every day there is at least one comforting occurrence for which one turns to the Lord in gratitude: the gift of rain for parched crops, or a child recovered from influenza, even a lost calf discovered stuck in a bog. On the whole I think we tend to be more grateful than sorrowful.

At home, the servants are adjusting to the new circumstances, of having a neophyte mistress, and rather like the idea of being in charge of themselves. It is they who instruct me, not the other way around. When occasionally I do make a request for a change of some sort — to have roast pork instead of the constant boiled venison, or to make new candles this week instead of next, as they are running short — they can be quite put out about it. It is amazing how much petulance one can put into a brief, silent toss of the head, or even a stolid contemplation of one's shoes. I keep having to tell myself that I am really the mistress and they the servants, so I do not have to give in to them all the time if I do not choose to. I will stand silently until whoever it is looks up, and then I look her (Cook usually) straight in the eye, waiting until she says, "As you wish, Mistress," and goes off. Still, I feel so young, and they are so — experienced. Only Nellie agrees to everything I want. She tells me I am a very fond mistress.

With all the to-ings and fro-ings, and new things to learn every day, I have written nothing in my journal to send out to my friends in England and Wales. So I pick it up again today, and try to give them a taste of Hartford:

June 5, 1639

"How can I describe the way we lead our lives here, in all its freshness and diversity? There is so much that is utterly new to me, mixed in with customs and activities that I know well. Naturally I am inclined to tell of all the novelties, but I will do my best to make a well-formed picture.

"There are 153 of us in the town now. That, of course, does not include the Podunk Indians who live in the South Meadows, but they are not very numerous, about thirty I am told. Seventy-five are freemen, of whom forty are church members. Here is the first difference between our town and New Haven. We do not require a person to be one of the visible saints in order to be a full citizen. Any planter or merchant of good character may be one. Everyone in the town, however, whether freeman or not, must attend the Sabbath preaching of the word. Our minister, Mr. Hooker, hopes that many more will be converted over the course of time.

"As for the rest of the population, many are young men without families, mostly indentured, but some are artisans. They are required to live with a family until they marry, which is a good arrangement, as it keeps them out of harm's way. (You know what I mean, of course: it is either amours with the serving-girls, or dissipation in the ordinary. We hear of such goings-on in Boston, but here the young people behave quite sedately.)

"Every planter is allotted a two-acre home plot, although some are able to purchase larger ones. A few, like my husband, have acquired acreage beyond the town for pasturage and crops. On both sides of the riveret, our home lots are long and narrow, and each is sturdily fenced in. This is so different from the English and Welsh countryside, where all is open, but then you do not have the threats we have here. It is hard to maintain a flock of sheep on account of the wolves that come boldly into town. We are paying a town wolf-catcher, and he does his best, bringing in two or three pelts a week, but he cannot be everywhere at once. I have been told that Mr. Willis, the pig breeder in Springfield just north of us, has changed over to black pigs so the wolves will not think they are deer and attack!

"My maidservant, Nellie, told me that she had heard that one night over in Roxbury a farmer had fired his musket to scare off wolves, who were after his calf. The townspeople were so alarmed at the noise that they thought it must be the Indians attacking. So, they all got out of bed and dressed and armed themselves, and sent a courier to Boston to ask for help. I laughed when she told me, imagining how foolish they must have felt the next day!

"With our rail fences and trim wooden houses, Hartford looks tidy and safe. Today there is not a house without its own cowshed, courtyard and little garden. Most houses have at least two rooms each with a small window, and a sort of mattress for a bed. In some of the houses I have visited there were more than six people in a room together, so they are more than snug, I think. It is a rule now that everyone must build a stone chimney, as there have been too many fires in the wooden ones and people suffocated.

"We have a constable to prevent unruliness from spreading, though I have seen little of that, except for the occasional drunkard singing himself home. He will be fined if caught; if there is a second misdemeanour, I am told, it is the stocks for him. So far the stocks have been housing only spiders' webs and dead flies.

"Constable Pritchett is supposed to be on Indian alert too. He checks each house to make sure that there is a supply of powder and shot. It is a town law, in case of an attack. People are still haunted by the terrible Pequot wars a few years back, even though the colony has been peaceful ever since. The only disaster to come from this rule was when Mr. Skinner left his gunpowder to dry in the chimney. The foolish man had obviously never handled the stuff before. The gunpowder ignited and blew out the gable on his house, severely scorching a maid and a baby on the face. The maid later died of her burns. The constable has been ordered to instruct each household on the proper care of guns and powder.

"I walk out every day in the fine weather, and even the rain does not often stop me. Sometimes I go out to the fields on the edge of town to watch the men at work. Most of the planting is done now, and the fields look beautifully tidy and well turned over. I watched a group plowing the other day before the planting was begun, and was horrified to see what difficult heavy work it is. It takes six oxen, three men and a boy a full day to complete an acre, and they look as though they are struggling against the resistant ground the whole time. The man with the shovel has the worst of it, for he must walk beside the plough and reach down to release the soil where it is stuck to the mould-board. And all the while the oxen are being driven ahead and the soil is piling up again. If they had to stop every time it needed scraping off, they would never have finished. They stop often enough to drag huge stones out of the way. They will make walls of them, but not right now. Getting the seeds in matters most.

"It is a busy time for everyone. The bell is rung through town every day now at five-thirty, and all are expected to be up instantly, to get dressed and be ready to attend to their duties. Those planting the fields are working till suppertime, a full day. They are so exhausted after their labours that they fall into bed right after they eat. There is no time for gaiety of any sort these days.

"We now have our own plough-wright and blacksmith, who are working day and night making or repairing the ploughs. In fact, the whole town is bustling with new activity. Although the English Parliament has forbidden any more immigration to New England, Hartford is filling up with people escaping the crowded Massachusetts towns. Just last week we welcomed a tailor, a rope maker, a second ferryman, and another shepherd, not to mention the stable hands and farm apprentices, of whom we already have a good number. We are still waiting for an apothecary and, everyone hopes, a teacher. There is no doctor, but we have two midwives, Mistress Pratt and Goodwife Chester.

"The General Court of the colony has made it a law that every family must plant a spoonful of hemp and flax seed, laying the seeds a foot apart. Rope and cloth are to be our most important exports, with tobacco next. To feed ourselves we plant barley, rye, oats, peas, and corn. You can make a strange but substantial bread from corn, said to be very healthy. Wheat is grown only on the best land, of which we have a good amount, so we are the envy of our neighbours. My husband has bought a grist mill, and soon we will be able to sell our flour, even in Boston!

"I can hear my readers saying, if that is all you have to eat, it sounds like a dull diet, but you are mistaken. Our meals are richly satisfying. For our meat we have venison, rabbit, turkey, and occasionally we slaughter a pig. Our fishermen bring in great barrels of cod, mussels, mackerel and haddock. I have become a keen fish eater, which I never was before. The fish taste fresher here, but perhaps it is just because the atmosphere in which I eat them is clearer!

"In my garden I have planted melons, and Nellie and I go out to pick wild strawberries beside the river. The cherry and pear trees that were already here now have buds on them, just waiting for the sun to warm them into bloom. Beside the kitchen, the yard boys have put in carrots, turnips, and potatoes. All in all we have a feast of flavours awaiting us in our little realm.

"So you see, what with the stores of sugar and spices, and butter and cheese that we have had sent to us, we dine like — Parliamentarians, I should better say. I will include in this journal our cook's recipes for Brunswick Stew (made with squirrels) and Pumpkin Soup, both of which are tasty and filling."

10.

IT IS HEAVY WORK digging in this tightly packed soil that no one has ever turned over before. That must have been the worst part of being exiled from Eden — going from a well-planted garden into a wilderness of clay and weeds. We must take Adam's and Eve's punishment literally, I think. For me this is hardship, but no punishment.

Sometimes when I am bent over with my small spade I think I hear rustling on the other side of the hedge, almost like someone whispering. I sit back on my heels and look up, but there is no one there. Another time when this happens, I catch sight of a pair of heads moving along quickly, as if afraid to be caught snooping. I make a game of it: I listen for sounds of someone approaching then wait a minute to see if he or she has stopped to watch me. Then, I jerk my head up suddenly to see if I can recognize who it is. It is not effective, so I change my method, and today I am successful. Instead of moving quickly, I raise my head just a little bit at a time, hardly any movement to be seen, and I catch them standing in the road talking to each other, glancing at me, and talking again. Mistress Simson and Mistress Lowe, two of the saints whom I have seen at the meeting house, but who have not paid me a visit. Mistress Lowe has a disapproving look on her face as she speaks. The other one looks benign. I wonder what they are discussing — me, of course, but what about me? They see me looking, bow curtly — really just a nod — and walk on sedately.

The next person who passes is a woman I have been longing to meet for some time. Elizabeth Johnson lives next door to Mistress Simson on the south side of the riveret. I have seen her several times from the garden, as she walked past the house pulling a small cart with a young child in it. She is short and wiry with long red hair, and she walks with a bouncy step, her head bobbing in rhythm. She looks to be about my age. Even from the back of the garden I can see that her face has a keen, intelligent look, and she seems ready to break out laughing as soon as you please. The child in the cart always sits looking straight ahead earnestly as if setting out for an important infant engagement.

I have noted that the pair pass by at about the same time on most days, so today I have already decided to try and intercept them. I take up my gardening efforts closer to the front gate, and when mother and child come by, I call out, "Good day!" in my friendliest voice.

She stops. "Good day to you, too. I guess you must be Mistress Hopkins, as this is the governor's house, isn't it? I am Elizabeth Johnson. I live just down the road."

Her freckles spread across her face like a sunburst. They make her look so happy. I say, "I know you do. I'm so pleased to meet you. Yes, I am Anne Hopkins. I've watched you going by often and hoped you'd stop. Would you like to come in and sit in the garden for a little while?"

"Thank you, that would be lovely. I can only stay for a few minutes, though. It's close to Angela's supper time, but I don't think she'll mind waiting. There is so much to look at in a new place. The garden is beautiful."

In fact, baby Angela has begun to look around with wonder at the apple blossoms on the trees, smiling as petals float down over her cart.

"Angela, that's a lovely name," I say. Then with hesitation, I continue. "It isn't a usual name around here."

"That's because she isn't a Puritan child. Neither my husband nor I are part of the gathering of saints here," says Elizabeth brightly. "I suppose it might be considered rather Romish: Angela — angels and all, but it isn't that either. My husband and I just thought she looked like an angel when she was born."

"She still does," I say softly. "And she behaves like one, too." I hand the child a blossom and watch her pat it with her fingers in deep concentration.

Elizabeth laughs. "Oh no, not all the time. She has quite a mind of her own, but we keep hoping she'll grow into her name."

We carry on from there chatting first about ordinary things — the arrival of spring, what new foods will be available soon, how dusty the town is with all the new building — and then gradually we begin to let each other into the more important nooks and crannies of our personalities and our thoughts. The more we talk, the more we realize how much we have in common. We read some of the same books, have many of the same ideas, the same love of the countryside. Elizabeth's husband is also a trader, and so she is often left alone while he does business out of town, as I expect to be too. Our meeting is a godsend.

Finally, at shrieking signals from Angela, Elizabeth stands up to take her leave, turning the cart towards the gate. I bend over and kiss the little girl lightly on the top of her head, which stops the noise, or perhaps it is the movement of the cart that does it. I promise to visit Elizabeth the day after next. I have every intention of seeing her as often as possible. She will surely become my best friend here, never a replacement for Jane, of course, but a different sort of friend and woman altogether. Is it because she is not one of the saints that she has such a refreshing attitude to life? If that is true, then woe is me, because in the company of so many saints I may lose whatever I have of my own person.

11.

WHILE I HAVE BEEN BUSY making my first discoveries about Hartford and finding new friends, Edward has been occupied with his grist mill, spending part of every day over there beside the river, watching and learning, because this venture is entirely new to him. The former miller has managed it well, and Edward is pleased with its profitability. Not only that, but I know he secretly enjoys the tactility of the operation. He brings some of the freshly milled wheat home for Cook, and I watch him sifting through it, feeling the grains slide over his palm as if he were stroking a silk gown. In public his fingers are the most flexible part of his body. Most of the time he holds himself as a prosperous merchant should, carefully formal. You might think, what a stiff man. But then, you would be missing the soft yielding centre he keeps hidden from public view.

You would imagine then, that being in the fur trade also, he would have an even greater delight in handling the pelts, but that is not so. Furs are exotic, sleek, and, to most Puritans, they smell like forbidden fruit. (Not to me: I adore furs.) No saint is permitted to wear such showy apparel. Edward, whose love of God is almost matched by his love of the sensuous world, tries to keep an emotional distance between himself and the furs he ships out of his warehouse as quickly as possible.

I found this out one night in bed. I was rubbing my hands along his back, relishing the smooth warmth of his skin and feeling his body melting to my touch. He turned and did the same for me.

I said, laughing, "You stroke me like a fur. Sometimes I think you imagine I am a wolf or a red fox."

"If you were, I'd have to leave you alone. I'm afraid to touch them because, you know, they are so tempting."

"You mean that those lascivious fingers of yours would lead you into some grievous sin?" I teased.

He laughed. "When you put it that way, I suppose not, but I still feel it's a devilish pleasure if I touch them too much. It's not the furs themselves, but what they stand for."

"I'm glad of that! Just keep your hands on the vixen beside you."

He complied instantly. "You are temptation enough for me."

"Good."

The fact that his senses now shape his life nearly as much as his reason, and his God, is in part what drew him to me in the first place. He does not put it this way, but that is what he means. He does say he loves the scent and stroke of my body just as much as the shimmering grace of my soul. (Those are his words.) For a normally private person, this sort of talk is rare and precious to me. I love him even more for it.

Most evenings I have Edward to myself, although more and more often, as people come to know him, he is called out on urgent matters. One night it is a distraught husband whose wife is giving birth, and there is no midwife to be found. Edward goes out to the house, taking Nellie with him. Apparently, she once mentioned helping to deliver her sister's child, so he rushes her along to see what she can do. The baby comes without a hitch. It turns out that one midwife is visiting her sister in Windsor. The other is later discovered in the tavern, so full of cider that she can hardly get herself home. She is publicly chastised and fined, and if she were not such a valuable part of the community, she would have been warned out

Another time it is a young woman who comes clattering on our door, frantic with fear. Edward calms her down enough to learn that her husband, John Munson, is at home, coldly and fiercely breaking the house apart with hammer and axe.

"He is quite distracted!" she cries. "We had a row over the accounts, and he accused me of being an idle foolish housewife. When I said that I was sure I had kept the ledger correctly, he became angry, and began to beat on the table. Then he took an axe to it, and after that started on the stool he had been sitting on. I was afraid he would hit me next, so I ran out of the room, and when I looked back he was slashing at the walls. I am afraid to go back there. I don't know what he will do."

"You shall not go back," I say, putting my arm around the young wife, whose name is Abigail. "You shall stay with us. Edward, what can be done?"

Edward is already putting on his coat and reaching for his walking stick. "I will fetch the constable and Mr. Wakeman and we will see to it. Don't be afraid, Mistress Abigail. You will be safe here."

"And my husband?" she asks, beginning to sob. "Will he be safe too? Will he be his own good self again?"

"You can be sure we will do everything that is possible to help him," Edward says, as he goes out into the night. I am glad not to be in his shoes.

When he comes in late, wearily unbending his body into a chair in the parlour, I see the deepening creases in his face and wonder if his role as governor is going to be too demanding upon him. I go and sit beside him, stroking the wrinkles out of his forehead, willing his tiredness to go away. Then, when it seems the right time, I ask him to tell me what happened. He says, "Let's leave it until tomorrow. I don't want to think about it any more." But I insist. "It's better to talk about it, it helps to relieve you. I can see how miserable you are about this." So he relents.

"It was even worse than Abigail told us. John was foaming at the mouth, and he couldn't or wouldn't speak to us. He just kept on hammering at one of the doors until it gave way. Then he swung at the doorposts with his axe. At one time he had the axe in one hand and the hammer in the other. We were shouting at him to stop, but whether he heard us or not we couldn't tell. The constable went to the next house and brought over Mr. Caswell, and the four of us managed to subdue him. We put my coat on him back to front, and then tied his arms down, but that did not hold him for long as he was so strong. We took him over to Mr. Talbot's place, where he has a good shed attached to his house with a bed in it. We had to tie him to the bed, and the constable will stay with him tonight to give him water, and bathe him if he gets into a lather again. He was quite mad. I don't know what we can do with him. There's no place to take care of him here."

"Perhaps it is just a passing spasm, and he will recover," I say hopefully. "I've heard that people can regain their wits if they are given rest and quiet."

"Yes, there have been some recoveries, but where could he go to be helped? We intend to take him to Boston for an examination, and if he is thought to be incurably mad, we will send him back to England. Mr. Winthrop, the governor's son, has learned some of the latest treatments in England. If anyone can help him, he can."

"Oh, poor little Abigail! What will she do?" I cry. Abigail is the first goodwife I have met who is younger than I am, therefore she is "little."

"The congregation will help her. We will either maintain her here until she is able to work, or we will raise the sum of her passage home. I think her parents are still alive somewhere in Dorset." He rubs his hands over his face absently. "Where is she now?"

"She's sleeping next door, poor thing. I heard her crying for a time, and then she stopped. She will feel a lot worse tomorrow when she hears what is going to happen to her husband and herself."

"I dread having to tell her, but I must. I will call on Mr. Hooker to console her later on, but I am the one who should deliver the news."

There are other evenings, the good ones, when no knocks are heard at the door, and we two spend the entire time together in the small parlour after supper. Often, we take turns reading to each other. Most often it is the Bible, and although we do succeed in reading it all the way through to the end once, we keep going back to our favourite books over and over. I love the narratives, particularly the gospel of Matthew and the story of Esther, while Edward, who is more inclined to think about law and civility, prefers to go over Paul's letters, looking for models and instruction for life. So we take turns choosing.

There are plenty of sermons to read also, which have been copied and sent from England to nourish the saints in their wilderness. We find this charitable gesture amusing, since we know that the best of preachers live right around us in New England. There are Mr. Cotton and Mr. Shepherd in Boston, Mr. Bulkeley in Concord, and of course our very own Mr. Hooker, the finest of them all. The sermons of these ministers are carefully copied and sent to all the churches in the colonies, but I am told that soon the new printing press in Cambridge will issue them, and send them to England to edify the brethren there! A fine exchange that will be.

We are fond of many of the same writers, which is a bit unusual between a husband and wife. Edward tells me I can order any books I wish from England, as I have more time to read than he ever will. I make my selections carefully, choosing several old favourites, and a few new books about which I have heard good reports. I choose, first of all, books we can read together: Plutarch's *Lives of Illustrious Men* with its comparisons between the Greek and Roman heroes, and Sir Thomas More's *Utopia*, I order a copy of Milton's *Lycidas*, , which comes in a little volume of elegies on the death of a young poet of his acquaintance. We read it over and over, marveling at the grace, timeliness, and wisdom of the poem. I often read Sir Philip Sidney's and Mr. George Herbert's poems to Edward. As the lamps are dim, and I am so caught up in the enchantment of the lines, I do not notice him nodding off from time to time. Then, looking over at his head bent over his collar, I close the book quietly and sit looking at the fire until the silence wakes him up. He says, "Oh, I'm sorry. I didn't intend to do that in the middle of your reading. Not your fault. Such a lovely soft voice."

"Let's go up to bed, sleepy one. I'll just have to read you that poem again tomorrow," I tease.

Some evenings, when we are both wide awake and in good spirits, we entertain ourselves with lighter fare. We read the stories of the exploration of this new unknown world, but now that we too are world travellers, we enjoy the strange accounts of the discovery of America. I have a copy of Richard Hakluyt's retelling of the voyages of early explorers.

"They said they saw leopards on these shores!" I chuckle. "Have you spied any near here?"

"No, and I haven't seen any of the Indians wearing leopard skins, either. For that matter, none of the tribes around here wear birds' feathers, which these travelers say they saw."

"Well, customs do change, of course. But I hear that the man who observed all these things — he was an Italian, by the way — was roasted and eaten by the Indians. That seems a heavy penalty for making up silly tales!" I am laughing now so hard I cannot finish reading.

Another time Edward comes home waving a paper. "Here's something to make you smile, Anne. It's a poem that has been circulating anonymously. The author sent it to England for a jest. It's called 'New England's Annoyances'."

I read it to myself, laughing out loud when I come to the verse:

'Stead of pottage and puddings and custards and pies,
Our turnips and parsnips are common supplies.
We have pumpkins at morning and pumpkins at noon,
If it was not for pumpkins, we should be undone.

"Well, I doubt it will discourage anyone from coming here, but they will probably bring some extra supplies with them," I say. After that, whenever I feel reined in by the sobriety of the colony, I read that poem again, which I have come to call the "pumpkin song," and realize that there is some humour in this way of life after all.

One evening I ask Edward, "Why is it you never married before now?" And he says, with all the charm I would expect of one of Charles's courtiers, "I could never find anyone as adorable as you before. I have very high standards." He chuckles at that and watches to see what I will say.

I think of replying, "It's a pity you had to lower them," but that would only be asking for a greater compliment. So I say, "Well, as to that, I thank you, dearest husband. But you must have attracted the eye of many a woman, I am sure, and they cannot all have been so unacceptable."

He looks a bit embarrassed, so I know it is true. He says, thoughtfully, 'There are many fine women in London, but none like you. When I saw you, I knew right away that you were the one I had been waiting for."

"Oh Edward!" I go over and throw my arms around him. "If I had only known you were waiting, I would have come sooner!" We both laugh, give each other a great kiss. We remain standing there with our bodies pressed together. I rest my cheek against his until he gives my back a few pats and says he must get to work. "I am sorry, my accounts call me."

"Silly old accounts," I say, and let him go.

The most sorrowful piece of news, which sends Edward into the bleakest mood of his life, comes from England. A cousin writes to say that Jonathan, Edward's youngest brother, has been killed in a military skirmish in Scotland. I come into the parlour as he is reading the letter, and know by his face, empty of all expression, that something really dreadful has happened. I say, "Is it Jonathan?"

"Yes." He hands me the letter, which does not take long to read. I stand there limply too, taking it in. "The utter fool, I told him not to go," he says.

"Oh, Edward, how tragic! The poor fellow, so young, and so good." I am speechless. We both are. I start to cry, and Edward who has covered his face with his hands, looks up. He seems close to tears himself. I go to him, and embrace him as hard as I can.

"He was only twenty-eight, and with a wife and three children…" his voice trails off, trembling.

"Whatever will they do? Oh, how bereft they must feel! They are a very loving family, aren't they?"

"They are, very. That was one of the reasons I told him to stay home and mind them." He pauses, thinking. "There's the farm. Now they will have to find someone to look after it for them. I will help, of course." He stops, and bursts out, "Oh, what a foolish war this is! When will the King learn diplomacy instead of rushing about brandishing his sword — as if he knew how to use it — and dragging loyal young men after him!"

With this outburst, Edward sits down and begins to cry, silently. It is the first time I have heard him say anything this harsh about King Charles, even though I know he thinks the King is taking bad advice from his archbishop and others. In a moment of pain like this, people are inclined to exaggerate what they believe; however, perhaps for others like Edward it is the beginning of stating the truth.

After an almost silent meal, our minds on brother Jonathan and his family, we spend the rest of this evening quietly reading some of the psalms. We go to bed, giving each other a tender kiss before rolling over and trying to sleep.

The next morning Edward tells me that he is sending over some money to his sister-in-law, and hopes to go over himself as soon as he can to make sure she is safe and well looked after. From that day on we hardly ever mention Jonathan, except in our prayers.

12.

SLOWLY MY LIFE TAKES ON a certain direction as I learn what is required of a governor's wife and mistress of a household. There is not much to the latter, especially as far as the culinary arts are concerned. Every morning after making my toilet, I visit the kitchen to make inquiries. "Is there anything I can do here? Shall I bring something from the butcher?" And Cook responds, "No, Mistress, we have everything we need. It will be gammon for dinner today." And I, in turn, say, "Very good, then." As for the rest of the house, Henry seems to run it effortlessly. I seldom hear sounds of frantic activity from the other servants, as though some undertaking were forgotten, or an object needed to be fixed before Henry cast his eye upon it. When I run my hands over the tables or the window frames, they are free of the dust that blows daily into the house. One of the young men sweeps the walk every morning, and another washes the hall and parlour floors. Happily I leave Henry to look after all of that.

It may sound as if I am lazy, but I am not. I have the garden to tend, and as soon as it produces in abundance, I will take bunches of herbs or vegetables to my favourite neighbours such as Mistress Goodwin. I have errands to do: when the ships come in from England and other ports, and the shops are full, there are supplies to purchase like needles and thread, quills and paper, and of course books, though I have already read almost everything that arrives. There are now a potter and a clockmaker, whom I visit occasionally just to watch them at work. In the market I buy baskets and once in a while pewter for the table, but never food; I leave that to Cook. A tailor newly arrived from Boston is doing very clever things with leather, so I commission him to make a smooth fitted coat for Edward.

No matter how many errands I have to do, or visits to make, or visitors to receive, I always find time for myself, to do what I love most: walk, read, and write. Edward is away most days from early morning until dinnertime; then he leaves again, and may not turn up until supper is waiting on the table. So usually after dinner I take a long walk, and then when I come home there is plenty of time to read, and to write about what I have seen and thought.

Much as I love passing through the town into the countryside beyond, I have developed the recent impression that people are observing me, as if I were doing something peculiar in sauntering about on my own. Women sweeping their doorsteps or hanging out their washing look at me strangely, as do some men walking to or from their fields, or standing along the river with their fishing rods. All of this sets me on edge. Some of them acknowledge me with a nod or a greeting, and a few whom I know now by name will stop and inquire about my health and exchange a few civilities. They are not excessively friendly, certainly, but I am beginning to think that effusive warmth is a rare commodity here. Hardship breeds restraint, I guess.

Sometimes I am faced with a tight, wordless stare. I suppose they are still curious about me, though why that is I cannot understand. There may be something about my walk itself that disturbs people. My step is bit too long for a lady, I know, but being so tall and slight, I am afraid I might trip over my own feet if I take shorter steps. Once I saw a bookcase, mistakenly filled with the thickest volumes at the top, fall over, and its contents scatter and slide across the wooden floor. I could topple over just like that, if I do not take care. As a result, I have found the right rhythm and length for my stride, and my body freely moving, I try to ignore these curiously critical watchers and just revel in the good spring weather. It is not always easy.

When I return from one gorgeous walk I write in my journal:

May 28, 1639

"It is nearly as beautiful here in May as it is in Wales. In this country of severe contrasts, spring comes in so suddenly, blowing away the gloom, tossing the branches into leaf, combing the grass upright. We notice its arrival with astonishment, and much cheer. In Wales we are less grateful, I think, for all that the land in May is sweeter there, both in sight and in sound. As long as I live, I will remember the dusty, scented rosemary and the gently swirling tendrils that surround the white jasmine blooms. I used to hide in the bowers of wisteria, and breathe in the whole springtime of the garden. The only gardens here so far, except for mine, are those that have been dug to feed us. Usefulness is the only reason to have a garden at present. My lovely wisteria would be thought frivolous or ostentatious, or both, although I am sure people are as eager to have flowers as I am, when they have the time to look after them.

"The beauty of this country is simple and uncultivated. The woods behind us are all in leaf, and dotted among the green are little hawthorns all dressed in sparkling white. There is a tree with magnificent large white blossoms as soft as silk. It is called dogwood, although it is nothing like our English shrub, and far more impressive.

"As today is Saturday, and everyone is occupied with baking and scrubbing for the Sabbath, I walk out to the end of town, and then take a rough path towards the forest. No one sees me go, and I know I will be home before anyone bothers to ask where I am. Going this far is not allowed, for fear of wild beasts and savages, but on such a day as this I cannot resist.

"It is still too damp to go far into the forest, even if I could. Ever since the Indians left this part of the land, the underbrush has grown back until it is well nigh impossible to pass through, especially in a wide heavy skirt. No one bothers to tend to the underbrush, because these trees will soon come down to make more houses, or be sent back home to build ships. So I am satisfied with wandering along the edge of the woods, peeking in to see if I can spot any unusual wild flowers. I intend to take home a specimen of every one I find to press in my book. Then I shall consider them carefully, so as to choose the right name for them. Afterwards, perhaps, I shall find out what names others have given them, the official names. We shall see whether they or I have done a better job of naming.

"I find a few, very tiny plants with miniature flowers, so precious. It is sad in a way that many blooms are so undernourished here compared to those at home. Winter is a fierce tyrant who forces us all to crouch instead of stand up for ourselves.

"This sparkling day and our warm little town have put thoughts of nasty old winter right out of my head."

In good weather, I have my favourite garden seat, under one of the apple trees. Seth built me a wooden bench that curves all the way around its trunk, so I can face whatever way I please. It is the perfect spot for reading and writing, and I usually sit for an hour or more at a time, sheltered from the afternoon sun by a sunshade over my cap, and by the interlacing branches. With my nose in a good book, or scribbling in my notebook, I can be oblivious to everything around me.

I have a few books tucked away for reading on my own, so I take these to the garden. It is not that Edward would disapprove of them, but he just would not understand why they appeal to me. Jane sends me writings by young women with unusual modern views of life, such as Rachel Speght, and Lady Mary Wroth. They are friends of some of our old friends, so there is the extra pleasure of reading poems and essays by people I know about already. The only book I would not tell Edward about is Sir Thomas Browne's *Religio Medici* , which I keep in my bedside chest. He might not approve, so that is why I do not say anything. I love Browne's writing best of all.

A few days ago, I was busy writing down what I had seen on my walk. I looked up for a moment and noticed two heads that seemed to be propped up on the fence, staring at me. It was that Mistress Simson and Mistress Lowe again. Both withdrew slowly when they saw me looking back. Yesterday, I noticed the same two heads appear, stop briefly, turn to each other, and move on. I am getting fed up with their surreptitious observation. Today, I decide to find out what it is that they want. I get up and go to the fence. As I come closer the women nod quickly, and walk away without speaking.

These peeping gossips are too much for me. I change my seat for the time being by going around the side of the house to the back where I know I can be hidden by a small shed. It is not nearly as pleasant, and there is no protection from the sun. I think I should have a parasol, but then I remember asking for one in a shop, and being told they are not being imported, as they are thought to be a frivolity here. So I must find out quickly what this constant observation is all about, or I will produce a larger crop of freckles than I have already.

The next time I see Mistress Goodwin, I ask her about the two women trying for a bland approach. "What do you think they were doing, admiring the garden perhaps? Except that they were not really looking at the garden, but rather, strangely, at me. At first I thought they would think me impolite not to go over and speak to them, but then, when I did get up, they just turned and left. They made me feel quite peculiar, as though I was behaving badly."

"I wouldn't think too much about it. They don't know you very well. They may have just wondered what it was you were doing there," says Mistress Goodwin.

"I was writing, that's all. I'm sure they could see that. I had my pencil and journal in my hands. How could that upset them?" I sense my tone is too crisp for my good friend, but she does not seem to notice.

"It's rather unusual to find a young woman sitting writing in the middle of the day. Most women don't write except for the occasional letter home. But of course you, being the governor's wife, probably have a good deal more correspondence than others do," she says calmly.

"Oh, I suppose that's true," I say rather vaguely. "Actually, I am writing a little book about life here to send to my friend in Wales, and there is so much going on that I have to keep at it every day, to try and remember what happened."

Mistress Goodwin is cautiously encouraging. "What a good idea. There have been so many distressing accounts of the colony that have been sent back, which have kept people from coming out here. I'm sure yours will not be one of those. But, Mistress Anne, do be careful of your health. People say that it isn't good to spend too much time writing and reading."

I laugh. "What a silly old notion that is! Don't you believe it. I am healthier here than I have ever been. I am not straining myself at all."

"Well, I will keep you in my prayers all the same, because I wouldn't want you to come to any harm," my friend says.

"I will always be glad of your prayers," I reply. "I'm sure the Lord listens keenly to what you have to say."

"Tush!" says Mistress Goodwin, who cannot help smiling.

It is not until after she leaves that I begin to worry about the discussion we have just had. Here are neighbours who are suspicious of my favourite activities, and a good friend who frets over my health. And yet, Edward and I spend much of our free time together reading aloud to each other. I am sure Edward approves of my writing, though he says little about it. Surely he does not think it is bad for me. All this talk about the perils of reading and writing is confusing, to say the least. No one ever mentioned it back home. I expect my behaviour just seems strange to people who are doing house and field work all day, but they will get used to it when they come to know me better.

13.

THE LOT OF A GOVERNOR'S WIFE is such that not a day passes without visitors. They turn up unannounced, and Edward and I, or I alone if Edward is not at home, have to drop everything and come to greet them. The servants know that the more distinguished people — ministers and their wives, merchants, members of the governing council — are to be shown into the large parlour, where they are seated and offered a glass of cider or a warm posset cup, depending on the season. The rest of the townspeople are received in the great hall, which, lacking any furniture but a couple of hard benches, keeps the visits brief.

There are a few people who, whenever they come to the house, examine the premises from top to bottom, as if they are going to make an offer for them. They do the same to me. I can never decide whether they are planning to eat me or molest me. It is an uncomfortable feeling either way, being sized up or stripped down. No one ever says anything untoward, and eventually I accept the scrutiny by imagining these are people from another race who have never seen a civilized white woman before. What is it about me that they find so fascinating? Their stares make me quiver. I wish they would just go away.

Some people's inquisitiveness irritates me more than others. At the top of my list are our nearest neighbours, the Woodsides. He is much older than his wife, and is as gaunt and stiff as a stovepipe. He speaks little and smiles less. When he opens his mouth there are several black spaces to be seen where teeth have come out. I suppose that is why he seldom smiles, although his disposition does not seem to be conducive to it either. His voice has an odd rusty sound, more likely a sign of ill health than lack of use. I try to pay attention to what he has to say, whenever he does speak, and not to be distracted by the look of him. Yet everything about him is dull and humourless. Even his "Good day, mistress," has an unwelcome tone to it, as if he begrudges the effort. It interferes with his investigation of the room.

Mistress Woodside looks like a small ferret beside her crow-shaped husband. She is almost half his height, with narrow features drawn together like a purse. She moves jerkily, but with great speed, as if she were on strings pulled by an agitated puppet master. I dread it every time she approaches me, as her manner is so shrill and snappish.

I am convinced that the woman has taken it on as her personal duty to discover everything she can about the Hopkins' life together. Mistress Woodside must believe that to be a model of Christian behaviour, which the governor's family should be, our life must be an open book, and she is the one to open it. Being the governor's family's minder gives her an importance she could not achieve otherwise, for, as far as I can tell, neither she nor her husband have any other special gifts by which to serve the colony. This supposedly high-minded obligation, which I would rather call prurient spying, seems to occupy Mistress Woodside's days fully.

As often as I can, I avoid that lady's frequent morning visits. The woman presents one spurious reason after another for her calls. This Monday, she tells Nellie, she has come "to inquire whether Mistress Hopkins would like some red thread, as I find I have an extra bobbin," and on Tuesday, "to tell Mistress Hopkins that a new shipment of wool cloth has just arrived in Saybrook, and the wagon has gone to fetch some," and on Wednesday, "to report that Magistrate Gurney's runaway servant has been returned," and then, on Thursday, "to invite Mistress Hopkins to attend the flogging of Magistrate Gurney's servant this afternoon," and "to ask whether Mistress Hopkins' health has improved" — this, after Nellie has excused my absence four days in a row.

I cannot remain sick forever, so on the fifth day I force myself to come downstairs, on being told that Mistress Woodside is here again. I ask Nellie to show her into the hall, the way of indicating that her welcome will be a brief one, even though she probably will not take the hint. However, if I were to receive her in the parlour, I would never see the last of her. I greet her in the hall with a quiet "Good morning," appropriate for one who has not quite recovered. Thrusting her arm forward Mistress Woodside hands me a bunch of roses.

"Now that you are well, you will not be needing these, I suppose," she says. "The scent is a good remedy for faintness, I am told. And you can use the rosewater for your other complaints, whatever they are."

"I have not been feeling at all faint, Mistress," I say, "but I do thank you for the thought. The roses are so lovely, aren't they? We have planted some like these in our garden, too. We put them at the back along the wall under the small parlour window. I want to take in the perfume in the evening."

Straightening up even further, Mistress Woodside sniffs righteously. "Perfume!" she exclaims. "What a frivolous notion. We left all those worldly adornments behind us when we came here. We do not pay attention to such things in the colony."

I am flabbergasted. "I think, Mistress, that you are confusing artifice with nature," I reply, rather sharply.

She looks puzzled for a minute, not understanding in the least. Then comes the ferret-nosed sniff again.

"Well, if it weren't for the rosewater they provide, which has its uses, I should think you should have them removed."

Being at least a foot taller, I stare down at her. She must recognize some menace in my look, for she takes a step back, and when I say, "I must not keep you any longer from your other duties," she turns towards the door in a hurry. I do not wait for the maid, but usher her out quickly myself. As soon as the door closes behind her, I let out my best, seldom practised growl. "Grrrrh! And grrrh again! What a nasty woman. How did we have such poor luck as to have her for a neighbour? I try to swallow my tongue, but even when I say nothing, I can tell she knows I can't bear her."

Talking to myself this way brings Jenny running, dusting cloth in hand. "Is there anything wrong, Mistress?"

"No, Jenny, nothing is wrong now. I am sorry you heard me. I was just thinking aloud. You can return to your work, and I will go back to my sewing." As I go up the stairs, I turn back slightly and see the maid shaking her head. She believes I have been having a conversation with an imaginary person. It would never occur to her that I might be pouring out some nasty feelings I dare not admit to anyone. We are not supposed to entertain such feelings. I have heard Mr. Stone say they are devilish.

14.

MISTRESS STONE MAKES her promised visit on a morning when I have no excuse not to receive her. The timid little woman whom I thought to be sheltering under her husband's wing turns out to be just as openly nosey about my surroundings as any of the other women who have come in like sanitation inspectors. Watching her scrutinize the immaculate state of the house and its furnishings, I cannot detect one admiring glance, one nod of approval. Not that I care what Mistress Stone thinks, but it might be wise to stay on her good side. I am beginning to guess that all is not sweetness and light among the saints of Hartford. There are a few people here who remind me of my New Haven connections.

So it is not too much of a surprise when Mistress Stone tells me how greatly her husband admires my stepfather.

"Mr. Stone looks on Mr. Eaton as a model governor," she says. For the first time her face loses its woodenness and her voice grows firmer. "The order of the New Haven colony is what we should be aiming for here. It is so smoothly run, there is no fear of violence or immoral acts occurring."

She does not know what I think, or she would not say this. I reply evenly, "I think Hartford is progressing very well, considering its youth and its size. We have few problems and they are small ones."

"There I would dispute with you, Mistress. I have been here longer and I know what I'm talking about. We have had a number of criminals brought to justice, and there will be more."

She sits up straighter in her chair and looks at me sternly. She copies her husband; she is getting ready to give a sermon. Horrors.

"It is because we allow any sort of riff-raff to become citizens. You can tell your husband this, if you like, because Mr. Stone agrees. In fact, it is bound to come up again at the council, even though Mr. Hooker does not wish it. If we do not restrict citizenship to the saints, we will end up with more murders, more runaway slaves, more attacks from the Indians, and," here she lowers her voice before continuing, "more horrible acts against women, You know what I mean."

I nod and keep quiet for a minute. How can I reply to this silly woman with her alarmist arguments? She frightens me. Her husband has probably put these ideas in her head, and she has exaggerated them. At least I hope she has. If Mr. Stone thinks this way too, we could be in for a hard time. I must say something, but without stirring the pot any faster.

I say, "You paint a grim picture, Mistress, but I am convinced that with your husband, Mr. Hooker, and my own good husband in positions of such respect, the colony will remain as peaceful as it is today." I tell myself I am not lying entirely. I mean two thirds of what I say.

Mistress Stone sniffs, not too convincingly. I can see that praising her husband has had some effect. "I wish I could believe that, and of course I do agree that the colony is in good hands. Still, if we would only decide to limit the town membership to the saints, it would be a lot safer. Some of those others — well, they may be good planters and well-educated, but I don't trust for a minute their intentions in coming here. Greed is insidious, you know, and it spawns other evils."

For fear that she is going to bring out another garbled version of her husband's sermons, I fake a cough, covering my mouth politely. "I am sorry, I think I am getting a cold. I'm sure it's not contagious, though." I cough again. How devious I am becoming!

Mistress Stone stands up. "Perhaps not, but just in case, I had better go. Is that your wedding ring?" She reaches out for my hand. "I am surprised you still wear it. Did they allow it in New Haven?"

"No. I put it on again when I came here."

"There, now, you see what I mean. No rings are permitted in New Haven, and yet some people" — she looks at me archly — "do wear them here. I say, what is ostentation in one place is ostentation in another. I'd advise you to remove it."

I make a swift, curt reply. "There's no ostentation about it. This is a symbol of my happy and Christian marriage, of which I am very proud."

Mistress Stone's voice rises so high it squeaks. I cover my mouth quickly so she will not catch my smile. "Symbol! Mr. Stone says the ring is a diabolical circle for the Devil to dance in."

Before she can launch into another tirade, I move towards the door. "Indeed," I say, with a finality that cuts her off. We say goodbye formally and frigidly.

Oh dear, I have made an enemy. I shudder at the effect of the last few minutes of conversation. She does not like me to begin with, I can tell, although she seemed pleased at the idea of instructing me. Well, I tried to avoid an argument, but in the end I could not help myself. Anyway, what business is it of hers whether I wear a ring? I begin to giggle, thinking of of my ring as a diabolical circle!

That night I raise the subject with Edward. "Do you think I shouldn't wear my wedding ring?"

"Why, what's wrong with it? Is it worn down?"

"No, but I wondered whether it was considered showy to wear one here."

"Oh, I don't think so. It is a very plain ring, after all."

"Mistress Stone seemed to think it was wrong to wear it."

"Ah, Mistress Stone. She is a bit difficult, isn't she? I wouldn't worry too much about her opinions. She can be very, um, insistent about them."

"She must get that from her husband," I say.

"That may be, but I don't think she has the mind her husband has. He always has good reasons for his opinions."

"Yes, some of the things she said were really muddle-headed. Well, I will pay no attention to her silly advice."

I had no idea there would be people such as Mistress Stone and Mistress

Woodside in the colony. I sense my euphoria about becoming one of the favoured saints nestled in the happy glades of this New England fading into a haze of wishful thinking.

15.

MISTRESS HOOKER HAS INVITED me to join a circle of women who come together each week for discussion and support. She tells me to "Bring your sewing if you wish. Most people like to be busy at something." I can't wait to go, for here I am sure I will be entering the hallowed circle formed by the wisest female heads in the community. The very next week I come to the Hookers' house, and am shown into the great parlour, a simple forthright room built with a craftsman's eye for detail. The mouldings are well-fitted, the floors finished to a fine glow. The women are sitting comfortably on settles covered with rugs, or on chairs with cane seats. A blue pottery bowl filled with nuts and dried fruit is placed on one of the square tables. Other than that, there are no decorative additions to the room.

I am the last to arrive. I find that I already know a few of the people sitting in the circle. Mistress Goodwin is there, as jolly and welcoming as ever. My heart sinks as I look at the others: Mistress Woodside; my other neighbours, Mistress Simson and Mistress Lowe; Mistress Stone, who gives me a forced smile. Then there is the tall, scrawny-necked woman I noticed on that first Sunday, whom Mistress Hooker introduces as Mistress Brigden. The latter examines me in every particular, her mouth forming a tight line when she spots the wedding ring. She says nothing, however, except the usual "Good day, Mistress." She has a face like a blasted rock. It is a wonder it can move at all. There are a few other new faces, ruddy and cheerful. They look more promising. I take an empty chair beside one of them, a Mistress Gordon. She is the only other person in the room who seems about the same age as I am.

Looking around a little furtively, I see that everyone, with the exception of Mistress Hooker and myself, has brought some handiwork. Most are sewing some ordinary article: a shirt for a husband, a child's shift, or an apron. One stout woman, Mistress Armitage, has a large basket of fleece, which she is carding and setting into small neat piles ready for spinning. There are a few small pieces of embroidery to be seen, whose makers are scarcely able to lift their heads for fear of spoiling such dainty work. These women take little or no part in the ensuing discussions. Mistress Hooker is sitting with her hands in her lap, holding a volume of Scripture. In my quick survey of the women at work, I have not spotted a ring on a single hand. Except my own.

Mistress Gordon beside me is sewing an infant's dress, and from time to time she starts to hum quietly to herself, quite unaware of what she is doing. When someone looks at her pointedly, she reddens, and stops abruptly. I find her humming a treat, the most lighthearted sound in the room.

Apparently, my arrival has interrupted a lively discussion, which, after a few polite inquiries as to my health and how I am getting along, starts up again with vigour.

"To think that he had been appointed a magistrate and all this lewdness going on right under Governor Winthrop's nose," says Mistress Lowe.

"If you are implying that the governor knew about it all the time and said nothing — well, that is almost libelous," Mistress Hooker says. "The governor acted as soon as he heard, and ordered the trial." I have never heard her speak so sharply.

"Oh, I meant nothing of the sort," says Mistress Lowe hastily. "Only that Mr. Humfrey must have appeared to be an upright, steady person to hold that position. Who would have known that he would neglect his children so carelessly, especially those two little girls."

"What happened to them?" I ask.

"Haven't you heard? These sinful acts took place in Boston two years ago, but they have only come to light now. This Mr. Humfrey used to go off to the assembly twice a week and leave his four children on the farm with no one reliable to look after them, just a couple of servants. So the children high-tailed it over to the neighbours', where the husband abused the older girl over and over, in what manner you can guess, and she only eight years old."

Mistress Stone takes up the story. "And that wasn't all. There was a labourer on the farm who also abused her, and later, a former servant of Mr. Humfrey's, who took the children in for schooling, did the same."

"How horrible! Why didn't she tell her father?"

"No one knows," says Mistress Stone. "They say that she came to enjoy it."

The women gasp and tut-tut, feeding on the illicit pleasure of the imagination.

"Then how did the governor find out?" I am puzzled.

Mistress Lowe says, "It wasn't until after Mr. Humfrey had gone back to England alone. The older daughter told her newly married sister, who told her husband. The three men who abused the girl, Dorcas, were arrested, and this week have been brought to examination. I am surprised that your husband hasn't told you of this."

"He has been very busy, and we usually don't talk of such things when we have time to be together."

I note Mistress Brigden's face twitching in a slight smirk, but she says nothing.

I go on. "Do the men admit to doing these things?"

Mistress Brigden says, "Not yet, but they will confess. In Boston, the penalty for rape is death."

I am beginning to feel somewhat uneasy. There is a catch in my throat that will not go away. "But this is the word of a child — how old is she now? Eleven? Does anyone support her story?"

"They say she accuses her two younger brothers of abusing her also," the red-faced Mistress Armitage says, looking up from her carding.

"There, now! Doesn't it seem like an incredible story?" My anger is barely controlled.

"You know nothing about it, Mistress," says Mistress Brigden sharply. "You weren't here. There are more and more wicked occurrences of this sort coming to light all the time. Most of them have been in the Bay Colony, but even here we have suspicions about certain people." She carries on with her sewing evenly, as do the others.

I cannot leave the subject alone. "Why did Mr. Humfrey return to England? And why did he leave such young daughters behind? The younger one, you say, is already married."

"Yes," says Mistress Brigden. "Mr. Humfrey arranged that before he left. He must have felt some guilt about what happened to Dorcas, and wanted to make sure the younger one was protected."

"Do you think he knew about Dorcas?" I am appalled.

"Suspected at least. Considering what happened to him, I believe he knew, and that is why he left." Mistress Brigden sews on righteously.

"Is there more?" I ask.

"Well now. That's what we were discussing when you arrived."

Mistress Stone's voice drips with pleasure. "He barely made it back to England, the voyage was so dangerous. But there were faithful people on board who prayed to have their lives spared, and the Lord heard them and calmed the waters. Mr. Humfrey was only just safely arrived when he discovered that his third daughter, still in England, had gone mad. So with that punishment from God, another daughter evilly abused, and two sons sent for correction at the minister's house, he is well-paid for his delinquent behaviour."

Mistress Brigden looks over at me, satisfaction smoothing out the clefts in her face.

I stay silent. I would not dare say anything more. True, I do not know the whole story, but neither do they. I look around me. I am in the minority here. Even Mistress Hooker is smiling ruefully, as if wishing it were not true. No one has expressed any doubt about the story. Perhaps in this company of self-appointed judges they are afraid to.

The next time I come to the women's meeting I bring my sewing with me. I hope that if my emotions ever come rioting to the surface again, I can bury my head in my work and not let them show. After one encounter with Mistresses Brigden and Stone, I am sure that there will be other serious disagreements. And even if I am the governor's wife, I will never be listened to with the respect given to the older women. I am too young, too new and, I already begin to suspect, in their eyes too frivolous.

The second meeting starts out better, because there is no gossiping. News has just arrived from England that King Charles has agreed to recall Parliament, after an eleven-year lapse. Most of the women have no opinions of their own, but freely quote their husbands', arguing whether the new Parliament will have a long life or a short one; what demands it will make of the King, and whether he will agree to them; and, whether this will mean a change of fortune for the saints at home, or will Archbishop Laud still have control over them.

I give my own view, that Parliament and the King will achieve a good settlement with regard to their differences for the sake of keeping peace in the country.

"Is that what your husband thinks?" asks Mistress Brigden.

"Oh, no, I wouldn't dream of speaking for him," I say.

"But surely you consulted him about this?" Mistress Brigden prods.

"No, I did not. I heard the good news, and then I just wished for a successful outcome. I do not really have any idea what will happen. Perhaps Mr. Hopkins does, but if so I couldn't say."

It is a weak response, and I know it. So does Mistress Brigden. "It is customary here to ask the advice of one's husband on such important matters." I feel harshly reprimanded, but because I have spoken so foolishly, I cannot help agreeing. "Yes, of course."

Once all the other husbands' opinions having been trotted out and bounced against one another, the subject is exhausted. The rest of the meeting passes amicably; even Mistress Brigden's manner is mildly ingratiating towards me. She has scored a hit; she can afford to be pleasant. I soon recover my equilibrium and converse with Mistress Gordon and Mistress Goodwin.

Near the end of the afternoon, the gossip begins. I have just accepted a glass of cider from Mistress Hooker, when I hear Mistress Simson at the other side of the room, say, "Do you mean Bridget Peirce, who used to live in London?"

"Yes, that's the one," says Mistress Woodside. "Did you know her?"

"Not very well, but she was always a vain woman certainly."

Mistress Lowe bursts in. "What happened to her?"

Mistress Woodside says, "Well, you know she was married to that ship's captain who they say is very rich. On his last trip, he brought her a parcel of very fine linen, which she had asked for. She wanted to show it off in good condition, so she had her maid wash and press it and lay it all out in the parlour overnight."

All the women have stopped chatting with each other, and are listening keenly to what is bound to turn out to be a horror story.

"The maid went in later that night, and managed to spill some ash from her candle on it without noticing. The next day Mistress Peirce discovered her linen all burnt to shreds."

They all shake their heads, some with undisguised satisfaction.

"Not only that, but the boards underneath were burnt through, and a pair of good stools as well. It is amazing that the people were not consumed in their beds."

The women gasp.

"Mistress Peirce must have been miserable, especially at the loss of her valuable linen," says Mistress Lowe.

Mistress Brigden, who has not spoken so far, has the defining word. "I am sure the loss did her much good. It doesn't do to prize one's possessions; it takes one's mind off the only true treasure," She glances over at my hand with its gleaming ring. "Vanity is close to pride which, as we know, is the root sin." I realize I am twisting my ring nervously.

"It was indeed the Lord's way of preparing her for a worse affliction," says Mistress Woodside.

"What else happened to her?" Mistress Armitage asks. All work has stopped now, hands are at rest, and eyes are fixed on Mistress Woodside.

"Her husband was killed on board his ship as he was trying to help some passengers disembark on Providence Island. It is a dangerous place to land. There is no word as to how he died."

"Poor, poor woman," says Mistress Armitage.

"Yes, but think how God helped her to bear the greater loss, by causing her a lesser one beforehand. Now she must understand more deeply the perils and griefs that we must endure in this wilderness for the Lord's sake." Mistress Brigden has the last word.

This time I am not silly enough to speak.

16.

IT IS THE TUESDAY following the meeting when I meet Mistress Hooker walking along the road, a covered basket on her arm, her face beaming at me.

"Ah, Mistress Hopkins, how nice to meet you! What a blessed day it is, don't you think?"

"It is that. It makes such a difference when the sun comes out. It seems to burn away one's worries."

"Oh, don't tell me you have many worries, not a dear young woman like you." She frowns slightly. "Not that we do not all have a few things to trouble us; that is to be expected, particularly in our present rugged lives. But you seemed to be getting along well, I thought. Is it more difficult to fit in to colonial life than I realized?"

I hesitate. Shall I tell the truth, or just keep mum? If ever I am going to say what I think, it must be now. I start out gingerly.

"I do not think I shall ever fit in completely." I pause. "Perhaps because I am so young, without the same experience as others here, but I do not always see eye to eye with many people here, women especially."

Mistress Hooker reassures me. "No one expects everyone to agree in all matters. How dull it would be if we all held the same views." She laughs easily, and I join in.

I say, "Very dull indeed." Then, soberly, I continue. "But Mistress Hooker, I find it hard to understand why people can be so critical of those who have been struck down by some disaster — like the man whose daughter went mad, for instance. And, why do they want to dwell on it so much?" I look closely at her to see how she is taking my words. She appears not the least disconcerted by them.

"Well now, this is one of the guidelines that sets the saints apart from other societies. We believe that as a community we are responsible for each others' lives. Our salvation will be granted to us as a community, and so no single individual must be allowed to go astray, as it endangers not just him but all of us. We must look out for the wanderer, and assist when possible. Mr. Hooker calls it the 'brotherly watch'."

I am quite taken back. All I can say is, "Oh!"

Mistress Hooker sees that I am not convinced. "Of course, some abuse that trust. You have noticed that people emphasize the horrors of sinful behaviour and the punishment rather than praying for help for the sinner. That shows them to be sinners, too, and we can only pray for them as we do for all of us."

I say "Oh" again, wondering how much divine petitioning it might take to change these women's gloating demeanour.

"Do you understand now, my dear, that even though we are called to be saints, we are a long way from sanctity, and need all the help we can get?"

"I suppose so. Yes, of course I do. I certainly need it."

"I too." She takes her hand, which has been resting on my arm, and rummages in her basket, coming up with a small crock. "There we are. I thought I had one left. This is the last of our apple butter. I have been doing the rounds of the sickbeds with it. I don't suppose it has any medicinal value, but it tastes good anyway. Here, try some with a fresh loaf."

I kiss her soundly on the cheek. "Thank you, Mistress, I am cheered up already."

"Prayer and apple butter. Not a bad combination."

And your hearty goodness, I think, as we go our separate ways.

17.

I F I HAD ANY HOPE of being respected for my opinions by the "Gossiping Gertrudes," as I call them privately, it is swept away by the news from England. Jane writes to say that the King has dissolved the Parliament within weeks of recalling it, Archbishop Laud is once again in power and there is great disturbance everywhere, especially in London where Jane had moved when she married. Jane writes:

May 10, 1640

Dearest Anne

Here in London there are people everywhere lurking about listening for contentious opinions. The Archbishop's "ears" and "eyes" penetrate even into our houses, fierce little weasels with no scruples at all. My husband and brother are afraid to speak in front of the servants, in case their views should be misunderstood, and passed along. It cannot go on like this much longer, or there will be no good people left in England, only spies and thieves and turncoats. All the rest will have fled to the continent or to New England.

I guard my tongue most carefully, politely agreeing with the accepted opinions about everything — the King, the Laudian reforms, even the disparagement of the sectarians, meaning mostly your lot (not you, of course, but your "Puritan" society). I feel like such a hypocrite, but am too afraid to differ openly. Of course if the Cromwellian party should succeed, then my silence will not argue well for me. It would not matter in any case. I cannot think in black and white. I could no more support

Cromwell wholeheartedly than I can the King. I know you think as I do, or I would not write this. Women are not supposed to have opinions about government, or religious divisions. But how could I avoid it, living in the middle of this disputatious society?

My brother thinks of coming to New England, but from what you tell me, life is harsh and the conditions for becoming a freeman are so stringent that he would never achieve the intellectual liberty he desires. Without full citizenship he would always be suspect, and what is more, he could never make a gainful living for himself without sufficient land to farm. Even though he is first and foremost a poet, he cannot live on his verses! So he, and the rest of us, tossed into the waters of these turbulent times, are caught between the Scylla-like Laudian monster and the Charybdis of dissension that seems near to pulling us all down into a bottomless whirlpool.

On a gentler note, I am sorry to hear that you are still unable to conceive a child. Perhaps it is these uncertain times that cause the difficulty. I will add my prayers to yours, and I am certain it will happen, as you would be the best of mothers.

Your affectionate cousin,

Jane

Holding Jane's letter, I am aware that my fists are clenched and my back has stiffened. I can almost feel the hatred and despair raging through the country, growing worse day by day. I think of Jane and her family, burrowing like moles underground, deprived of any light, of reason, or of hope. Then I begin to cry, quietly, dismally. Poor old England, merrie no longer. All the while that I am struggling to find a way to live as contentedly as possible in this unfamiliar place, at the back of my mind there is always the faint but constant dream that I will return to England some day. Not to a divided, cruel country, but to a place where religious differences have been settled, the King's desire to make wars has waned, and he and the Parliament together govern a quiet land. Above all, I want to see my beloved Wales again.

What a foolish woman I am to believe such a fairy tale. I am just as deluded as those who expected that this wilderness would be a new Canaan. In contrast to poor old England today, perhaps it is. What are a few silly rules and squabbles compared to the picture Jane draws of England? People are snoopy and curious here, but surely not malicious. They are just starved for something else to think about besides the daily chores and frequent preaching. I suppose they look into their neighbours' lives, hoping to find something more colourful than what is in their own.

18.

W E ARE HAVING DINNER, a good one, fish from the river, and fresh vegetables from our garden. However, Edward notices that I am merely pushing carrots around on my plate.

"What's the matter, Anne?" You're not eating. Aren't you feeling well?" he says, puzzled.

"Oh no, I'm fine. I am just not hungry." I look at him. The answer does not satisfy. "Well, I am feeling a little disheartened … not your fault," I say quickly. "I am sure I will get over it."

"Don't try to pretend with me, dearest. Tell me what's wrong. Please."

"I didn't want to bother you with it." I stop, not wanting to go on, but then I do. "It's those women at Mistress Hooker's circle. I can't believe how cruel some of them are." I tell him about the conversations at the last two meetings, and finish with, "They seem to relish the misery of the people they deem wicked."

Edward starts to reply, but I carry on. "No, I am not exaggerating, if that's what you are thinking. You should have seen one woman — I won't say who — smirk as she told about the linens burning. As if she were perfect herself."

"Now you are exaggerating, dear. No saint would ever think she was perfect," Edward says.

I agree, reluctantly. "Well, she does act superior to the rest of us — some of us anyway. Me certainly."

"She wouldn't think that. These women hardly know you," he says gently.

"And when they do? I am beginning to think I should never let them know me truly. I can see already how different my views are on many things."

"Then go softly, Anne. That's my advice. Don't rush in with your opinions until you know more about the people you are meeting. I would not want to see you making bad friends here."

"Of course, you're right. But don't let it worry you. There must be plenty of people in Hartford who will make good friends. I just haven't met them yet."

"Well, in the meantime, don't give up on these women entirely. They are some of the mainstays of the saints and the community, so as the governor's wife you will be seeing a lot of them, one way or another."

I sigh. "So it seems. I'll do my best to get on with them. I do like a few of them very much."

"Thank goodness for that. I would hate to think you weren't enjoying yourself somewhat." He stops, realizing what he has just said, and goes on with his meal. Enjoyment is not something we talk about in the colony. Edification, yes; pleasure, no. Edward cares so much about me that he breaks the unwritten rule.

I say, "Oh, I am," and give him a huge smile. Then I pick up my knife and spoon and try to put away some of my now cold dinner.

19.

HOW CAN I MAKE people see that I am a helpful governor's wife, capable of being a good housewife? I think I will give a party. Edward agrees that this is a good idea.

I decide to hold it on a Friday, not to interfere with all the other village activities, such as laundry day, baking day, market day, the Tuesday meetings (not just the Gossiping Gertrudes, but other little groups of women who meet to study the Bible or do their stitching, or both), and, of course, the Thursday evening prayer meetings. Friday seems the only free day really. I thought to have just women; later on, when I am feeling more comfortable in my role as mistress of the house, Edward and I will have an evening supper party, perhaps for the counsellors and their wives.

This is to be a purely social occasion, so no knitting and no Bible study, just pleasant conversation about, well, that remains to be seen. I want to get to know these women a little better, and let them see that I am not as wayward as some of them believe me to be. I never stopped to ask myself how I am going to convince them of this.

Eight women seems like a good number to have. I invite Mistresses Goodwin, Simson, Lowe, and Armitage; Mistress Hooker, who cannot come because she is in Boston; Mistress Stone, reluctantly, and Mistress Brigden, even more so. Perhaps the latter two are just as unwilling to come. I ask the nice young Mistress Gordon, and Elizabeth Johnson. I deliberate about inviting Elizabeth when all the other women are such ardent saints. But then, I decide that she can handle them with her winning manner, and, perhaps, after meeting her, they will not think she is so wicked, or stubborn, or whatever it is they think about her.

Being uncertain about what to serve, I ask Nellie and Cook to find out for me what is customary for an afternoon's gathering. I know they chat with other servants, and hope they will be discreet about their questioning, so that the word will not get back that I do not know the right way to do things. Both come back saying that for an afternoon gathering, a glass of wine with small helpings of cheese and bread would be suitable. No cake, of course. The saints disapprove of such luxury.

Jenny makes sure that every stick of furniture in the parlour gleams with sweet-smelling wax, and the Turkey carpets that my grandfather let me take from Plâs Grono are given a good beating so the colours stand out gaily. We lay the Brittany linen cloth on the folding table, and set my precious Venice goblets on it, Edward's wondrous wedding gift. The last thing we do is place the eight chairs. I do not want them in a circle, the way they are at the Gossiping Gertrudes. We try different groupings, but they look like a stage set, which would upset my guests straight off. Finally we just set them in a row along two of the walls. That way people can move them about as they see fit.

Oh, how stupid I am! They do not see fit at all. Everyone arrives at the same time, and each one goes to sit down in the chairs just the way I have placed them. For the whole time, no one moves scarcely an inch to turn and face someone beside her. It looks like a schoolroom, or a meeting house.

They all know one another, although they make a pretense of not knowing Mistress Johnson, I suppose this is because they have never been introduced. They must have passed her in the road many times, or at the market, or even noticed her sitting at the back of the meeting house on a Sunday. Still, I have to introduce her, and almost every person nods her head soberly when I speak the name, without even raising her eyes to look at my friend. Right away I begin to feel my stomach throb, and sense a chill in the room that has nothing to do with the temperature of the day. When I get to Mistress Goodwin, she does look up and say, "Good day, Mistress," to which Elizabeth replies, "And to you." It is not much, but it is better than nothing. Mistress Gordon also looks up and smiles shyly at Elizabeth, but does not say a word. I think they are friendly with each other, but Mistress Gordon does not want to admit that in such company.

I am in such a hurry to warm things up that I decide to serve the wine right away. Jenny carries it round, and I see everyone taking one of the glasses in her hand gingerly, and looking at it as carefully as if examining an insect through a microscope. As I see Mistress Simson run her thumb along the side of the glass, I say, "These were my wedding gift from Mr. Hopkins. You are very the first to use them. Aren't they beautiful?" I suppose I look quite proud.

Mistress Simson nods, and Mistress Stone says, " So that explains it."

I look puzzled, and she goes on, "These are rather elegant for such a humble colony, I should have thought."

Without thinking, I say, "Anything to brighten up the place. It's so dull around here."

All eyes are upon me. I stop, raise my glass quickly, and say, "To your good health, ladies." They drink obediently. Then there is silence.

Mistress Brigden finally says, looking around her. "You brought quite a lot of furniture with you from London, I see." She is staring at my court cupboard with the colourful dishes and the pewter, and then down at the carpets. I feel as though my house and I are being undressed at the same time. I fiddle with my wedding ring, and wish Mistress Brigden to a fiery unmentionable location.

Mistress Goodwin, bless her heart, steps in. "I think Mistress Hopkins has made her house as handsome as it should be, since she and her husband will likely be entertaining all sorts of important people in the future." She changes the subject mercifully. "Isn't the spring lovely this year? So many birds have come back, more than ever before. I love to hear them singing, it makes every day so cheerful."

I say, "Today I saw the ducks migrating. Did you see them? They came in enormous flocks, hundreds at a time. I'd guess there were two thousand of them."

I would have liked to go on to tell them how they soared, each group making a different swirling formation. I think the ducks must have an alphabet of their own, with each flock acting as a single letter. Then, when all the flocks are together, they form a word, their whole name perhaps, or a greeting word for us. They were calling as they flew, just one sound, but because they all cried at different moments, it was almost like a chant. They could have been calling "Ultreia!" (meaning "Onward!") like the Compostella pilgrims. To me their appearance was a vision, the most heavenly I will ever have, until perhaps I get there truly.

I am getting up the courage to say more, when Mistress Lowe speaks up. "Is that so? Well, now, all the men will be gone from dawn till dark with all the ploughing and planting to be done."

Why is it that people cannot enjoy the beauty around them, just because it is there? Instead ,they have to make even the joyful arrival of spring into a work project. Back to the grindstone everyone, eyes down, stick to business. The conversation goes from bad to worse.

"My husband can't do any heavy work yet, because of the fall he took this winter. I don't know how we are going to get along," puts in Mistress Gordon.

"Ah yes, he was fixing the chimney, wasn't he, and fell off the roof. Did he break his back? I've forgotten," says Mistress Stone, almost casually, as if the remark had interrupted her other thoughts.

"Yes, it's almost healed, but not enough to go with the plough," Mistress Gordon answers pathetically.

Elizabeth says, "My husband has hired a man to plough for him. I will ask him if he has time to help you out, if you like."

Mistress Gordon flushes. There is a brief pause when no one says anything, and then she turns to Mistress Johnson. "Oh, thank you, that's so kind of you to suggest it, but really we'll manage somehow." She looks agitated, and I fear she will spill her wine.

Elizabeth can take the hint, and only says, " Well, just let me know if you change your mind." She sits back in her chair and sips her wine, acting as if nothing untoward has happened. The subject is finished. I feel sorry for both of them, having to pretend so. I know that Elizabeth will do as she has suggested, and that Mistress Gordon, when the time comes, will accept the help gratefully.

I am waiting for Mistress Brigden to get in again. She cannot bear to be left out of the conversation for long. Usually, it is she who introduces a subject, and also concludes it with her own moral wisdom. Today she has to take what she's been given, and so she does. Fixing her gaze on the far wall, she intones, "I remember the first year we came here, there was that young man, what was his name, who tried to replace some stone around the top of his chimney, just as your husband was doing, and he fell down and broke his back in two places. It never mended."

Mistress Gordon cries "No!"

"I am afraid so. But, of course it may not happen to Mr. Gordon. We must all pray that it does not." She looks directly at Elizabeth, who, in turn, gives her a little smile and tips her head slightly. I take this gesture of Elizabeth's to mean, "I'll do it my way, but at least I am sincere about it, whereas I doubt that you are." I love Elizabeth's way of treating these slights, quietly in control. I wish I could learn her skill.

I said, "I'll certainly pray for a swift recovery. Shall we have some cheese now?" I get up, as Jenny has left the room, and pass it around to everyone. Some decline, but other take a piece with a bit of bread, probably just to avoid having to say anything. This party is not going well, and I know it, but I cannot think what else to do. I wish I had not decided to do this on my own.

I look around me, and see a smile spreading over Mistress Lowe's face. "Are you planning an excursion this spring, Mistress?" I ask.

"Why would I do that? My family is here, and I have everything I need in Hartford. I do not have to run off to Boston for special goods, or for a diversion." The smile is still there, but I recognize it as a somewhat sardonic one. I think she must be criticizing me, the nasty woman. Or maybe she is directing her comments at someone else. I look around the room, and realize that it is either Elizabeth or myself who is her target. I decide to pick up the challenge. I will try an equally devious reply.

"Yes, Hartford is the heart and centre of our lives. It is a pity that some of us, such as my husband, have to go to Boston to have those goods sent here that we all enjoy. I guess if there were no Boston to supply us, there would be no Hartford.

"You are so fortunate to have all your family in one place. I do wish I could persuade all of mine to plant here, but the Lord has other work for them to do." I finish with my best, not too supercilious, smile. Another conversation stopper, I think. My clever reply is not going to improve my standing with these people, but I cannot help myself.

It seems to me that there is a certain amount of fussing going on, the brushing of crumbs from clothes, the changing of sitting positions, the scraping of feet, as though everyone is preparing to leave. This is not to be. How could I have forgotten? The last word has to be — whose will it be, Mistress Brigden's or Mistress Stone's? I always think of the latter as standing in the other's shadow, deferential, while trying to let on that she is the one in charge. So it is that this little dance is performed here, as the closing scene in my pathetic party.

"I think that we have taken up enough of Mistress Hopkins' time today. She must have many more tasks to finish before supper," Mistress Stone says.

"I think rather that this afternoon has put her to enough trouble for one day," says Mistress Brigden. "It was good of you to invite us to see your house," she says to me.

My face smarts at the implied criticism, delivered as if it were a proper thank you. All I can say in return is, "I do thank you for your visit."

One by one they say their thank yous, with Mistress Goodwin pressing my hand warmly. Elizabeth, who is the last out the door (she knows they will all want to walk away without her beside them), kisses me softly and says, "Good for you, Anne. Don't mind the dreadful ones. Some of them are really quite sweet." I almost cry.

Later on I do, volubly, torrentially. Red eyes at supper. I say nothing to Edward, not wanting to upset him again.

From that moment on, as I go about the town, it seems to me that they are watching me more intently, to see what mistakes — errors, in their books — I will make. Are they storing up each blunder for a time when they will need to use such instances against me for some mean cause of their own? I begin to wonder about this a lot, but I know if I start thinking this way all the time I will get sick.

20.

I HAVE BEEN SO BUSY with all these new activities that I have abandoned my journal almost completely. Now I take it up again, with a difference. I look back at the first pages I wrote when I came here, and am stunned at the change in me. The rapture that breathed through my first writings after I arrived in Hartford has gone. Just as, when you first enter into a part of the country you have never seen before, all you have eyes for is the briskly waving cornstalks, the rich brown earth; and the bright headscarves and aprons of the women bending and tossing the corn into their baskets. When the sun sinks lower you are able to see much more closely. Many rows hold stunted plants, and there are gaps where the corn did not grow. The earth has dried between the rows, leaving gaping cracks. And the women, whose clothing gives off an air of cheerful harvesting, are bent over because they must. There is not a straight back among them, so knotted and gnarled are their spines and knees.

So I watch the sun fade over my first exuberant impressions of the new land, and begin to see the dryness, the cracks, and the crookedness that I have come to learn is part of the little colony's life. I write:

July 12, 1639

"How thoroughly unfit we are for this raw primitive life. Every day I hear of another misfortune caused by ignorance or carelessness on the part of ordinarily sensible people, or so one would think. Last week, a man was carrying a heavy load of lumber up the river in his canoe, and, as a result, the boat tipped over and he fell out and drowned.

"People do not treat fire with the caution it requires. A poor family tried to make a fire in their house to keep warm, as the nights are growing cold now. They had never put in a chimney before, so, of course, their little frame house ignited and burned down. They were able to get out just in time, but now they have nowhere to live. Also, down beside our jetty, a sailor on a small pinnace lit up his pipe while standing beside a barrel of gunpowder, and blew up the boat. He escaped, but at the loss of both his hands and his feet. How he will survive in this condition I cannot imagine. He has been sent back to his family in Boston, who will have a hard time of it now.

"When I hear our ministers and magistrates talk about having been called forth into New England to be a light for the old country, I wonder if they still really believe this. It seems to me, either the Lord has made a great mistake and pointed his finger at the wrong people, or he is trying to teach us a lifelong lesson about the folly of self-importance. I might think he has an awful sense of humour, were it not that our fumbling efforts to build a colony have such unhappy, sometimes tragic results.

"What makes these terrible events even worse in my eyes, is the sanctimonious way in which they are explained. When the governor of the Bay Colony's children were saved from mishap, it was the Lord's providence that did it. They had been plucking birds, while sitting under a great pile of logs. The feathers from the birds were flying into the house, so their mother told them to move over to the other side of the yard. They had just gone, when the entire heap of logs fell down. Clearly, they would have been crushed to death. The governor said that it was the special providence of the Lord that allowed them to escape.

"On the opposite side of the Lord's providence, His blind side, I guess, was the godly family down at Weymouth with three small children. The parents left them at home all alone, would you believe it, while they went to the Sabbath assembly. While the eldest was outside, the middle boy aged five, took hold of his father's fowling piece, and set it ready to fire on a stool, pulling up the cock and putting down the hammer. Then, imitating his father's actions, he blew in the mouthpiece, and with that stirring, the piece, being charged, went off, shooting himself into the mouth and right through the head. It was the littlest child who saw the whole thing, and tried to tell his father what had happened when the parents came home.

"I confess I do not like the notion that the Lord moves in mysterious ways, which is the explanation given when terrible accidents like this happen. I would rather blame the latter occurrence on the negligence of the parents, and the former on the watchfulness of the governor's wife.

"Today, I walked out of town towards the forest, through mile after mile of open country bereft of everything except the stumps of trees. It is hard to imagine that any of the saints here who can leave such a wasted scene behind them are capable of creating a fair and verdant land."

III
Hartford, 1642

1.

WHEN JANE'S LATEST LETTER arrives, I read it immediately, but the news she sends is hardly cheering.

September 10, 1642

Dear Jane,

I was so happy to receive your letter, which took only six weeks to arrive. Travel is certainly faster these days, and safer, but not in the late fall or winter on account of the storms at sea. People are still foolhardy enough to start out, though; we hear rumours of ships lost, and all their passengers drowned with them. Once in a while they say that God's special providence has saved a ship, but I am beginning to be quite skeptical of this explanation. If all these stories were to be believed, one would believe God to have a capricious character. Adding it up, I would say that he lets three vessels sink for every ten he saves.

Of course I am glad to hear that Archbishop Laud is still in prison, and is to be held accountable for his actions against all nonconformists. I do not see how the Parliament can impeach him for high treason, though, as he has been one of the King's most ardent supporters — unless they intend to attack the King also.

The impending civil war will not help the King: from what you tell me, he cannot win it. He has made too many enemies. He has certainly behaved badly and foolishly towards Parliament, but I think it would be wicked if it were to do him any harm. I hope he will see the error of his ways, and agree to make concessions to save the country.

News of the preparations for war had already reached us, and we have already had two days of humiliation and fasting, to ask the Lord's forgiveness for our sins, and pray that he will bring the war to a swift end. So we think of everyone at home, and pray for your safety. Please do write again soon, and assure me that you are well looked after.

I am glad that you liked *A Connecticut Spring*. As you can tell by the date, it took me a good while to write — almost three years! — and then I had to wait to find a trustworthy courier for it, because I was not entirely circumspect in what I wrote. I will have to be even more careful with this letter, I fear, as my first impressions have changed somewhat, and I would not want anyone to discover my true opinions about our life here. I think I shall wait until I visit David in Boston to give it to him to send; he has good, unaligned people travelling frequently back and forth on his business who could take it.

When I say that my first impressions have changed, I do not mean every one of them. Some things that one expects would change, do not. People are still oblivious to the dangers of living in this primitive town surrounded by a vast and implacable wilderness.

Today, for example, I learned of another ghastly family loss caused by sheer ineptness in New Haven. A man was cutting down trees; his four sons were with him, either helping, or watching. One came in the way of a tree being felled, and, as it toppled over, it struck him in the head and killed him. I heard that he was only six years old.

This past winter, a number of people have been reported missing after they wandered off into the forest without telling anyone and lost their way. Two men I know of made their way back to town barely alive. And one man was discovered in the snow by another cutting wood; his hands and feet had frozen and had to be amputated. Then there were the frequent unguarded fires that destroyed houses and left families homeless in the perishing cold. This past winter was severe, but not nearly as bad as the one two years ago when so many people starved. I feel a certain shame about all this as we are shipping our beaver pelts to England to be made into fashionable coats and hats, while our Puritan consciences will not allow us to wear them for fear of ostentation. Think of how many poor people were perpetually chilled to their bones for want of a fur coat.

Actually, when I consider what we have endured, I should write another journal and call it *A Connecticut Winter*. Edward is away so much, all the day at his mill or his counting house, and sometimes he goes to Boston for a week to look after the shipping. So, I have plenty of time to write these days, almost too much time.

Winter seems an unlikely subject at this time of year, as I sit in my steamy chamber trying to take my mind off the heat and swatting mosquitoes every few minutes. They are so lazy and confused they fly into my nose, and I sneeze to expel them. It is so humid that it is impossible to do very much. At the height of the day I lie on my bed with the curtains drawn and fan myself with a book. I wash my face often, but in the same precious water, for the wells are nearly dry.

Many farmers are trying to work in their fields, with no protection from the sun. The ground is cracked and hard as flint, and many crops burnt, but they are starting to harvest what they can and hope for rain soon. Before this drought began there was such an abundance of green growing things, it looked as though we would be living in Eden at last. But the Lord's providence, you know, is not just for saving us but also for testing us. We do seem to have plenty of tests. If I were a cynic, I would ask, how many tests are enough to prove our faithfulness? (Jane, please do not repeat this comment; it would be considered blasphemous here.)

September 18

I suppose I should be called out for my blasphemy. Last week, on account of the drought, we gathered for a day of humiliation, to seek the Lord, and ask him to forgive our sins and to relieve our sufferings. The next day we had a good shower of rain. In the days that followed, we had so much rain that the corn is now fully revived, and we can count on an exceptional harvest. Still, I am undecided about providence, even though it appears that our prayers have been answered.

The town has grown in the last few years, despite Mr. Cromwell's refusal to allow more emigration from England. I cannot understand this hostility to emigration. Edward says that we are becoming too prosperous and have attracted all the best farmers and artisans from overseas. Why should Mr. Cromwell begrudge us some improvement in this difficult place? Edward says that comfort is not the Puritan way, although he hesitates when he says so, seeing that we are in fact rather comfortable and certainly well-to-do.

What we lack in grandeur we make up for in cleanliness. It seems to be an unwritten rule here that everything we walk on, sit on, or are likely to put a hand on, shall be scoured, polished or at the very least dusted every day. This includes most, but not all, of my body. My gowns and bed coverings are aired daily. It is not for any spiritual reason that we do this; it is to prevent disease from entering the house. In a new land, who is to say what infection may lurk in the ground, or in the very wood our houses are built from? This routine keeps the servants busy for a good part of each day. Still, there is a lot of sickness in the colony, such as fevers and aches and influenza, though no one knows why. I have had nothing but a red face and an itchy back, on account, I suppose, of having my outer layer of skin scrubbed away regularly.

Our numbers have grown, owing to new births, and also to the arrival of families from the other colonies, particularly New Haven and Boston. The civil order in those towns is much stricter than our own, especially with regard to citizenship. There you must be a visible believer in order to vote; here any freeman who has been approved by Mr. Hooker and the council may vote. So we have many planters who are not saints.

A few of our most rigid members think this will lead to trouble, but so far nothing of the sort has occurred. We have had no murders, few run-away servants, and very little theft — not that there is much to be taken. The worst sins are between husbands and wives; my Bible-study circle reports with a touch of glee any story of infidelity or fornication. They all trooped out of the meeting last week to look at a woman who was put in the stocks, supposedly for incest. However, the truth is, she is a widow whose husband was recently lost at sea, and his brother had come to visit merely to commiserate with her. As the brother had returned to his own town by the time the suspicious neighbours had reported on them, there was no one to support her statement. The council, uncertain of what to believe, decided to forgo a whipping and placed her in the stocks for half a day, just in case. I did not go with the women, but went home instead.

My departure was noticed, of course, and added to the list of peculiarities for which I am becoming known. Others you will recognize as the Anne Hopkins you know so well — reading, writing, musing, and, worst of all here, speaking my own mind, rather than deferring to my husband or our revered minister. I am learning to curtail the latter, but for me to attempt to put away the other harmless activities would be to cut off my life's blood. I know that the most severe saints do not think of these activities as harmless, or even peculiar, but as sins. I believe their theology is misguided, but their voices are loud and insistent. So, although I will never give up my dear pursuits, I try to hide away from prying eyes. Privacy is another grey matter, morally speaking, as communal life is to be chosen above personal habits. So, here again I walk near the border between the country of the saints and that of the misbegotten. Sometimes my whole being rebels at the subterfuge I must maintain. I find myself shaking with fury at the need for it. Then something lovely takes place and I feel free again.

Despite my complaints, I can say that we are, on the whole a much more lenient and forgiving town than any in the neighbouring Massachusetts Bay Colony, no doubt because of the influence of Edward and Mr. Hooker. One of Edward's merchant partners in Salem told us of a monstrous cruelty imposed on a Samuel Gorton whose loudly pronounced opinions were considered blasphemous. As punishment, the colony's ministers ordered the fort in which he and his family lived burnt down, with all of them inside! They escaped the fire, so the ministers put them out of the town, each one, children included, wearing an iron on one leg. The children are punished for the sins of the father, or so it is believed. But I cannot imagine any person's blasphemy that would deserve this treatment. I read somewhere about a group of French heretics who were burned to death inside a church by the Inquisition a long time ago. Surely we have become more humane since then. Do you not think that to burn someone alive is far more of a blasphemy against God's creation than any words, no matter how damnable, could be? Thank God I live in a colony where nothing like this could happen.

Now that the depression is over and the harvests, up until now, have been good, everyone is much happier, and we do not have so many willing poor in the colony. There is work for all, though it may not pay more than sustenance wages. I have heard Mr. Hooker say that we recognize God's glory by the wonderful ordering of his creation, with rich and poor living out their callings, each different from the other. He is a fine and noble man, who would not do harm to anyone, but I do wish that he would get closer to his people, to see what their varied lives are really like. No one surely could call an arrangement wonderful where folk are so poor they must eat plant roots and corn husks in a bad season, and where they sew cast-off strips of leather together to make soles for their children's shoes. On the matter of God's glorious order, I wonder: surely he would have shown his wisdom and glory more fully if he had not included the level of the suffering poor. If I were to speak out and say this, Mr. Hooker would say that God created the hierarchy this way, and so it is bound to be good. There I go again, the silly goat thinking crooked thoughts.

As I say, we are at present quite free of the problem of the poor, and the whole colony prospers. We are shipping more wood than ever to all parts of Europe: pipe staves to Spain for their wine barrels, and great masts to England. Between supervising the milling and transporting the finished lumber to his ships, Edward is so busy that he fears his duties as governor are being slighted. I assure him that his assistant and the council are looking after our affairs very well, and that he cannot do more than he does. These days he rarely spends a full evening at home.

I try to keep occupied. When it is cool enough I weed in the garden. Next month I will be able to pick our apples, which Ardyth can make into cider. So far, no one has told me I must not climb a ladder.

Of course I have my regular outings: to the assembly on Sunday, the "Gossiping Gertrudes" on Tuesday, the market on Wednesday, the lecture on Thursday evening. On Monday, I pay visits to the sick and the very old.

On Saturday, we are all supposed to be getting ready for Sabbath. That is when I try to take my country walks unobserved, because most people are inside doing chores, and will not catch me going off. I feel like a criminal climbing through the bars of the jail, but sometimes I just have to get away.

That leaves Friday with no demands. I can write or read (in private, in my room, or at the back of the garden under the willow) and see whomever I wish. Have I told you about my friend, Elizabeth Johnson? She is just my age, and has a wonderful sense of humour, even though her life is not always easy. She and Mistress Goodwin are the people I can really trust, apart from Edward and Nellie and Mr. Hooker — but of course I cannot tell them everything. I know that, even when we do not agree about something, these two women will never discuss it with anyone else. That precious silence is hard to find here.

I am sorry to send such a gloomy letter, but do not be upset about all my complaints. I am sure matters will improve. I am praying with all my might that they will. Still, I cannot keep my memories of home far from my mind. I do wish I could see you, and all my friends there. My thoughts and prayers go with you.

Your loving cousin,
Anne Hopkins

2.

IT IS SATURDAY and I am looking forward to my usual walk. I decide to take a different direction this time and follow a footpath along the river. It is warm in the sun, so I am dawdling, stopping to pick a few wildflowers and take in the scents of the good earth. Ahead of me a small brown animal, one I have never seen before, jumps out of the meadow and runs off along a smaller path that angles away from the river into the forest. In seconds it is gone, and, curious about where the new path leads, I follow. It is much cooler here, and I begin to shiver. I am almost ready to turn back when I see a bright clearing some distance ahead and run towards it. Overhead a crow squawks a warning.

Abruptly, I arrive at the edge of an Indian village. I stop in alarm. About a dozen wigwams stand in a half-circle around an open space in which a few people are kneeling on the ground working. They leave off what they are doing and stare at me.

This is a fine pickle. What should I do, and what are they likely to do? I cannot guess, and my shivering body grows even cooler with fright. Do not be silly, I tell myself. I am not coming to harm them, and they surely know it. What threat could a defenseless woman be to them? They do not look fierce. I look more closely. They are all women. I will speak to them, and if they are not friendly, I'll just go home.

I say, "Good morning. I was just taking a walk and lost my way. I am glad I found you."

The women look at me in silence. I take a couple of steps ahead. "Could

I see what you are doing? It looks very interesting."

The women say something to each other that I cannot understand. Their voices are low, and the sounds they make come from deep in their throats. Of course, none of them speak English. I shall have to try another way.

I move further into the clearing, pointing to myself and saying, "Mistress Hopkins. Hopkins."

The word seems to have some effect. They repeat it to each other, and finally one woman stands up and beckons me to come and sit down. I squat beside them. But then, another woman goes inside a wigwam and brings out a deerskin. She lays it on the ground, and gestures for me to sit. All of them are looking at me, at my dress as well as my face, though not critically as the saints do. They are wondering about the stuff my clothes are made of, and whether my face is painted. I return their looks, and motion for them to carry on with their work, which they do.

They are preparing hides, which I find out later are moose. Two of the women are scraping the hair off the outside of the skins with a sharp knife, careful not to score the skin beneath. Then they take them over to the side of the clearing where the sun is brightest, and lay them out to dry.

Two other women nearest to me are kneeling on the dried white hides, which look like thick parchment. They are rubbing grease into the hides to make them supple again. Then they scrape off the extra grease with a blunt paddle, leave the hides to dry, and repeat the whole process. It looks like hard work. The heavy smells that I am not accustomed to make me sit back on the deerskin as far as I can. I am tempted to move over to the furthest side of the group, where women are cutting thin strips from the tanned hides, to use for lacing, but I think that might not be polite.

One of the women leaves the group, and returns with a wooden bowl holding some boiled meat. She hands it to me graciously, making hand-to-mouth gestures. I thank her, and start to give it back, while trying to express the idea that I am not hungry. Then it strikes me that this is a special act of welcome, and I cannot refuse. I will just have to try and eat it, and hope I do not vomit. I take a piece, bite gingerly, and discover it is excellent. I smile and pat my mouth, trying to convey my appreciation.

All the women, who have been observing me, make you-are-welcome sounds, or so I guess.

When eventually I get up to leave, I wonder, how can I repay this gift of food? I have nothing to offer. I reach for the wildflowers I picked, and hand them to the woman who brought the bowl, holding out the other hand as well to show it is empty, I have nothing else. It is difficult to get across the idea of, "Thank you, I will be back, and the next time I will bring something better"; but I think I am understood, and I say goodbye, waving.

This is one of the happiest days I have spent since I came to New England.

On the way back I decide that I must not tell anyone where I have been. I have been warned about the danger of visiting the Indians — what foolishness! — and I know there have been rumours of Indian attacks. Not these Indians, surely. Still, Edward would probably insist that I keep away from them. Best not to say anything.

3.

THIS EVENING AFTER SUPPER we are sitting contentedly in our small parlour. I am just about to put my nose in a new book when Edward says hesitantly, "How are you getting along with the servants these days?" I look over at him sitting carefully with the air of a diplomat embarking on a treacherous assignment.

"Oh, very well. Nellie is such a gem, and the others are all fine, too. Not that I see a lot of them. They do their work so well that they are almost invisible. At least I have seldom any fault to find. Have you?"

"No, they are well-trained, and fastidious in most things. But do you think you should be taking more of a hand in the household? If you were there, perhaps doing some little task you care for, you would be able to watch in case anything should go wrong. All may appear to be well on the surface, but sometimes there could be trouble brewing, and if you aren't there, you won't spot it."

"You think I should be their sly supervisor, a sort of kitchen constable?"

Edward laughs at that. "Well, no, I wouldn't say that exactly, but you must not be so trusting, Anne. Even honest servants are likely to behave in rather foolish ways."

"As do we all," I say. "Well, now that the weather is changing, I suppose I will have to spend more time indoors anyway. I hope my presence won't make them uneasy. It has been so lovely, just looking after the plants or sitting in the garden reading or writing."

"I know. Some of our good church people have commented on it. That is why I mention the idea of spending some more time looking after the house."

I am horrified. "Do you mean that someone has told you I am a layabout and should be doing housework? Oh, Edward, how could they? And why do you pay attention to them?"

Edward looks crestfallen. "I don't mean to upset you, my dear. It is for your own good, I think, not to spend so much time with your head in the clouds. You know what Mr. Hooker would say about using your imagination too much: it is God who is the creator, not we, and we should be satisfied with the world he made, and not try to dream up another one."

I start to interrupt, but he continues gently, "I know how much you love to write your little books, and your letters, and to read the good authors, but you need to balance your life, don't you agree? I know that Cook and the others would be glad to see more of you."

I cannot speak. I feel as if my inner world has become utterly unbalanced. Edward is speaking to me as if I were an untutored child. And it is not as if it was his idea; it is the nosey neighbours who put it into his head. Has he spoken to Mr. Hooker about me? Why are they so worried? I will not ask. I do not want to know. Edward is wise in most things, so perhaps he knows better about this than I do. I thought I was getting along very well, and that the house was running like a good clock. Well, I will listen to him and try to change. I could be wrong, after all about the inner workings of the house. My mother used to tell me I could not see beyond the end of my nose. I hated it when she said that, but that does not mean it is not true. One thing I am beginning to learn, certainly: keep out of the way of the neighbours. "I'll do my best," I say. "They may regret it, though, when they discover how ignorant I am."

"I don't believe that for a moment."

The next morning after breakfast, I walk into the kitchen. Cook, who is standing over a wooden slab on which she is cutting up a large piece of meat with a cleaver, nods a "Good morning, Mistress," and keeps on chopping. I stand well back, afraid that if I disturb her, Cook might make a serious mistake and hurt herself. As I see the assured way in which the

woman handles meat and blade, I decide that Cook is too steady to be in danger of an accident. Whereas I, who have never held a great cleaver like that, would be so nervous that I would probably lose a finger. Wielding such an implement takes experience, brawn and nerve.

I watch fascinated until Cook has finished. Then I say, "Where is Ardyth? Shouldn't she be helping you?"

Cook says, "She's in the larder making butter. We're almost out."

"Oh, good. I'll go and watch. I've always wanted to know how it's done."

Cook mutters, "It's not so difficult to figure out. It just takes time and elbow grease."

"Well, then, perhaps I can help." I go through the door into the larder, turning my back on Cook's puzzled face.

Ardyth is hard at work. I stand beside her, caught up in the solid rhythm of her churning arm. Once, when she stops and lifts the cover off the churn to check her progress, I peer in too, but can see nothing but foaming cream. "How long will it take before the butter comes?"

"Oh, it will be a while yet. It always depends on the cream, and the weather, and how fast you churn it."

"Would you like me to take a turn and relieve you?" I ask.

"Oh, no, Mistress, this would be too tiring for you. Me, I'm used to it." Ardyth looks me up and down as if gauging my weight. It is true, I am almost as thin as the churn, but much taller. Is that what Ardyth is thinking too?

"Let me try. I'm stronger than I look."

Reluctantly Ardyth gives me the plunger, shows me where to place my hand, and then stands back. I begin to churn the cream. It is not that heavy, or difficult, but it does use my arm in a way it has never been used before. I switch hands. Soon I am feeling a little sore, then a bit more, then my arms really hurt. I hand the job back to Ardyth. "I guess that's enough for a first time."

"You lasted very well, Mistress. But you needn't bother with it. I can do all the churning we need. It's easy for me." Her arm flies up and down.

"So I see," I laugh. "Well, I will just have to find some other way to help out." I go off to find my journal, in which I will describe my first and only day as a dairymaid. As I hesitate in the hall, wondering where I left it, I hear Ardyth say to Cook, "What was that all about?"

"I don't know, but I think the master has had a word with her about looking to see what we're doing in here."

"He wouldn't do that. He's not the suspicious kind."

"No, but perhaps someone else is, and has put the idea into his head. There are some powerful big snoops in this town, who would love to see the mistress embarrassed."

"That would be cruel!" cries Ardyth. "She doesn't know much about housework, but she is a good kind woman."

"She'll do me a kindness if she stays out of my kitchen," said Cook, regaining her usual huffiness.

"My kitchen" says it all. Cook is not that hard to get along with, but after being left in charge of the food stores and the meals for so long, she does not want to be displaced, especially by someone who is more likely to be a hindrance than a help. I decide that I must tread lightly.

I continue to visit the kitchen, but my offers of help are politely and firmly refused. I know enough by now not to argue with Cook. The best I can do is to inquire as to the menu and, once in a while, to suggest a small alteration. This is acceptable. Since Cook and Ardyth are now of the opinion that someone has forced me into this attention to the cooking, they take my inquiries with good grace. I am sure they say nothing to anyone else. To them, loyalty and privacy are still virtues, and for that I prize them greatly.

Sometimes I will stand beside them, ostensibly to see how a special dish, such as a boiled sallat with spinach, is being prepared, with all the cooking, chopping, reheating and mixing with the other ingredients. If it takes a long time, my mind draws me somewhere else, and I leave them, rushing up to my chamber to write down whatever thoughts have come to me in the kitchen. I agree with Cook and Ardyth's unspoken opinion that I am not cut out to be a cook, with the result that my visits to the kitchen become shorter and less frequent.

4.

IT IS EDWARD'S BIRTHDAY, and, thinking back with longing about some of the heartwarming celebrations our family had held in Plâs Grono, I decide to make a special pudding. It is the least, and the most, I can do. Cakes and fancy pastries are frowned upon in this ascetic minded colony, but once in a while, for a good cause, sugary, fruit desserts are deemed acceptable. I venture down to the kitchen, and make my proposal to Cook, who hums and haws, looking glum and apprehensive about the whole thing. Finally, she has to give in; it is not her house, after all, or her husband's birthday.

"I suppose you will want a recipe, then. I doubt I have anything that fancy," she says.

"Oh, but I don't need one. I'm sure I can remember it. It was my grandmother's pudding, and we served it often in Wales. I helped make it a few times."

Cook looks even more skeptical. "You'll be using up all the eggs, probably. And the butter — we'll be running short of butter if you take most of what's there."

"I don't need very much," I say. "I'll go and see what is in the larder, and then I can tell you." I hurry out of the room before she can make another objection.

The larder door is heavy, made of three thick layers of wood, in order to keep the food cool. It has a solid iron latch and below that a firm handle. Still, it is not a difficult door to open, and I tug at it rapidly and go inside to get the butter. It is sitting on a shelf at the back of the little room, and just as I reach it, and am lifting it down, the door closes with a bang. (I was told later that one of the young servants passing by and seeing no one inside, thought the door had been carelessly left open and shut it quickly to keep the room from warming up.)

I stand there frozen to the spot, holding the butter mould in the pitch darkness. Waves of terror come over me, and at first I can do nothing. Then the fear rises to my throat and I begin to scream. I drop the butter. My screams turn into short, choking cries. It is useless to try and move, to find the way out. There is no way out. My body trembles violently in a dark cold cell.

I am very small and cold, standing in my bed gown shut in an old room. I try to turn the door handle, but it will not move. My hands are sore from beating on the door. No one will hear me. No one will come. I cannot scream any longer, my throat is dry and hoarse. Where is my mother?

The two women in the kitchen must have heard my faint cries, because they come to open the larder door. Tears are pouring down my face, and the mould of butter is splattered at my feet. I cannot speak. The women draw me out of there, and Ardyth disappears, returning with Nellie who, seeing me, looks frightened to death. Nevertheless, she takes charge, leading me upstairs to my chamber while asking Cook to prepare a soothing broth and to send someone up with hot bricks for the bed. All the while she keeps talking to me: "There, now, Mistress, don't worry. You will be warm again soon. Here, don't cry. Put on this nightgown over your clothes and get into bed. I know that's improper, but you do it anyway. It'll warm you up quicker."

I do as I am told. It takes me a while to recover myself, and I am surprised to find myself in my own bed. Then I remember going to the larder, but after that I recall nothing. "I was going to get the butter," I say vaguely.

"Don't you worry about the butter, now. Cook says it is all right about it, it's not spoiled or anything."

I stare at her. "Spoiled? Why should it be?"

Nellie can hardly disguise her alarm. "Of course it shouldn't. I don't know why Cook would say that. She did say to tell you that she would make your pudding for you, as you looked as though you could use a rest. You have been doing too much."

I say, "Oh, not so much, really, but still, I do feel tired." And with that, I fall asleep.

The strangest thing is that when I wake up, I still cannot remember what has happened. This is the most upsetting part of the whole business, and it continues to plague me, until finally the whole incident comes back to me. Now I am even more worried. In my journal I write: "What was this, a memory or a phantasm? Does that mean that my mind is going too? I refuse to believe it. What am I to do? Edward wants me to be a model housewife, but how can I be one now? After what happened in the larder, whatever it was about, I will not try to cook again ever. Besides, Cook and Ardyth do not want me to. And I am certainly not going to sweep and dust; we have maids for that. I can sew a little, gather vegetables and fruit from the garden, and that is about all. What a hopeless housekeeper I am turning out to be."

At supper I am recovered, and so after we have finished Edward's birthday pudding, I present him with a good belt buckle I bought in town. He thanks me with a somewhat absent-minded kiss, and then turns solemn. I know he has been told about the episode in the larder. I jump in before he has a chance to mention it.

"Edward dear, I am so sorry. I feel that I am letting you down all the time. Every time I try to do something like baking, it turns out to be a disaster."

He looks at me in astonishment, and says, "Oh that. It doesn't matter at all, your not making me a pudding, although of course it would have been a treat to have it. What is worrying me, and Nellie, and Cook as well, is why you were so disturbed over the butter. Cook says you were screaming and crying over the broken mould."

"I wasn't crying over that," I say. "I was..." and then I cannot finish, because I do not know why I was crying.

Edward looks anxiously at me, and I say, "I don't know what it was. All I know is that it was a horrible experience, standing there in the dark. It was as though I was a helpless child again." I begin to shiver, and Edward comes to wrap his arms around me. I start to cry. "I don't know, I don't know."

He holds me closer. "There, now. It's all over. It won't happen again."

I look up at him, sniffing back tears. "Are you sure? I'm not."

"Yes, Anne. Just think of it as a bad dream that will never return."

"I pray not."

5.

A LL THE OUTSIDE DOORS are kept locked day and night: the back
gate to the stable yard, the shed, the storeroom, and the larder. The
main doors to the house are always locked of course, including the one at
the top of the outside staircase that leads from the yard to the servants'
quarters. Inside, the parlour and hall have locks, and the kitchen too, but
these are seldom used except when everyone is away. Cook, who has a key
to the kitchen and all the cupboards, can often be heard moving about far
into the night, and again before sunrise. Jenny, who is not the speediest of
workers, often washes clothes by the light of the moon. She says she likes
to work then, the light is so gentle on her eyes; but, as I said to Nellie, it is
not strong enough to illuminate the stains that come back on the freshly
laundered garments as visible as ever.

Only Edward and I have keys to the whole house. I wear mine around
my waist in case someone should need a cloth for a table or a jar of physic.
When asked, I open the right chest, hand out the requested article, and
lock up again. The servants have been told that no one suspects them of
being light-fingered: some stranger might break in and make off with the
household's belongings. Fear of outsiders governs a lot of our behaviour
in this colony.

Owing to Cook's industrious habits, the kitchen is seldom vacant except
in the middle of the night. I cannot risk going down there then, even
though Edward is a sound sleeper, because the stairs creak and the walls
are paper-thin. So, on a Thursday lecture day, I invent a bad headache

and an uncertain stomach as an excuse to stay home. Naturally I have to put up with having a dose of treated rose-cake bound to my head, and instructions to lie flat on my bed, before everyone leaves.

After they have gone, I unlock the kitchen door, and go over to the barrel where the salt is stored. I rummage around to find a small sack, into which I scoop a fair amount of salt, though not enough to be missed, I hope. Then, locking up again, I take my precious bundle back to my chamber, hide it in the clothes press under my heavy winter things, and go back to bed.

On Saturday, with Edward gone to his counting house, I gather up the sack of salt wrapped like a parcel in a piece of cloth, and leave the house. By now no one thinks this unusual, as I walk every Saturday if the weather allows, and could be gone for ages. I head out of town towards the Podunk village. The town is quiet; as far as I can tell, I have not been observed.

This time I walk right into the clearing, stand still, and say cheerily, "Good day to you all."

As before, a few women are sitting in a circle working around a fire, on which something is simmering in a large kettle. I cannot tell whether they are the same women as before, but I recognize the woman who comes forward as the one who greeted me the last time. Unwrapping the sack of salt, I hold it out to her. The woman, whose name I learn is Wacusa, opens the sack, wets her fingertip to touch the salt, tastes it, and smiles broadly. She points to it, and looks questioningly at me. I say, "Salt. For fish. And meat. Salt."

"Salt," Wacusa repeats. She leads me over to the group of women to show them the sack. "Salt," she says, and they copy her. "Salt." Everyone is now looking happy.

I had read a traveller's report that indicated that the Indians in Massachusetts were just learning how to preserve their meat and fish by salting it. He said that this method of keeping food was the greatest boon one could bring them, to prevent sickness and starvation in winter. By the women's smiles I see that he is right. My Connecticut Indian women know how to use salt, too.

The deerskin is brought out for me to sit on, and I watch the women sew skins together for capes or stitch soft leather stockings to go inside their heavier boots. My hands are not idle long, as Wacusa who seems to be the cook of the day, reaches into the kettle and ladles out some richly aromatic stew for me. I waste no time in scooping up the meat with my fingers. It is wild turkey, I guess, cooked with unfamiliar herbs. I wonder how to find out what is used, and then, how to pass on the recipe to Cook without saying where I found it.

I have had no trouble teaching the words "Hopkins" and "salt," so I decide to continue with the English lessons, slowly, a few words at a time. Over the course of my visits, I manage to teach the women about one hundred words, I reckon. I learn none of their language, but with gestures and their small English vocabulary, I am able to understand quite a lot about their lives. I try to tell them something about myself, but because I have little to show them, I think they scarcely understand. I cannot take them to my house, show them my garden, my books, and tell them my thoughts about living in New England. I discover, though, that they can understand some of my feelings, since, after all, our feelings are similar. At times they laugh at me; for example, when I show fear about the possibility of meeting a bear by shaking and putting my arms straight out in front of me, or hiding my face in my hands. The word "bear" is easy; bearskins abound in the village.

I, on the other hand, can see how the Podunk women live, watch their children play, and, once in a while, see their husbands come home from fishing and greet their wives and myself gravely and with respect. I grow very fond of them all, my "secret family," as I think of them.

The only person who knows about them is Nellie. I want to bring my new friends something to repay their hospitality, some new matter from my life must enter theirs, just as I have been taken in and shown their ways and works. But all I can think of is food; I do not have much else to give away. So finally I have to bring Nellie into the conspiracy to rob my own kitchen. I cannot keep on playing sick every time I need supplies.

Nellie's forehead wrinkles as tight as a prune when she hears my description of my visits, and my proposal to take foodstuffs from under Cook's nose. "Oh mercy, Mistress, you can't keep on doing this. People will find out sooner or later, and tell the governor, or someone else, and you will be in trouble. Everyone is afraid of the Indians. They don't know what they might do."

"Not these Indians," I say. "They are the kindest people I know. They don't intend to trouble anyone."

"That's not what I hear. People say that there are no Indians you can trust, that they are all wolves with men's brains. They say that even among themselves the men can get angry and fight each other over their women and lots of other things; and the women, well, they aren't so bad, as you would know."

"I've never seen any of them fight. In fact I've never heard an angry word spoken. And they don't fight over women, either. They all seem to be very happily married."

"I'm glad of that, Mistress. But anyway, I'm afraid to take food from the kitchen. Cook is sure to notice, and I will be sent away."

"Don't be silly. That won't happen. If she does find out, I'll admit to taking the things. I'll tell her I took salt to put on the slugs in the garden." At that we both giggle, and the matter is settled.

In the next few months I carry more salt to the Podunk which is well-received. I also bring plums, apricots (a few), apples (which they cooked into a broth-like consistency), sugar for the apples (which is quietly rejected), and more salt, as winter is coming on. If Cook notices that her stocks are gradually dwindling, she says nothing either to Nellie or me. We hug each other like schoolgirls who have stolen the teacher's birch rod from behind his back and buried it in the potato patch.

Even though Nellie pretends to be excited and proud of the way in which the kitchen thievery has been accomplished, I can see that she is growing more and more uneasy every time another midnight visit is proposed. I know she is not just afraid for herself, but for me too. She is taking a greater risk than I am, for I would never be thrown out of the house if caught. I wish I could reassure her, but I would be lying if I tried. At the very least

I must let her see how much I value her willing nature and kind heart.

One afternoon, when Nellie is putting away some of my clothes in the press, I say, "I'd like you to have these. To wear on special occasions. There is a little break in one of them, but I'm sure you can mend that easily." I hold out a fine lace collar and cuffs.

Nellie looks at them and her face reddens like a pomegranate. "Oh, no! I couldn't. I mean, you must not. They are beautiful, but — I just couldn't. It isn't right."

"Why not, you silly! Of course it's right if I say so. I have ordered a new set, so I won't need these any more."

"But Mistress, you know it is not permitted. A girl like me, a servant, does not wear lace. I would be whipped if I were caught wearing them." A pathetic tone creeps into her voice.

I am furious. "That's just wrong! Why, at home, in England, you can pass on anything you are finished with to the servants, or anyone you please. It would be wasteful not to. These are still good, which is why I want you to have them."

"It is a very kind offer, but I cannot take them, although I would like to so much." Nellie looks wistfully at the delicate pieces.

"Then what shall I do with them? Feed them to the sheep?" My anger turns into a petulance I remember adopting as a child.

"Why not give them to the Indian women?" Nellie suggests timidly.

"Of course! How clever of you!" I laugh, and Nellie, feeling slightly better, joins in. "But Nellie, I am so sorry you cannot have them." I am sober again.

"Don't be bothered, Mistress. Think how lovely the lace will look on a bearskin mantle." Picturing this starts us up again, and we laugh till we hurt.

6.

ONE DAMP AND GLOOMY Thursday as Edward and I are walking towards the meeting house for the weekly lecture, I see that there is a crowd standing about in the square instead of going inside. Oh dear, this means there is to be another punishment. My stomach begins knotting in anticipation. Public shame and physical abuse are what I hate most about the colony. If someone has done wrong, give him a fair trial, a suitable penalty, and time to repent, so he will sin no more. But to humiliate him in front of the whole community is far worse than to inflict any sort of pain. A person might never get over it. I know I would not.

Edward, being deputy governor — the law permits only a year's term as governor, and then you must wait a year before being re-elected — is not required to stand beside the accused. Nevertheless, he has to take his place at the front of the crowd. I steel myself to endure the hurtful scene. I am determined not to look to see who is being punished, but I cannot help myself. To my horror, I see that the figure tied to the whipping post is Wacusa. I let out a cry, which, fortunately for me, is drowned out by the governor's announcement. "This woman has been accused of thievery and fornication. She is to receive a dozen strokes for her wickedness."

Wacusa's head is turned away from me, but at the first stroke of the whip, her head turns in the other direction, and her eyes find mine. Without thinking what I am doing, I scream, "Stop! This is wrong!" All heads in the crowd turn towards me, eyes sharp with anger. I faint.

When I come to, I am aware of two servants carrying me into the nearest house, which is Mr. Hooker's. They put me down on a settle. As soon as they are gone, and I am alone, I begin to sob, my whole body trembling with grief and fury. The sobbing possesses me, it seems I will never stop.

Eventually I weaken, and it ceases. Forlornly I ask myself, what has happened to this good place? How could it have changed so much, and become so blind and cruel? How could they treat Wacusa this way? To punish a woman in public for actions I am sure she has not done. And to think that Edward, who is the soul of justice, would be one of those who condemned her. He has never been cruel to anyone before. What is happening?

Poor Wacusa! How it must have hurt. And she saw me there, watching, doing nothing but cry out. Even if I try to tell her how wrong I think it was, we will never be friends again. This thought starts me crying again.

I try to pull myself together sufficiently in order to get home while everyone is still in the meeting house, I make my way slowly, and once inside, go straight to my chamber. The shock of that scene and my anguish for Wacusa leave me so limp that I lie down and fall asleep.

Waking up feels like creeping out of a black and chilly tomb. I sit by the window numbly, wondering what to do. Edward finds me there hours later.

"Are you recovered, my dear? You gave me a fright, screaming and falling down like that. I would have brought you home, but when I saw you were awake, I thought I should stay there and do my duty while you had a rest. Did you hurt yourself at all?" He puts his arm around me tenderly, just in case.

"Only a few bruises. But Edward, the whipping of that woman. That was a terrible thing to do. I cannot believe it was done."

"I know it seems cruel, but it is the only way to teach these people that our laws must be obeyed."

"But how did you know that she had done these things?"

"She was found with some articles of clothing — lace pieces, I think — by one of our freemen who saw her on the road." I groan. "She was with two other men, and was laughing and showing off her finery. They were touching her in very unseemly ways."

"And from this the court deduced that she was a fornicator? What did she say?"

"She denied it."

"Did she understand what she was accused of?"

"She must have understood. She could speak many words in English, although not a full sentence."

"That's all she knows, a few words," I burst out.

Edward looks at me aghast. "How do you know?"

"Because I taught her," I say defiantly.

Then the whole story has to come out, right from the beginning. As Edward questions me more closely my tears start to flow again.

"And the lace pieces are yours," he says finally.

"Were. I gave them to her," I say in a whisper, "for all she had done for me."

Edward gives a deep sigh, and sits back thinking, rubbing his chin with one hand. I stay silent. There is nothing more to say. It is up to him now.

His voice is soft but firm. "I can see that an injustice has been done to the woman with regard to the theft. However, the heavier sin is that of fornication, and she was correctly punished for that."

"But what if she did not do it?" I look at him at last, through eyes still moist and blurred. "From all I know of them, the Podunk are pure-minded and faithful to their own spouses. They only have one wife each, and they do not try to use others' wives or husbands. The men could have been her husband and a brother perhaps. Wacusa couldn't deny the charge because she didn't understand it."

"There is no proof that she did not do it, either, just your word for it. Anne, the punishment has been given out, it's all over. I can do nothing to change it." I try to interrupt, to protest, but he holds up his hand to stop me, and says, "To right any part of the wrong, your visits to the Podunk would have to be disclosed, and you would be admonished for having gone there. I will not let that happen to you."

He reaches over to touch my hand, and then he remembers who he is. "You have put yourself and the community in great danger. But despite my obligation as deputy governor to to make these facts known, I am not going to do so, for the sake of your reputation." Now he looks severe, but his voice is mild. "I must forbid you to visit these Indians again. I am sorry, because I believe they have been good to you, as you have been a friend to them. But you have no idea what might be in store for you if they came to distrust you."

 "I think they distrust me now, after today," I say piteously, turning away to look out the window into the distance. "What a miserable outcome for us all. We could have done so much to make better relations between our two settlements, and then we wouldn't be so afraid of wars."

"Perhaps one day," Edward says mildly. "Mr. Hooker says that some of them — but not your village, I think — are ensnared by the Devil, and we must make every effort to bring them to Christ."

I nod. I am too exhausted to reply that, if the Indians were in league with the Devil, they wore a very Christlike disguise, and that Christ never had anyone flogged, except himself. But I will say no more.

Edward straightens, then bends down and pulls me to him. "In the meantime, I will simply tell people that you are disturbed sometimes at the sight of blood."

Shocked at this, I nod. Edward, the man of integrity, is lying to protect me.

A few days later Constable Pritchett, who was sent to the Podunk village to warn the Indians against coming into town, returns to report that they have all vanished. There is no sign that a village has ever existed, except for the trampled grass and a burned area where once there must have been a fire.

7.

FOLLOWING THE DISAPPEARANCE of the Podunk, my spirits fall further than they have ever done, as I think about the drab future before me. Only now do I realize how much I came to depend on these visits to give me the pleasure of undemanding company that I so sorely miss in Hartford. I had laughed, sung, tried to tell stories, learned, and taught, all without criticism or qualified acceptance. I had enjoyed myself more than at any other time since I came here, Edward's company being the one beautiful exception.

I realize that in public I have become quieter, and my face feels stiff and unanimated. In the women's meetings, the atmosphere seems tenser, as if someone might be ready to pounce on me if I open my mouth. I am not sure they believe the excuse about my squeamishness. So I keep my opinions to myself, while inwardly I am itching to debate.

One time, for instance, Mistress Simson tells of the success a Mr. Grey, a farmer, has had in rooting out sorcery. One of his heifers was ill, and Mr. Grey was certain his jealous neighbour had bewitched her. So he beat the animal, and sure enough, his neighbour fell down in great pain. The proof of the man's sorcery was plain to see.

What about the poor beast, I think. Surely she was in agony too after that flogging. I wonder if any of her bones were broken. If that is magic, Mr. Grey's is worse than his neighbour's.

Mistress Stone, steering the conversation away from sorcery, which intrigues the women far too much, she says, tells of an example of God's punishment on those who defame the work of the colonies.

"My husband has heard from Mr. Hooker, who has heard from Governor Winthrop himself, about a certain tanner's servant who left the tanner at the end of his term of service and went to work for anyone who would hire him. He earned so much money that he determined to go back to England, where he could spend it. On the boat and on shore, he told many wicked stories about this country, and how pleased he was to leave it." I can hear people making clucking sounds between teeth and tongues.

Mistress Stone goes on. "No sooner had he landed and gone a little way, but some cavaliers came up to him and took all his money. Then finding that he could not regain what he had lost in England, there being very little work he could do, he set sail on the next ship and returned to Boston. The news of his foul speeches came back with him, so he would be hard pressed to find work.

"So the Lord punishes those who speak ill of our holy endeavour," she concludes.

This time I can barely hold back. I want to say, "Surely the man must have bragged about his earnings, and someone overheard him and robbed him? It would be his boastful words that caused his loss, not his criticisms of New England."

Just as I am about to speak, Mistress Brigden says, out of the blue, "I understand that it was your lace that the Indian woman stole, Mistress Hopkins?"

Trembling at the half-lie I am about to tell, I say, "Yes, it was."

Mistress Brigden persists. "Did you not notice it was missing?"

I say, "I hadn't worn it for some time. It was put away."

"And your maid? Doesn't she keep count of your clothing?"

"She does. She may have mentioned it, and I forgot. Yes, I believe she did," I say, trying not to squirm in my chair. I am not going to bring down anyone's wrath upon Nellie.

I have to divert Mistress Brigden. "In any case, I cannot wear it any more after all this. I have ordered a new set."

I hope the conversation will turn to a discussion of the best lace-makers, but instead the women choose to go over the trial and punishment of "that thief and fornicator." I suspect they derive more pleasure from this than from any other subject. I try to ignore them and concentrate on my sewing.

I am so upset that I decide at last to confide in Elizabeth. I tell her about my visits to the Podunk, about the condemnation of Wacusa, and about the remarks made by the women in the church circle. "I am sure they know that I had something to do with all of it. And oh, Elizabeth, I feel dreadful about it. It's all entirely my fault. I wish I had never gone to their village and started the whole horrid business."

Elizabeth shakes her head. "It was not your fault, Anne. Don't think so for a moment. It was the judges and the rest of those narrow-minded people who made false assumptions and also these rigid rules. They are to blame."

"I should have known better. If only I had told Edward that I was visiting and taking gifts, but I thought he would not like it. So, you see, it is my fault." I am sure that the shame and dejection I feel are written all over my face.

Elizabeth speaks tartly. "Sometimes one must depend on one's own judgment, not one's husband's. One has to stand alone and take the consequences."

"I agree, but if the consequences fall on others who are innocent?"

With a wry smile, my friend says, "God sees the sparrow, but He also sees the hawk, and the rabbit. Innocents don't get spared in his plan, do they?"

I say, "Does he see the savages?"

"Yes, and they aren't really savage, are they? At least not the ones you speak of."

"Of course not. It's just our way of speaking — oh dear…!"

We sit silently for a few moments, thinking about the awful power of language.

8.

E DWARD IS BEING CONSIDERATE of me these days. Not that he is not always a fond and dutiful husband, but with so much on his mind, he is bound to leave me alone much of the time. I can tell he is worried about me, when he comes home and finds me moping about the house, doing nothing in particular. He probably thinks it is because we do not have a child, which is certainly a part of the melancholy I feel, but not the whole cause of it.

"Have you been out today, dear?" he asks, knowing full well that I have not. I know he speaks to Nellie about me. She is also looking concerned.

"No, I didn't feel up to it," I say. "I will go out tomorrow." After I have said this several days in a row, even I begin to question my chances of improving my state of mind. My whole body seems to have collapsed as if the blood has drained out of it. As for my soul, I dare not think of what is happening to it.

"The good people you used to look after must be missing you. Why don't you pay some of them a visit? They have problems of their own, but even so, I'm sure they would return your kind efforts with some comfort."

I nod. "I will. But — and I hope you won't be angry — I do not want to entertain any more visitors for the time being. Or, if you think you must, would you host them alone, and say that I have a severe headache? I do not think I could face new people right now, and I am certainly not good company."

Edward's expression is grave. "Of course we will not entertain until you are ready. I only wish I could help you, but I can't truly understand what it is that makes you so miserable." He looks quite woebegone himself.

"Don't worry, Edward. I'll feel better, sooner or later." Now I am the one patting his face, trying to cheer him. But it is no use.

So we carry on, he with his work and his anxiety about me, and I with my dismal sadness following me around like a shadow. In our conversations, which are seldom lively now, he skirts around subjects that might distress me. Sometimes, though, they cannot be avoided.

For instance, one Sunday after the morning sermon, I am sitting at dinner eating slowly and without interest. Ordinarily I love good meals, and Sunday's is always the best of the week. Today, I pick at my food listlessly. I can hardly bring myself to answer Edward's questions. He knows I am puzzling over something, but when he asks me what it is, I say, "Oh, it's no matter, really," shutting him out of my thoughts.

The matter is that this morning Mr. Hooker was away preaching in Boston, so Mr. Stone gave the sermon. It was as long as usual, poorly constructed, moving from subject to subject without any clear connection between them. The only assured quality of the sermon was its tone, which was a loud, severe, uncompromising rant. I stared at the floor, tried to shut him out, even willed him to stop. Please God, you cannot really want this man as your mouthpiece, your knight errant! If only Mr. Hooker could hear him, he would put a stop to this battering speech. That is why Mr. Stone waits until he is away to declaim like this. I tried to think about something else: Mr. Stone's hair is wispy, and so is his wife's. I wondered if they rubbed their heads together at night and scoured it off? I noticed, too, that he had pimples on his pate, which were the result, I reasoned, of hairs being yanked out.

"They are the source of vice in this community, those who hold us back in our sacred quest." Mr. Stone looked to the back of the room where behind the poorest of the saints sat those who were not church members. "Those of you who call yourselves planters have even more to answer for, since you can read and understand Scripture, but you do not believe. You turn your backs on the Lord's salvation, and walk away, refusing to acknowledge yourselves to be miserable worms, sinners in need of repentance. Woe to you, and," he turned to scan the entire assembly, "woe to those who associate with you. They are beguiled by your good manners and riches. They think that you are the Lord's elect also." Now he addressed the front seats directly. "Do not be led astray by those who have no desire and no will to follow the Lord, who do not repent and pray for the Lord to come to them; who do not belong among this gathering of visible saints. I know that some of you have allowed yourselves to take recreation with those who profess no true faith. This is dangerous for any whose own faith is delicate; and you are now warned, not to have any more connection with these unacknowledged sinners. Leave the task of bringing them to see their errors and wickedness to those better equipped to do so." Mr. Stone ended with a triumphant flourish of his hand, certain that his words had been driven deep into every heart.

I had been struck indeed by his sermon, and also by the looks some people gave me as I stood outside with Edward acknowledging greetings. No one said anything directly, but I was sure that the sermon was intended for me, among others. I knew it when I saw Elizabeth Johnson and her husband walking swiftly away as soon as they came out of the building. All of the people in the community, whether church members or not, were required to attend the Sabbath lecture. It was hoped that by hearing the sound interpretation of the word of God, they too would wish to become saints. Mr. Stone's sermon surely had had the opposite effect.

Finally I break my own silence. "Do you know Mr. Johnson well, Edward?"

"Yes, I suppose I know him as well as any other trader here."

"Do you think he is a good man?"

"He is certainly honest and honourable in all his dealings. Why do you ask?"

I ignore his question. "Do you think he is the cause of any wrongdoing in Hartford?"

"I do not. Whatever gave you that idea?"

"Mr. Stone," I say.

"Oh, the sermon. Well, Mr. Stone is overzealous sometimes. He does believe strongly that those who aren't church members should not be citizens. He thinks they bring wrong ideas into the town."

"You don't agree with him, do you?"

"You know I don't, Anne. Nor does Mr. Hooker, but we think that everyone in the congregation need not hold exactly the same views, except on the most fundamental beliefs. Mr. Stone has a small following, but most of us think that any upright person who has the means to benefit the colony may become a freeman."

"But surely you can see that Mr. Stone's judgment is wrong, not just different — entirely *wrong*!" My temper is rising, and I pound the table with my fist.

Edward is startled. "Anne! Calm down. The servants will hear you."

"They should, and they should pay attention. Mr. Stone's attitude is a stain on this community." I pause, amazed at myself.

Edward looks at me thoughtfully, for once trying to see my point of view..

"You may be right. Such a harsh position is likely to drive good planters away, not convert them. I think we should pray for Mr. Stone." I notice that he does not add, "And for conversion of the Johnsons or other heretics."

Much calmer now, I say, "Mistress Johnson has become a friend of mine. I am very fond of her."

Edward says, with audible relief, "I'm so glad you have found someone you like who is your own age."

"She told me that in England she had been an Anglican, but here there is no place to worship, so she has stopped thinking about religion altogether, except when she listens to the sermons on the Sabbath."

"Today's would have given her little cheer," says Edward dryly, "but of course it wasn't supposed to. No, I see nothing wrong with your having Mistress Johnson as a friend, though I wouldn't devote all your time to her, to the exclusion of the other women. Then there would certainly be trouble. But it will be good for you to see her from time to time. You lack company, especially of women who have the learning you do."

"I am not a good model of a governor's wife." I look at him apologetically. "Perhaps you should never have married me."

"What nonsense! Of course I should have, and I have never regretted it for a moment. Nor, I hope, have you." He reaches over the table to touch my hand, and I feel myself letting go bit by bit. Oh, he is wonderful, the way he can sweep away my anxieties in an instant. My words burst out, like a stream suddenly cleared of tangled brush. "I love you, Edward, and I always will." There is just time for a quick embrace, a moist, rather tasty after-dinner kiss, and a moment of hand holding, before Jenny comes in to remove the dishes. At times like this I forget my sadness, and just dwell in the moment.

9.

A STRONG WIND PULSES tonight, as ghosts moan their soulless half-lives and press against the trees for solace. I can hear the trees bending, with the odd crackling protest, but mainly they are in sympathy with the wind-riding ghosts. Once I think I hear a human voice cry out, "Anne! Let me in!" and I fear it is my father trapped between life and death. Coward that I am, I hide my head under the quilt to muffle the sound. I do not know what would happen if I opened the window; in my blackest fantasy, I can see his cold grey swirling form catch me in his shadowy arms and sweep me outside. A father truly alive is one person, strong and affectionate; dead, or partly so, who can say? I only know I will go to hell before I will open that casement.

What is my imagination doing, bringing up such alarming thoughts? I can hardly remember my father, and certainly I never feared him. I suppose it is because Edward has been called out, and I am alone in the bed. I wait, sleepless and shivering from these dark hauntings, but still he does not come. Finally, I fall asleep, only to be wakened by the quivering of the person who now lies beside me. I cry out, as in my barely conscious state I think it must be that ghostly voice now given bodily form. But it is Edward, cold and trembling, his eyes open and staring straight ahead as if he too has seen a ghost.

I reach over to comfort him. "My dearest, what is wrong? Why are you shaking so? Tell me."

He does not move, but he says, "Oh, Anne, I have seen the most horrible sight. That such things should happen to innocent people!"

"What things?"

He shakes his head.

"Tell me, please."

He turns his head towards me. "I hate to trouble you, but you will surely hear about it from someone. And I cannot get it out of my head."

I pull the coverlet up higher around us and move over so that our bodies touch. "I want to know."

"You know that Constable Pritchett came to fetch me because the Wimsatts' house had caught on fire. When I got there, there were half a dozen other men trying to form a line from the well to the house, but they had only three buckets, and the fire was spreading faster than they could quench it. I sent Pritchett, who is quite useless in emergencies, to find three more men and six more buckets, but it seemed at that point to be almost hopeless. I joined the men myself, but with so few buckets what could one do?

"I said to the man beside me, where are the occupants, and he said he didn't know. The next man along said, they must have gone into someone's house for help. They have two small children who would need to be sheltered. Did you see them leave, I asked, and he said no, he had not. In fact no one had seen them.

"At that moment I heard a cry, and looked to the upstairs window. Mistress Wimsatt was standing there, holding up her little girl, and calling, 'Help, someone, catch her!' Two of us ran over to stand below, and just as she was about to lift the child to the windowsill, she fell back, and I could see flames appearing around the window, and a dreadful red glow all behind it. I heard the mother scream, but not the child. It was only a few minutes later that the whole front wall of the house collapsed, and then the roof, and the rest.

"We all stood there helpless, and every man had tears in his eyes, both from the smoke and from the pity of it all. I suspect we will find the other two bodies, father and son, when the fire dies down. Or we may never find them. It was so hot, I could imagine what the flames of hell would be like. It was horrible, horrible."

His eyes are full as he looks at me, and I wipe them with my fingers. "Oh Edward, what a dreadful thing! I cannot even bear the thought of their agony! Poor, poor souls! How could such pain be inflicted on human beings? No one deserves this, no matter how wicked they are."

"No, and the Wimsatts were certainly not bad people. I must say, I cannot myself understand how the providence of God comes into it."

I say, "Nor I. The divine will may be mysterious, but surely it is not cruel, and has no reason."

"There must be a reason, of course, a part of the plan for the world, even if we cannot know it fully," Edward says, recovering his composure somewhat. "Mr. Hooker will explain it, certainly."

When consulted the next day, Mr. Hooker cannot explain it, except to say that God's intentions for his creation are unfathomable, but we are assured, quoting the saint, that all things work together for good to them who love God.

Discussing this privately, Edward and I are not so sure, but we cannot conceive of any other way to look at it.

10.

ONE SABBATH AFTERNOON when Edward and I are taking a tour of the town boundaries as we often do after dinner, we meet Mistress Hardy and Mistress Burnham going in the other direction. Mistress Hardy is the widow of one of the magistrates, and still acts as if she has the authority of his position. With her grand proportions and upright bearing she is quite formidable. She intimidates me so much that however I try, I always say the wrong thing to her. Then she looks at me as if I am an ignorant serving-girl. I am sure that the woman only speaks to me at all because I am Edward's wife.

This afternoon, I feel quite without armour and I dare not chance saying a word to her. Instead I turn to little Mistress Burnham with whom Mistress Hardy is now living. Even so powerful a woman as Mistress Hardy is not permitted to live alone.

"What a fine bright bonnet you are wearing, Mistress Burnham. Did it just arrive from England?" I say, reaching out to touch its brim. Mistress Burnham pulls back, ever so slightly.

It is Mistress Hardy who replies. "On my word, Mistress Hopkins, you shame Mistress Burnham, and yourself, too, in saying such a thing. Governor Hopkins, you must be careful that your wife is not considered vain for praising such things."

"Mistress, I assure you that Mistress Hopkins had only good will in her heart in greeting Mistress Burnham. She is the least vain of all women. In fact, she hardly notices how she is dressed, and sometimes—" Edward breaks off, thinking better of his next words.

"What is that 'sometimes,' Mr. Hopkins?" asks Mistress Hardy peremptorily.

"It is just that sometimes" — Edward fidgets slightly — "she will wear the same gown from Monday to Saturday until I ask her to choose another."

I feel my face flushing with shame and embarrassment. In the first place, Edward has told a lie, something for which he will repent grievously. In the second place, he has probably unwittingly made matters worse. To say that I am oblivious of what I wear only confirms what I'm sure some already believe, that I am not capable of being the wife of a governor, if I cannot even remember to change my outfit.

These two will think I am too scatterbrained by far, too ignorant, and too self-indulgent. And now I am forced to confirm my husband's lie by becoming careless about my person, something I loathe to do. Mistress Hardy is halfway right; I do love fine clothing suited to the occasion. Unfortunately there are few occasions anyway, so it hardly matters what I wear, except to please myself, which I would never admit to anyone.

In this town of busybodies who dress their curiosity in religious drapery, I wonder if I will ever get anything right. It is taking me so long to learn what I may or may not do, or how to present myself to others in this demanding community, that I am afraid I may become despondent before long. I feel at this moment as if I am on the side of a steep cliff, with the rock wall on one side and the sea on the other. When the path along the side of the cliff ends, I will have to choose how to fall. Or else I can just stand still and let fear and weariness do the rest.

Poor Mistress Burnham, whom we have forgotten, chooses a pause in the conversation to explain herself. "Mistress Hopkins, I must tell you that my bonnet is an old one of my cousin Helen's who lives in London. She sent it to me because she said it was no longer in fashion there, and she couldn't think of walking out in it any more, even if it is still good and has several years of wear in it still. I am very glad it is not fashionable, as what would a woman in my position do with such a thing? It came just in time, because my old one had been mended several times, and had worn so thin in places that it couldn't take another patch."

She ends breathlessly, amazement at her own audacity written all over her face. Probably no one has ever heard Mistress Burnham make such a lengthy speech. We stare at her. I smile as encouragingly as I can, inwardly thanking her for taking attention away from the subject of my own vices, which surely is what Mistress Burnham intended to do. What compassionate shrewdness lies inside this timid little woman!

There is another lesson learned. How difficult it is for me to curb my tongue, but curb it I must if I am not to get into more trouble. I will not always be saved by the kindness of people such as Mistress Burnham. How was I to know not to give Mistress Burnham some attention? Because that is what the matter was really about: Mistress Hardy's jealousy. I think I will end up saying nothing at all, and people will take me for an empty-headed creature.

Right now I have to say something, to repay Mistress Burnham for her thoughtfulness. "The bonnet suits you well, Mistress, and is in such good condition you can hardly blame me for thinking it is new. Of course, I know nothing about London fashion, our life is so much simpler here, isn't it? I am glad not to have to be bothered about such things." I am telling the truth.

Mistress Hardy lets me go with that remark, although I can see she is dying to find a way to take another swipe at me. Fortunately Edward is there, and he leads the conversation away from fashion, bonnets, and jealous women. I feel only a slight, chilly breeze drifting over from Mistress Hardy when we part.

On the way home Edward is too embarrassed to say anything about his part in this little encounter. So we make up our chitchat as we go along.

That night in bed I say, "Dearest man, you don't have to defend me the way you did this afternoon."

A pause. "Hmm." He pretends he is falling asleep, and then does.

11.

OVER THE PAST FEW MONTHS I have been practising discretion in my speech, at least in public, but here is my dilemma: No one is supposed to have any secrets in this congregational family of Hartford. That is more than just refraining from telling lies; we deny each other nothing in the way of information. Our ministers may call this the "brotherly watch," but, in my view, we are the magpies of humanity, deviously collecting and then chattering about it. Of course, there are a few matters between husband and wife that are not open to scrutiny, at least publicly, because they would appear vulgar. I have yet to discover the line drawn here between vulgarity and truth, and between the common good and sheer inquisitiveness.

Nowadays I answer questions truthfully as best I can, but I tell no more than is required. The more I can keep my thoughts to myself, the less I will be subjected to public embarrassment and mental anguish. Normally, I love a good battle of wits, or a fair discussion, but in this community , at least among the women, such discussions are unlikely to take place without some moral outrage or condemnation attached. I am afraid that people would think I am stupid, but it is worse than that. They are beginning to be suspicious of my reticence, believing that I am hiding some shameful behaviour from them all. They are too much in awe of Edward to speak outright, but they circle me like wolves around a deer. The women are especially curious, some licking their lips at the thought of my exposure as a "crooked" woman. I am ever polite to them, speaking quietly when spoken to, offering a "Good day," and "I hope you are well," and closing my mouth when almost any other subject is raised. It amuses me to wonder what they think I may have done: am I thought to be avaricious? A glutton? A whore? A witch perhaps? Sometimes I feel like giving them a little grist for their fantastic mills. Life is so tedious and difficult here, you need a flowery imaginative life just to survive. (A most heretical thought!)

The certain bane of my life is Mr. Stone, who is a slimy, hard-nosed worm — can there be such a thing in all creation? Every time I see him I want to shrink into myself, close my eyes, stop my breath, and pray he is not there. But he is, and his greeting is always the same: "Good day, Mistress, may the Lord keep you from all evil." I want to say, "If this means you, then thank you, that is what I would like." But, of course, instead I bow, and say something stupid like "It doesn't seem like a day for evil does it?" And he, of course counters, with the statement that the Devil is all around us, seeking whom he may devour. He leans forward a bit to look right into my eyes with that stony gaze he has; he thinks he is seeing right into my soul, but he is the last person in the world whom I will allow in. I can lock him out, even if I cannot get rid of him altogether.

Sometimes our conversations stop there, as I nod and pass him quickly, heading in the opposite direction. Once in a while, he manages to prolong them, trying to win my confidence by asking whether I found Mr. Hooker's sermon, or the last meeting of the women's circle instructive. Of course, I must reply, but when he refers to the sermon again, I know he is going to launch into a ponderous analysis, telling me in his own pedantic way just what Mr. Hooker has said so persuasively. Then I make some excuse for having to depart, saying that perhaps we can continue the subject at another time. I hate myself for lying, but to tell him the truth would be so much worse. Unless, of course, he is so self-impressed that he would not believe me.

Today, which is the Sabbath, Edward takes me aside after I have been quieter than usual following the assembly. This is the time when people's tongues are loosened and wag most freely; four or five hours' sitting does that to you. Then the news of the day or the day before is chewed over and spat out for general consumption. The women live up to their name — Gossping Gertrudes. Without them, I believe the men would hardly know whom to chastise, or defame, or arraign, although they seem able to show esteem without the women's help. The spirit of "neighbourliness" inhabits the sexes differently, it would seem.

"Are you feeling well, my dear?" he says. I assure him that I am fine. "In that case, perhaps you could be a little friendlier to these women when they speak with you, the way you used to be when we first came. These days you seem rather dour and distant, and they have been remarking on it."

"I don't think they like me at all. All they want me to do is gossip the way they do, and tell tales of others' misdemeanours. So, because I won't do it, when I say something by way of making conversation, they pounce on my every word."

"I don't believe that," he says, somewhat abruptly." You must be imagining it."

"You have never been to one of their circles, to see how uncharitably they speak about those who don't belong," I reply with asperity. "Even if you are at the meeting, you aren't safe from their criticisms."

"Be careful, Anne, you are speaking about many godly women, magistrates' wives among them. I am sure that if they are critical, it is meant to help you." His tone grows sharper.

"You see?" I retort. "When I do tell the truth, even you get angry. Just imagine what they could do to me." I can feel the fury starting to whirl around in my stomach.

"They will not, and I will not let them." He is alarmed now at the thought of it. His tone changes as his anger dissipates. "I will have to think about this. Let's say no more about it for now." He takes my arm, turns me around, and walks me home. We hardly speak, but I know, just by the way he holds on to me, matching his pace to mine, that he is not annoyed with me. I feel like a child, whose father is going to set things right with the other grown-ups so they will not hurt me. Is that what I want or need? I would like to say no, but I do not know how else I can survive in this vicious circle,

We take our dinner together, conversing amiably about the garden to be planted, laughing about the attempts of our neighbours and ourselves to make a truly frightening scarecrow, and the hopelessness of all our efforts. It seems that New England crows are almost fearless — either that, or they do not recognize a scarecrow when they see one, believing it to be just a bunch of rags on a pole.

12.

THE DAYS CREEP ON like an old nag pulling a cart of firewood. I am that nag, I think, dragging myself around thoughtlessly all day, doing this and that. The times when I feel unburdened are rare; the best are when Edward appears at meals, and on the evenings when he is not called out on some community business. I do not know what I would do without him, probably expire. Seeing Elizabeth cheers me wonderfully when we are together. We can usually find something amusing to laugh about, or at least we can groan together about matters that distress us. We talk about books and politics with no fear that our views will be reported and condemned. After each happy meeting I am more downcast, knowing I must spend so much time between visits with difficult company — I mean the Gossping Gertrudes especially. I have not the courage to stop attending the group, and to be fair, I do admire several of the women. It is too bad that the stiff-necked critical ones always dominate. I wish someone would put them in their place — a busy barnyard with a lot of scrabbling chickens would be fitting.

I am afraid of the dark now in a way I never was before. I do not mind the gradual descending darkness; in fact, I love the calmness that seems to settle over everything, as colours fade and birds finish their evening salutations to each other, then go to rest. It is the sudden plunge into the dark that terrifies me; I could never go into a mine, or a cave, or even a dark room. I freeze at the thought. Now I insist on having two candles in my room every night, in case one goes out. I wake often, just to make sure that they are still alight. I chide myself for being so nervous, but there is some terror deep inside me that I cannot quell. There is a familiarity about it that tells me it has always been there, but never with such a grip upon me as now. If only it would go away. I am now beginning to ask the Lord in my prayers whether I have somehow committed some unrecognized sin, and if this is the retribution for it.

Apart from the time I spend in my chamber writing in my journal and reading, there is a great void in my everyday life. I have taken to wandering about the town again, at times when I am not likely to meet many people. So I am quite surprised this morning as I am returning home to see Mr. Hooker approaching. He must be coming from our house.

We greet each other warmly, then I say, "I suppose you know now that my husband has gone to New London today to see about buying some pigs."

"Yes, your housemaid told me, but actually it was you I was coming to see." He gives me a little smile, a half-smile, as if he wants to be serious but not unfriendly.

"Me? Well, that's very kind of you." I sound a bit puzzled, I am sure. "Won't you come back to the house, then?"

"Thank you, I suppose I should," he says, then hesitates, "but perhaps we can talk here just as well." I wait, looking at him for some indication of what this is about. I am always pleased when he speaks with me. He is another of the sun's beams that breaks through my gloom.

"Edward tells me that you have not been your usual bright self recently." I nod. How can I deny it? "I don't know the cause of course, but from what he says you seem to be quietly struggling with something close to despair, which is the worst condition the soul can experience." I nod again, sober now.

"Let me reassure you, Mistress, that every saint must at some time or another pass through the bleakest part of the wilderness; it is a stage of one's growth in holiness. However, God always gives nourishment enough for the journey, just as he sent down manna for the children of Israel. No despair is too deep that he cannot lift us out of it. Do you believe that?"

I say, "Yes, I think so."

"Then I urge you to increase your prayers for the faith that will shield and encourage you. Will you do that?" His voice brooks no refusal. I say, "Yes," and mean it.

"Good. I shall pray for you also, of course." That rallies me, though I cannot explain why. Are some people's prayers more effective than others'?

"Now," he says, "we have tackled the heart of the matter which is the soul's health, but we must also consider the body. If you take a drink of white wine and water once a day, I am told it will reduce your lethargy, and you will be out chasing the cows around the fields any day now."

We both laugh at that, and with a few more pleasant words, he leaves me.

I try my best, with the prayers and the white wine, and thoughts of what a fine Christian man Mr. Hooker is to pay such kind attention to my troubles. But, I must say, that I am not feeling much better for all that.

13.

THERE IS SOME CONSOLATION in writing down my thoughts. As I read them over later, I see that I am trying to put the best face on things, as if that will make everything better. I write:

March 16, 1644

"In spite of the loneliness of this sequestered place, there are little chinks and corners of my life in which I am quite content. Edward, for all that he cannot understand me or fathom my misery, loves me well, and is a comforting presence when he is at home. He is even more admirable for loving me without understanding why I am sometimes strangely sorrowful and out-of-sorts.

"Sometimes, in the evenings, I come over to his chair and squeeze in beside him on the cushions, just to feel the warm sureness of his body. We sit then, just the two of us, beside the hearth, watching the fire burn and thinking our own private thoughts.

"I can guess what is on his mind. First, the events of the day — a ship safely harboured, a cargo delivered, the accounts rendered. He will be examining himself to see whether he has been fair in all his dealings, whether he has shown a loving disposition to all those he trades with. If he were to ask me my opinion, I would say 'Yes,' every time. He, however, is never sure, and that is what makes him one of the most respected of all the saints to everyone here; a saint among the saints, I would say.

"After he has examined his conduct he will go on to prepare for the next day's court. There might be a dispute between two planters to settle, several misdemeanours to judge, a letter from the magistrates of another town to be read and discussed. He will be asking himself how to handle the rise of drunkenness and all the quarrels it causes among families and neighbours. He will be questioning whether the court is being too severe on the impoverished, those willing poor who cannot find work. Should they be sent away, or is there some work in town to be found?

"All these matters and more will be going through his head as we sit here. I wonder how he can rest so placidly, patting my arm while he smokes his pipe and looks into the flames. Then, wrapped in the warmth of his body, I know how much I do love him, my spouse of these eight years. If only … no, I will not bring any sadness into this good memory. If only there could be more moments like this, I think I could put a better face on my existence here in Hartford."

One night I talk to Edward about Plâs Grono and my beloved Wales. I describe, as I have no doubt done before, our old stone house, its gardens, and the hustle and bustle of the many people who lived there, about twenty of them, I think. I say that I can see in my mind's eye, the round low hills protecting the smooth valleys where the sheep grazed, each one seeming to possess a feeding space of his own. I talk about the skies that could show all moods at once: over here a lowering storm cloud, over there a few little puffs in a pure blue sky.

"It was such a fine peaceful land to live in," I say. I wrap my arms across my chest, hugging myself, relishing the memory. "And so happy. Everybody was full of gaiety — except my mother, of course. But the rest! We had such merry times, with our feast days and harvest days and, oh, the Mayday celebrations! They were the best of all. There were always lots of people to talk to, in the town and in the country too. You could say anything you pleased, and no one would frown or correct you." I look longingly at Edward. "I wish we were there now."

Edward says evenly, "Anne, you were just a child when you left Wales. It would be different now. The war has changed many places, including Wales. You would be surprised if you went back there. It's not nearly as peaceful as it is here in New England."

"That may be, but if only we could transport some of the joy of that old country into this new one." I look at him confidently, almost as if I believe in what I am saying.

He corrects me gently. "This is not the time for joy, Anne. The world is in a dreadful mess right now. Brothers are fighting brothers, commoners are fighting nobles, and the King is still at loggerheads with Mr. Cromwell and the Parliament. Here we are being spared all that, even though we take what is happening in England very much to heart. You should be thankful to be here at the present time. It is the best place to be."

"Well, it's not a very good place here, either. What became of the promise that we would be the city on the hill, or the candlestick to light the world? Our candle is short and smoking, I think." Unwittingly, a new brittle note has crept into my voice.

"We are trying our best, but as you well know, we say only that we want to be that candle, not that we have become it. Our sinfulness holds us from it."

I consider this. "Do you think Mr. Hooker would agree with you?"

"I suspect in his heart of hearts he fears we cannot achieve this goal, at least in our lifetime. The city is to be entered in the hereafter. Even so, that will not stop him from showing us the way towards it."

I think, if we could become the good city, what would it be be like.

14.

IT SEEMS THAT EDWARD has consulted Mr. Hooker again about me, with the result that he tells me he has invited my mother to come for a visit. He must be desperate to find something to improve my disposition, for he knows how coolly my mother treats me most of the time, and he is not all that taken with her either.

I am astonished to hear that she set out as soon as she received Edward's letter, as if she could hardly wait to leave New Haven. I am even more amazed at her mood when she arrives. I can hardly remember an occasion when I have been hugged by this woman. Today, she folds her arms around me, holding me tight and close. Her coming is a mystery to me: even though Edward asked her, why did she agree, when her daughter's well-being is usually the last thing on her mind? There must be more to her coming than the force of parental obligation; indeed, she seems genuinely glad to see me.

It does not take me long to realize that my mother has come to Hartford, not so much to succour as to escape. At the dinner table, she entertains us with New Haven stories. Like a chirpy sparrow, she prattles on about everything from the latest shipwreck to a new improvement in washing powder. She makes no distinction between the importance of the two, and treats all subjects she mentions with a guileless lack of concern. When has she ever cared enough about domestic affairs to think about washing powder? I guess that she is disguising some serious troubles of her own. Her hair, now almost completely grey, lacks sheen and substance. In the candlelight, her skin has the dry translucency of old parchment, a sure sign of an unhealthy body, or is it the soul — or both together?

Her behaviour in church the next day confirms my suspicion. All through the service, especially during the sermon, she fidgets, with her hands, her Bible, her skirt. I notice her taking notes during the sermon, and then watch in dismay as she crosses out many of the lines she has written. Eventually, she puts down her notebook, squirms some more, and then seems to stop paying attention. How can she not listen to Mr. Hooker? I have never heard him speak so brilliantly as he does today. I am sure he is a far better preacher than her old Mr. Davenport. What is the matter with her? I hope old eagle-eyed Brigden is not watching.

After the service, Edward and I introduce her to all the leading families, who speak very respectfully to her as the wife of one of the most important governors in New England. Mistress Hooker, whose manner seems to me to be serenity itself compared to my mother's jumpiness, invites Mistress Eaton to the next meeting of the women's circle. My face falls, as she accepts with apparent pleasure.

At the meeting, Mother is all smiles as she is introduced once again. It is customary to begin with a Bible reading, followed by a discussion of the passage, which is led by either Mistress Hooker or Mistress Stone. After this, the Gossiping Gertrudes hit their stride, with the conversation taking any direction they please. This is where I expect trouble. It begins well before that, however.

Mistress Hooker, in deference to the honoured guest, asks Mistress Eaton to read the biblical text. It is the parable of the labourers in the vineyard. She reads it well; it is the story of workers who are hired at different times during the day right up until the last hour before quitting time, and all are given the same wage. Those who have worked all day complain to the owner of the vineyard, who says, "That is the amount you contracted for. I am not cheating you. Is it not lawful for me to do what I will with my own?" The passage concludes, "So the last shall be first, and the first last: for many be called, but few chosen."

The women listen intently. It is a familiar parable, thus the discussion is sure to be lively. As soon as the reading is over, several people lean forward almost sliding off their stools, eager to start in. Mistress Hooker says blithely, "Who would like to begin?"

Mistress Stone, who is halfway out of her seat, is cut off by Mistress Brigden. "This is a difficult parable," she says. Clearly, she believes she is the only one to do it justice. "But our Mr. Stone has rightly given us the correct meaning of it, I think. The lord of the vineyard is the Lord God Himself, and in this parable He judges those who murmur against Him, who complain against His laws, and reject His gift of salvation. The parable is a warning, which has not been heeded, to the established church in England and to the church of Rome, that although they were called first, they shall be last to receive his mercy."

"In fact, they stand in peril of losing God's favour altogether," says Mistress Stone. "My husband says we should pray for their salvation." Everyone murmurs agreement. Some of them have relatives in England who have still not become visible saints.

Mistress Hooker speaks next. "I don't doubt that Mr. Stone's understanding of this parable contains truth, but I think it misses a very important point. Mr. Hooker says that the different hours of the day when the workers were hired refer to the history of redemption from the beginning of time until our own calling. So it is that we who are the last shall be first rewarded. As for those who complained, they must learn that God shows His mercy equally to everyone. In the story, all received the same wage at the end of the day."

My mouth opens in amazement. In all the time I have known her, this is only the second time I have heard Mistress Hooker put together a reasoned argument. She is usually in such a rush to do ten things at once that I have wondered if she ever gave herself time to think at all. Here is the evidence that she does, even if it is just to repeat what her husband said.

"This is a more compassionate God, then, who does what he wants with his own," I mutter. A few women look at me, but their attention is taken quickly by Mistress Brigden, who addresses my mother. "What does Mr. Davenport say about this Scripture, Mistress Eaton?"

Her reply comes quickly. "I neither know nor care what Mr. Davenport thinks. I rely on no man, including our illustrious minister, to tell me what to think." Although her voice is soft enough, there is a slight inflection on the word "illustrious" that might suggest its opposite.

A chorus of gasps and "Oohs" ensues. Miserably, my head sinks down on my chest. She continues evenly, "It is the Spirit who guides me in everything I think and do. He will lead me into all truth." She turns to Mistress Brigden directly. "How can you presume to be so sure, when you do not have the Holy Spirit in your heart?" The challenge, though spoken politely, is there.

Mistress Brigden is taken aback, and for once, indecisive. I can imagine her reasoning; it would be a grave error to insult the wife of such a strict believer as Governor Eaton, but how can she let these remarks pass? She decides she will have to, but the spirit that burns inside her must be searing with fury.

The meeting is a shambles. People begin speaking to those next to them in undertones. They have never witnessed such a confrontation. What an exciting story it will be to take back to those who missed the incident. Mistress Hooker sits there, a faint, dubious smile on her face, hoping that order and decency will be restored, but she is, for once, unsure how to bring it about.

It is Mistress Goodwin who comes through. Leaning over and smiling at my mother and me, she says, "It is a long time since I have been in New Haven, but I am sure things are said and done differently there than they are here. Your words have given us something very important to think about when we go home. Would you agree, Mistress Hooker?" As she speaks I raise my head, staring between people, not at them. Mistress Goodwin has saved the day, for now at least.

Mistress Hooker agrees gratefully, and, turning to the whole group, asks about the health of absent members. Some sort of calm is restored, even though certain feelings are hurt irrevocably, and the thought of retribution is surely simmering.

My astonishment at my mother's outburst shifts quickly into fear of what may happen next, to both of us. I am sure that news of the incident will get back to New Haven. I am just as certain that my mother's outrageousness will be chalked on the slate of peculiarities already listed against her daughter. For the rest of the meeting, I keep my head bowed to my sewing as much as possible.

We say little on the way home. Mother remarks that I have some interesting friends, and I say that most are only acquaintances. My closest friend is not of their religious persuasion. She says that the same is true for her; her best friends are not saints, and leaves it at that.

In the evening, after Edward has gone out to one of his meetings, Mother inquires about my health for the first time. We have been sitting by the fire mending some old shirts, when she says, "You seem much more subdued than you used to be. Is it the difference in the climate here? It is very damp, which is not good for one's humour."

"I don't think so, Mother."

"Then perhaps you are not eating well. I noticed that you left a lot on your plate this evening."

"I wasn't particularly hungry. I never am after one of those meetings."

"Ah, the meeting! If you are afraid that those women will harass you because your mother is an independent thinker, don't worry about that. You and I are both governors' wives, and to be treated with respect. Your reputation is safe."

My mother an independent thinker? I can hardly keep from laughing despite my mood. Her thoughts have always resembled milkweed down, clinging to any plant in sight until they are blown off. Something strange is happening to her. I wonder if she can tell me.

Mother puts down her work, and looks me in the eyes. "You are a fortunate girl, to have a husband who loves you and treats you tenderly. I have made two unhappy marriages, which I shall always regret."

I look at her in astonishment. "What do you mean?"

"My first husband, your father, was a lovely man, but he died so young, and left me to my fate: a poor widow with three little children to raise. Of course it was not his fault, and had he lived we would have been happy all together. By now we would have all been living in the country, back at Plâs Grono." She looks as if she is going to cry.

She loves it too, the dear old house. All I can remember of her there is her weeping and wailing in her widowhood, and complaining that she would never find someone to marry her, hidden as she was in the Welsh country.

"Then I married again. I was so grateful for being given a second chance to lead a good life, to have a position in society, and to have enough to support us all.

"When I married, I had no idea that Mr. Eaton was planning to move to the colonies. Perhaps he didn't then either, but soon afterwards he and Mr. Davenport made up their minds to leave the country. That's when everything began to go wrong.

"Mr. Davenport — I blame him most for the difficulties of my marriage — was determined that New Haven would be the true city on the hill, the only true city. We would show the others in Boston and elsewhere how weak in faith they were. So he and my husband began to make laws for the saints and for the colony that were more severe than for all the other towns. They wanted to be sure that the Devil could not enter our colony by any door, or window, or crack in the wall.

"I could tell that my husband wanted to be the most highly esteemed of all the governors, and so he would be if there was no unacknowledged sin or crime or heretical idea to be found in New Haven. That aim of his affects everyone at all times: in the assembly, at work, at home. To me, his courtesy is unfailing, his demands are heavy, his watchfulness is constant."

I am hearing for the first time the voice of a woman who can think for herself. "How horrid that must be! Can you do nothing to soften him?" I ask.

"With that mother of his approving his every move? Not a chance. She has never liked me, and now she has the opportunity to treat me unkindly if I step out of line, which of course I do. Then there are the children, too."

"But surely they bring some light into the house? I remember how fond you were of little Hannah."

"Hannah has become her father's daughter. She cannot help it, she's so young. He has forced her to become a sober, dutiful child. There's no playfulness or joy left in her. Ellis, the baby, is unaffected so far.

"The servants are his spies. Sometimes they are surly, and seem about to refuse to obey me, when they think better of it, and slink off and do their work. I had to slap one of them, for refusing to fetch water for me to wash in. Said she didn't have time to get it right now. She looked so hostile afterwards, and I am sure she told Mr. Eaton about it. He hasn't said anything yet, but he will. Oh, I am so glad every day when he goes out and leaves me alone. I told him so once, when I was at my wits' end. He told Mr. Davenport, who admonished me, and said that wives must honour and obey their husbands in all things."

"What did you say to that?"

She smiles. "I told him that the Holy Spirit guided me, and if I was led to obey my husband, then I would do so without fail. I let the other 'if' go unsaid."

I laugh out loud. "I do admire your courage, but I'm afraid it will get you into trouble. From what you say, Mr. Davenport is not to be contended with."

"Mr. Davenport and my husband are good friends. I think I can count on that to spare me any indignity. Although Mr. Eaton is a strict man, he is not harsh or mean, as I am sure you know."

I nod. "That's true. Still, I would guard my tongue, if I were you."

Mother says, "I trust in the Spirit and with a few good friends to support me, I will survive. As I said, you are lucky to be here, with such a husband, in this free and lively community."

I say, "More or less." I am not going to foist my own confusion upon her; she has difficulties enough of her own.

The rest of her visit passes amicably. It is in fact the pleasantest time we have ever spent together. She does not unburden herself further, nor does she invite me to do so. We make calls upon Mistress Goodwin and Mistress Johnson, whom, my mother declares, is "the liveliest person in Hartford, and the pleasantest, even if the Spirit does not dwell in her as yet." I am delighted at her approval. When the time comes for her to leave, I wish her a fervent Godspeed. I am truly sorry to see her go, and ask her to please hurry back as soon as she can.

The next meeting of the women's circle comes all too soon for me. I am dreading what people may say about my mother. To my surprise, Mistress Eaton is not mentioned. Of course, I wonder what the silence indicates: is some nasty plan of revenge being prepared that I am not to know about? The only question directed at me comes from my neighbour Mistress Woodside, who asks rather pointedly whether I am not gaining a little weight. I say, "No, I don't believe so," and immediately realize that the question is an oblique way of asking whether I am pregnant. So I smile enigmatically, and the subject is dropped. That will give them something different to gossip about. I wish it were true, though.

15.

I AM GETTING TO BE such a worrywart, looking for trouble from
every side. The Gossiping Gertrudes and Mr. Stone bother me most,
because I expect to receive more harm from them. I do not expect harm
from Mistress Hooker or Mistress Goodwin, of course, who are closest
to my heart after Edward. And Elizabeth too. I visit her occasionally, but
after Edward's mild warning, I am afraid to see her more often for fear
of criticism coming down upon him as much as on me. Elizabeth seems
to understand the predicament without being told, so gradually our lives
became more and more separate from each other, though we remain the
best of friends.

As for the rest of the community, though I have met many other decent
women, there are none I can call my friend. I did not realize when we first
came here how different I was with respect to age, station, and learning.
It is a small place, a true farming village. London must have formed my
tastes and habits more than I realized. So for one reason or another, my
mother's departure leaves me on my own most of the time, with no one
to talk to except Edward, when he is at home.

I continue my meandering walks through the town, which now stretches
out far west of the river, and south of the Little River. I walk past the
burgeoning farms, so well-ordered now that even the apple trees form in
identical ranks like well-trained schoolchildren, forbidden to wave their
arms about or put a foot out of line. I walk over the meadows speckled
with daisies, trailing purple vetch and the odd spontaneous sapling of

sumac or elderberry. I go as far as the edge of the forest, which from now on I will never enter. Some days, I hate the silence that lurks over me like an unspoken judgment. That is when I miss the old sounds of the Welsh countryside, the merry tripping and clop-clop of horses' hooves, the lively undisciplined dogs barking as the carts go by, and the sense of wonder I used to feel at the simplest joys of creation. Here, where horses and dogs are rare beasts, the ratcheting of saw on wood may be the only sound I hear for an hour or more. Is this place holding its breath, waiting to pounce on me, like some of its inhabitants? What foolishness. Yet, I have never before felt such a cool withdrawal of all things that make up one's everyday life.

I think about the Vale of Clwyd near Plâs Grono. There were the farmers, father and son, bent over, picking up stones and heaving them into barrows behind the patient oxen. There were the carts bumping along the winding tracks and disappearing into the green hills. I remember the trees drunk with rain, shaking themselves with every surge of wind. And I can almost feel the comforting breezes that followed and parted the clouds to let in slips of sunshine.

Then, there were the times when I walked through those fields of grass and clover and furze, and the sheep, disturbed, picked up their feet in front of me and stomped on ahead. Sometimes, I felt my body open up and spread itself across the horizon, attempting to enter into that green world, body and soul together. Then the smell of wet, dirty fleece, the glancing strokes of crisp grasses, and the buffeting of winds from nowhere, would be proof enough of the distance between my life and the world I trod in. Even though I have been assured by preachers on both sides of the ocean that I am at the apex of creation, just underneath (the thumb of) man, some rare days arrived when I wished this hierarchy were not so, days when this unique time and this particular place and my love of the country hinted at a strange harmony of a different sort.

The strangeness that is Connecticut is not the same, although once in a while, on a wet day, I do catch a wisp of an old Welsh memory in the fields and woods around me. Mostly though, the sky is broader here, its ceiling far higher than in the Old World. It is vast enough to frighten me sometimes, to put away any remaining sense of a connection between the elements of the natural world and myself. The winds of the New World are harsher, more insistent, moving like a line of soldiers with their muskets raised. They do their worst and then, as if they have been ordered to, die away completely. Driven before the onslaught, in the war between woman and wind, I am always conquered.

All these thoughts, perilous though some of them are, I record in my journal. As the days grow more monotonous and my encounters with other people fewer and less satisfactory, I write more and speak even less than before.

16.

IN THE SPRING, after the sheep have been sheared, I decide to take up spinning yarn. It is not a suitable occupation for a lady in England now, as there are women working in their cottages for wages who can supply the gentry well enough. Here it is quite another matter. For most women, it is either spin or be cold. For me, it is something I can undertake that even the Gossiping Gertrudes would approve. It gives me something to do, and, as I discover, engages my mind entirely. Edward is delighted. One might have expected him to be appalled to see the governor's wife at such humdrum work. Instead, he is pleased that I am pursuing a new and useful interest. He hopes it will keep my mind occupied with housewifely things, instead of so much writing and daydreaming. He is coming to share the common opinion that excessive reading and writing are bad for a woman's health.

Spinning is not a skill easily acquired, I find out, although it looks so simple. I write Jane:

April 26, 1644

"...My first attempts were horrible. The fleece refused to help by allowing itself to be guided into an even thin line on my spindle. It must be stretched and flattened first, and combed into neat airy packets to sit in my basket. This manoeuvre is called 'carding.' Then, I take each packet and try to join it to the end of the previous strand of yarn, easing gently with one hand, neither loosely nor tightly, while the other hand starts the wheel turning and my foot pedals it onward. It is a slow process, trying to get the rhythms right all at once, almost as difficult as when you first attempt to use both hands to play the virginal. I must say that on the day when I produced a long strand of wool without lumps or breaks, I was almost as pleased with myself as when I learned to play Mr. Byrd's *Pavana* for the first time, almost correctly."

The wool I am spinning is coarse and rubs harshly on my hands, even after Nellie has washed it several times and laid it outside to dry. Farmer Montrose, a distant relative of Mistress Goodwin's, hearing from her of my efforts, offers to send me some fleece from his own flock. It is much finer, he says, with a longer staple that makes it spin up quickly, and is far better suited to delicate hands I am so grateful, as I do not think I can last any longer with the scratchy, tough wool from our own flock. Nellie has to wrap my hands every night in cloths spread with honey, but it doesn't help much. Nellie says her mother has a better remedy for roughness and blisters, which she will bring when she goes home for her day's leave, in three weeks. I wish it were sooner.

Edward beams when he sees me at work, and declares that I am getting my colour back and looking much healthier. It is true that when I am forced to watch what I am doing every second of the time, never looking up or letting go, I cannot concentrate on anything else. When I rest though, my sorrowful, guilt-stained thoughts come back instantly, as if the wheel has chained them to it, and in stopping has let them fall into my lap like a heap of dirty fleece with bits of weeds entangled in it.

I think about my mother's unhappiness, and how painful it must be to have to disguise it in that sternly critical family. I was unable to recognize it when I lived there, or perhaps had not bothered to notice, being so uneasy myself. Would it have helped if I had cared even a little? Then I think about the punishment inflicted on Wacusa, my Indian friend, and myself the unwitting cause of it. How no sorrowful apology I might make can wipe away the cruelty the Podunk must feel. It does not matter to me in the least whether they blame me for it; I blame myself.

Then I go over the time, years ago now, when I came to Hartford as an eager young bride, stepping blithely into this community of brotherly love and holy watchfulness, as one of the written covenants described it. And how I came to see that brotherly love had its price, and holy watchfulness ensured that those who would not pay it were chastised or cast out. I wonder where the fault really lies:, in those who set down the rules for mutual love, or those who will not keep them?

I had hoped that these seething thoughts might subside if I ignored them for a while, but it does not seem to work that way. I am as miserable as ever; the spinning only a temporary diversion.

What would be the use of trying to explain all this to Edward? He sees me changed, domesticated. He would never notice the anguish simmering under the concentration, because he wants so ardently to have a new Anne who will be his helpmate in the community. How I wish I could be what he needs, but the Anne I really am must come out, otherwise I will go mad.

On one of her frequent visits — "I just happened to be passing" — Mistress Woodside arrives bursting with excitement, like the King's herald about to announce a royal marriage — or an execution. She looks admiringly at the skeins of yarn piled up beside the spinning wheel, her surprise at my skill barely hidden. She says, "What do you intend to do with this yarn?"

"I don't know. I haven't given it any thought." I am so intent on trying to improve my skill, and don't really think the result is good for anything, until I look at the number of neat skeins lying in the basket. I realize they are quite respectable, good enough to be made into something serviceable, which is all that is required in this society.

"Perhaps it could make a blanket," I venture.

Mistress Woodside laughs. "A blanket? What you have there might be enough for a border, or to cover a cushion. In a year or so you should have enough for a blanket."

"Oh well, then perhaps I should settle for a cushion. Who knows where I'll be in a year's time, perhaps nowhere."

Mistress Woodside looks at me strangely. "Well, I don't know what you mean by that. Just because your mother is having her troubles is no reason for you to be so morbid."

"What do you know of any troubles of my mother's?" I snap.

This is apparently the moment Mistress Woodside has been waiting for. "Oh, didn't you know? I am sorry to be bringing you the news. I thought you would have heard already."

"What news?" I ask. My body shivers with apprehension.

"Well, it seems that your mother has become associated with some Anabaptists, some women who have tried to convince her that she has not been truly baptized. She says that infant baptism is no true baptism. One must be baptized by the Spirit. She is causing quite a furor in New Haven."

"What sort of furor?" I do not want to hear what is coming next, but I cannot stop myself from asking.

"Well," Mistress Woodside is trying not to let her titillation show, "evidently she has been getting up in the middle of the service just before the sermon and walking out. Mr. Davenport is, of course, upset at her behaviour. He has tried to reason with her, but she will not listen."

I recall mother's attitude towards Mr. Davenport. "And Mr. Eaton? Where does he stand?"

"He must stand with Mr. Davenport, because your mother is voicing heretical opinions and will not be guided by him either. Yet I hear he is reluctant to divorce her."

"Divorce? He would not!"

"He may have to. They say there is going to be a trial, and she is likely to be excommunicated if she does not recant. He would certainly be forced to divorce her if she were found guilty. A governor could not harbour a dissident under his roof."

I am not listening any more. I am thinking about my poor mother, caught in the tentacles of that rigid community, in a household that is inimical to her at the best of times, and certainly hostile now. I cannot imagine how she ever thought she could get away with voicing these ideas in such a place as New Haven. Did she truly believe what she said when she was here, that being the governor's wife would keep her immune from criticism and judgment? If so, she was very silly indeed. The governor is supposed to be the model for others, his household beyond reproach. I wonder what has addled my mother's mind, or what has driven her to this extreme behaviour? I shall write to her immediately, and I shall pray for her safety and courage.

Mistress Woodside having said everything she knows, thankfully, is spent of enthusiasm. Seeing that I am not paying attention to her any more, she decides to make a polite exit.

"Mistress Newby next door to me is an excellent weaver," she says. "If you wish, I'll have a word with her and see if she will weave you a blanket when you have enough yarn — or whatever you decide," she finishes.

"Thank you," I say absently, and show her to the door. Now I am certain she will have something to report to her friends Mistress Brigden and Mistress Stone that the governor's wife is becoming more and more distracted, just like her mother.

Although I am deeply disturbed at Mistress Woodside's news, I am not completely surprised. I knew my mother was headed off in some strange direction, but I never thought the outcome would be this drastic. What can I do? I can think of nothing.

I am sitting staring blindly out the window when Edward comes home. I turn to him, and I can tell by the look on his face that he knows I have heard the news. I say, "How long have you known?"

He, reddening a little, says, "Just a few days. I, uh, did not want to upset you."

"And did you intend to keep it from me forever?" I demand, crossing my arms like a fishwife.

He hesitates. "I suppose that wouldn't have been possible, but "he sees my chest heaving, ready to burst, "I truly thought it best —"

"Best not to tell me something so vital, so urgent about my own mother? Oh Edward, how could you?" I shout now, my eyes glaring, my body stiff as a starched collar.

He puts his hands out, palms up. "Please, Anne, please don't take it so hard. I am sorry, truly. I thought the news might be too much for you." He looks intently at me. "I am afraid I was right."

The wind goes out of my furious sails as I take in his meaning, and I sink limply back into my chair. I try to speak calmly.

"No, it is not too much for me. It is terrible, such a prospect for my mother. I grieve deeply for her. But also for myself. To think that you will not trust me not to go to pieces when I receive bad news. I cannot decide whether you think I am a child or an invalid."

The last remark astonishes him. He sits down beside me, and following my example, stares out the window, debating his answer.

Eventually he says, "I am sorry, my dearest Anne, if I misjudge you. You are stronger than I sometimes think. No, you are neither child nor invalid."

"You always want to protect me from hearing anything offensive, miserable, evil, or disastrous. But I hear them anyway, you know. This is a chattering town."

"I know that, but still I hope, perhaps foolishly, that you won't learn of every nasty thing that takes place in Hartford. You seem so, so weighed down much of the time. I don't want to burden your mind further."

"You would have me believe we live in a fine righteous community, untroubled by any wrongs? A kind of Eden, except that there would be only one person in it — me? Edward, as horrid as it may be, I need to know the truth about life."

Just before I can reach for his hand, he shifts away from me, tilting his head backwards and staring at the ceiling. I feel him turning over the idea in his mind. He is not happy about it. He truly wants his little bride—as he still thinks of me — to be spared all unpleasantness. Me, the little bride, who cannot manage to fit into this alien town.

"I will try my best not to hide things from you, but you must let me use my own judgment about that. Sometimes you seem so wan and fragile — no, not an invalid, but a tender person who can be easily hurt, and then you might become ill indeed. I do want to make sure that doesn't happen."

He takes both my hands in his, and gives me a rather wistful smile, hopeful that I will accept his compromise.

It is the best he can do. I hug him fondly. At least I have spoken and he has heard me.

We turn back to my mother's plight, and Edward agrees that there is nothing to do except wait for the court's decision. He is sorry, because, since her visit, he has grown fond of her. He finds it difficult to believe that she would speak out so boldly in New Haven.

17.

EVERYWHERE IN TOWN I am sure that Mistress Eaton is the chief subject of conversation. Her presumed defection is, after all, the most exciting occurrence since the Pequot wars. When I do go out occasionally I sometimes overhear the odd phrase, which is broken off when the speaker notices me: "…slapping her mother-in-law at the table…," "…servant refused to obey her…," "Mr. Davenport…." Voices are lowered, and then the chattering resumes: "…tried twice to convince her, but now the trial is to take place next week." Once I hear, "Poor Mistress Hopkins, it must distress her terribly. And she not in the best condition herself … pregnant perhaps?"

In haste I write to David in Boston. He is the clever one of the family; he will think of something to do. At least he will share my anxiety. I give him all the details I know, describing our mother's visit to Hartford as well, and end writing, "Dear David, if only you can think of some way out for her, to get her away from those miserable creatures who trample on her good nature. Please, please try."

On a dismal autumn day, I receive his reply. The rain has been pouring down as if all the washerwomen in the world are emptying their buckets over the little town. The streets run with mud, keeping most people indoors. Earlier this morning, I saw a small errand boy slide and fall headlong, his parcel burst and all the mackerel inside slithered onto the street. Poor child, he will have some explaining to do when he hands those to his mistress, and he will probably be beaten for his carelessness.

I am wrapped up as well as can be against the damp, with a thick woollen cape I purchased from Cook's half-sister Bridey. So far, my spinning has not resulted in any garment, as Mistress Newby had enough to do for her own family. Today, I am so chilly that the rough fabric does not even feel scratchy. Edward says the colour becomes me, probably because it is not showy, I think. It is soft apple green, dyed from local leaves.

I am sitting by the fire in my own chamber, with only my hands peeking out from the cape to hold on to my book. I am reading the memoirs of Lady Arethusa C and thinking wistfully about the difference between the writer's amusing life in London and my own in this wilderness. For the Englishwoman, every day is different: today there is an assembly at my Lady H's, tomorrow a ride in the park, then to the theatre to see the new play by Massinger. She takes a day at home without visitors to arrange for the next — a dinner given for her husband's City friends. Then, they pack up the furnishings and move to Scotland for the hunting.

What a contrast between her life and mine. Here, except for such horrid things as my mother's trial, one day is the same as the next. The events may change, but their complexion is as drab as the mud outside my door. It does me no good at all to grieve over my situation, though. These memoirs at least are not dull. I can spend some time in Lady Arethusa's company to take my mind off the present.

I am reading a hilarious account of Lady Arethusa entertaining a would-be suitor for her patronage, of his putting on obsequious airs to gain her favour. I burst out laughing, a rare act for me, and just at that moment someone knocks at the door. I call "Come in," and Jenny appears. She looks around, surprised. "Oh you are reading, Mistress. I heard you laughing and wondered if you had a visitor."

I smile at this strange comment. No one but the servants is permitted upstairs. Surely Jenny does not think I have invited a guest to visit me privately?

"I had just found an amusing story in my book," I say.

The look on Jenny's face changes from skeptical to grave. "A letter has just come for you, Mistress. From Boston."

I reach for it eagerly. "Thank you, Jenny. I have been waiting for it." I dismiss her with a nod, turn away and break open the seal as fast as I can.

August 1, 1644

Dear Sister,

The news you sent me about our mother does not surprise me. I had already heard rumours about her public opposition to infant baptism, and her refusal to attend the ministers' sermons. I believe she has some intelligent and well-respected lady companions, but I do not think they can withstand the might of Mr. Davenport and the whole gathering. I feel some sympathy, as you do, with our stepfather's conflict, caught between his principles and his wife.

At present, I do not see any way of helping. If she should be excommunicated, and if Mr. Eaton should put her away, then we will have to find a place for her, either here or in England. In your position, you cannot take her in, and she would be in an even more damaging situation if she were to come to me. We can only pray, dear Anne, that the worst will be avoided.

From the hints you dropped in your letter, I guess that your own life is not as content as it once was. What a pathetic family we are! You at least are not taken for a heretic, as mother is, and as I fear I will be soon. Only Thomas seems to sail over these anxious seas, oblivious to all the storms. He always found life less complicated than we do.

I am sorry to write such a few lines, but I am engaged in a struggle of my own against the colony's magistrates. I will not bother you with that now, except to ask your prayers for

Your loving brother,

David Yale

My tears are coursing down my cheeks and onto the paper as I read. What is happening to this world? First my mother, and now David is in trouble. He does not even tell me what the matter is, which makes me worry even more. I simply must find out. I will write him again, or perhaps, when Edward goes to Boston next, I can go along and stay with David and his wife, Ursula. Oh dear! Everything is turning sour.

Tonight, in bed, I tell Edward about David's letter. He says — and I am sure he is telling the truth — that he does not know what trouble David is in, but he will try to find out. After all, he was David's friend before he knew me.

I cannot help it; I am letting my emotions get the better of me, so I must speak what is on my mind. I say plaintively, "What are we doing in this place? Why can't we go home?"

"Anne!" He is shocked.

"I mean it. I am sorry, Edward, but I can hardly bear it any longer, the way things are going. There is something terribly wrong with this errand into the wilderness. Perhaps it has all been a mistake. There is no room for different opinions, different ways of worshipping, or different approaches to praying. If you don't conform you are likely to be put on trial, or worse. People are quarrelling with one another all the time over the most trivial things. Not that they think these things are in the least bit trivial as even the slightest mistake is taken to be a huge grievous sin. And there are more real sins all the time, with murders, and rape and theft and drunkenness. It's not getting any better, either. It's getting worse."

He is silent, taken aback by my outburst. I cannot stop there.

"Every time I do something, I am criticized for being ignorant, or foolish, or just plain sinful. If I laugh, people suspect that I am making fun of something. If I cry, I am not in control of myself. 'Control!' I hate that word! Is there no room for freedom, for laughter, for tears, for simple enjoyment? Can't we have pleasure, hard work, piety, and God all together? Why must we choose?"

Edward gets out of bed in his nightshirt and starts pacing the room, saying nothing. When he comes over and sits on the bed beside me, I can see dimly by the candle's light that he is seriously worried.

"I suppose that the news about Mistress Eaton and David has brought all this out," he says. "But I know that's not the only reason." I nod.

"You've not been having an easy time of it, ever since the beginning, have you? And I'm only just beginning to recognize just how hard this life has been on you. It is my fault. I have been too much preoccupied with the business of the colony to pay enough attention to my own darling wife."

"It's not your fault, it's mine. I should have made more of an effort to run the house, even though the servants are better at it. I didn't want to be shown up for my ignorance, but instead I am criticized for laziness. I try to be a good hostess, but that has failed every time. But the worst thing is, I have such contrary opinions to the rest of the people I know, with few exceptions. I have been trying to keep them to myself, but then I am thought to be foolish or obstinate, because I simply cannot agree with everything others believe.

"Now, because of the other Yale family troubles, I will be seen to be a heretic like the rest, just you wait and see."

I am so overcome with self-pity that I am dribbling tears. The salt runs into my eyes so that I can hardly see. I feel a pair of large comfortable arms envelop me.

"Don't, please, my dear love. Don't accuse yourself like that. It's not true. Come, now." He kisses my eyes, wipes my cheeks, and then just sits with his arms about me until I stop sniffing

"Thank you," I say, in a very small voice.

"This is a terrible time for you right now, and it's no wonder you feel so intensely everything else that goes wrong. This may be the worst moment in our life here, and perhaps God means it as a test of our faith, even though it takes such a toll on those we love. I do believe that this colony was founded through God's will, and that it will succeed eventually. I would like to continue on here and help it to become whatever God had in mind for it. It is a slow and rocky path we will have to take, though, I do admit."

Placing his hands on my shoulders he looks closely at me. "I am hoping that you are willing to share that path with me, Anne. I don't claim to know better than you about your own situation, and yet I am sure you are loved and respected by many, though right now you cannot see it. Shall we wait until all these troubles have been sorted out and, let's hope, disposed of, and then think some more about the future?"

"Yes, that's best," I say.

"In the meantime, do try to spend time with those you love and admire, and try to ignore the attitudes of the rest, if you can."

"I will."

Finally, he is beginning to understand how it is for me. I hope that will open his eyes to the devilish things that are spoken and done here. Edward always likes to think well of people. That is one of his great virtues. Right now, I would trade some of that goodness for a clearer understanding of our little world and our part in it.

18.

MISTRESS GOODWIN ASKED ME two days ago if I would like to go to the shops with her today. She is going to be measured for a new pair of boots and would like my opinion as to the leather and cost. Of course I said I would go with her. She has had such trouble walking recently that properly made boots may help, if only a little. I know nothing about the art of cobbling, but perhaps my presence as governor's wife will help to ensure that she will be given a good product at a fair price.

When she arrives I am shocked by her appearance. Her face is red, and she is breathing fast. "Come in, my friend, please, and sit down. You cannot go to town yet. Stay awhile and then let's see about it." I take her arm firmly, and she offers little resistance.

"Thank you, my dear. I think I should rest for a minute or two. I seem to have picked up a bit of a cold." She turns her head to blow into a handkerchief.

"Oh, you certainly have." I feel her forehead. "And a bit of a fever too, I'd say." She is blazing hot. "I think we should postpone our shopping for a day or two. Why don't we have a nice camomile tea instead. It may help your cold, and we can chat as well here as anywhere."

I hope I do not look as alarmed as I feel, but she does not notice anyway, and simply nods her head as she fumbles with a clean handkerchief.

I go out and find Nellie. "Can you bring us some tea, any remedy you know for a fever? I think Mistress Goodwin has influenza and I'm very worried."

Nellie puts her head in the door, sees Mistress Goodwin looking at her, and ducks out. "She looks bad, Mistress. I will make up a remedy, and then we should take her home to bed."

"I don't want to worry her. She thinks she just has a cold."

Nellie says, "Oh, no, she doesn't. She knows she is ill." That girl is growing wiser by the minute.

"Then why did she come to go shopping, I wonder?"

"She didn't want to upset you, she's that kind."

"She is, " I say. "You are right. So she will care for me rather than herself." Nellie nods.

I say nothing , taking this in. Then, "Hurry, girl, let us have that tea."

Mistress Goodwin and I have trouble finding much to say to one another while we wait, and then drink our tea. The fever dominates in her head, and I cannot think of anything but how she must be suffering, and of the worst that could happen. I can hardly wait until she has taken the last sip to suggest that I accompany her home. She agrees without protest.

Nellie and I each take an arm, and walk her the hundred yards or so to her house, step by creeping step. She tries to make light of it. "If only I had those new shoes we could have run home," and Nellie and I both force a laugh.

"Next week we will try that," I say.

At the door, Constance, her maid, reaches out to help her inside, her face pinched with worry. We say a quick goodbye.

We are both quiet on the way back. Just as we are turning in at our gate, I cry, "Oh, Nellie!" and she squeezes my hand quickly, and takes it away.

"Don't worry so, Mistress. She is in the Lord's hands, and he will surely look after her. She is one of the best."

I nod, and rush to my room, just as the tears come. A while later I am still sitting there, my forehead cradled in my hand, drained of all but a dull sense of — what? Loss? Abandonment? Misery, anyway. I will the feelings to go away, but they will not. I pray instead.

"Dear Lord, don't take her away. What shall I ever do without her?" How selfish of me!

"Lord, make her well, so she can serve you, and be a light to people like me who only think of themselves." Still selfish, only sneakily this time.

"Dear Lord, if you must take her away, help me to bear it." Really!

"Lord, it is up to you. She will be content whatever you do. And I will just have to get by. There, that's the best I can do right now."

19.

M R. HOOKER HAS BEEN AWAY in England for several months, preaching and bringing encouragement to the churches there. Reports tell us that civil strife still disrupts the country, and there is ongoing conflict between Anglicans, Presbyterians and the saints, whom everyone over there now calls Puritans. People have become discouraged, their lives a shambles, their faith crumbling. On his return, full of pity and grief for those he has left behind, Mr. Hooker calls for a day of humiliation to seek the Lord on behalf of the poor churches overseas.

I am so overjoyed to see him again, that, for the first part of his lecture I pay little attention. I try to listen, but inwardly I am absorbed in my own satisfaction that now there will be someone who can help me. I need someone to understand what a mess things are: my mother's possibly impending trial, my brother's troubles, and my own status in the community as an object of criticism soon to be an object of disgust due to my family's deviance.

Then I start to wonder, should I tell him all that? Should I divulge how I feel about living in this community among so many censuring people? Should I say that my only real friend, apart from one who is dying, is outside the fold, a heretic whom he will think should know better? That I am sometimes so homesick for my native land I would rather be there, even if it means putting up with all the conflict he has been speaking about?

All of this I want to tell him. Mr. Hooker will understand and not condemn. He speaks now, words I can hear:

"I have listened to many people overseas, both high and low born, and all they speak about is the evil of the times: the lives that have become dissolute, the families that have been divided amongst themselves, the once faithful who have gone away in anger and contempt. They say that the Lord has left them to their fate, and has removed his protection. They say that he has turned his face from them and towards us, and that it is here that he will make his New Jerusalem.

"What they are saying is true. When we left our beloved homeland, we were sorry to go, but we knew that the Lord was taking us away in order to accomplish his new purpose here. As he did to the children of Israel, he drew us into the wilderness where we should be tested and humbled and learn true repentance for our sins. But he did not leave us to wander around unprotected. Around this New England he has set a hedge, to keep us safe from our enemies without and within.

"This hedge that surrounds us represents the laws of God and the magistrates who carry them out. You can see how well they safeguard us. We have fought against the savages and conquered them. We have survived every terror this wilderness holds. When lives have been lost, it has been God's purpose to humble us thereby and persuade us to trust in him. During all these perils, the Lord has been a sun and shield to us, keeping our hedge tall and whole.

"In our earliest days, the hedge was there to protect us from enemies beyond its limits. Today we must plant it more closely, in order to keep us safely within the bounds. Our colonies today are an assembly of the saved and the unregenerate. Even our churches contain some who are faithful and sincere hearted, some counterfeit and false hearted. The laws of God and the counsels of his magistrates and ministers are there to prevent the faithful from becoming corrupted by those unbelievers who would tempt them away from the truth."

Oh, but see what this hedge has done to my mother. It has closed her in so tightly she cannot breathe. So she has tried to break through, and its thorns are tearing her to pieces.

"Our church is the fruitful garden that God has surrounded by his hedge.

Beware of trying to go through that hedge, for the thorns in it will prick you, and you will bleed miserably. And do not think for a minute that this hedge should be torn down. If that were ever to happen, our plentiful garden would be overrun by the wilderness beyond it."

As people bend their heads to thank God for his hedge of grace, and to pray for their continuing safety and deeper faith, I know without a doubt that I can not confide in Mr. Hooker, good man that he is. This hedged in society that is cause of my misery is his delight. The thought only adds to my misery. There is nowhere else to turn.

IV
Hartford, 1645

1.

TODAY EDWARD AND I return from Boston during the heaviest rainstorms of the season. The carriage ploughs and stumbles its way through the mud-soaked roads, but even the driver's care for our well-being — holding the horses to a walk over the worst spots — does not help much. The new, highly praised main road to Hartford must have been laid without a layer of stones, because it is jarringly uneven and broken by deep hollows in places where there are old rotting logs underneath, which formed an earlier track. Edward tells me it was built by labourers from the Bay Colony, so it was not his fault the construction was so poor.

It is a wonder we are not stuck in some muddy trough and have to wade to the nearest refuge. Rain and brown water come through the gaps in the thick curtains, spattering us steadily. Occasionally, when the carriage dives into a deep gully, water comes in over the floorboards. Our cloaks, my safeguard petticoat, and everything underneath including my shift are blotched and sodden at the hems. Edward's cloak and breeches, made especially for the Confederation meetings, are probably ruined. No wonder highwaymen look so pathetically bedraggled, a far cry from the gallant figures of the old tales.

It is dangerous to look outside, for fear of stones or flying mud dashing into our faces. So, for most of the two-day thirty-mile drive, we travel in deep gloom, not knowing where we are, or even the time of day. The moist stench of a spring slow to cast off its winter bindings seeps inside. I hold Edward's hand for reassurance, but from what peril I cannot say.

From time to time he pats my shoulder, in an attempt to calm my silent trembling. It is almost supper time when we arrive in Hartford, and dark as deepest ignorance, as Mr. Hooker would say.

At home at last, the prospect of having the first moments to myself in almost ten days revives me. It surprises me how glad I am to be home, an uncommon sensation of late.

The first thing I do after closing the door of my chamber is to look for my journal. It had been decided before we left, by Edward in consultation with Henry, that in our absence all the rooms would be given a good spring cleaning. It did not surprise me that he did not ask me about it, as he knows how much I dislike telling the servants what to do. They think they know better than I, and of course they are right most of the time. With Edward it is quite another matter: he is the master. When I heard about the housecleaning, I took Nellie into my chamber and closed the door carefully. "Please, Nellie, take my journal from here" — I showed her its hiding place — "and put it away safely in your room during the cleaning. When my chamber is finished, you can put it back. Whatever you do, do not let anyone see it."

"I'll hide it well, mistress," she said. "I know how you treasure it."

"Sometimes I think that it is the only thing that keeps me sane," I said.

"It wouldn't do that for me," Nellie said. "Reading and writing as you do would drive me mad."

I laughed. Nellie's open nature and kindheartedness are good for me. Each morning she bustles around the room, bending like a wishbone to pick up a piece of lint or a dropped pin, as if her entire though unexamined aim in life is to keep me in a state of chaste cleanliness.

She was as good as her word. The journal is tucked between the layers of the cushion on the commode chair, a seat no one uses but me, and is the most private place in the chamber. I feel the relief sweep over me. This journal is my dearest possession. I don't know what I would do if I lost it.

Nellie has taken my mud-stained clothes to see what can be done for them, and I tell Edward I need some time to rest after such an unsettling journey. Ever since our visit to Boston, he has become even gentler towards me than before, if that is possible. He has always been the kindest of men, even if at the same time I wonder how much he understands me.

I would like to begin to record the events of the last week, but I am too tired for that. Tomorrow I will make a start at it. Perhaps by then I will be able to determine what it all means, and what I can do about it.

It is now a week later, and I still have not been able to write a word since Boston, on account of a cold I caught on the way home. Everyone worries about my health, expecting the worst ailments to follow the least ones. So I have been visited hourly by both Ardyth and Nellie with posset ale for my dry throat, syrups for my cough, and salve to place on my forehead in case I cannot sleep. All these remedies, especially the consumption of ale and aquavit, make my head ache, which, when I mention it to Nellie, brings out another odd-smelling substance to be pasted on each temple. With all this to-ing and fro-ing, and the overwhelming waft of competing smells, sleep is impossible, even though I feel as though I have spent every day in a tavern. From then on, when they ask me how I am feeling, I say, "Much better, thank you." If I were to mention that my back is sore, or my stomach upset, or, worst of all, that I cannot keep my head up straight, it would be sure to bring on another consultation, followed by some noxious mixture which I must, in order to placate them, consume.

Today I am a lot stronger and clear-headed, despite the physic. The one good thing that has come out of the last five days of treatment as an invalid is that I have been unable to think about anything except the immediate needs of my body. The anxiety that plagued me during the Boston visit has been kept at bay, and seems to have quietened down for the present. This means that I can begin to set my thoughts in order without the heavy chill of fear bearing down.

When Nellie comes in to tidy the chamber, I am dressed and sitting in a chair at the open window. Seeing Nellie's concern deepen into a frown, I say, "I feel so well today, I think some fresh air will do me good. I am going to go and sit in the garden for a bit. You needn't fuss about me. I have my cloak and the sun is plenty warm enough now."

I go downstairs, the sounds of Nellie's tut-tutting following me. Beside the little orchard at the side of the house, near the back, we now have a new, smooth cedar bench in a bower of lilacs and honeysuckle, where I can be invisible to both the occupants of the house and the passersby. I wrap myself snugly in my thick kersey cloak. This part of the garden is a good place to sit and think. I am not ready to put anything on paper yet.

How does it happen that an excursion that should have brightened my dull spirits has turned out to have exactly the opposite effect? Why am I now, after a week of entertainment, warmth, and civility, unhappier than before I left home? And why is it, after such friendly advances from the finest, most charitable people, that I am less inclined than ever to expose my feelings to anyone, feelings that sometimes probe and scrape at my body like knives? If understanding the reason for these feelings will not make them go away, it might at least give me the means of controlling them. I will not let these passions get the better of me, if I can help it.

It all began so well. When Edward first suggested that I accompany him to Boston, I was delighted. We were sitting after dinner in the parlour, a modest fire burning on the hearth. The circumstances were so unusual that I knew something important was afoot. Normally we do not sit in this room during the day, so the fire is never lit this early. That Edward would stay at home after his noon meal was also peculiar. He looked a little apprehensive, but at the same time rather pleased with himself as he leaned back and grasped the arms of his chair.

"The governor has invited us both to stay with him for a few days next week before the Confederation meetings begin, and I have accepted for both of us. We will have enough time to look around the city and admire all the new construction. And I'll take you down to the harbour to see my ship, which should arrive from the Bahamas while we are there. You would like to go, wouldn't you, Anne?"

"Of course I would! But I'm astonished that the governor asks us to come for a visit, when he has so many more important matters to occupy him, with the meetings and all. He has always been generous towards us, though. I am quite honoured."

"It is an honour, but as you say, he has always had a tender regard for little Hartford and for us." His smile betrayed his pride in the matter.

"And I will be able to see David, too!" I was sitting up straight now, even more excited. This would be my true pleasure in this visit.

"Most certainly. In fact, Governor Winthrop has suggested that during the four days when the New England Confederation meets, you should go and stay with your brother. It seems like a good arrangement, as I will be busy day and night with the other governors."

"I would love that. It's been over two years since I have laid eyes on him, and his wife, and now there's the new baby." I think back to our last visit; it was so brief. David was on his way to Springfield to meet some new suppliers and he stopped in for a quick chat.

I continue, excited at the prospect of an imminent visit with my brother. "He writes me that they have named their baby David too, and that he is very lively and acts just like his father. I must think of something to take him: perhaps I have time to sew a little smock before we go." I was already thinking about the fine wool and the silk thread I would use. I wondered if there was enough cloth in the chest, or whether I would have to search out some more.

Edward, bending to poke the fire, replied evenly, "I shouldn't attempt that, Anne. You haven't had a needle in your hand for months. Perhaps you could ask Nellie's mother to make something for you to take."

I leaned forward abruptly. "Oh, but I would much rather make something myself. After all, he's my first nephew, and the son of my favourite brother." My voice came out in a rushed, staccato, which I knew was not a good sign. I tried to stay calm.

He looked down thoughtfully, as if making sure to use the right words. "No, I really must insist on it. Your health is so delicate, and the strain of doing such careful work in a hurry would take its toll. It might even make you too ill to travel."

"It's only a wee smock," I said, with a bit of a whimper, "Well, I suppose I must give up the idea. Perhaps there isn't enough time." I settled in the chair limply, but not too dramatically, so as not to draw attention to the dejection I was feeling. This was an outcome I was accustomed to. Many things had become forbidden for the sake of my health.

Ever since the incident with Edward's birthday pudding, I kept away from the affairs of the kitchen, to everyone's satisfaction but my own. I would have loved to learn from Cook how to prepare a few choice dishes to present to my husband. The question of my health has affected everything I do.

For a time, I continued to attend the women's circle. Then, several weeks in a row I came home in a great hurry, running down the walk and into the house, my eyes burning with angry tears. I could not bear any more talk of the Lord's horrible yet providential punishments of heretics and backsliders. Whenever the gossipers came round to discussing decent people I knew, the Johnsons in particular, I could hardly restrain myself from shouting at them, "Stop it, you whited sepulchres!" I did not report any of this to Edward as he would have thought I was exaggerating. He noticed my behaviour, though, which convinced him that the meetings were a terrible strain on my health, so he suggested I give them up. I was so grateful that he had relieved me of going that I was happy with any excuse he would make for me, even if I disagreed with it. He said that he explained to Mistress Hooker that I was undergoing a difficult period, and said no more. Tongues must have wagged deliciously at that cryptic statement.

My health, my health! Some days I would have gladly allowed my body to collapse to its weakest level, for the chance of a few moments of joyous living. Body's life for the soul's life — a holy exchange, one would think.

Edward was speaking. "We must try hard to keep you well. You will have enough on your mind, deciding what to pack for the journey."

I knew it was not my body he was worried about, but my mind. Though I was as capable of reason as always, he seemed terrified that something might snap, and I would be lost.

With that, the subject of the smock for baby David was dropped, and we went on to talk about Boston, how much it had changed since my last visit, and what we planned to see. I duly spoke to Nellie, whose mother produced a fine, soft smock, neatly sewn, for the new nephew. He would never know the difference between her work and mine anyway, I told myself, so why should I be unhappy about it?

Edward was right. I did have plenty to do with regard to arranging my wardrobe. A visit to the governor's house in the most important town in the colonies meant that I must look my best. Looking over my clothes with Nellie, I saw how shabby they had become, like those of a woman who had laboured on the farm from dawn till sunset, and had lain down on her bed too exhausted to worry about her appearance. But how unlike my life that was: it seemed as if the gowns had gone out to work and left me behind, neither they nor I noticing what was wrong. Nellie would have her days full, and her evenings too, just trying to repair and refresh the collars and aprons, the stockings and petticoats. After all that effort, the shabbiness would still not have disappeared.

I was relieved that I had kept one gown aside out of those I had brought from England so long ago now, to be saved for an important event. Edward told me that Governor Winthrop was giving a dinner for all the governors and their wives. The gown was certainly old, but hardly worn, and not too frivolous for Massachusetts society, with a good lace collar but little embroidery. The lavender silk was appropriate for a formal dinner, so I would not disgrace Edward on this occasion. For the rest of the week, dowdy little Anne Hopkins would have to do. I wondered whether people would think it was piety and not negligence that made me so.

The party gown having been decided, there was the question of what to wear for the journey. After examining everything carefully for indelible stains, patches, and worn spots, I saw that I had no other choice but the green wool costume, which I had sworn never to wear again. Pushed to the back of the closet, I had made myself believe it was out of sight, out of mind. Now I stared at it once again, willing my anxiousness to go away. It would not.

I am back on the Hector, pacing the deck. It is March 15, 1638, a date I will never forget. I recall the swollen lurching of the sea, the rumble of the sky overhead, the slapping of wood on wood, the squealing of ropes in tension, my mother dragging me into the cabin, and then everything stopped.

What I refused to allow breathing room for was the surge of terror that had started to engulf me at that moment. I determined to wear the same clothes again to Boston. Everything was different now. Edward would keep me safe this time. Perhaps. I was not quite sure.

2.

I PULL MY CLOAK AROUND ME, to hold myself together. The garden is not as peaceful as when I first sat down. A few bees are nuzzling on the first of the apple blossoms, and a pair of robins race back and forth. They are big red-breasted birds, so unlike the charming little robins I loved in Wales. These two are carrying beakloads of cumbersome building materials for their new home in the chestnut tree. From the dairy comes the regular thump thump of the churn, which is Ardyth giving it her sturdy best. There is no butter like the Hopkins', I have heard it said, but if you look at the meadow our cows graze upon, it stands to reason. In the distance, I hear two lads bantering in the stable yard, then splashing sounds, and then more laughter. More water goes on them than on the horses.

I turn my mind away from the smooth familiarity of the present, and back to the troubling events of the week in Boston. By starting at the beginning I may discover the root of my discomfort.

We travelled down on the packet boat *Eliza*, arriving at the harbour just at dusk. Edward had ordered a carriage to be made, to be the first of its kind in Hartford, and we were to travel home in it. The little *Eliza* was quite comfortable, much more so as it turned out than that new carriage on the body-shaking journey home.

Boston had grown quite large. Edward told me there were almost six hundred households in the city, and building was proceeding at a furious rate. On landing, we found a cart driver right away who was willing to take our trunk and boxes to the governor's house, a fair distance from the jetty. Edward insisted that I sit on the cart with the driver, and as there was no more room, he walked beside it. I said that I could use the walk too after the boat trip, but later when I saw how far we had come and how steep the climb, I was glad to have been talked out of it.

It was almost dark by the time we reached the Winthrops' house, so I had no chance to see any of the shops or new enterprises that had been opened since my last visit. As the next day was the Sabbath, shopkeepers were putting up their shutters early, and hurrying home to finish their preparations. In Boston, they were even stricter about Sabbath observances than in Hartford.

The governor himself and Mistress Winthrop came to the door to greet us. The Winthrops were noted for their lack of pretension, and yet this was the couple deemed to be the royal family of New England, even if such words were never spoken. I warmed to them both on first glance. The governor was a handsome, well-formed man who carried himself upright, but not stiffly. He wore his long brown curly hair swept back off his high forehead, setting off widely spaced eyes above a fine straight nose. A carefully trimmed moustache and beard did not disguise a mouth that I soon discovered could indicate tenderness and firmness at the same time. His wife was a fair match for him. When she stood beside her husband, who was quite short, she seemed much taller. Except for a few scars on her face left over from the smallpox, her clear grey eyes and gently curving mouth gave her a noble appearance. As the days went by, I watched for the twinkle in those eyes and a twitch of her lips hinting that she found something amusing — something that she should not be entertained by — though she would not say so out loud. Her covert sense of humour kept her human, though certainly not ordinary. Luckily for me, Mistress Winthrop was not the perfectly pious woman I expected. She became one of my favourite people.

The Winthrops welcomed us warmly, the two men embracing, as good friends. This was unusual in New England, where bodies made barriers, not bridges. We were offered a glass of cider and then, after a short discussion of our journey, I was invited to take a rest before supper, which I accepted with relief.

"Don't bother to change out of your travelling clothes," Mistress Winthrop said kindly. "We shall have a light supper, just the four of us, and after that you can have a good long sleep. I am sure you need it."

The maid, who was to attend me, showed me to my chamber, where my clothes had already been taken from the trunk and placed in the press. I lay down on the bed fully clothed and in what seemed like an instant later, there was a knock on the door, and Edward came to take me down to supper. Mistress Winthrop had spoken the truth: it was a light meal of fresh cod and mussels, with some hearty vegetables and a little candied fruit. Except for the great feast on Tuesday evening for all the governors and their wives, the meals at the governor's mansion were filling but not elaborate. I was told later by one of the wives that the governor had become quite impoverished as it had taken so much of his fortune to look after the affairs of the Bay Colony. They said that he never turned anyone away from his door who had need.

That night at supper I had little to say, as both my body and mind were weary, the one from the exertion of the journey, the other from trying to adjust to the new circumstances. There was a certain formality that we lacked at home. Every statement was taken as seriously as if it were a minister's pronouncement. When the governor asked me what I thought of the new government's views on the education of children, I looked at him uncomprehendingly. I was so bewildered and exhausted that I could not even remember what those views were. So I simply said, "I don't have any children to teach."

Mistress Winthrop looked at me sympathetically. "Don't trouble Mistress Hopkins with questions tonight, Mr. Winthrop. She is very tired and should sleep."

"Of course, I shouldn't have been so thoughtless. Let us finish off now, and let you go," he said patiently.

After reading a few short psalms, and leading us in prayer, the governor stood up, and wished me goodnight. "I hope I may keep your husband with me for a while longer, Mistress. I value his opinions, and I am certainly in need of them right now."

"Of course you may." I bowed, and bade them all goodnight, went over and squeezed Edward's hand, and left the room.

Mistress Winthrop followed me into the hall to say, "Please ask if there's anything you need. I hope you will have a very pleasant visit in Boston."

"I'm sure I will, thank you, Mistress. It was so kind of you to invite us here."

"Goodnight, then." She smiled in that way she had, that made you think that you and she were sharing a little secret, and left the hall in the direction of the kitchen.

I slept so soundly that I did not even hear Edward come into the bed.

Sunshine poured into our room the next morning, as if to celebrate what Mr. Hooker calls the "magnificent day." Besides announcing the Sabbath, it seemed to me that the sun was shining on the next days' ventures, or so I hoped. I got up early so as to take in as much of our surroundings as possible before being summoned downstairs.

The chamber we were given was a large one, with a high-beamed ceiling and two great windows. The furnishings were grander than ours, no doubt the work of some highly skilled Boston craftsmen. I ran my hand over the satin surface of the chest, traced the faultless carving with my fingers, and sighed with pleasure. All the hangings, about the bed, on the windows and covering the clothes cupboard were of a rich blue linen. On a bright day such as this, they were the colour of the distant bay. The glass in the windows was thick but clear, so I could see perfectly the ships floating serenely at anchor. On the street in front of the governor's house all was quiet too. Even the dust seemed to have settled. The town was preparing for divine service.

As we descended the gleaming oak staircase, I was able to have a better idea of the whole mansion. The rooms were spacious, the proportions well-suited to their use, although with such high ceilings the rooms must be impossible to keep warm in winter. I admired especially the small parlour with its narrow leaded glass windows, and the woven woollen hangings on the walls to keep out any draughts. There was a high backed settee beside the fireplace where Governor and Mistress Winthrop usually sat in the evening, side by side. They were very loving towards each other. I could see this in little ways, as when she leaned over to catch his eye, or came around to straighten his collar, and he smiled back at her. Edward told me that they read together almost every evening when they were alone.

We had a scant breakfast in the hall, a glass of cider and a fresh roll. Then, as soon as the town bell began to toll, we set out all together for the church, about a quarter of a mile away. The two governors walked first, then Mistress Winthrop and myself, and following behind were all the servants in their proper order. As we started out, I could see that we were not the first to stir. The streets were already crowded with families, mostly on foot. Those who must have come from a distance, trotted along on horseback. Nary a carriage was to be seen; only one donkey cart bringing two old, rheumy and infirm people. No one seemed in a great hurry, Friends waited for each other to catch up, and conversed along the way, sedately as befitted the day. I felt a twinge of something I would hate to call jealousy, for the way in which they seemed to get along with each other in such congenial fashion. I wished it could be the same in Hartford, but then I left such a depressing thought alone.

In my Sunday best — a black flannel dress and small lace cap — I slipped into the crowd outside the door quite unnoticed, as all the women looked pretty much the same. Mistress Winthrop took me by the hand, and to my surprise led me down the aisle and into the front pew. Then all eyes fell on me, I was sure, even though I could not see them. It was such an honour to be placed beside the governor's wife. I looked across the aisle slyly, and out of the corner of my eye I could see that the governor had put my governor beside him also. A great day for little Hartford.

Mr. Cotton was a fine preacher, almost as fine as Mr. Hooker. I had heard him once before in England, but never at such length. Although he used an hourglass to time himself, when the top half was empty he absentmindedly turned it over again and continued to speak. The sermon was based on *Luke* 17:4, and verses 7-10, on brotherly correction and service. His manner of speaking, plainly but without severity, made the first hour go by painlessly, but when he turned the hourglass once again, I grew restless, although I tried not to show it. Guiltily, I admitted to myself that I could not remember anything he said in that last hour. I was sure it was important, and would have enlightened me, but my body was crying out, please stop.

Eventually the service was over, but we could not go back to the mansion to eat until the governor and his wife had greeted many people, and introduced Edward and me to most of them. I bowed to Mr. Cotton and thanked him for his uplifting words; then I stepped back quickly for fear he would ask me which words lifted me up the most. I could not have told him to save my soul.

At dinner, in the great parlour, we were all supposed to discuss the sermon too. Fortunately Edward had listened well, so he could hold up the family's honour. I was terrified that I would be asked to contribute, and tried to think what I could say: "I am sorry, but my mind wandered. I was thinking what a lovely day it was, and how sad to have to be sitting inside where we cannot see the flowers and the fresh new grass. On one tree whose limbs stretch across the window on the women's side of the church, I saw a squirrel stop on a branch, shake his bristly tail, and sit up straight as if he were taking in the words of life. I thought then of the squirrels at Plâs Grono, playing at being circus performers among the oaks in the great park. I chased away the memory of my old Welsh home before the longing could overwhelm me."

I could not tell them that. So when I was asked a question, I kept myself to short remarks. If they thought that I had an empty head in which nothing of interest lodged — well then, so be it.

They were ten for dinner: two merchants whom Edward knew, and their wives, and the governor's son, Mr. John Winthrop, the younger, and his young wife, Elizabeth. Young Mr. Winthrop and Edward were old friends, having made their first voyage to New England together the year before our marriage, but I had not met him before. He was rumoured to be as capable as his father, perhaps even more so. Already he has been elected assistant to the Bay Colony and was certain to be a governor himself one day. Edward had remarked on his abilities in law and medicine as well as his experience in business affairs. He sat beside me at the table at dinner, so I was able to judge his character well by the time the day was over. I found him very amiable.

In between the two meals I rested in the beautiful blue chamber and then joined the others in the hall for the walk back to the church for afternoon service. Mr. Winthrop surprised me by asking if he could walk with me to hear some news of Hartford. The talk at dinner had been general, and I took little part in it. This was the first time we had conversed together. So, with Edward walking behind us with young Mistress Winthrop, we strolled along the road, he thoughtfully matching his long, springing stride to mine while I tried to answer his questions as best I could. The trouble was, I did not know very much about the town's activities, since I seldom went out in company any more, so there was not much I could tell him. He must have realized that, because he began to ask different questions.

"I hear that you are a prolific writer, Mistress Hopkins. What sort of writing do you do? Is it stories for children? I know there are many helpful children's books written now, both here in the colonies and in England." His eyes under the heavy brows were deep brown, but when the sun struck them I thought they were more like agates, streaks of blue and green whirling around in a pool of chestnut. His interest in what I said was keen, his eyes told me.

"I have never written for children. You must be a mother to do that." My eyes were beginning to burn, and I felt tears coming on.

He waited for me to say more, but I could not speak as I was trying to stop myself from crying. I was not going to tell him how hard Edward and I had tried to have children, without success. That every time we decided to try again, we became more and more discouraged, until we decided it was making us both so unhappy. Not that it was my fault, Edward insisted. It was simply that God did not will it.

We walked a few minutes in silence. He seemed to understand what was happening to me. Finally, he asked gently, "What do you write, then?"

"I don't write very much now." We took a few more steps, and then I said, "I did compose a journal a while back about spring in Connecticut. There was one after that about the following winter."

"Were they printed at the Boston Press?"

"No, I sent them to a friend in England who had them copied, and then passed them around to some of her acquaintances. I don't know what happened to them after that."

"I should like to see them," he said warmly.

"I don't have a copy. My brother or my mother may—" I stopped abruptly. I should never have mentioned my mother, especially among the rulers of the colonies. How could I have been so foolish? My nervousness will ruin everything. I was trembling now, and even closer to tears.

Mr. Winthrop looked grave. I said, "I am sorry. I shouldn't have spoken about her right now."

He nodded, and said, not unkindly, "Her troubles are in New Haven, not here. We are all praying for her. Don't be upset at speaking of her. She is your mother, and I am sure she is a good one."

I had only time to give a weak smile, and a "Thank you," because we had arrived at the church.

Later I wrote this in my journal:

May 1, 1645

"It is remarkable how one's emotions can change intensity and colour so quickly under different circumstances. My sadness, which, despite Mr. Winthrop's kindly manner, was growing with every step I took along the road to church, was torn away as if it had never existed, once we went inside. As before we sat in the front pews, and because of this, I was forcing myself to listen with all my wits, so as not to shame my husband or myself. Then the singing of the psalms began.

"I could hardly believe my ears; in fact, it pained them so much to hear those sounds that I wished I could stop them up with wool to keep the noise out. There could not be any worse singing in the entire New England. To begin with, the singer who 'lined out' the psalm was tone deaf, I was sure, for he could not find any sort of tune no matter how he struggled for it. So the congregation had to begin its part with the group of misaligned notes he offered them. Then, since each person chose his or her own tune to follow, and all began on different notes, the result was a caterwauling that to my mind was more like the noise one was likely to hear below, not on earth. I could not believe that those who decided'on this sort of singing thought they were praising the Almighty. It made a mockery of freedom of worship. I kept my head down, so people would not notice that I was silent.

"I was so furious at the damage that was being done to our sensibilities and to the good name of music that all thoughts of my own unhappiness were driven off. It took me well into Mr. Cotton's sermon to quieten my heart and my nerves after such a travesty. In the end, I was calmed, and ready to ask forgiveness for my anger, which I hoped did not show. I would not insult my hosts for anything, or the good people of that place. I only wish they were more in tune with the true sounds of God's creation.

"The best part of the whole day was meeting young Mr. Winthrop. I felt as though he could read me, quite uncritically, and that he liked what he had learned."

After supper, my mind was still tossing around the contradictory events of the day, as Governor Winthrop began the evening prayers. He thanked God for the blessings of this Sabbath, and for the boon of godly company to share it. Then he asked that divine love and grace be bestowed upon the King, the Massachusetts Bay Colony, and the rest of the colonies, especially Connecticut. He prayed for the souls of their families, for those in peril of their faith, and for those in doubt or despair. Finally, he commended all the saints to the Lord.

I heard the words that seemed directed towards me personally, a lump rose in my chest, and tears welled up in my eyes. As we finished our devotions my predicament was obvious, though I tried to keep my hand over my face for a time as if I were still praying. I did not think anyone there would understand, and naturally I dared not explain. I thought, if only young Mr. Winthrop were still here; he would have recognized the cause of my unhappiness, remembering the words we had had about my mother. But he had left right after the service.

For the third time in the last twenty-four hours I was left with nothing I could say, and emotions I could not give way to. The room felt suddenly oppressive. I stood abruptly, said, "Please excuse me," and left. Once inside my chamber I sat on the bed, my heart pounding, my temples throbbing.

That night my sleep was disturbed by dreams vivid enough to wake me, and make me wonder if they were real. In most of them the people were unfamiliar, the places unknown to me. But in my last dream, I was following my mother into a room crowded with strange, staring faces, when the door was closed against me, leaving me outside. I woke clutching the bedclothes.

3.

THE NEXT DAY, the sun came out even more satisfyingly than on Sunday, and Edward proposed a visit to the harbour and the shipyards. Not only had his ship come in from the Indies, but he also had an interest in another ship being built there, the first in Boston designed for Atlantic crossings. His enthusiasm for the project was apparent as he discussed the plans for its future voyages with Governor Winthrop over breakfast. The governor had a small share in the new vessel, and pitched in eagerly to the conversation. He had not had time to visit the shipyard recently, and was keen to hear from Edward how the work was progressing.

Edward and I went first to the harbour where his own ship, the trusty *Susannah,* was berthed. Several other ships had arrived from the West Indies, bringing sugar, a small portion of which would stay here, the rest going on to England where sugar was in short supply. On the *Susannah,* the unloading of her cargo was finished, and the heavier task of bringing the colonies' goods on board was underway. For this time, the *Susannah* would be carrying masts of pine to outfit ships of His Majesty's navy. New England was now the best supplier of pine, her forests still rich with the tall species needed for great vessels. Part of our wealth in Connecticut came from these noble giants.

We strolled along the jetty, Edward pointing out the sailors of his own ship as they hoisted the long, stalwart trees on their shoulders and walked them carefully to the ship. Their backs were straight as washboards, and the muscles on their arms rippled like waves. I thought them handsome, especially seeing how their sun-baked skin glistened with their exertion.

"When will they embark, and to which port do they sail?" I asked.

"Tomorrow, for Portsmouth. It will take them over six weeks with this full cargo."

"Will the sailors stay at home for a while, or must they turn around quickly and go to sea again?"

"Except for the captain and his officers, the sailors have only been hired for this one triangular voyage, from England to the Bahamas, then to Boston and back to England. If they have proved themselves they will be hired on again. The captain decides who goes and who stays."

"Let's go and speak with them, Edward, and ask where they come from. Perhaps some of them live in Welsh country. I would love to hear some news of my old home!"

Edward caught the mute pleading in my eyes, and dismissed it quietly. "We cannot disrupt their work for that, Anne."

"Could we go on board when they have finished? Just for a short while?" I had already guessed that my request was hopeless, but still I had to ask.

"They will be exhausted by then, and I can well imagine they will be putting away many tins of ale. You have no idea how befuddled these men can get. They would be far more likely to toss unseemly compliments to you than to satisfy your curiosity about Wales."

"I wish I could return with them," I said in a whisper, turning my head away, for my eyes were filling up again.

It came back to me then, just a glimpse of an old lost time, a memory I had buried until now. There was a round cool bay with a tiny white boat dancing far out on the water, almost at the edge of the world, and I was jumping up and down on the sand waving it home. I was so excited I thought I would never be able to wait until the person in the boat came to shore. Then the picture was gone.

Edward had heard me. "I know you do. Perhaps we can go back for a visit before too long. Right now, our lives are in Connecticut, and there is much to be done here."

That is true for you, I thought. My life is as empty as a beggar's palm.

With Edward guiding my steps, we made our awkward way along the harbourfront to the shipyards on the other side of the bay. Every sort of maritime activity was taking place, along with the loading and unloading of exotic cargo. Men were mending sails, replacing ropes, painting and patching the boats. We had to make a wide detour around the smoking barrels of pitch, where frenzied men were dipping in their swabs and rushing to coat the sides of the vessel with the thick hot substance. Other obstacles lay in our way: coils of rope, or boxes and barrels abandoned on their sides, some split open by mischance and their contents spread over the dock. There were mounds of slippery grains, a case with bottles of India ink fortunately still unharmed, and another whose pretty wooden dolls had cascaded onto the boardwalk, their painted faces scored and chipped, orphans ready for a foundlings' home.

I hardly noticed these things, except when someone, seeing me about to catch my foot on a piece of sharp debris, would shout, "Watch out, mistress! Take care, sir!" I was back dreaming again of Colwyn Bay, not far from my old home. It was not the cool breeze of Massachusetts Bay with its smell of salt and rotten fish that blew sand into my hair and across my face; no it was the lovely wind coming off the Irish Sea, blowing the sand into my hair and across my face. The bay I saw in my mind's eye sparkled with small fishing boats, such little slivers of wood, taken from nature, then formed and given back to another element, the sea. I was thinking that the trim little boats were humanity's contribution to the greater realm, an enhancement offered to the love feast of men and sea together. I brought myself back to the jetty where I stood. Here were wooden vessels too, built to travel great distances, to bring wealth and civilization, to dominate the ocean and survive its perils. I feared we would lose our fondness for the sea if we treated it only as an instrument to help us prosper.

The new ship, when we finally reached the yard where it was being constructed, was a remarkable sight. The longest vessel ever built in New England, its skeleton stretched along the ground like a mythical beast come to destroy the world. It lay inert as it waited for its skin to be hammered on like a suit of armour. Then, it would take to the sea with such strength it would force the winds to let it pass. I saw it, not as an economic venture bringing great rewards, but as a monster whose allegiance would be uncertain. I did not voice these unreasonable thoughts, however, but stood in silence looking at the mighty hulk. Edward probably took my speechlessness for admiration, not shuddering awe. I could see how pleased he was with it, as he strolled its length, hands behind his back, nodding courteously to the shipbuilding crew.

It was a long walk back from the shipyards along Cornhill Street and its bustling commerce. Strangely for me, I hardly glanced at the shop windows displaying the latest English imports, except when Edward drew my attention to something — the handsome gallyware dishes decorated with blue birds sitting among ferns and flowers from Master Wilhelm's Southwark workshop, a silver knife, a pair of soft leather shoes whose workmanship had not yet been mastered in New England. My mind kept shifting elsewhere, although I must say I did covet the shoes.

Every so often we would be stopped by some worthy gentleman who grasped Edward's hand genially and bowed deferentially to me. My husband was well known in this town, having travelled back and forth on business affairs several times a year. To me, these merchants were strangers, their lives occupying another atmosphere than mine. I had no distaste for them; their remoteness carried no weight of emotion at all. I smiled a "Good day" as best I could, aware that my greeting had probably missed its mark.

4.

I N THE GARDEN, the sun has climbed to its noonday height, yet I shiver a little, rememberinghow cross Edward had been with me. He is,
overall a fair-tempered man, but sometimes he finds my behaviour trying,
especially when his pride is involved. Oh yes, he was proud enough to
want to keep up appearances. A governor's wife must act in a particular
fashion as he plainly made clear: "Can you not make a greater effort to
be courteous to these gentlemen? They are the leaders of the community.
I wish you would not snub them so." At times like that, he forgot about
my supposedly delicate health.

I cannot recall my answer, except that it did not satisfy him, and he
wore a pouty disapproving look for some time afterwards. How was I to
explain that my silence did not mean disrespect? That it was hard for me
to send words over such a vast distance, like moths in the gloom, fluttering
in and out of some formless cavern? I could not tell him then, or now,
that those traders and I had nothing in common, and that the tongue we
shared, though English, was not the same at all.

Here in my own little orchard I am aware again of the brisk humming
of the bees, the sharp pebbles probing the thin soles of my boots, the
fading apple blossoms falling on my hair. A tiny chipmunk scoots along
the walk in front of me, and beyond in the cowshed, a mother moos over
her infant. I let the whole bucolic atmosphere enter my being. I could be
so happy here, if everything could stay like this always. With just Edward
beside me, and my books I should never get tired of it. But I fool myself

to think that such a life could be possible. Even if we two could live like our first parents, it would not be paradise. My fears and my memories, all my blunders and regrets, will always keep me company. How I wish we had never come here!

Putting these thoughts away, I turn reluctantly back to my recollections of Boston. It was the evening of the formal dinner that Governor and Mistress Winthrop were giving for the heads of the other colonies and some of their assistants. I spent quite a lot of time in my chamber, dressing myself with care. This night I must do my best, both for my husband's sake and my own too. I would make up for any earlier lapses in social behaviour. After all, I knew how to act; it was only some mistake, some accident, that had prevented me from doing my part well up till now. When we came in from our walk a few hours earlier, I barely greeted the governor, my thoughts being miles away. He probably thought me rude, but I would show him I was indeed a congenial person, and could appear quite comfortable in company, even if it was just a pretense.

At dinner I was seated facing the governor who was resplendent in his scarlet jacket, and a deep ruff bordered with delicate lace. The place opposite, on the governor's right hand, would by rights have been occupied by the guest of the highest standing, the wife of the governor of New Haven, my mother. As she was unable to appear at public functions, at least for the time being, Governor Eaton had brought his mother instead. So I found myself facing my step-grandmother for the first time in six years. I had not anticipated this meeting.

After a lengthy grace, the meal began and so did Mistress Eaton. "You have changed a great deal, young woman, and not for the better. Your complexion is pasty and, "she peered across the table," your hair is quite lifeless. What have you been doing to yourself?"

"Nothing in particular," I mumbled, glancing at a spot somewhere below her wobbly chin. Her eyes, sharp as a starling's, were best avoided.

"Are you getting up early and seeing to the household, or are you just sitting about reading all that nonsense the way you used to do?"

"I don't read as much as before," I said. I remember rubbing my finger hard where, hours before, I had removed my wedding ring. The Eatons did not approve of such ornamention. I felt odd without it, as if I had lost an important talisman.

"Well, that's better anyway," the old woman snapped. "Too much of that sort of thing will burst your brain. I do not believe in a lot of thinking, either. Look where it got your mother —" she broke off, having caught the warning eye of Governor Eaton.

Mistress Eaton's body crackled like the carapace of a beetle. I caught myself smiling at the resemblance one often sees between the human and the animal, which does not always favour the human. Across the table one of the assistants saw me smile. "You found my remarks entertaining, Mistress?"

"Oh no, I am sorry. I wasn't listening for a moment. I was…" I paused, "thinking how good it is to be here with my husband."

The old brown beetle glared at me, and began to say, "What a…" when John Winthrop the younger interrupted. "It's easy to see that you are a very devoted wife, Mistress Hopkins."

Mistress Eaton cleared her throat, noticeably in disagreement, wiped her mouth with her napkin, and collapsed back into her chair.

Evidently, Governor Winthrop decided it was time to intervene before a battle started, and he began a monologue of his own directed to both of us. He offered Mistress Eaton and then myself a dish of roast duck, all the while describing the farm from which these splendid fowl had come, the barnyard they foraged in, the grain they were fed. He then went on to tell about the farmer who had raised them, his children's names and abilities, and after that subject was exhausted he came back to the dish we were eating and praised his cook. He ended by saying, "I don't consider it gluttony to celebrate the gifts of nature, and the skills that make them suitable for us. What do you think, Mistress Hopkins? Do you agree?"

"Oh yes," I said. "The farmer is to be congratulated. This is very tasty."

"Then why are you fiddling with it?" my step-grandmother said. "You will let it get cold on your plate."

"I am sorry," I said, looking at the governor instead of my critic, "but this is all I can manage. I have a very small appetite. But I did enjoy it," I finished.

The governor smiled, Mistress Eaton harrumphed, and I sat with my hands in my lap, hoping that something or someone would come along to help me. I would have given anything to be away from there. I imagined Pegasus as a daring white knight, sweeping down to take me on his back, giving my step-grandmother a little tap on the head with his hoof as we flew away, just to reprimand, not to hurt her. Or, more practically, I wished Edward would stand up and say, "Thank you for a lovely evening, but my wife and I must leave you now. We wish to have some time alone together." I wished fervently that frosty Governor Eaton, who had barely said good evening to me, was far away, sailing back to England with his mean-mouthed mother. Then I could perhaps enjoy myself here. The Winthrops were so good, and all the others truly warmhearted. Only the Eatons cast an icy spell over the feast.

Conversation at the dinner table moved along vigorously among the men. A few of the women, those who were among the first planters in the colonies and could lay claim to years of experience here, joined in. In such a gathering, talk naturally revolved around the welfare of the different colonies. Everyone was eager to speak about economic progress, and the individual planters' successes; in passing, they admitted their few failures, but did not dwell on them. They spoke about each town's expansion and the threat this posed to the conventicles. Some were in favour of allowing two congregations to be formed in the same town. Others disagreed, saying that they feared the division into two would lead to disputes among the ministers, and the breakdown of consensus about beliefs and rules of conduct.

Someone declared, and the rest concurred, that there had been a disagreeable change of attitude overall in the colonies in the last five years or so. The newer arrivals were not the only ones at fault; some of the older settlers had become dissatisfied with colonial life, or bored, or lazy. Some had gone back to the old country, but there were plenty still around whose lives were no example to the young.

"Only last week, for instance," said Mr. Shipley, an assistant from New

London, "I caught sight of an old widow flaunting herself in front of a gentleman farmer half her age. Fortunately, he is already intending to marry someone much more suitable. What do you think should be done about the widow? I am in a quandary about it."

"Is she a church member?" Governor Eaton asked.

"Yes, and before she was widowed she was very faithful, very respectable," answered Mr. Shipley.

"Then I should speak to the minister about a public admonishment. If she has tried to take matters further, paid the farmer a visit and so forth, she should be brought to court, and most probably whipped."

"She is quite small and delicate," Mr. Shipley protested.

"Well then, the stocks would have to suffice," Mr. Eaton said. "In New Haven, we would certainly make an example of her."

During this exchange I had been asking myself what might be meant by "flaunting herself." Not one of those listening seemed to have been interested in inquiring. My stepfather's attitude I knew very well.

It did surprise me, however, that Governor Winthrop could be just as harsh in his judgments. The discussion moved on to other examples of laxity, moral or mental, which often turned out to be the same thing.

"My old accountant died two months ago, " Governor Winthrop said. "He was an excellent worker, constant and of a good nature. I had to take on a younger man, who told me firmly that he could handle the work. There is a great deal of work, I told him, more than you perhaps realize. All to the good, he told me. I like to be fully occupied, he said. Three weeks later he had proved so incompetent that I took him to the court, who ordered his ears cut off. I do not think he will boast of his skills again."

I shuddered. How could they have been so cruel, these upright godly men? What made their minds so narrow, their thoughts as rigid as the pine planks they tread on? My stepfather determined the punishment before he heard the case, assuming he knew all he needed to. And the governor's poor accountant was guilty of what? Misplaced confidence? Lack of ability with figures? What grievous sins are these, that he should be mutilated and humiliated so? If these were crimes, then how should I fare if I were to voice my opinions? Better to let on that I have none, even if they think of me as a ninny.

The others nodded knowingly at Governor Winthrop's recounting, and told similar stories. Edward, who had said nothing, looked across at me and I could see he was worried. I knew he was afraid that I was drawing into myself, which usually was the beginning of a prolonged silence. I had been doing this more and more often when something disturbed me. Latterly, I had trouble breaking out of it. Edward was thinking that this would embarrass both of us, though I was sure his concern was more for me than for himself. He rose and went to my chair.

"It is rather late, Governor, and my wife has had a full day exploring the city. Would you excuse me for a moment while I escort her upstairs?"

The gentlemen rose, and as I passed by my stepfather I paused. "How is my mother?" I asked quietly.

Looking me in the eye, he said, "As well as can be expected." His tone was rusty, like the sound of walnuts cracking. I thought, there is a fondness in him that wars against his judgment. I was sure he loved her still.

"Please tell her I think of her every day, and hope to see her as soon as possible."

"I will tell her, and I know she will thank you for it." He bowed, and turned his head away. Enough had been said here.

As we made our way upstairs, we heard the others shifting in their chairs and preparing to take their leave. Edward went on ahead to be sure the candles were lit. A few fragments of conversation floated up the stairwell. Stopping for a minute on the landing, I heard, "…such a pretty woman … it is a pity … been distracted for some time." And another voice said, "…she should not wear lavender, she is already too pale. It makes her look like an invalid … worse than ever … takes after her mother." And yet another voice that said, "…it really is too bad … .poor man … no children … a blessing perhaps…."

The speakers came through the doorway into the entrance hall, and I fled as quietly as I could before they saw me.

5.

IT IS GETTING CHILLY in the garden now that the sun has almost set. Soon I will be summoned to supper. Perhaps my memories are making the air seem colder. I shiver as they arrive haphazardly, in no particular sequence. It is as though time has been forced out of its regularity by vivid pictures that keep reappearing in my mind, sentences like doomsday warnings, words that sound like tolling bells. I hear "distraction" sputtering as if it is slithering out of a hollow in the ground. Then the ground seems to rumble with "just like her mother" and then "not like her mother." I sense a faceless crowd repeating these two phrases over and over like an antiphon and responsory. Then, at last, come the prolonged sombre notes of "melancholy" resonating in my ears and fading gradually into the distance. I cannot make sense of it all. Some of these are not even my memories, but strange images that intrude and push aside my personal recollections. The cacophony keeps growing louder, although I fight against it. I must stop them pursuing me. I stand up, swaying forward on my toes and back again. I am a little light-headed, but I straighten up, pulling my cloak around me for comfort, and turn to the house. Tomorrow, I will begin to set down my thoughts in my journal.

April 28, 1645

"Tuesday. What a torrent of words I seem to have built up inside me. My head is tossing about with fragments of thinking never quite assembled in the right order. It must be because I have kept back so much for so long that I cannot form a complete idea except by letting it loose in speech or writing. Writing is safe since no one sees it, but even so I fear my mental brooding must stop. I have built repressive dams that will not withstand much longer the pressure to let go and speak out, whatever the consequences. At least I have the channel of this journal, along which I send little rivulets of myself. To write here is better than to do nothing at all. I must be careful, though. Something is happening in this house that I do not understand, but I think it will affect my daily routine in some way. I will stay alert, and wait.

"Whatever is taking place, it comes as a result of our trip to Boston. It was such a peculiar visit in many ways. While I did enjoy the first part of my stay with the Winthrops, and meeting all the leaders of our colonies, nevertheless, I was uncomfortable at the best of times, except when I was alone with Mistress Winthrop or conversing with young Mr. Winthrop. It seemed as if everyone else had their inquisitive eyes on me, waiting for me to say something bizarre or stupid, so they could nod their heads at one another and join silently in an already agreed upon view of my behaviour. I grew so agitated at this curious way of treating a guest and a stranger, that my mind froze and I could say nothing except platitudes, or even less.

"Once I remember someone voicing a rather silly opinion, and I laughed outright. A woman across from me at the dining table declared that there had been a spider in her porridge that morning, which through divine providence she had been permitted to see before she swallowed it. She had been spared a dreadful poisoning through the mercy of God. I could not help laughing at the idea. Why should it take the Almighty to intervene when all she had to do was look down at her bowl, instead of chattering to those around her? As soon as I laughed, I knew it was a mistake. Everyone at my end of the table turned to look at me. I saw Edward's frown, and so I quickly said, "Excuse me, I have the hiccoughs," and tried hard to imitate one. It did not sound much like my previous laugh, so I do not suppose I persuaded anyone. It was the first time I have ever told an outright lie, but then what else could I do? I certainly could not explain, even if I wished to, why I could not take the relationship between spider, porridge, and God seriously. I would have been sternly reproved, and then reminded of the love of God for falling sparrows. How could I have explained the difference?

"There were other instances when I thought people were looking at me pityingly, as if I were a helpless cripple or a stupid child. There were a number of allusions to my mother when Mr. Eaton was not present — at least I took it that she was meant — and to the need to stamp out heretical thought. I could not hold back my tears, even though I tried to look away so they would not be noticed. But they were seen, and yet no one seemed to realize their cause. Why would they not direct their discussions away from such a disturbing subject? It seemed as if they did not know how much it upset me, or else they thought it should not. My own mother condemned as a heretic and excommunicated; how could these leaders of our towns not recognize the pain it caused me to hear any talk of heretics? I was left to my silent misery without any word of comfort. Mr. Winthrop seemed to be the only one who understood, and yet, in this public conversation, he said nothing to me.

"What I did do was take my mind away from any discussion likely to upset me. It seemed the only safe thing to do. Then all that would appear on the surface was a young woman so polite and demure that she left the conversation to those who knew better than she. This was the impression I hoped to leave, rather than one of a person easily distraught and unable to control herself. I think I controlled myself well, except for the few occasions mentioned.

"Yet I still feel uneasy about my visit there. The Winthrops were so kind, and I would have no concern about them, were it not for my feeling that they too pitied me. Our farewells were cordial, even affectionate, yet I thought it was as if we were saying goodbye for a long time, perhaps even for the last time. They embraced me, and invited me to come again whenever Edward came to Boston, but it seemed like a hollow invitation. I may have mistaken pity for affection. I do not think I will be visiting them again.

"Even Edward seems different since our return. I catch him when he does not know I am looking, with a deep frown on his face, as if he is trying to decide what he should do. Perhaps it is about an important matter of government. He does not discuss these things with me any more. More likely it is about me.

"The last part of our week in Boston was the best for me, staying with my dearest David and his family. All is certainly not well for them, but even in the midst of their anxious life, they made a comfortable place for me, a haven after the strangely disturbing events at the governor's."

6.

I WAS RATHER LOW in spirits when I came to David's house, but the mood soon passed in the company of my brother, his welcoming wife Ursula, and, above all, the darling baby. I took to him instantly. He was such a roly-poly little treasure, there was hardly a squeal or a cry out of him except when something truly frightening happened. The first afternoon I was there we were all were sitting in the parlour, and little David tumbled off the chair Ursula had set him in. He turned so red in the face with crying that I was quite worried. But Ursula picked him up and embraced him close. A few soothing pats and he stopped almost immediately. Once again, his face shone like a sunburst, and he found life just as satisfactory as before.

Before long I realized that beneath the surface all was not as content in this house as it seemed at first. When the Yales were not playing with the baby, or making a special effort to please me, which they most certainly tried to do, David and Ursula seemed preoccupied with something they could not shake from their minds. I saw Ursula glance at David with such concern that I decided whatever it was, it was serious indeed. And David frequently looked so angry that he might snap at the next person who spoke. He held back, however, and since I was often the one who spoke next, he tried gamely to brighten his expression and answer me as mildly as he could. I knew him too well to be deceived by this attempt, but accepted his good intentions for the moment. There would be time enough to discover what lay in his heart. At least he had seemed to have reined in his emotions somewhat. His explosive temper used to get him into such trouble when he was young. Every ridge and angle of him, from his tightly locked legs to his set backbone to his unruly black hair that splayed out in wiry coils every which way, spoke of a person trying with all his might to keep control.

Most of the time, despite these persistent rumblings of unspoken woes, the house was filled with merriment and lighthearted occupations. Ursula showed me many little secrets about caring for baby David, and after a day or two he came to recognize me as part of his inner circle of loved ones. I was thrilled when one day, taking him for a ride in his carriage, he held out his tiny hand to me instead of his mother, as if he would include me in this, his favourite pastime. Even if I could not be a mother, it was lovely to be an aunt!

David was usually gone from the house in the daytime. He told me that not only was this a busy time for his overseas trading ventures — he had ships arriving at least once a week — but he had other meetings he must attend that could not be put off, not even for my visit. When he referred to these meetings, I saw Ursula's anxious expression appear again, but I did not think it right to inquire about the subject of the meetings, not just yet.

Meanwhile I was still troubled by the occurrences at the Winthrops', and so I waited impatiently for a time when I could tell David about them. Of all the people in my little world, David was the one whose judgment I valued most — even before Edward's, I must admit.

After three days had slipped by, I knew I would have to ask him to stop and talk before my time ran out. I could almost hear him sifting over in his mind all the matters he must put aside in order to accommodate me. He grimaced once, thinking of some business of his own, but when he saw me observing him, he changed his expression to an odd smile, like one of those stone gargoyles forced against its true nature to view the world cheerfully.

"Come into my study, Anne. You're right, our talk is long overdue. I'm sorry, but there are a number of pressing things on my mind." He sank into his deep arm chair, the one luxury in his rather austere house.

"I've noticed that you seem preoccupied a lot of the time. Won't you tell me what is bothering you?"

"Perhaps I will later on, but now it is your turn. I also can tell when something is worrying you." He smiled genuinely this time, and I returned it. This was the brother I loved: sunny, tenderhearted, and alarmingly astute. I decided not to mince words. "David, do you think I am distracted?"

His laugh came immediately. "Distracted? You? My dear sister, you are the least distracted person I know. All the world first, but never you!"

"What about melancholy? Do you think I have fallen into that state?"

"For goodness' sake, no. Certainly not. Whatever makes you ask such questions? This is so unlike you, Anne."

So I told him all about my visit to the Winthrops': the incidents when I felt myself to be curiously observed, the snatches of conversation I overheard, my little moments of weeping and their cause, my reluctance to say much in any company in case I was misunderstood.

All the while I was talking David listened carefully, sometimes looking at me intensely as if to fathom the meaning of what I was saying. Occasionally, he raised his eyebrows and leaned forward as if to interrupt, but thought the better of it, and heard me out to the end. As I finished, a puzzled frown creased his forehead. He uncrossed and then recrossed his long legs.

"I am hard put to understand all this. There is no doubt in my mind that your manner and speech have been completely appropriate to the situations you found yourself in, especially when you have so little in common with most of the people there. There is nothing strange about your actions, they are perfectly rational. Why anyone should think you were distracted is beyond my comprehension. Still, as you have described it, it seems that people do believe that."

I could not help myself. I began to whimper a little, a wave of self-pity washing over me. Here, finally, was someone who understood. I had been so alone, bereft of comfort until now. I pulled out my handkerchief and dabbed at my eyes.

"There now, it is probably not as bad as it seems," he said, not altogether convincingly. "Don't be alarmed. We must put our heads together and see what we can do."

I said, "I feel so helpless. I think that even Edward believes now that I am in danger of losing my mind, judging from the way he treats me, like a delicate creature ready to fall apart at any moment."

"Then you must convince him that you are not. Was there no one there who understood you, who did not treat you like a weakling?"

"The young John Winthrop was the only one who conversed with me about anything except the weather, or the meal we were eating. He must know that I am not distracted, because he asked me about the books I had written."

"If we cannot find a solution ourselves, then we might ask him to intervene with Edward," said David. "Meanwhile, this is what I have been thinking."

He said what I knew he would, that I should attempt to participate more in community occasions and to polish my social manners. He said that with my powers of observation, I should be able to imitate the subject and style of the conversations of my neighbours, or my husband's professional acquaintances, or the leaders of the community and their wives, for instance. I could see that he was trying to make an intellectual game of it, and so I said that I would make an effort, although I did not like the idea of playing a part, even if it was amusing to try. David told me that I had no choice.

"I know you find this strange, coming from me. I have always believed in saying truly what I think. But in this community, and most likely in Hartford too, honesty will get you into trouble if it speaks against the views of the rulers. I have paid dearly on several occasions for it." His expression was angry again, and for a moment I thought he would tell me more, but he calmed himself and let the subject slip.

Then he said that what had been worrying him about my situation was that it must have begun much earlier than just this last week. He asked me whether I had noticed any peculiarities in my neighbours' attitudes towards me in Hartford.

I said, "I've often noticed odd looks directed at me, but I'm accustomed to them. People always think me different, I suppose because I am the governor's wife and don't have to do any heavy work, having servants to help me. Also, I think they find it strange that I spend so much time just thinking about things, and writing them down. One or two people who have come to the house remarked that Edward had gathered quite a sizeable library, and they were shocked when I told them that the books were mostly mine." Then I told David about the Gossiping Gertrudes. "I've made too many mistakes with them. I couldn't fool them with a polite performance. They are like hawks watching a rabbit; they wait for my every misstep and then pounce. Especially since our mother's excommunication. They expect me to fall, too." I corrected myself. "They aren't all like that. Some of them are fine people, but there is no one in the group that I could call my friend. So I have given up going to their meetings." I looked forlornly at him. "I have made only two real friends in Hartford, and one was carried off by influenza last year."

Thinking of Mistress Goodwin, I began to sniffle again, then collected myself to listen to David. He told me that it would be a good idea to go over everything I could remember about the past few years in Hartford that struck me as odd. I should pay special attention to signs of animosity or sharp criticism. Perhaps something would come to my mind that would help to explain what was taking place.

I told him that I had kept a journal ever since I left England.

"Oh, so you have kept that up. Well, that is helpful. Why don't you read it over again and see what you can discover? Perhaps the answer lies in there, under your very nose."

"I can hardly believe that, but of course I will go over it. If the answer is there, I will find it."

"Let us hope and pray for illumination, then, as soon as possible. From what you tell me, I don't think your life has been happy altogether of late." I hesitated. "Come now, sister, we have always shared our secrets. You know you can trust me with them."

"Oh David, let's not talk any more about my unhappiness. It is too painful a subject on top of this new anxiety. You are quite right, though, my life in Hartford is not what I hoped it would be."

Before he could ask, I said quickly, "It is not my husband's fault. He does all he can to help and please me. I am afraid the problem is much greater than that. I should never have agreed to marry and come to New England. I am not either by my nature or my faith, shallow though it may be, a true Puritan, although I have certainly tried."

David's face took on the gargoyle look, as he laughed sardonically. "You too? Well, I see that we are just as much alike as ever! No wonder we are both in trouble."

"What trouble are you in? Surely you are not following in our mother's footsteps?"

"Good heavens, no! Me, an Anabaptist? No, my beliefs are as far apart from those wild sectarians' as New England is from — Japan. Why our mother became associated with them is beyond my comprehension. I have been to New Haven and tried to reason with her, as have the ministers there, but she refuses to recant. I can't make any sense of it."

"What will happen to the governor? Will he be able to continue, with his wife under condemnation?"

"I don't know, and to be honest I don't care very much about his welfare — an unchristian thought, I know. It is what will become of our mother that concerns me. New Haven is, as you very well know, the most intolerant of all the colonies."

"She must be going through a horrid time, but I do think Governor Eaton will not desert her," and I told David about my brief conversation with him.

"That raises him in my estimation," he said. "Perhaps, in time, it will all be smoothed out then."

"I do hope so. I have missed seeing Mother so much, but she is not permitted to visit us, and Edward will not let me go to her."

"That is just as well, Anne. A visit to New Haven would make you even more unhappy."

I could not help agreeing. "Please now, David, tell me where you stand towards the saints."

He sighed, stretched, and leaned back again. " I do not want to go into it fully right now. At the present time we are in a bit of conflict, and no one knows which way it will be resolved."

"We?"

"A group of dissatisfied citizens, some of them rather well known. We are trying to convince the leaders of the assembly to make some important changes to the rights of citizens, but so far we have been unsuccessful."

"Are the assembly members angry at you for your proposals?"

"They try to be calm and rational towards us, but inwardly they are probably seething, just as we are about their intransigence."

"I hope you won't get yourself into trouble over this, David."

"Oh, I expect I will, but there is too much at stake not to try. If this colony will not change its narrow-minded ways, I don't think I will be able to stay in it."

"But where would you go? There are no other cities as prosperous and as suitable to your business as Boston."

"I will return to London. Not yet, Anne," he said quickly, seeing my look of consternation. "The time is not ripe, the government too unsettled. No one knows what will happen to the King, except perhaps Cromwell. I don't trust him entirely."

"If you do return, take me with you," I said, knowing perfectly well that it was impossible. "I could not bear to stay here, knowing you were so far away."

"Don't be so distressed, Anne. Everything may turn out well. It may be that Edward will want to return to England too. He is a supporter of Cromwell, I know, and could be useful to him. Besides, Thomas is here. He's got a good warm shoulder and a soft heart. I know he won't understand why you are so upset, but he'd certainly help you if you asked him."

"I would do anything to go home," I said.

"Let us look forward to that day, then. My business is not finished here, and perhaps if the assembly begins to give way on these grave matters, I will be content to stay. But I very much doubt that change will occur, at least in my lifetime."

So we ended our conversation with a tearful embrace, and a weak attempt at smiles on both our parts. I went away more upset than before, but confident as always in the affection and assurances of my brother.

And so Edward and I left Boston, both of us with heavier hearts than when we came, and jolted our way back to Hartford, which I now must call home.

7.

I COULD HARDLY WAIT to see Elizabeth again. The entire Boston trip has confused me utterly. I thought of all those good people (a few not so welcoming), with their mixture of curious looks and understanding smiles, as if indulging a slightly backward child who did not know what she was doing. Even David's confidence in me was overpowered by my feeling that everyone else was, in a kind way, against me. I try to describe it to her.

I say, "I sound as though I am being disloyal, but I know you won't betray me."

Elizabeth says, "I've been wondering all along how you can bear these people. You are not like them in almost every way, and yet I see you struggling to belong. It must be tearing you apart."

I say, "Oh, it's not really like that all the time. And truly, the Boston people were not like some of the people here — you know who I mean." She nodded. "They were much nicer than that, and they did try to show an interest in me. But all the same, I could sense an undercurrent, some sort of implicit agreement that I couldn't detect clearly."

She says, "You will probably figure it out eventually. Anyway, I am glad you are back. It's been quite boring without you."

"Boring, ha! Lucky you. For me life is never so ordinary as that. There are some days when I could wish for boredom instead of these horrid events that intrude upon our lives. Something happened just after we got home that has me wondering about this belief that some of us are visible saints. Shall I tell you?"

"Of course."

"Perhaps you have heard about it already, that is, about Mistress Gordon's little boy?"

"No, I haven't seen Mistress Gordon for at least a week. In fact I've been wondering where she was. What happened to Dudley? Nothing bad, I hope."

"It is very bad. I am sure that if Mr. Hooker or Edward had been here it wouldn't have happened, but they were both away. Nellie brought me the news. Apparently, he tried to run away — no, no, of course he didn't really mean to. It was just a child's fantasy. I remember I, too, once set off to leave home in Wales, but really all I had wanted was to have a little picnic in the great park. Dudley would not have gone far, and he would have been so frightened he would have tried to come home. He is only eight, after all. Anyway, someone found him going along one of the trails in the woods and brought him home. It was decided by the council, on Mr. Stone's advice, that he should be shackled for a month to teach him a lesson. To make it even worse, his sister was going to go with him and explore in the woods, but her mother called her in to do a chore, so he left without her. She admitted this, and so she too was shackled as a warning. Now everywhere they go they must drag their chains. Look! Here they come, the poor little things!"

The two little children are rattling along the road, heads hanging, moving dully like a pair of rag dolls. I rush out to hug them, but Elizabeth runs after me. "Don't, Anne. You mustn't be seen doing that. I know that much about what is forbidden. You could be in trouble for that."

I say, "They wouldn't touch me, I am the governor's wife. This isn't New Haven, you know." I am thinking, of course, of my mother.

"Oh, Anne, how naïve you are! I fear for you."

Her face is all wrinkled up in an effort to stop the tears from falling. I put my arm around her. "Don't you fret, now. I will be all right." I look at the children clanking past and silently say a prayer. "Please God, look after them." Then, as an afterthought, "And me, too."

How is it that Elizabeth knows these things, and I do not? Am I really naïve or just uneducated? Are there things Edward should have told me, and would not? I know he hates to see me unhappy. "My little jonquil looks wilted," he said once, and liking the comparison, he used it over and again. "I see the little jonquil is drooping her head today. Is she very tired?" "My jonquil is smiling, it will be a sunny day." The metaphor always makes me feel about eight years old. If it were anyone but Edward saying it, I would want to box his ears. With him, I just smile faintly — like a fading jonquil! — and hope he will give it up soon.

The next time I see Elizabeth I tell her that Mistress Woodside has informed me that Mistress Gordon is no longer a member of the Gossiping Gertrudes. By a majority vote it has been decided to ask her to withdraw. "For good?" I had asked.

"We will decide that later, when we learn of her repentance," Mistress Woodside had said. For what, I was going to ask, but, thinking of Elizabeth's comments, I refrained.

8.

I CANNOT MAKE SENSE of what has happened since we came home. Every time I try to look at it from the other side — from Edward's point of view — I fail to see any connection between what he thinks and what I know. I go over it all again and again, hoping that something will come to light that I have not thought of before.

Edward's behaviour has completely changed ever since we came back from Boston. He seems agitated, unable to settle down and read, or just converse with me. He wipes his forehead frequently, as if to erase a painful thought. I have asked him several times if something is bothering him, and he evades the question, saying at one time that he is a bit overtired, at another that he has had a hectic day, or that there is something he is trying to work out. None of these explanations satisfy me; he seems too overwrought for that.

Finally, one day he sits down beside me in the parlour. I have been sitting staring at nothing, my mind puzzling over these recent occurrences. He takes both my hands in his, saying, "Anne, there is something important I have to discuss with you. I'm sorry, because I know it won't make you happy, but still it can't be helped."

I stiffen immediately, alarmed, and pull back my hands. "What is it? Has anything happened to my mother?"

Quickly he says, "No, it's nothing like that." He pauses a second or two. "It's about you, your health, that is."

"I am healthy. I feel fine," I say.

He looks at me strangely. "Now my dear, do you really think it is healthy to be so bottled up most of the time, when you are out in company? And then, every so often, to break out crying, or speaking abruptly, and then go silent again? That's not like you."

I begin to say, "But you know…" but he goes on.

"And there are those times when you have started to scream, and then blacked out, do you remember?"

"Of course I do. I'm not losing my mind." I look for agreement, and see nothing. "You know why I behave as I do." Again, no confirming nod. "Apart from those blackouts, that is. I can't understand why they happen. But they don't come often."

Edward says nothing, so I go on, trying to convince him that I am as sound as anyone else. "I have to keep my mouth closed, because whenever I say what I truly think, someone finds fault with me, and if this gets worse, I will be judged a heretic, and then I will be in the same pickle as my mother. And so, I have to keep my views to myself, and then there's nothing else to talk about except whose cow is bewitched, or who is misbehaving, or who is accused of some evil doings, and then I am expected to join in with the condemnation — condemned without evidence or trial, by most of the people I know — and I simply won't do it."

I am running out of breath, but I go on. "Of course, I have some good friends, and some other people I like well, but I wouldn't want to turn them against me, so I don't speak my mind to them either. And I certainly can't tell anyone, except you now, at this moment, how miserable I feel." I am drained now. I slip down in my chair, reach for Edward with one hand, and cover my face with the other.

We sit together in silence. His hand is trembling almost as much as mine. Finally, when he says "Anne," I open my eyes and turn to him.

"I do believe you when you tell me how difficult it is to keep your views to yourself, and how unpleasant it is to be criticized. I wonder then if it is wise for you to do so much reading? It must surely influence your thoughts, perhaps taking you in directions you should be wary of, or even avoid. You are a very intelligent woman, but your mind may be leading you astray."

This cannot be happening, I think. Edward has never cast aspersions on my reading or my ideas, although I admit I do not share the most outlandish ones with him. He is not finished either. He speaks calmly, as if telling a story.

"When we were in Boston I had the opportunity to speak to both of the Winthrops, father and son. It was on the night of the formal dinner, after everyone else had retired. Actually it was Governor Winthrop who brought up the subject of your condition."

"'My condition?'

"Well, your health, let us say, but young John Winthrop did call it a condition."

"What is 'it'?"

"He seems to think you have what he calls a wavering mind; that is, you tend to see-saw from one emotion to another, from laughing to crying, and in between to have the appearance of no feeling at all." I raise my hand to protest. "You know it's true, Anne."

I am unwilling to concede. "Once in a while it's like that, but only after I have had one of those horrid encounters with hard-faced people. I laugh because I am uneasy, and I cry — well, for all sorts of good reasons."

"Mr. Winthrop thinks there is another cause besides that. You know he has just returned from England, where he studied the latest medical findings at Cambridge."

I say, "I like Mr. Winthrop. He was the only one in Boston who didn't treat me as either a child or a fool."

"Then you will trust what he says. He has learned that the brain of a woman is much smaller than a man's, which is why women's work is, or should be, more circumscribed than men's. He says that if a woman tries to do more than her capacity allows, she runs the risk of overtaxing her brain so much that it falters and begins to lose its reasoning power."

I stare at him apprehensively, not knowing where this is leading. "And so?"

"Mr. Winthrop thinks that by reading and writing so extensively you have exerted yourself beyond the ability of your brain to perform."

Incredulous, I say, "But there's absolutely nothing wrong with my brain.

I am writing just as I always have, and I certainly comprehend everything I read — except for a few turgid theologians whom no one could fathom."

"You do write very well, and your understanding seems good. But do you see, when you speak so vaguely to others, and fail to pay attention to what people are saying, together with your sudden bursts of emotion, it betokens a weakening of the mind."

I shake my head, speechless. Edward goes on. "Mr. Winthrop is troubled by this, and so am I. He believes that you must shorten your periods of reading, and of writing, for fear that the condition may become more drastic, and eventually untreatable."

He stops now. His voice has become less and less assured, and I see a few tears gathering in his eyes.

"But that is my life! Those are the happiest moments of my day, when I can forget my problems here, and enter into other worlds—" I break off, fearful that I have offended Edward. I cannot be too blunt about my dislike of this place. He still loves it, although he is beginning to see some of the cracks in the walls of this perfect city.

He takes my hands again, and I let him. "I do know that, Anne, and I am so very sorry to bring this news to you, but I do believe we cannot ignore what young John Winthrop is saying. He thinks that if you were to restrict yourself to two books each month, and to write for perhaps half an hour twice a week, you might begin to regain what you have lost."

I shudder, and he goes on, trying to reassure us both, though I doubt he believes what he is saying. "Then we will see you regain your eagerness for life in this country. I miss your sparkling self, your joy when you first came here and promised to be my helpmate in this new adventure. I know it has not turned out the way we prayed it would, but we do still have hope that we will create a strong and holy community in this fine land. When you are better, you will help to make that happen."

I can read the "if you get better" thought in his mind. What can I say or do? I am sure he is mistaken, but is that a sign that my mind is failing and I cannot think straight? I cannot believe that. Yet I do have these horrible surges of anger, of fear, of even hatred, though I will not admit to that out loud. Do such feelings indicate a weakening of the brain, or a natural response to what is happening to me? John Winthrop hardly knows me, so how can he determine what is wrong? On the other hand, he is trained in medicine and can perhaps see a problem before anyone else can.

I look at my darling husband, who seems even more distraught than I am, if that could be possible. I must comfort him, reassure him, so that he does not feel guilty about what he has said. Is this the sign of a sick mind? Hardly.

"My dear, don't worry about me. I am not distracted, only confused and rather unhappy, except when I am with you. I really need my books for companions, and couldn't bear my life without them. Still, if Mr. Winthrop thinks that reading less might help to correct some imbalance in my head, I will try it, for a while."

"That's my dear girl, so good, so brave." I look into his face, which is not the picture of happiness. "We will pray that this condition lifts, and that you are your lovely sunny self again soon."

We clasp each other, each thinking our own thoughts which are neither lovely nor sunny.

After I go to my chamber, I push my head as deep into my cushions as I can, so no one will hear me sobbing.

V
Hartford, 1646

1.

I AM, AS IS USUAL, happy to receive a letter from Jane, but soon disturbed to discover that the letter seems to have been opened by someone before it was given to me. It gives me pause and I shudder.

June 5,1646

Dear Jane,

Thank you for your letter, which arrived last week, and the book, which was delivered today. It seems odd that they did not come together. The parcel was quite damaged, so perhaps someone had opened it by mistake. Your letter, too, had been resealed.

We are so relieved, as you must be even more so, that the war is over. Now that the King is in the hands of the Parliament, he must surely agree to their terms, and will be allowed to go home to his family and resume his rule. Edward says that Mr. Cromwell has presented him with a proposal that is fair-minded. But rumours have floated over the ocean that Charles continues to assert his God-given right to rule, and will not agree. Some here think there are worse days to come. For your and everyone's sake, I dearly hope they are mistaken.

There is not much to tell you. The summer is very hot this year, and I have great trouble sleeping. At first I cannot fall asleep, and then I wake up in the night with my bed gown soaking wet and my hair stuck to my head. I must look a sight, for one of the servants found me outside one night — the stars were brilliant, and it was much cooler than my room. He was agitated when he saw me, and ran in calling for his master. Edward came, and after making sure I had not been sleepwalking, he took me back to bed. I cannot imagine why he would think I was doing that. I have never walked in my sleep. I told him I came out to look at the sky and to cool down. He looked puzzled, but I think he believed me.

The hardest part about life here is the tedium. Every day is the same, except for the occasional visit by a trader or a minister, or the arrival of some good merchandise from England. We are not called the land of steady habits for no reason. I do not have the solace and inspiration of many books now, as some people have told Edward that reading is too hard on me. I had to beg Edward to let me have the book you sent.

Do you remember that I told you of two good friends, Mistress Goodwin and Elizabeth Johnson? Sadly, the former died last winter, and the latter is having her fourth child any day now, which keeps her busy. As soon as she is delivered, the family is moving to New London for the sake of her husband's business. Even though, recently, we seldom see each other, she always lifts my spirits marvellously. I do not know what I will do without her.

There is the occasional diversion, though not nearly enough of them to suit me. We had a fine feast to conclude the training days for our young men. We still need a large militia here, even though there is less fear of Indian attacks than before. I went to see the men parade, and was so excited to hear a marching band for the first time in ages. I was humming and tapping my foot as they went by, and started to follow along, until I caught the eye of some people beside me. They were staring as if they thought me a weird woman so I gave up the idea, and stood there like a dull statue. Some people cannot enjoy the simplest things.

I have some good news. A teacher has been appointed to start a school here. His name is Mr. Andrews, and he comes from Somerset. Since he is not married, he is to stay with us until some other arrangement can be made. I am told he is a clever young man, and well-read. I hope he proves a stimulating guest.

The only news I have from New Haven now comes along a chain of rumours, so I hardly know what to believe. It is said that my stepfather keeps my mother confined to the house, and prays over her daily so that she will repent and give up her false beliefs. In such a prison I cannot imagine how she will survive; you know what I thought of that house at the best of times. I long to hear from her, but no letter comes.

The other sad news you may have already heard, as word of any disruption in the New England Way always seems to fly home quickest. David and several others in Dr. Robert Child's group, whom they call Remonstrants, have been tried and heavily fined for disturbing the peace of the Bay Colony by their insistent petitions. They want to extend citizenship beyond the confines of the saints, to include all Englishmen, that is, all men of substance. The narrow-minded General Court will have none of it. Dr. Child has been jailed, a dreadful affront to such an upright man.

I fear David will make good on his threat to return to England, and then where will I be?

How I wish I could see you, and that green and familiar land where I used to live. Despite all the turmoil you write about, I still prefer it to the stolid unrelenting monotony of where I am now.

I shall write in better spirits next time, I promise. Keep this letter to yourself, dear Jane, as I would not want anyone else to read it.

My fondest affection and truest prayers go to you.

Your loving,

Anne

2.

M R. ANDREWS IS a pale sandy-haired young man with a receding chin and a tentative smile. There is nothing tentative about his approach to his work, however. He arrived at the house with a trunk full of books, and another that he ordered sent over to the meeting house. That trunk contained paper, quills, and schoolbooks for the children. He told Edward that he intends to start classes as soon as the summer fruit has been harvested and preserved; the young people are needed for such work.

At supper the first night, he eats carefully, picking at his food. I think he must be shy, so I chatter away (not my usual habit these days), hoping to put him at ease, but it only seems to make him more reticent. To all my questions he answers in the shortest possible sentences, with a "Yes, Mistress" or "No, Mistress," or "It could be," or "I don't know, I haven't read them." This last reply is in answer to my question, "Don't you admire the poems of Mr. Milton, the 'L'Allegro' and 'Il Penseroso'"?

I am disappointed in the clever new teacher. I had so been looking forward to having conversations with another keen reader, but we seem stalled before we have even begun. I try again, asking him what he will be teaching the children. He says, "Their letters. And sums. All that is necessary. We have hornbooks and primers, thanks to the generosity of your husband."

"And the older children, those who can read; what will you give them?"

"They will begin to read Scripture," he says, lifting his head briefly from his plate, and then turning back to stare fixedly at the pile of turnip. He must think it is the golden fleece.

"You will have your work cut out for you, Mr. Andrews," says Edward. "Most of the children are completely unlettered. We have had no time to teach them."

I speak up quickly. "That's just what I was thinking. It won't be easy with so many to teach. I would be glad to come and help. I could get the little ones to repeat their letters, but I would be better with those who can read already. I do a lot of reading myself — or at least I used to." I look expectantly at the teacher, then at Edward, who is frowning. Mr. Andrews is watching Edward, waiting for his reply.

Edward says, "This isn't a dame school, Anne. It is for children of all ages, so it would be out of the question for a woman to teach there. And, as you know, your mind is already burdened enough. Your offer is kind, but Mr. Andrews will certainly receive help if he requires it." He looks at me quite reprovingly. I can read his mind: he is annoyed that I am forcing him to be firm, when he hates it so.

A slight flash of defiance rises in my throat and fades away as I recognize the finality in his tone. Is he right? I do not think so, but these days I have my bad moments when I think either the world is going awry, or I am.

The rest of the meal was is as joyless as a fast.

3.

THEY SAY IT IS the sign of a weak mind if you talk to yourself, but these days, for want of any companions, I am doing so more and more. It comes naturally to me, thinking aloud, puzzling over this life I seem to be losing my grip on. This harmless habit may lead to trouble, I know. One day, Jenny was walking by my room and must have heard me talking, because she peeked in and seemed surprised that I was alone. The whole kitchen will know about it by now. I can hear them now: the foolish ones will say I have lost my wits; and Ardyth, the only true believer among them, will tell everyone that what Jenny heard was the good and bad angels fighting over my soul.

I tell myself that I must give up this habit, and so I take up my journal instead:

October 21, 1646

"Sometimes I cannot stop myself. My sadness pours out like a river to the ocean, spilling its banks and making sodden everything around it. I flounder in it, thinking that drowning is the only ending. And yet, exhaustion keeps me from the brink — but of what? death? Inescapable madness? My husband thinks I am headed that way, with no likelihood of return.

"I can tell by the way Edward looks at me these days that he is worried sick. He takes me walking. 'Would you like to get some air, my dear? I think it might do you good.' There is no more chance of my skipping out by myself as I used to do. Someone is always around to keep track of me.

If I were to go out, a servant would offer to accompany me, 'to carry your parcels, Mistress.'

Now Edward makes our walk a regular part of his week — not every day, but often. So we go out arm in arm, trying to make a pleasant stroll out of a duty. We do not walk on the main street in case we should meet someone of importance and be required to stand and converse. Edward does not trust me to say the correct thing at the proper time. I know this from the way he tries to avoid people we know. He would never say so, of course. That would be undignified, harmful to us both. Still, there are enough people about that we must speak to some of them, keeping to quick remarks about the weather, and how nice it is to see me out again. I smile and bow, say thank you. Their expressions belie their good wishes — knowingly suspicious, if not frosty and severe.

"Our shoes are squelching with mud, as it has rained all week. I miss a board that someone has laid over the worst pothole, and fall in, ruining the front of my gown, apron and cloak and all underneath. Edward humours me as he would a sick child.

"'Dear, dear, what a pity your gown is soiled. I shall have to order another right away. Would that please you, Anne? A tiffany silk one perhaps, or a fine light cotton? You deserve a new gown in any case. We had better go home now, so you don't catch a chill. Nellie can bring up a hot posset cup.'

"I say, 'Yes, thank you, that would be fine.'

"Once, in my room I cannot wait to close the door. Taking off my wet things I am shaking, more from the fall, I hope, than from the unhappiness I cannot contain. It is so horrible here in this muddy pathetic little town with its dismal weather and these pointless outings to look at nothing in particular, kind but futile attempts to lift my spirits. And always I sense in the background the wide grey river rushing through town to the ocean, calling me home. Oh, Plâs Grono, oh my beautiful Welsh land, how I wish I were there!"

At supper Edward tells the teacher about our excursion. "We had quite a stroll, Mr. Andrews. The air was pleasant after the rain, and there were quite a few people on the streets who bowed and spoke graciously to both of us."

I do not know how he can be so blind. Most of those people dislike me utterly. They think I am either proud or a madwoman, but they do not know which, and that makes them even more annoyed. I can hardly tell them, or even Edward, what I really think: that those who are not utterly horrid are dull, dull, dull and nothing I could say to them would change that.

After supper, Mr. Andrews disappears into his room and we move into the small parlour. I shut the door tight, and stand with my back against it, waiting for Edward to take his usual seat. When I do not join him he looks over at me in surprise. "Why don't you sit down, Anne? What is the matter?"

"The matter is, Edward ... oh, I don't know what it is. Everything's the matter." I shake my head vehemently and begin to wring my hands. He stands up and comes over to me, holding out his arms, but I hold him off. "No, don't. That won't help. I'm not an infant."

"Of course you're not," he says soothingly.

I flare out. "Then why are you treating me like one? Making up stories to calm me down when all that does is rile me even more. I can't bear it."

Edward says, "I am so sorry, my dear, if I've offended you, but I don't make up stories, truly."

"Then you mustn't see very clearly," I retort. "You think the women in town like me. They don't. They hate me. They think I'm mad. They don't want me here. Some of them wish I would die." I stop suddenly. I know I have gone too far.

He looks at me intently, taking in the collar of my gown that is askew, my sleeves pushed up to my elbows, tight and wrinkled. I am standing with my feet wide apart, glaring at him almost saucily. This is shrewish behaviour, I do admit, so unlike my usual manner. I can see Edward is troubled by it, perhaps wondering if I am truly in a distracted condition.

He raises his voice authoritatively, hoping to stop me from ranting and to settle me down. "Anne, you must never say such things, or even think them. No one wishes you ill."

I keep on with my harangue as if I have not heard him. "Why do people want to bring me down? I can't do anything I really like, I can't say what I mean, and every time I try to keep quiet and act as if nothing is wrong, people assume I am being devious, or that the Devil has got hold of me. I can't even read without someone thinking I'll lose my wits. As for teaching the little ones to read, which I would love to do, why, that's impossible. Even you have given up on me. I hate this place. It's just as mean and narrow-minded as New Haven." I end with a loud flourish.

Now Edward is furious. "That's enough, Anne." He leads me across the room and places me firmly on a stool. "Now listen."

I look up at his face, see the poppy-red colour of his face swelling up with blood, and my anger subsides. I am afraid he will collapse. With both hands, I reach up and grasp his arm. "Edward, please. Don't look like that. I didn't mean it, well, not everything I said."

"I think you did. You always tell the truth." He sinks into a chair beside me, his body limp after the strain of such alarming emotion. He has never been so angry before, and that disturbs him. His tone is softly contrite. "I am mortified, Anne. I don't know how I could have lashed out at you, of all people. I pray you to forgive me. It will never happen again. And I will never speak to you like a child again, I swear." I nod, dry-eyed.

"I know you are unhappy about many things, dear. And I know that some of the saints here are harsh and unbending. Every town has people like that, and you have come up against quite a few of ours. But you also know others who are kind and moderate and good company. Isn't that so?"

I nod again, a little hesitatingly. There were a few, a very few.

"Then why not spend some time with them, and stay away from those who aren't so easy to get along with? You do need some good company."

I wonder how I can ever avoid Mistresses Brigden and Stone and their followers, even without going to their circle? I should not let them into my thoughts, but I cannot help it.

Edward goes on, the weariness in his voice the only indication of how much he dislikes having to say the rest. "As for your reading, and the idea of teaching the small children, I do hope you understand that it's only because I want to see your health improve that I have said no to both. I have it on the best of advice, from Mr. Winthrop the younger, whom you like and respect, that if you give your mind a rest, your spirits will soon recover and you'll be your usual bright happy self again."

I begin to interrupt, but he says, "You may not believe me now, but when you get better you'll understand why these restrictions are necessary. And one day you may begin to take up your reading and writing again — although not nearly as rigorously, of course. There now. Does that help?" He wears a pleading look that I can hardly resist.

"I don't know, Edward. I don't think so, but I know I can always count on you to care about me." It is almost the only good thing left.

He takes me in his arms, and I sink my head on his shoulder. My body is still heaving with the last tremors of my outburst. "I will always love you to the best of my power, and care for you until I die. After that, it is in the Lord's hands."

"Amen," I say softly.

4.

MY LIFE CANNOT GO ON like this. I can feel the anger inside me crackling like chestnuts in a fire, but how it is going to emerge I do not know yet. I have been a docile young woman, a pathetic example of a governor's wife, for too long. I have taken the censure cast on me and on others with scarcely a word of retort. I have been constrained, forced to give up my books, my friend Elizabeth, and my frankness. I have played false to my true nature, which is to be loving, thoughtful and open.

The urge to do something to help myself has been coming on for some time. I felt it when Edward told me I could not teach the children because they were not in a dame school. That was just an excuse to keep me away from them, so I would not overheat my tiny little brain. I could have taught them something interesting. Then, when we had the great argument about how much the women dislike me, there was this sense again that I would not let myself settle back into my old ways, but I would act, take charge of myself, and refuse to be so compliant. Still, I did not know what it was I needed to do until today.

Today, I blurt out, "Edward, I want to go and see my mother."

He looks at me as if I am daft. "You what?"

"Yes, I do. I want to go and see that she is all right. I have heard nothing from her in almost a year, and I don't like it. I must go to New Haven. I will go alone, if you don't have the time to come with me."

Now he is really frowning, shaking his head. "But Anne…"

"No, don't try to make me change my mind. I am determined to go."

"So I see, but I think you will have to wait. I can't go with you right now, as you say, and you certainly could not travel alone."

"Then Nellie will come with me," I say, smiling triumphantly. I have my answer ready, so surely he will agree. "If I send a letter right away, then Mr. Eaton will have someone come to meet us in New Haven. I know there is a good boat leaving on Thursday that can take us."

"You have been busy," he says reluctantly, but I can see he will yield.

"Yes, and Nellie can pack in an instant. I've already warned her that we might go soon."

Edward is flabbergasted, I can tell. "You have planned all this? Anne, I am so surprised. I haven't seen you this active in weeks. You must really want to go to your mother."

"I do," I say emphatically.

"Then by all means go, and I hope you find her situation much improved." Impulsively, he gathers me to him, and gives me a hug. How Edward responds to any signs of life from me! I hug him in return, and then rush out to finish my packing.

5.

RETURNING TO NEW HAVEN is not something I look forward to with any pleasure. I prepare for it by reminding myself how chillingly austere is the atmosphere of that household, and how much more guarded I must be than in even the strictest company in Hartford. Am I going back here to punish myself for some hidden unexpiated sin, I wonder? Or is my reason the opposite: that I want to confront these severe saints, in order to assure myself that I am in the right, and they are the misguided ones? I examine myself carefully, and say no to both these arguments. I go to comfort my mother, even to defend her if necessary from the snares of the righteous.

Summoning up a mouthful of fleeting courage, I knock on the wide imposing black door of Governor Eaton's mansion, and am ushered by a servant in to the large hall. Sitting by a paltry fire, covered in layers of shawls is Mistress Eaton, the miserable matriarch, with her son facing her in his armchair. Hannah, working at a table with paper and quill, scarcely lifts her head to look at me. My mother is absent from this family scene.

Governor Eaton comes to greet me. "Mistress Anne, we only received your letter yesterday, so there was no time to stop you from coming."

I step forward quickly. "Why shouldn't I come? Is there something wrong? Where is mother? Has she gone away somewhere?" Then, more slowly, "Is she staying with David? With Thomas?"

He measures out his words as if he has few to spare. "She is not. She stays here in this house. But I cannot let you see her."

"Not see her! Of course I must see her, that's why I came. Is she ill? Has she caught the influenza — or is it something worse?"

"Please do not raise your voice. It's not her body that is ill, it is her soul." I glare at him. "She must remain alone until the Devil leaves her."

"And when will that be?"

He misses my sarcasm, and replies earnestly, "After prayer and fasting have brought her back to the true faith in the Lord, and she has repented of her false beliefs." More softly, he says, "We are all praying for her and have every confidence that she will return to us very soon."

The shock of what he has said makes me feel weak, and I collapse into an empty chair without being invited. Nellie, who has been standing at the back of the hall, comes to me. "Are you all right, Mistress? Should you lie down?"

She looks at my stepfather, who says, "I have prepared a room for you, in case you wish to stay."

He is hoping I will decline, but he knows very well that I cannot get a boat to go home right away.

I say, "I must see my mother."

"You may not. She is to stay by herself in her room until…"

"I will not leave until I see her."

He hesitates. "Mr. Davenport must be consulted about this."

"Mr. Davenport has no authority over her, since she is no longer one of the saints." That is not true in this colony, most likely, but Mr. Eaton must see I will not be dissuaded.

He is quite exasperated. I am sure he is wondering now, how can I get rid of this woman? He must have decided the sooner the better, because he says, "You may visit her briefly, but I will hold you responsible if anything should happen to make her worse."

"Thank you," I say politely. He has overturned his own convictions, so I must not appear ungrateful.

As I leave the hall, I pass Mistress Eaton, who turns away from me without a word. At least I am spared one of her nasty glares. I follow my stepfather up the oak staircase with its heavy hand-carved railing. Once again, I think to myself how well-constructed are these stairs, as not a board creaks. We go along the familiar hall, and turn a corner into a narrower one where I have never been. There are two doors at the far end. Mr. Eaton opens one, steps just inside, and says, "Here is your daughter come to see you. I trust she will not stay long." He backs out, motions me inside, and closes the door.

She is standing with her face to the narrow window, a grey wool garment wrapped around her. I say, "Mother," and when she turns around, I see it is a blanket. Beneath it, she wears a white bed gown. On her feet are the old rose wool slippers I have seen so often.

"Anne, is it you?" It is such a hoarse voice, unused and unloved. I look at this figure, familiar and yet disturbingly strange, and gasp. Her face has lost its colour, and it seems as though the bones will pierce the skin. For the first time I notice how her eyes are hooded: surely they were never like this before?

"What has happened to you?" I wrap my arms around her, and feel how thin she is. "What have they done?" I lean back to look at her, but she does not want to meet my eyes. She turns her head away.

"It is nothing. It will be over soon." She starts to shake.

"Come now," I say, leading her over to the bed. "Sit down and tell me." The bed is hard, its planks skimpily covered with a straw mattress. There is no comfort to be had here. I stroke her back. "Now, I want to know what is going on."

The shaking subsides a little, but she still will not look at me, bending her head down until it almost touches her chest. I wonder if she does not have the strength to keep it upright for long.

Finally she says, "Don't blame my husband. It isn't his idea."

"What isn't?"

"Keeping me in here alone all these days, with … just a Bible and … some water, and…" she breaks into tears, and cannot go on.

"What are you getting to eat?" I ask, suddenly feeling the panic rising in me.

"A … little broth, and some bread, and a bit of meat … once in a while."

She finally lifts her head. "But it won't go on much longer. I know the Lord will take me, and hide me, and they will never find me."

I am speechless, but suddenly she is not. "Then I will enter the pastures of the blessed, and all the angels will say, 'Welcome Ann, welcome to your heavenly rest. And you are no longer Ann Lloyd Eaton, but once again you are Ann Lloyd Yale, whose father was a bishop and whose husband was a bookbinder of good lineage'." She looks at me strangely. "You are of good lineage, too. You look like a fine daughter."

"I am your daughter. I am Anne Yale, now Hopkins."

"I thought you might be." She smiles.

This conversation takes me aback. I touch her forehead, and it is as hot as live coals. No doubt she is feverish, which is why her thoughts are wandering. I go over to her washstand and dip a cloth into her water jug. I return to the bed and press the cloth on her forehead. She smiles again.

"You never did that when we were back in ... what was it called? Oh yes, my father-in-law's house, with the ivy all over the brick walls, and the birds sitting in it singing and making nests for their chicks. Wasn't it lovely? Though I wasn't always very happy, even when you children were behaving yourselves and Mr. Yale was teaching you to read. Do you still read?"

"Yes, I read and I still write in the journal he gave me." I will let her go on talking, if it helps take away the anguish of the present. But oh dear, she must get help. She must be taken out of here.

"I started to read after I came here. I never was much of a reader before, but a friend gave me some wonderful books, about true faith, and how one may be saved, and I read them with such eagerness, and that's how I ended up here...." She trails off, and starts to tremble again. I envelop her with my arms. "I feel cold."

I say, "It is quite cool in here. I am going to go and ask for another blanket."

She grasps my arm. "Don't go, Anne. They will never let you back. They will just lock me up again, and tell me to get down on my knees and ask the Lord's forgiveness for saying unholy things against them. They will tell me they are praying for me, but they aren't. They are praying that I will say what they want me to. They don't care about me at all. They just don't want the governor to have such a crooked wife. A man in his position deserves respect, not rebellion. I am sure they hope I will die, and I will, so that will solve their problem."

"You will not die. You must not. You will not give in to them and their wishes. I am going to do something about this right away. No, don't worry, I will come back, and I will bring help. Let me go now. I will be back in a short while." I unclasp her arm, and open the door, the sound of her moaning "Anne!" following me down the corridor.

I burst into the hall. "Mr. Eaton, I should like to speak to you in private, please." My peremptory tone brings him to his feet immediately, and he points to another door that takes us into his study. I close the door behind us, look around me hurriedly at the room with its shelves of books, the large writing desk, and the high-backed wooden chairs that line the room.

"She cannot be left like that," I say. "She is ill. Never mind about her soul, it is her body that is wasting away. She is feverish and almost delirious, from lack of food, sleep, exercise, and loving care," I finish boldly.

Mr. Eaton looks worried. "The last time I saw her I thought she looked pale. I thought she had been praying for too long, and I told her she must not stay up all night. She agreed with me, and told me that the praying had done her no good."

I say, "She is so hot at one moment that it hurts to touch her, and then she is shivering with the cold. She must receive care. It can't wait another minute."

He replies, "Mr. Davenport thinks that such a fever is the Lord's way of telling her she must repent. I agree with him."

"Well, you shouldn't. If she should die, you will be accused of having neglected your spouse, because she would not agree to say she believes in something she does not." This is harsh, but if it takes harshness to move him to act, then I dare even more. I went on. "I am going to summon Mr. Hopkins to come to New Haven, and we will bring my mother home with us if nothing is going to be done for her here."

Mr. Eaton straightens up. This is too much for his pride. "She cannot leave here. She is not well enough for that. I will call in a doctor to say what can be done."

Ha! I have caught him up. He does know her body is ill. Finally, he will not leave it to the Lord's good pleasure to heal her, or, blame it on the Devil if she does not get well.

"I will wait and see what he has to say, and then if need be, I will stay on to nurse her. I doubt there is anyone else in the house who is willing or able to do so."

"You do us wrong. I have some very good servants who can look after her." Now I have made him angry, which is no help to my mother.

"Still I must know what the treatment will be, and whether she will be able to regain her health."

"Of course." A pause. "Anne, I am sorry that this has happened. I do hope you realize that I was only thinking of her salvation, which is far more important than any fever."

"Your view of salvation is not hers, and I doubt that you believe in forced and therefore false conversions anyway."

"No, I do not." A great sigh. "Well let us attend to her bodily needs right now. As for the other, I would be deeply sorry not to be able to see her back with us...." His voice trails off.

I am satisfied. I have done what I had to do. I am not triumphant; it is too soon for that. But I can sit at table with Mistress Bad Mouth Eaton and know I cannot be cowed by her any more.

Four days later, I go to take my leave of my mother. She has gone back to her own spacious chamber with its view over the green valley and the trees stretching out as far as one can see. She is wearing a soft blue dress with an even paler shawl of the same tone, and the old rose slippers. Perhaps it is the dress that has made the difference, but I do think I see some colour in her face, and that the shadowy pasty look seems to have disappeared. Or perhaps I just wish it so. In any case, she smiles when she sees me, and it is the old smile, usually reserved in the past for little Hannah, never for me. Then she remembers why I have come and the smile disappears.

"You are leaving me," she says.

"I must, but I know you are in good hands now. Soon, you will be well enough to come and be with me when I need you."

I see the worry cross her face. "Do you need me now? I think you are sad too."

"No, no," I lie. "I am fine. Hartford is a lively community, and there is plenty to do to keep me happy." It would be cruel to say anything different. I look at her, imagining what a struggle lies ahead for her, and realize that she will never be able to help me. I kiss her goodbye, wondering if it is the last time we will meet.

6.

N O SOONER DOES THE *Arbuthnot* dock at our wharf than I spy Edward, his eyes shifting from one passenger to another until he finds me waving. He has brought Zachary to take my box, so we keep our conversation brief and stay on neutral subjects until we are home and closeted inside the small parlour. I can hardly wait to tell him about my visit. I describe everything, right down to the blue veins on my mother's hands and the rash of red spots on her ankles. I do not omit the bitter look on Mistress Eaton's face when she learned what I had done. Her hatred of my mother was engraved in the deep ridges of her frown. I tell him that Hannah never once went to see her mother, no doubt persuaded by the old crone that sin was contagious. That Mr. Eaton came around slowly after I had been there a while, but that his faith tugged him one way, his loyalty to his wife another, and he was in great turmoil. I finish by saying, "It is horrible, Edward. She is ill and stubborn, he is utterly convinced that his is the only faith. I don't know how it will end, but I see no hope for her happiness — nor for his."

Edward scratches his head. "I wonder…" he is thinking aloud, "whether there is any connection between his treatment of Mistress Eaton and his business affairs."

"How could there be?"

"I don't know, but perhaps it isn't just a coincidence that his shipbuilding enterprise has been failing and may have to be closed down."

"I heard nothing about it when I was there."

"You would not. For one thing, Theophilus wouldn't discuss business in front of women. And for another, he would probably be embarrassed to do so. Did you know that he asked me if I would join him in this undertaking, and I refused?"

"He did?"

"Yes. It wasn't that I didn't trust his abilities, and I know him to be utterly upright in his dealings. I said I had too much on my plate already."

"Thank goodness for that!"

Edward rests his chin on his palm, thinking. "It is odd, isn't it, that Theophilus, who is a sound governor and a devout saint, is doing so poorly in his trading ventures, and yet David, who has rejected the Puritan way and been judged for it, is thriving? I know it is said that the Lord's ways are not for us to fathom, but it does seem sometimes that the Lord tests his most devoted servants severely, and lets the heretics off lightly."

"I've often wondered the same, but I have never heard you say so before."

"I have occasionally thought so too, but I haven't asked the question out loud till now. It shows my lack of faith in God."

I say gently, "I think it shows something quite different." He raises his eyebrows. "It leads me to think that God is not cruel, and so He does not order these disasters. We bring most disasters upon ourselves, or we are the victims of other people's actions, not God's."

"Mr. Hooker would never agree with that, Anne."

"Perhaps not yet." I leave the rest of my thought in the air.

Edward seems tired of the discussion. I think it is the strain of having to reconsider such important beliefs that wearies him, because he concludes with a sigh and, "Well, it bears thinking about."

That night and for the rest of the week I wake up from nightmares so potent that I can hardly shift from the dream time to the waking, they seem so connected. Each time I find Edward awake beside me, and in a frenzy I tell him what I am dreaming. The images are legion: of two-headed black horses; of frogs leaping out of the butter churn; of Governor Eaton and Hannah going downstream on a raft, turning end to end and almost tipping into the rapids; of my mother in her white nightgown and grey blanket lying in a burnt field beside a cow's skeleton. And, in almost all of them, I make my way frantically up jagged cliffs, through thick reedy marshes, or I run along a road towards what I do not know ... the dream never takes me there. All these images jostle against each other, and time and place are jumbled together, so everything I blurt out must seem like nonsense to him.

After a few days, I realize, from his haggard appearance that he has stayed awake much longer than I have. He must be worrying about me. I take him to task. "Edward, dear, you eyes are so droopy you can hardly see to put on your boots. You must try to get some more sleep. I am sorry about my dreams, but I am sure they will go away soon."

"I do hope they will. I should never have let you go to New Haven, it has upset you too much."

"If I hadn't gone, we would have been attending my mother's funeral by now," I say. "I wish I could think of a way to stop waking you up. I suppose I toss and turn and say things?"

He nods.

"I am so sorry."

"It can't be helped. But I wonder if you would mind if I were to sleep in another chamber, just until your dreams calm down?"

"I suppose it is the best idea," I say evenly, though I hate the thought of sleeping alone.

He must have read my mind, because he says, "Why not ask Nellie to stay with you for the time being? It won't be for long."

I agree. Nellie will be better than no one, and she will not waken easily. Still, I feel abandoned, even though I know he loves me just as much as ever.

7.

M Y NIGHTMARES CONTINUE. I wake up often to feel Nellie rubbing my shoulders and saying, "There, there, go back to sleep now," and eventually I do. As if to make up for his absence from our bed, Edward is spending more time at home with me in the evenings. I think he is watching me carefully for signs of melancholy. I will not show any. It seems to me that no matter how often I explain why I behave as I do in public, he still sees me slipping into the darkening gloom of distraction. I hope that our conversations will change his mind. He is certainly changing his view of the colony, and for the first time in over a year he discusses his work with me.

One evening he drops weakly into his parlour chair and gives a deep sigh. I notice how his body has sunk, as flaccid as a cushion with all the feathers coming out of it. I wonder about his health; is he also having bad dreams? Evidently, it is the events of the daytime that are upsetting him.

"The most unpleasant case came up before me in court today. I can't get it out of my mind. I know I shouldn't discuss it with you, but…"

"You can tell me. You know I'll keep my own counsel."

"Well, then … there is a widow in town, whom I shall not name, but she is one of the saints. I used to think that she was an upright person of clean habits, but then I hear that she is pregnant. That's serious enough, but when she is brought to court, she declares that the father of her child is one of our richest planters and a member of the assembly. He, of course, stoutly denies it."

"Whom do you believe?"

"We are still looking for witnesses who may have observed any man entering her house. All her neighbours say that the planter she named has never been near the place."

"Can they be sure?"

"Not absolutely, of course, but one of them swears that the woman has hinted that she will have a rich husband one of these days."

"So you think she is accusing this man in order to get hold of his money? Would he have to marry her if no other man is found?"

"That's what I have to determine, along with the other members of the court. It is not clear yet what is the truth of it, and it may never be. And the worst part of it is that this woman is devout; she has given great service to the saints all her life."

"Yet, she may be also an avaricious and cruel liar."

"Yes."

We both sit still, considering this twisted story. Edward says, "I don't know what to make of this colony these days. Cases like this — and there have been others — and the experiences you have had with some of the women, leave me wondering where we are headed. I try to govern well, but the standards I came to Hartford to uphold are falling every year."

"I wish I could disagree, but I cannot. Still, I know you do your very best in this imperfect place."

"I like to think so, but I'm not so sure." He has something else on his mind, so I wait for it. "When I was in Boston last month for the governors' meetings, Governor Winthrop spoke out about the growing faithlessness in the colonies. He said that people should be asked to state what work of grace the Lord had wrought in them. It struck me then, and I still wonder, how could I reply? What have I done that I know to be the Lord's work? I couldn't think of anything."

"Edward that is so foolish of you. You are one of the dearest of the saints, the humblest, the most dedicated. No one does more of God's work here than you do — except Mr. Hooker, devout and thoughtful though he is."

"You are mistaken, Anne, but kind all the same. I suppose it is this woman's

behaviour that has set me thinking about the colony and my part in it."
He stands up and takes a candlestick. "I will keep on praying for a right
judgment in the case, and hope to be able to tell when we have found it."

"I will pray for that too," I say, carrying my candle up the stairs. "Meantime, sleep long and well, my dearest."

"And you too," he says.

8.

THE SABBATH IS NOW the liveliest day of the week for me. On the other days, except for the time Edward spends with me, I am languishing more and more without any sense of purpose or joy, often just wishing for night and sleep to come. With the loss of my two good friends, and the limitations on my reading, I actually relish the idea of keeping house, but I have been effectively banned from the kitchen. Even my offer to pick apples from our own trees is rejected: Nellie, who encourages me at every turn, is adamant this time. "You are too delicate, Mistress, your back is weak and the ladder too unsteady. I couldn't catch you if you fell. Wait until you feel stronger." So I am left with a few little tasks such as mending, the occasional trip to the market, and short walks along the river. I keep up my spinning as it takes concentration, but because it goes so slowly and I have nothing much to show for my efforts, I give up easily. Often I steal away to my chamber on some pretext or another, and manage to write a few lines in my hidden journal. If I stayed there too long, though, the servants would think I was ill, and that would make things worse, as I would be kept inside with absolutely nothing to do.

On Sundays it is different. The day is filled with the usual attendance at the services, and conversing with members of the congregation afterwards. We do not spend as much time as we did in the past, but still Edward must shake many hands, listen to requests, and make promises to look into certain affairs. I am usually approached kindly by some of the women in the old circle. Even though I stopped attending after my mother's defection from the straight and narrow, there are a few good souls who do not hold that against me, and sympathize with my delicate position. I return their bland and courteous remarks with fair words of my own. If I see one of the more critical Gertrudes looking at me, I turn around and face the other direction.

The highlight of the day is, of course, Mr. Hooker's sermon. One morning, sitting in the pew beside Mistress Hooker and Mistress Haynes, the alternate governor's wife, my mind begins to wander off into pleasant pastures. Mr. Hooker is preaching with his usual dramatic zeal, his voice sounding out like a bell heralding a festivity. He is like an actor lacking a stage, I imagine. He could be the Duke in *Measure for Measure* — no, the Duke's too reasonable — or, better still, Antony. Yes, he is a man in love, except that God demands a stronger, purer faithfulness than does Cleopatra.

I catch myself about to smile at the delicious wickedness of comparing the minister to a character in a banned play. No Puritan would ever go to the theatre. Reluctantly, I turn my mind back to the preaching, not the preacher. Mr. Hooker is well into his subject for the morning, the covenanting as God intends it to be, His treasure that he wants to gather to Himself. Despite the sins the saints have committed, he tells us that through true humiliation we are able to glimpse the salvation that is offered in the life eternal. "Grace is the porch, as it were, glory the palace."

Oh dear, does he mean this? Does he consider this congregation to be filled with grace? I think of some of the people I know, the ones who have treated me as if I am both ignorant and wicked. Am I living in the suburbs of happiness when I am with them?

Mr. Hooker does not think so. He is trying to urge us all, using the most radiant of images, the heavenly mansion, to repent and be humble, and allow truth to guide us. He reminds us over and over that we must help each other, and be helped. "See a need of Christ in all," he says, "and see greater beauty in Christ then in all, and be led nearer to Christ by all, or else you get nothing by all that you do."

I take this in humbly. It is true, I do not look to see Christ in everyone.

I am much quicker to take offense and see the sin in my neighbours than to look for the spark of Christ. Still, the devilish parts do stand out without my searching for them. I do wonder if this is the best I, we, can do? Surely we can make a better job of this little Canaan we are planting.

My mind floats off again, and does not come down to earth until Mr. Hooker has finished speaking. I feel a little guilty about that, and a bit sorry, as I love hearing him, and never fail to be moved by his words. This time, however, I am concentrating on new ideas of my own that stimulate me well enough. I can hardly wait until the next day when the servants will be occupied and I can spend time writing them down.

I take my journal from its hiding place and begin:

January 9, 1647

"This is probably the silliest idea I have ever had, but I will write it all the same: 'If I were a magistrate:'

"I would make sure that everyone in our town was warm, well-fed, and safe. I would start with the houses, and rid the town of shacks and those pathetic burrows dug into the hillsides. There would be no more thatched roofs, and every house would have a brick chimney. If the occupants could not afford it, the town would supply it. Fire is everyone's concern. Then, to let people live more cheerfully, I would insist that all be allowed larger windows so that all the houses would be free of perpetual smoke. Large windows should not be an exclusive item for the wealthy. As the town grew richer, we would import more glass to construct a 'glass room' on the side of every house. Here one could be warm in the spring without having to use our precious wood.

"In winter, I would allow all people to wear furs and skins, as the Indians do. They are always much warmer in their houses than we are, as they sleep under skins, and wear furs instead of wool. I do not consider this ostentation, as our rulers do, but commonsense.

"I would arrange for the sick who have no families to be cared for in the town. The last time the council sent a poor old man away because he was incurable, I felt ashamed that one of my family was party to the decision.

I heard that he did not make it back to England, but died on the ship.

"Every time I go out of town and see the trees circled with metal hoops, I know that another waste land is being created. I would clear the stumps from the old fields, and begin to plant young trees again. We must not lose our wilderness. It is our fair inheritance.

"I would try to persuade people to consider how we could make our town more pleasing to the eye, not in a frivolous way, but in a helpful way. Here, everything we have built around us is serviceable, and plain. We need to set aside land for parks, to be free to everyone. Our best philosophers know that a garden inspires meditation on the deepest matters of the heart. We should listen to them.

"In my town everyone, including women and servants, would be schooled, taught by men and women!

"I would invite the Indians to come and live in town if they chose, although perhaps they would not.

"Everyone would be taught to swim. We have buried too many people who fell out of their boats.

"It is not as easy as I thought it would be, to figure out how I would change our town. I have plenty of time to think these days, so I am going to work on some new ways to order the community, and the church. I will try out some of my ideas on Edward — not the outrageous ones, like having women on the council, of course."

9.

ONE SUNDAY, after evening service, Edward is approached by Mr. Stone, the morose Mr. Woodside, and Mr. Brigden who lags behind, heaving himself along with determination and difficulty. They request a meeting right away, saying that their business is important and cannot be delayed any longer.

Edward says, "Very well." He takes my hand and says, "Do go on without me. I'm sure I won't be long."

What could be so important that these men must discuss it on a Sabbath? No one talks about business then. Perhaps there is a serious illness in town, and Edward must find people to care for the sick. Or there is news of a great disaster. But why these particular men, of all people? Whatever it is that they want, it does not bode well.

I go home by myself, the rest of the household having gone ahead to set out the supper. We wait a while for the governor, until finally Cook asks if she might bring the food, as there are essential evening chores to finish. I say, "Yes, leave it on the table. I will eat when Mr. Hopkins arrives."

I sit in the small parlour, restlessly shifting around in my chair. The waiting seems endless.

Some time later, Edward marches in, his eyes ablaze. His face is the colour of a lurid sunset before a storm. I get up quickly and put my hands on his shoulders. "What is it, Edward? What has happened? Is there going to be a war? Please, please tell me!"

He inhales deeply, saying nothing. Then finally his breathing grows calmer, and his colour subsides. He sits down at the table, wipes his face with a handkerchief, and says, "No, there will be no war."

That is all. I wait silently, throbbing with anxiety. He picks up a knife and spoon and begins eating. I start in too, but lose my grip and the knife falls onto my plate.

Edward puts his own knife down. "Why don't we try and eat and let this whole affair pass?" he says. I hear the buried rage within him, powerful still.

"What affair?" My tension is rising to equal his own.

"What I've just been through. Never mind." He shakes his head. "It's over. Best left unsaid."

"Edward, that's not fair. You come home looking like a man driven by the Devil — no, no I don't mean that you are bad, just that you are troubled by something you cannot fight. Isn't that true? I know you so well. You must tell me what it is."

"I cannot." His head is turned away, so I do not see the expression on his face.

"You can. I insist. What troubles my husband is my trouble too."

Edward laughs sardonically. "Yes, that's true. Well, since I know you will press me until I tell you, I will do so. The subject of my discussion with the elders and ministers was yourself."

"Me?" I am startled. My face begins to burn.

"Yes. Three of the men at the church wanted you to give a public relation."

"What!" I cry. "A relation! Never, never! Why should I?" I stand up, stiff with fury.

Edward rises too. "Calm yourself, Anne. It will not happen. Mr. Hooker and I made sure of that." He takes my arm, urging me into my chair. "Sit down, dear, and let me finish."

I sit. My hands are trembling, my legs too. I can feel my heart beat, and can hear the blood rush through my veins.

"I'm sure you know why they were asking. Because of your mother's beliefs, and also because of David's trial. They want to be assured that you do not think as either of them does. I told them that you most certainly did not."

I stare at him disbelievingly. "They wanted me to get up in front of the whole congregation and tell how I came to have faith in God?"

"Yes."

"They don't ask women to do this, ever."

"I know."

"If they do ask for a relation of one's faith, it is given to the minister in private."

"They asked for that too, when they realized that neither Mr. Hooker nor myself would consent to a public relation."

"And then?"

"Mr. Hooker said that was quite unnecessary, that he knew the nature of your faith, and that there was no wandering thought within it. He was firm with them, and chided Mr. Stone for agreeing to suggest the relation." Edward keeps his voice level, reassuring.

I shudder at the mention of his name. "Mr. Stone does not approve of me at all. I wonder if it was his idea entirely."

"Perhaps so. He is a devout man, but he has many narrow views."

"What can I do? I can't bear to be suspected like this."

"We can pray that these people become more understanding, that is all."

I shake my head, disbelieving. Is there nothing or no one to protect me from these sanctimonious old crows that sit on the fence waiting for me to drop something they can feast on? Edward has been able to stop them this time, but he cannot change their opinions.

I say, "Yes, I guess so. I've tried so hard to say and do the right things, and to hold my peace if I disagreed with their views, but it's hopeless. I guess I'm a failure."

"Anne, Anne, don't think that way. You are a fine Christian woman, and my good wife."

I smile wanly. "If you think so, Edward."

"Yes, I do. Now come, let's put away these thoughts, and eat some of this cold dinner. See, the grease has almost hardened. That's what we get for wasting time on bad thoughts."

He is trying to cheer me up, I know, so I give the little laugh he is hoping for. Inside, I feel a chill all around my heart.

10.

I WILL ESCAPE from them all. I will not have anything more to do with them, these iron-clad guardians of the truth — their truth! I will turn my face away from them whenever we meet, and if they speak to me I will stare at them with eyes like coals and lips as tight as a hasp. Edward may chide me all he wishes, but deep down he knows now why I cannot abide them.

Now what can I do with my rage? I will not scream, or throw kitchen pots, or beat on doors; then they would be sure I had lost my wits. I will cease to think about them, as much as I can, and turn my mind to other things. I will try to imagine — what a forbidden word that is! — my new utopia. I will dream and dream it until perhaps it will come true, or seem to at least.

So I write some more:

March 7, 1647

"I can see this beautiful countryside, fresh and green again as when we first came, a privilege and a sanctuary. In the middle of it, all the inhabitants of the town live in houses of substance and beauty. They obey the few rules that are necessary, because they have made the rules. Those in authority have been elected by every single person, man, woman, servants, Indians too. All who call Hartford their home have a say. In this way those who hire servants or Indians will become more responsible to them, and will see to it that their lives will be enhanced.

"Ministers must give good counsel to their congregations, but they must not command them. Free will is God's most important gift to mankind, after salvation. Without free will there is no salvation. We shall not be slaves to our ministers.

"There shall be no public shame or torture of the body for any crimes committed, with the exception of the most heinous. Let a man keep his ears, a woman her nose. It is devilish to mutilate the body that God has given us. We shall not punish someone because one person alone has given witness, as that witness may be false.

"In this new city, we shall resolve arguments through discussion and prayer. We shall not invent a new rule to cover each fresh dispute. The Indians have their own ways of healing; we should not decline their instruction because they are heathens. Men and women will sit down together harmoniously, to listen to each other's thoughts, and build upon them.

"Before all else, in my utopia, I would abolish the brotherly watch."

I underline this last sentence heavily, the black ink seeping through the page.

11.

MOST OF THE TIME, I would not know if Mr. Andrews was even in the house. He is such a quiet man. He comes regularly for his meals, as he should, says little, and disappears afterwards either to his classes or to his room. I try hard to engage him in some conversation about books, but he usually manages one brief sentence before rushing away. I cannot see how I could have intimidated him. He is not so shy with Edward, but men often do speak more easily with each other, just as women do with other women.

One morning, a large package of books is delivered to our house, addressed to Mr. Andrews. Jenny takes it to the kitchen, where she cuts open the linen wrappings under Mr. Andrews' excited gaze. I see the parcel arrive, and, guessing what it holds, I stand in the doorway watching too. As the teacher picks up each book lovingly, opens the cover and reads the title page, I come quietly closer until I can read some of the page for myself.

He is so busy examining the books that he does not realize I am there, until he hears me give a little cry. He looks up, clasps the book he is holding to his chest, and says, "I beg your pardon. I will leave immediately."

"Oh no, please don't go on my account. I am the one who should leave. They are your books, not mine." I cannot help but add, "It looks like a fine collection."

He nods. "Yes, indeed. Your husband has been most generous once again." He gathers them up hurriedly, almost dropping one as he does so, then says, "Excuse me, I must go," and leaves the room. I would have offered to help him take the books upstairs, but I do not dare.

Later the same day, I cannot help myself. I go to the teacher's door and knock. It takes him a few minutes to answer, and when he sees who it is he steps back, his face aghast. I too am taken aback by his look.

"I am so sorry if I disturbed you." I can see that he has been reading as there is a book open on his table in the window. "I came to ask you whether you would let me borrow one of your books when you have finished with it. I saw that you received a copy of Sir Walter Raleigh's *History of the World*, which I would dearly love to read."

Mr. Andrews is upset. He holds his hands in front of him as if in prayer and lowers his head, which he does whenever he does not know what to do. I have seen him do it often. He says, "I — I — I..." and cannot go on.

I say, "Of course, I don't mean immediately. Please don't hurry on my account. But I have heard so much of this great work and would love to read it."

Now Mr. Andrews is in a quandary. He must know that Edward has curtailed my reading, fearing that my mind is weakening on that account. He tries to get out of the situation gracefully, but he is not skilled in the art of telling an untruth as if it were the truth. All he can think of to say is, "My mother ... she wants to read it also. I must send it on." He finishes pathetically, "I am sorry."

I take the hint. Knowing his plight, I feel sorry for him, although I am even sorrier for myself. Still, he has probably been told not to give me books. I say, "Of course your mother must have it first. I do hope she enjoys it." I walk away quickly before the teacher can see how pained I am.

This is my journal entry for the day:

May 3, 1647

"In my ideal community, I would have a library to which all could come, and read as much as they wished.

"I would have a circle of women writers, painters, and composers of music, who would gather to listen and look at one another's work, offering praise, encouragement, and help when asked.

"I would even have a university for women!

"Right now, since I cannot have these fantastical things, I wish for a continuous supply of paper and ink. I would like a quill that could be made to hold plenty of ink, as it would save much time when one needs to write a lot.

"I would like to have a writing room of my own, to spend all the time I wanted there.

"I would like to have a ship that delivered me a perpetual supply of new books of all sorts. I would like to read the writings of women, no matter how heretical their opinions.

"I would also like to be able to hear the latest musical compositions
to have a good friend
to have a feather bed
to have a shorter dress that does not get muddy
to have dances and Maypoles and Christmas feasts
and, to have my health again."

12.

A FEW MONTHS LATER I write:

July 3, 1647
"Wednesday. Mr. Hooker is ill with the influenza that has infected the town. They say some travellers from the port at Boston brought it with them."

Monday, July 7, 1647
"Last night Mr. Hooker died. The holiest man I have ever known."

13.

T HE WHOLE TOWN has been in mourning for weeks. As if to assist with the process, summer rains have drowned the fields, and washed the streets clean. Now that the sun has broken through at last, people are walking about, picking up broken branches, tying up scraggly plants, and slogging through the muddy fields in a hopeless attempt to salvage the crops that have rotted and sunk into the ground. All people, whether they are covenanting saints or simply concerned inhabitants, are feeling the loss of our leader, like children suddenly orphaned. No one has anything but praise for this godly man, who lived his life as faithfully as he preached. Wherever you go, people are talking about him: in the kitchen, at the market, and especially at the meetinghouse.

For a while I could not talk about him at all, and stayed in my chamber as much as possible, bemoaning my loss. I have no pride in this; I know others are as bereft as I am. But for me, as for all the rest, the loss is personal as well as communal. I ask myself, not only what will happen to this place, this gathering of saints, but what will happen to me? My faith, my hope that the future would bring me some relief, some slight happiness, was founded on the assurance that Mr. Hooker would be there to support me. Even though I could not trust him with my most disturbing thoughts, I believed that he would not let any more harm come to me from those punitive people that he could so firmly keep at bay. Now, there is only Edward. Thank God there is Edward.

I know I must say my condolences to Mistress Hooker, but I keep putting off a visit. How can I go to her and say, "I'm so sorry about your husband, Mistress." It sounds so formal, so unfeeling. But if I say what I mean — that he was the greatest source of light in my life, apart from my husband, and now that he is gone I am sure to sink into despair without him — well, I would surely burst into tears, and so would she. I start to cry. Tears come easily these days.

Then she would probably tell me what a terrible state is despair, and that I should never sink that far away from God. And, of course, she would be right, and I would tell her so and thank her — but I would still be so deeply miserable that one may as well call it despair.

I suppose I should not put it off any longer. I should not be so self-centred: think how unhappy she must be, worse than any of us.

The visit takes place more or less as I had imagined it would, except for one thing. I had forgotten what a strong, faithful woman Mistress Hooker is. It is she who comforts me, and not the reverse. I leave her far less downcast than when I came there, seeing in her the same spirit that used to dwell in her husband.

14.

THE GOVERNOR AND COUNCIL have declared that the official mourning period is over, and those who continue to grieve excessively are in danger of succumbing to melancholy. Edward and I have been trying to take up our regular life once again, and to subordinate our feelings for Mr. Hooker to the soundness of reason. Neither of us is finding this easy to do.

So, one evening, after supper, Edward and I go into the small parlour intending to carry out some ordinary tasks, mainly to keep our minds away from unhappy thoughts. Edward is consulting his notes for the next day's council meeting, while I am starting to mend a few little tears in a petticoat. I am grateful for Edward's company right now, for he is still called out often of an evening. The emergency calls never stop day and night, whether to ask him to settle family disputes, to provide a remedy for someone taken ill, or to round up the constable to deal with some drunkards tumbling out of the tavern.

Even though a fire is the last thing we need on this hot night, by old habit we draw our chairs close to the chimney place, and set the candles down on the hearth. There is not enough light to see properly for mending, but since the darns will not be visible under a skirt, I do not mind. Clothes matter little to me these days. Edward is squinting down his nose at the papers in front him. His newest spectacles have helped his sight a little, but not enough for close reading. He will have to send to London for a thicker pair. I worry about this. "You must not get eyestrain, or your sight will get worse."

"I know it, and you are right, but this paper must be finished tonight," he says. "There are never enough hours to accomplish what I have to do."

"One day I hope you will not be governor, or deputy, and then there'll be more time for — everything," I finish weakly.

"Of course some day I will be too old, but right now there are still so few men able to act in this capacity that we first planters have to carry on a while yet. Especially now," he says, and then bites his lip. Saying this brings the loss of Mr. Hooker to mind.

He breaks off, as we hear a wild sound outside. I get up to look out. The wind has come up, surging now through the trees, bending and cracking the branches, and battering at the windows. Heavy clouds cover the sky, lending a ghostly light to all below. Usually I love a good storm; its power and its lawlessness astound me. Like the sea, it has the freedom to do whatever it wills with us puny creatures and all we have built to protect ourselves. It is such a contrast to our constrained lives. Tonight, however, I feel my anxiety rising with the wind's efforts.

Edward says, "Listen to the gale out there. I had better fasten these shutters securely." Just as he stands up, the window flies open, extinguishing the candles. The room goes completely dark.

I stiffen, fear clutching my stomach. My hands turn to ice in the engulfing blackness. Without warning I find myself trapped in a fathomless space, bleakly cold, alone, and terrified. Yet I am not alone. Behind me someone lurks, a terrible someone I do not know, or perhaps I do. I begin beating my hands on something solid in front of me.

Then I scream and scream as if the Devil is after me — at least that is what the servants said later that it sounded like. Finally, I must have fainted, because afterwards I cannot remember anything.

Much later when I come to, I am exhausted. The sounds have stopped. I am enveloped in a coarse and heavy blanket. My forehead is being cooled with a wet cloth, yet I shiver. I feel arms around my shoulders. Finally, I dare to open my eyes. I am still in the parlour, the candles have been lit again, and Edward is standing hesitantly in front of me, his eyes red with tears. He speaks softly. "Are you recovered, my dear? How do you feel now?"

"Very tired," I say, "and sore." I pull my hands out from the blanket and examine them. They are covered with bandages. I look at Edward , who says, "You were banging on the windowsill and hurt yourself. Perhaps you thought the window needed to be closed."

I say, "No, I wanted it open, but I don't know why. Sometimes, I think that something dreadful must have happened to me a long time ago, something that has put the fear of the dark in me. I don't know, though, as I cannot remember at all."

"Don't think about that now. It's all over. We will talk about it tomorrow. Now you must sleep. Come."

He puts his arm around my waist and helps me up from the chair. I am like a bundle of rushes that has been dragged from the marsh and left to wither and rot. Nellie, who has been bathing my face, takes my arm, and the three of us stagger up the stairs and into my chamber. Edward sits down on the side of the bed, and promises, smiling anxiously, that he will stay with me until I sleep. I fall asleep seconds after lying down, but not before asking him to assure me that the lamp will not go out in the night.

My sleep does not last long, or so it seems. I may have been dreaming, or still recovering from the evening's events, but something wakes me up abruptly, a loud shrieking sound close to me. I sit up directly and open my eyes. The shrieking stops. Then I realize that I have been making the noise, which will certainly bring everyone back into the room. Quickly, I try to recall what it is that caused me to cry out, but I have only the slightest hint of some picture that recedes from my memory just as I think I have it. All that remains is a sense of another time and another darkness, but where or when I do not know. I am driven by the need to remember it, but nothing will come.

When Edward comes in, he finds me lying awake in bed, my hand on my forehead. "I am so sorry to disturb you, but it was the pain of a head-ache that made me cry out. I think I will be better with a little hot drink. Would you ask Nellie to bring me something, if she is there?"

He gives me a long worried look. I am not sure that he believes me, but it is the best lie I can manage given my state of mind. I smile at him, to let him know that I am going to be fine. He sits down beside me and smooths my forehead until Nellie arrives.

"Good night then, Anne. I will pray for a better tomorrow."

"God willing it will be so," I say weakly.

What if I am to be plagued every night, my mind like an abandoned house invaded by wandering evil spirits? It would be unbearable. But what have I done to bring on such hideous visions, if a sense of utter blackness can be said to be a vision? Is this a premonition, warning me that my understanding is going to be annihilated, cast into outer darkness? Whatever happens, I shall not rest until I find out what it means.

VI
Hartford, 1649

1.

A WEEK AFTER CHRISTMAS — another Christmas that never was — I write in my journal:

January 1, 1649

"They have taken the rest of my books away, and will only allow me one every month. This time I chose my own, dear Thomas Browne. I could hardly be without him. I asked for my Bible, and reluctantly they handed it back to me. It was the cause of my weakness, they said, too much study, even if it was Holy Scripture. It was Mr. Stone who came and spoke to Edward about it. Then he dragged Mr. Andrews with him to carry the books away. They could use them at the school eventually, Mr. Stone said.

"Nellie brings me writing paper hidden in her dust cloths. I keep it with my journal under the commode chair cushion. Ink is a bigger problem. The only source I had was David, but now that he never comes here any more, I must make do with what I have left. Fortunately, I can make it last a long time if I think carefully about what I am going to say, and then write it in the closest possible way, in very small handwriting. I do not know what this will do to my eyesight, but I must keep on writing. If I do run out, I may have to resort to taking some from Edward, even though that is stealing.

"Yesterday, Edward asked me what I did in my room most of the day. 'I watch the people going by, talk to my ghosts, read a little, and have a rest. Then it's suppertime.' He was not pleased about the ghosts. But it is true, except that I leave out that I am writing about the ghosts, my people from another dearer world than this present Connecticut."

I have been sitting most of the day in my chamber just looking out the window. The snow, first of the season, falls like shreds of cotton and taps the glass softly. It seems to cover the world's grime and grit like a blanket of benediction. That is a phrase I used in my last book, which no one will probably ever read. I am not sure that Jane ever received it. She certainly has not written to say that she has.

By suppertime, the whole street will have vanished, leaving ghostly humps of what once were solid objects, like the sheet-covered furniture in the large parlour. It is seldom used now, so it is better to wrap up everything, as it saves dusting and prevents bleaching from the sun. Not that the sun has much chance of creeping in through the dense linen curtains, designed to keep the heat in and God's benevolence out.

Two children, hand in hand with their nurse maid, are jumping and cheering and jostling each other along the road, revelling in its downy surface. Their coats and hats are so drab against the snow. Children should not be dressed gloomily in dingy browns and greys, as if they are always attending funerals. If I were to choose their clothing for them, I would make sure they had happy colours, poppy red and lovely azure. But then I will never have the opportunity, being, if not barren then certainly unsuitable for motherhood. I might present my husband with another melancholic. One to a family is enough.

The children are out of sight now, the freshness of the day urging them along. When I was about their age, how I loved being a child, especially during those years at Plâs Grono. Every day there was something new to do, another excursion to take, and the whole of Wales to explore. I remember the holidays when my cousin Jane came to stay in the other Yale house across the hills. Together we would go off with Matthew the coachman in the cart for a whole afternoon in the country. We would get him to stop every so often and wait while we tried to capture a bird, stealing up behind it with our makeshift nets. We were never successful, thank goodness, so the menagerie we planned never came to anything. We did not mind; the fun was in the chase.

Other times David, Thomas, and I drove out with our grandfather to visit the miners' cottages. He always had fresh cheese to take as a gift, so that our visit and his grandchildren's curiosity would not seem an imposition. Everything about their lives was strange to me, and a little bit frightening. Tucked into the side of a hill were the lead mines with their tall chimneys for smelting the ore. Some days, I would see the tiny boys, who had been sent up inside the chimneys to clean them, slithering down covered with soot, looking like the devils I already believed in. The fumes from the furnace, and the land around them, blasted and bleak, made me certain that this was what hell looked like. I was glad when we left the mine and went into the cleaner, friendlier cottages for a drink of milk and some bread and cheese. I never forgot the sight of the mines; sometimes here, when a preacher, on a day of humiliation, begins to paint the picture of hell, I think of the Welsh mines, and the boys whose faces were blackened out, with only the whites of their eyes gleaming in the dismal scene around them.

Jenny tiptoes into the room, afraid of waking me, and when she sees me sitting here, she hands me a letter from my mother with the date December 25, 1648, heavily underlined. To my surprise it has not been opened. I was sure that everything that came to me in writing or by word of mouth was censored for my protection — what an euphemism that is!

Dearest Daughter,

I have heard from David of your unhappy state of mind and your constrained manner of living. Both resemble my own situation, although from different causes, so I can sympathize fully with you. David tells me, and I believe him, that there is nothing wrong with your understanding, and that you are merely trying to guard yourself from harm by your reticence. The Puritan venom I know well; you are wise not to engage those whose poisonous attacks masquerade as rigid piety. Of course they will mistake your behaviour, not knowing the reason for it, and call it something unwholesome. You will just have to put up with that as there is no way out. You must pray that the colony will bring in a replacement for your present minister, a hardhearted man of extreme opinions, as I recall.

As for me, I also lead a quiet life, for the most part under my own roof. My good Mr. Eaton — for he has been very good to me indeed ever since your visit — will not divorce me, he says. I have been a good wife to him, except for my clinging to a religious "aberration" — he doesn't even call it heresy — and he still loves me. I see how tormented he is by his choice to stay married to me. I have even told him that if he must, he should send me back to England to preserve the integrity of his faith and the purity of the colony. He thanked me and said he would consider it. I could tell he was relieved at my suggestion.

Mistress Eaton has taken ill with a serious influenza, and the doctors fear she will not survive. I have thought many harsh things about her in the past, but I don't wish her a lingering or a painful death. I must say honestly, she has been a horrible thorn in my flesh, particularly in the last few years.

I wish I had some comfort for you, or some hopeful message, but I would not tell an untruth. Be brave, my daughter, believe in your own good power to reason, trust in God, and say a prayer from time to time for your unhappy but affectionate mother,

Ann Lloyd Eaton

Reading the letter beside the window with the pure snow erasing the dirt of ordinary living, brings a slight queasiness to my stomach, nothing more. Am I so sated with my own misery that I cannot sympathize more fully with another's? I go over the letter again, and this time I see in my mother a serene confidence that is new, which I believe will serve her well in the future, whatever that is to be. I wish I had the same.

2.

IT IS GETTING MORE and more difficult to write without being seen. I have never been caught yet, but I have taken precautions. I have devised a strategy.

Today, I hear footsteps approaching my room. I am prepared, my mending beside me, the needle already pointed into the cloth, ready to hand. If someone were to come in, I would make a little cry, and pretend that I had pricked my finger, and say, "It's nothing really, I just looked up for a second when I heard the door. Please don't worry, there's no blood, and the chemise isn't spoiled." If it turns out to be Nellie, of course I would have no need for subterfuge.

The steps pass my door and go on into the maids' quarters. I pull the journal out from under the pillow on the chair. It is much more difficult to put it away now, since my door is supposed to be kept unlocked. There are only a few seconds after someone knocks to delay my answer, then push the journal into a safe place as quietly as I can. Also, I must say something. I try to keep them waiting as long as possible. I have thought of lying on the bed and groaning as if just waking up, and then calling out, "Who is it?" Sometimes I say, "Just a minute," and make some rustling sounds as if making myself presentable. But I am afraid that sometimes I will not be able to think of anything to do except say, "Come in."

I live in fear of the day when someone dispenses with knocking and enters unannounced. It is not customary to intrude on the mistress, but I know that they are beginning to think that such a courtesy does not apply to me. For the sake of my health. For my own protection.

This time the footsteps belong to Jenny the housemaid. I am sure it is her sound, a determined but not commanding one, not like Cook who pounds, or Ardyth who scurries. Jenny would not disturb me, and even if she had a message, she would wait at the door until I am ready to open to her.

Jenny is not my friend, but she is not my enemy either. If she should catch me out, she would not tell anyone. I suspect she is still a churchwoman at heart. If so, there are words she cannot say, just like me. I am not the only one with something to hide.

My journal and my maid are my only confidantes now. There are some things I will not tell Nellie, even though I know they are safe in her keeping. But even saying them out loud is too difficult. I spend a great part of the day now sliding between dozing and dizziness, caused no doubt by being near immobile for so long. Apart from going to services, I take short walks with Edward or Nellie, or if they are busy, Jenny may tag along behind me. I am never out alone. My writing has become even more important to me. If they took away my journal, I would surely wither up and die.

So I tell my journal:

January 21, 1649

"I have become a sneak, a liar, and a spy. It is the last way I would have expected myself to behave, but I have no choice. I can sit here day after day, pining for what has passed, my mind starving for lack of something to stimulate it. Had I something to think about — some new ideas to consider, even some good discussion of town events — then perhaps the mournful nostalgia that accompanies my thoughts would dwindle. It will never go away; for lack of other food, my mind preys upon the past, swallowing again and again the same dreary mess of pottage. I grow weak for lack of mental nourishment. So I become a spy, lurking and listening in dark corners.

"After service, people make only the blandest remarks to me, as if they were speaking to a three-year-old. No one will tell me anything of importance for fear it will unhinge my already feeble mind. I may not hear about weddings because I will be sad at not being able to attend them. If a notable preacher comes to town now, I am not told of it as his fiery sermons would disturb my teetering equilibrium. I might even speak out in the assembly, or cry distressfully, bringing shame upon my husband. According to Nellie, when the spiritual gentleman remarks on my absence, my husband says delicately that I am unwell. The visitor probably believes that I am soon to give birth, and Edward never corrects him. It is easier for him to let the implication stand than to say, 'My wife is losing her reason,' which he is now convinced is happening little by little.

"Some local news is censored by those who care for me. I am not told of the lashings given to Mr. Timmins' runaway slervant, Joel, nor even that he has tried to run away. When I remark that I have not seen Joel tramping by with his sacks of grain for the Timmins' cows, I am told that he has been sick and is resting. Listening on the back stairs to the voices coming up from the kitchen, I discover that the open sores on his back have become infected, and he cannot do heavy work again. His contract has been sold to a poultry farmer, and he is not seen in town again. Joel was one of the sweetest souls I knew, always greeting me politely. One day, I remember, he handed me a bunch of lily of the valley, 'For a kind lady,' he had said. I shall miss him.

"Edward has taken a chamber to himself for good, it seems, because I am so restless at night, so Nellie continues to sleep in my room, just in case I should need anything in the night, they tell me. But I know they suspect I will harm myself by jumping out the window or setting the house on fire. She tells me her secrets and I tell her some of mine. I know, for instance, that she has been stealing out at night to meet a young fellow in the barn. I tell her she is a fool to do this; someone will catch her, and she will be severely punished. Being a servant out of doors, in the dark, most certainly will bring on the lash as punishment. For an unmarried wench to lie with a man? The penalty would be much worse. I heard someone tell of a woman who was warned out for becoming pregnant. She had nowhere else to go, and the man would not marry her, as he was married already. I ask Nellie how she would like to be sent away from Hartford all alone, and she hangs her head and says, 'I couldn't bear that, Mistress.' Then she says reluctantly that she will not see this young man again except after church. I doubt she can keep her promise; when she speaks of him, she is as gay as a lamb bounding through clover. I tell her that if she ever goes out again she must be very careful. I can see the excited glint in her eye as I speak."

3.

I MISS THE LOCAL NEWS because it cuts into the everyday tedium, but, more important, I long for news of the wider world, of the other colonies and the homeland. Since it seldom comes my way, I go after it on my own. I am now a confirmed eavesdropper, listening on the staircase, and even more boldly at half-open doors. I look for the post to arrive; even sealed letters can reveal something. I watch arrivals at the house from my window, and the comings and goings along Governor's Row. My hearing has become acute, as I have trained myself to listen for regular and familiar sounds, and those unusual ones that suggest some variety, a little excitement in our ordinary lives.

When the crier calls to waken the town at seven o'clock, I am out of bed immediately, hoping to have a peek at someone trying to steal home after a night of unlawful merriment, or something even worse. I grasp at any new occurrence that might enliven my day. Everyone in Hartford works strictly by the clock. This makes spying a lot less difficult than one might think. I know at what hour Edward will confer with Cook, then with Henry and Nellie; at what time on Thursdays the farm overseer will come to report, and when on Fridays the mill manager will bring the accounts. Edward's own counting house is now located just across the yard from the house, easy to keep a watch on. Edward leaves for the mill every day except Sunday at eight-thirty and returns at ten to have breakfast with me. Afterwards, he goes back to the mill, or on some days to the meeting house; later, the man arrives with fish, the boy comes back from the root cellar with vegetables, and Cook begins preparing dinner.

Some days, though not often now, Edward receives a trader from Boston or New Haven, and holds him for dinner. Sometimes, on those days, I eat in my chamber, and Edward makes excuses. It depends on how I have been behaving that day. If the men stand in the hall, I crouch on the stairs above and can usually catch most of what they are discussing. I learn a great deal from these conversations, although the news is not always heartening.

It is while sitting hunched on the stairs in a bundle of clothes on a cold February morning that I hear of King Charles's execution. At first I am mystified, not knowing of whom they are speaking.

"They say he behaved nobly right to the end. I would have expected that of him," says Edward.

"Noble is as noble does," the New Haven merchant says. "He was a proud and intransigent man, cruel to many, especially to us. I cannot shed a tear. He did deserve to be punished, and if Mr. Cromwell made a mistake in sending him to the block, the Lord will correct it in heaven."

Edward, ever tender-hearted, sighs. "I hope it was not a grievous sin to do so. King Charles was not a good man, but perhaps we do wrong in deciding what God's judgment might be in such a crucial situation."

King Charles executed by Cromwell! My heart races, and I am overcome with such tremors that I nearly fall down the stairs. Hastily, I try to pull myself up and make for my room, but my shoe knocks at a railing, and I am heard.

Edward looks up, surprised to see me. "Anne, what are you doing there, my dear? You look pale. Don't you think you should lie down? There's plenty of time before dinner."

"Yes, I will. I was just coming to get some water to bathe my forehead."

"But I think you have a pitcher of water in your chamber," Edward says anxiously.

"Oh yes, I forgot. I'm sorry," and I turn away quickly before I find myself saying anything more. Stupid, stupid excuse. I only make things worse. I can almost feel the looks they are exchanging behind my back: my husband's smile of pity, the merchant's solemn and uncertain smile in return.

Charles, King of England, defender of the faith, dead at the hands of the dissenters, with Mr. Cromwell in the lead. I cannot believe what I have just heard. It is unthinkable that any Englishmen, or Welshmen either, would kill their anointed sovereign. Even if he were a monster, which the King was not, it is a sin against God's law. The King stands alone, under God, above the law of the people. If he fails in his duties, it is to God that he must answer.

In my mind I argue with the executioners, willing them to undo what has been done. Finally, I let my tears of outrage and sorrow stream down. I push my head into the pillow, and pull the bedclothes over so no one can hear me. I do not want them to find out that I know about the King, but for what reason I cannot say.

I mourn him as silently as I can, alternating between sadness and disbelief. As the truth sinks in firmly, I begin to ask, what will become of us now? If we are capable of regicide, of what other wickedness might we be capable? It is not just the proud King I mourn, though I regret the killing of any man, but the death of the one anointed to wear the crown. How can we survive when we have turned against the one God has chosen? How can we claim to be a Christian kingdom? With this murderous act the whole known Christian world seems to have collapsed.

I send word with Nellie that I will not attend the men for dinner, as I am unwell. The exhaustion of grief brings sleep, and when I wake up it is the next day. Nellie has come and gone, and has left a cold meal on the stool beside my bed. I cannot believe it, but I am famished.

Later, at breakfast, Edward decides that I need some fresh air to revive me, to give me some colour. Would I like to take a little ride in the cart with him, down to the mill and back, just an hour, no more? I consent; it is an opportunity to get out of the house, perhaps to improve my gloomy disposition.

All along the main street men are standing in little groups, their faces concentrated on the matter being discussed. Of course, it is the news of the King's execution that they are talking about. They give us hardly a glance as we pass, and no one raises his hat.

Is anyone going to tell me about the King, I wonder? Probably not. If there were an earthquake, or a fire that consumed all of London, I think they would not tell me. If the angel of death were to carry off a child from every seventh household, they would spare me the news. If the Second Coming were to happen—well, I guess there would be no hiding that event.

Later that year, when a plague of grasshoppers cleans out all the spring crops, I remember what I had been thinking on this day when the regicide was reported. The plague serves us right. It must be God's special withholding of his providence.

It is a week later, and the thought of King Charles's execution still continues to plague me day in and day out. It is not the poor soul's fate so much as our own that disturbs me. Finally, I cannot continue any longer to pretend I do not know what happened, and speak to Edward.

We are sitting down by the river on my old bench, wrapped up against the wind. I say, "Do you remember the morning you found me on the stairs coming down to get water?"

"Yes, I think so. Yes, I remember."

"I wasn't coming for water. I was listening to you and Mr. Oldacre. You were discussing the execution of the King."

Edward grimaces in dismay. "You were not supposed to…"

"I know, and I know why. You don't want to upset this delicate equilibrium that keeps me sane. Well, I can tell you that I am upset, and still perfectly sane, but keeping up a pretense of ignorance is not helping me at all. I do want to talk about it."

A pause, while he considers this news. Then, "Since you know, the worst harm has been done already. Did it sadden you very much? Now that I think about it, you do seem to have been very low in spirit these last few days. I have hardly been paying attention to you, I have been feeling so sad myself. I cannot keep my mind on my work for thinking about it."

"Yes, I am sad for the King's sake, but more than that I am appalled that Mr. Cromwell and the Parliament should overturn the law of God whose anointed deputy the King is."

"You are not alone in believing that. It was certainly the view of the Anglican members of Parliament, but they were kept out and not allowed to vote. Some Puritans did not agree with the trial either and voted against it. I would not have voted for it had I been a member."

"Of course you wouldn't have! It was a foul, unchristian act, unjust and — wicked!" I wind up out of breath.

Edward looks alarmed. "Now, now, dear, calm down please. I agree with you, but do at least try to understand that these men believed they were doing what had to be done for the sake of the people of England. They believed that Charles was a traitor and a tyrant, and could not be stopped by any other means."

"I know nothing about that, not hearing any news from England," I look pointedly at Edward before continuing, "but even if he were what they say, he should not have been executed. Killing a king in cold blood — why, look what it says about us Puritans and our righteous ways."

"It is a horrible blot on our conscience and our cause. What is worse for me is that a large number of people here are satisfied that justice was done."

"The circle around Mr. Stone, I suppose?" He nods. "Of course. Well, if this is the way of the saints to the new Jerusalem, I am stepping off the path."

"Don't say that, Anne dear. You know that most of the saints do not think the way Mr. Stone's followers do." He pulls me towards him, his arm sheltering my shoulder. We sit quietly for a moment, and then he decides to continue.

"I am afraid that the community is splitting apart, and the sides are growing more acrimonious every day."

At last I can speak with some authority. "It was bound to happen. My own experience with the Gertrudes told me so."

"The who?"

"The women's group. I call them the Gossiping Gertrudes."

Edward bursts out laughing. "That's rich. I guess they deserve that name."

"Oh, indeed they do!"

Our troubling conversation over, we walk back to the house chuckling together as if we have no worries in the world, all the while knowing that the moment cannot last.

4.

THERE ARE TWO YOUNG men for dinner today, our perpetual guest, the wan and silent Mr. Andrews, and a stranger whom Edward introduces as Dr. Lord, recently arrived from England. What a contrast between these two men: the one so pinched and sallow, carrying his thin frame like a bent pole; the other as robustly composed as our young oaks. I cannot help being drawn to him, not only for his appearance — silky dark hair, true blue eyes and a face creased with smiling — but for his cheery conversation.

Unlike the teacher's indifference to everything except his pupils' achievements, Dr. Lord has an inquisitiveness that comes from his appreciation of everything under the sun: the rich milk we serve ("What do your cattle feed on?"), or the fine wood of our dining table ("Is this native oak or English?"). He brings the teacher alive, asking him about his pupils and how well they write. He even offers Mr. Andrews a new graphite pencil to try that does not smudge like the old ones.

For the first time in I do not know how long, I find myself having a pleasant, almost jolly conversation with this man. He eats his food briskly, but with an enthusiasm I can see in his face. Then, having finished every morsel on his dinner plate, and scooped up the last of the pudding, he asks me, "Did you make that wonderful syllabub, Mistress?"

"No, I don't do any of the meals. Our cook does it all."

"Well, you have no reason to then, since you have such a good cook. I wish I could find someone as skilled as yours to cook for me."

I am almost at the point of saying, "I'll look for someone for you," when I remember that I do not go out among people who might know any more, and I have not any friends I can ask. The sudden dismal look on my face is not lost on him, so he quickly changes the subject.

"Would you allow me to have a peek at your garden? I see from the window that it is beautiful." He addresses me, not Edward, so I answer instantly, "Yes, we can go out here," and I move to the parlour door. Edward says, "I'll join you in a little while."

Dr. Lord is truly interested; he is not just being polite. He walks along under the apple trees, admiring their flourishing growth, and he notes with pleasure the little grove of honeysuckle and lilacs I planted when we first arrived. When we come to my roses, he asks me for the names of the few he does not know, which I happily supply. No one has ever shown such interest before. "Are you a botanist?" I ask.

"No, I'm just an ordinary physician, but in Cambridge where I studied, we had masses of roses. I've always loved them."

"Me too."

"You must have to spend a lot of time taking care of this lovely garden."

I hesitate, then blurt out almost ashamedly, "I hardly touch it any more. I'm not allowed to do much, because I'm supposed to be so delicate."

"And are you?"

I consider this. He is a doctor, so what should I tell him? Am I going to make it worse for myself if I say what I think? "I suppose I am now, but I never used to be. You see, I get these nightmares, and sometimes I black out, and no one knows why." I stop, and then rush on. "People think I am melancholy because I won't speak to them, but I am just afraid of saying what I think, which often goes against what they think. And now I'm not supposed to read much or write, because it's hard on my brain."

At this Dr. Lord shakes his head as if perplexed.

I say, "I'm sorry, I didn't mean to spill out my troubles like this. But I hate just sitting around getting worse and worse. I'm afraid to lose my mind altogether."

He says, "There's no danger of that, as far as I can tell. You seem perfectly sane to me. The only things that worry me are your nightmares and blackouts."

"They make me think I'm going mad."

He says sternly, "Not so fast, Mistress. We may find a cause of these and a remedy just around the corner." He gives me a smile that would put the sun to shame.

"Do you really think so?" I can hardly believe it.

"I do. Let me scratch my head a while, and consult my books, and I promise I'll find something." Another all-embracing smile.

"Oh!" I smile back, tentatively, and then as the thought grows in me, another gleeful, "Oh!"

Dr. Lord takes my arm. "I am so pleased to make your acquaintance, and I thank you for trusting me with your difficulties." Edward then appears in the garden. "Would you permit me to ask your husband for some help in deciding what to do?"

"Of course. Edward will be so relieved to know that something can be done for me," I say gratefully.

"Then perhaps you would give us some time together?"

"Yes. And thank you … for trying." I go inside and wait in the small parlour.

The two men stand for a long time beside my reading grove. I can see from the window that Dr. Lord is asking questions, and Edward is wearing his thoughtful look, as if he is struggling for the correct answers. Then they start walking along the path beside the house. When they reach the window where I am sitting, they stop again, unaware that I am there. I move to the side, and listen with one ear next to the window frame. Dr. Lord is speaking.

"There is one thing you haven't tried. I think it will surprise you when I suggest it. This isn't a new remedy, but one said to have been helpful in earlier times."

Edward interrupts him in some agitation. "I hope you don't mean some magical cure, some potion concocted by a witch. Because that definitely would not do, in my position, even if it were supposed to do good. Besides,

I don't believe in magic. It's an illusion of the Devil."

The doctor says, "Good sir, I would not think of suggesting such things. I am a man of science. I don't believe in magic either, even if I am not always sure where the dividing line is."

Edward says, "Thank goodness. Well then, what else is there?"

Dr. Lord continues. "What I am suggesting is perfectly natural, sensible, and within every man's power to grant his wife. In fact, I have read that without this act, women are apt to become melancholy. I refer to the act of intercourse."

I peek out. Edward looks utterly astonished. Dr. Lord says, "What I don't know is whether this will turn back the clock, so to speak. I have never read that the loving act would cure the condition, but in your situation, sir, I suggest that you have nothing to lose by trying it."

Edward sounds anxious. "Don't you think that she will become too excited? We have lived as celibates for several years now."

"I understand. No, I think that if she is aroused, it will do her some good. And at her age she is unlikely to become pregnant, or if she does, she will lose the child in the womb."

Edward says, "But…" The doctor interrupts. "Don't worry. In my opinion, that will not happen."

They move out of earshot, and soon after I hear Dr. Lord saying goodbye.

I decide to say nothing about what I have heard. No matter what the reason, it will be so marvelous to have Edward with me after such a long time of abstinence. Already I can imagine how it feels to be embraced, to be kissed long and tenderly and to return his kisses, and to have him enter me fully, giving up something of himself to me.

This very evening I hear Edward say to Nellie that he is going to sleep in his wife's room, "to give her some needed comfort."

Nellie, who is nobody's fool, suppresses a smile and says, "Yes, sir." I can see her making plans to meet her young man tonight.

Edward is so gentle with me. He gives no reason for being in bed with me except "I've missed you." I reply, "So have I, my dearest husband." I embrace him with my thin arms, but being so weak, I cannot hold him for long. He, knowing how easily I tire, tries to hold himself over and above me as long as possible, until he cannot wait any longer and thrusts himself inside me. I lie quietly rigid, making no sound, although the pressure on my small body is painful.

It is soon over. Edward sighs with the exquisite pleasure of release and I echo him. Then, reluctantly, he leaves. "I must not tire you any further, my sweet," he says.

"Goodnight, Edward. I do love you so."

5.

THESE EARLY SUMMER DAYS I am in the garden, wandering idly about, looking to see if any new shoots have appeared since the day before. Although the trees and roses are thriving beautifully, there is not much left of my original flowerbeds now. After ten years, many plants are exhausted and have disappeared, replaced by invading wild grasses. Later in the summer, they will be dragged down by the bindweed that draws them to itself. I can see what has happened, but at present I lack the strength to attack the mess. The weeds are too tough for me; their roots are planted deeper than mine. If I stood too long in one place, they would have me, too. I poke a bit at the creeping Jenny, yank at the wild carrot, but it too is adamant. Is it the flowers that were not meant to be here, or is it myself?

One day I feel quite faint, even a little nauseous, sitting on the garden bench. It is not very hot, and the sun is hardly visible through the apple trees' foliage. I go to get myself some water, and decide to lie down until the faintness passes.

The second time it happens, I begin to worry. I am thin, scrawny even. Am I coming down with the ague, which goes after the weakest first? That morning I had called a greeting to two children who were passing in the road. When they saw me peering over the fence, they squealed like little piglets and ran off. They must have thought I am a witch. After they had run away, I looked at my reflection in the windowpane once, and did not recognize myself. Indeed, I am like a witch, or a changeling. This queasiness is what comes when I am being transformed from one body to the other.

I stop myself abruptly. I must not go on thinking like this, it is the worst sort of heresy. Dr. Lord would be annoyed with me. He has given me hope, just a thread of it, but I must not let go of it. Besides, the memory of being together with Edward restores me a little. I hope he will come to me again soon. Then my nights will continue to be calmer, as they have been since the first time, and then he will stay with me to sleep by my side. So I tell no one about these odd spells, not even Nellie, for fear of being dosed with something nasty.

I might have told her, but when I get to my chamber, Nellie is waiting for me. I see immediately that this is no time to divulge my own worries, as she is in tears.

"Nellie? Whatever ails you?"

"Oh, Mistress, it's so horrible! You were right, and I was wrong, and there, it's gone and done now. There's nothing that can be changed, and I'm so sorry! It's just horrible!" She was beside herself, sobbing and putting her hands to her face, then twisting them together.

I do not find it too hard to guess what has happened. "You've been found out."

Nellie nods.

"Where were you, in the barn?"

Another nod and a sniffle.

"You were with your fellow?"

Nod.

"Were you...?"

Nod, and another burst of sobbing.

I put my arm around Nellie, who shakes me off. "No, Mistress, you shouldn't do that. I don't deserve it. I'm bad."

"You're very silly, that's what you are." I sigh. "I've been wondering how long it would be before you were caught."

Nellie eyes me. "I know who did it."

"Did what?"

"Told on me. It was Zachary. He was jealous because I wouldn't go to the barn with him. So he told Henry."

"Zachary! He's just a boy. You're much too grown up for him."

In spite of herself, Nellie has to smile.

I say, "I wonder what is going to happen now?"

Nellie starts to cry again. "The master says I must leave town. He says he's sorry, but he's obliged. He says he knows you will try and persuade him, but he'll have to refuse you. I don't know what I will do. My mother will be so ashamed, she won't speak to me."

I say, "Oh Nellie, we must do something. I can't bear it here without you." This catches Nellie's attention. "Maybe we should run away together."

Nellie is appalled. "No, no, Mistress, you can't leave here. It wouldn't do, you're too ... too delicate for hard work, which is what we'd have to do to get a living. Don't worry, I will get along. I just hate to leave you, that's all."

"Perhaps you won't have to after all," I say. "Now dry your eyes, and we'll see what I can do when Mr. Hopkins comes home."

Edward is hardly in the door when I come down the stairs determinedly. His look is grim but I start in on him anyway. "Edward, dear, it's about Nellie."

"I know it is, Anne. I am deeply sorry, but she must go. No, don't speak. I would keep her here for your sake, although if she were to be pregnant I would have to send her away before it was known. But the whole affair has been made public, and she will have to come before the court if I don't get her out of town before that can take place, because it would mean a nasty punishment."

I say, "Oh," in the most forlorn voice I have ever used. I know he is right.

"Now I have an idea. I am going to send Nellie to Boston with a note to David, asking if he will take her in. I am sure Ursula could use her help. In that way you can still keep in touch, and one day perhaps see her if you go to visit David. I hope that cheers you up a little."

It does. "Oh, Edward, you are such a dear, kind man. I really don't know how you can be with so much on your mind." I give his arm a weak squeeze..

"There, that's better. Now why don't you put Nellie out of her misery, and tell her where she's going?"

"I will, I will." I hurry to my chamber to give Nellie the news. Only later did my own misery at losing my dear companion come over me.

Inside Nellie's bundle of belongings that she carried to Boston is this letter:

June 18, 1649

Dearest Brother,

I fear that this may be the last time I will write you my true feelings, for my secret messenger, Nellie, who has always found a way to send my letters to you, leaves me to go into your care. I know you will find her trustworthy and good-natured. Please be good to her for my sake.

In her place they have hired an Indian woman to be my maid. She looks well-meaning and kind, but I have said I will not permit a stranger in my bed. She will have to sleep in the next room. There are things I do not want her to know.

I grow weary of this life now and sometimes wish it would be over. If I were to have an accident, or become ill, no one here would care except my dear husband — and you, of course, but you are far away. If I could only see you, there is so much I would tell you. But perhaps it is just as well this way. You have your own troubles.

I give you my fondest affection,

Your loving sister,

Anne Yale Hopkins

6.

THE NAUSEA I HAD begun to feel before Nellie left assaults me every day now, and it finally dawns on me that I am pregnant. At last! After so many fruitless years, Edward and I will have the child we had given up hope of ever seeing. It is not too late after all. I start to dance around my room, until my stomach starts to churn, and I rush for a basin.

Weakened and lightheaded, I begin to take stock of myself. I am too thin, and have little appetite, no strength in my legs, and even my arms are weak. This is no condition in which to produce a healthy baby. I must remedy it as soon as I feel better. At least I can start to walk out again in the afternoons. I decide not to tell Edward until I am much better, as he would worry even more than he does now. When he sees me going about outdoors it will encourage him.

What an odd life I am leading now: the mornings so wrackingly miserable I can hardly bring myself to get out of bed, and the afternoons beginning to take on a happy countenance as I think about the Hopkins family of the future.

For a time this is the pattern, a predictable see-saw. Then my dreams begin again, fearful dreams in which everyday happenings shift over into macabre scenes where I am either the victim or a terrified observer. I wake often in the night to find the Indian woman, Rebecca (she has been baptized), bending over me, smoothing my forehead, rubbing ointment on my throat and face. In the morning I remember only snatches of these nightmares.

In one, Mother and I are walking on the sand. A big black shadow swoops over us; it is a large bird. I run away, and then I am in a room of blue mirrors. My body looks distended, my mouth is wide open, screaming. I wake up, and I am really screaming. Rebecca gives me something and I sleep.

At first, the scenes in my dreams have no relation to my condition. It is as though in sleep I have another life altogether. Most dreams are filled with horrors; in yet another, I feel an army of spiders crawling over my body and spinning a web of fine wire. In another, I see my husband paddling in a light craft, heedlessly rushing towards a steep waterfall.

This time when fear wakes me, I have trouble knowing where I am, believing I am on the riverbank frantically calling Edward. Only his voice as he stands beside my bed, asking if I am all right, brings me back to the present.

I note these dreams sketchily in my journal, along with the reason for brevity, "I am running out of ink."

The last dream I record in my journal changes everything:

June 30, 1649

"I am in a cave. It is so dreadfully dark I can only see tiny white flashes of some weird thing, but I do not know what it is. It seems to be waving, which is why the light comes and goes. In the dark it cannot see where to go. It is hopeless."

At this I wake, shaking. I am the cave. This thing, this creature, my child, is inside in the dark. It is alone, cold, trapped there. It is frantic, beating at the walls. I must let it out.

The more I feel this, the agony of my unborn child, the more I know I must do something. Each day makes it more urgent, as the child is flailing about, turning helplessly over and over. I can think of nothing else, and barely answer Edward when he speaks to me. He is really worried now, because he does not know why I am so distant. Rebecca, mother of six, knows very well.

"Do you feel bad, Mistress?" she asks. "This sickness will be over soon. I can give you herbs that will help."

I shake my head. "It will never be over unless I let it out."

Rebecca looks puzzled at first, and then she understands. "You don't want this child?"

I correct her fiercely. "Of course I want it, but she has to come out now, right now, or she will die in the dark. It is a terrible thing to have to stay in the dark."

Rebecca says, "If she comes out now she will die."

"No. If she stays in there she will die." I start to cry.

Rebecca says, "I can give you something to help her come out, some herbs I know. Do you want me to do that?"

I nod my head vigorously.

"Then I will go to my village and bring some for you." She leaves the room.

In the afternoon, I swallow the herbal drink Rebecca brings me. Then, I lie down, to wait for my child to be let out of the cave. The vision of the cave and the little thrashing limbs obsesses me now. I live only for the moment when the child will be free.

There are new rumbling pains in my stomach, now here, now there, as if an argument is going on within. With whom? The child herself? The Devil and the Lord? I am shivering with fear. Perhaps I was wrong. The child is stronger than I am. She wants to wait, to be born at the proper time, to be sure of her life. She will hate me if I do not do as she wants.

I try to make myself vomit, to bring up Rebecca's potion, to correct my terrible mistake. But it is too late. Nothing will come back. The disturbances in my stomach tell me that the process I have begun is unchangeable.

What have I done? Who might this child have been? A better person than I am certainly. A happier person? Or would she have inherited all her mother's persistent anxieties and sorrows? She might have carried the burdens of a woman's life here more resolutely, or perhaps she would have learned how to refuse them and brave the consequences. She might even have brought in new ideas, and made great changes for our betterment.

Would she have been loved? Of course! I would have loved her with all my heart.

My sobs seem to quiet the movement in my stomach for a while. I lie there, remorse battling against the determination that the child must escape the fearful place where she is trapped. Life, if there is to be any, is outside the cave.

By suppertime nothing has happened, and Rebecca comes to say that Edward is asking for me. "Come, Mistress. Have supper. You may have to wait a little while for the drink to work. Don't let your husband be anxious."

I get up woodenly and let Rebecca arrange my clothes. I have difficulty trying to think about anything else except what is going on inside me. I make my way to the stairs, start down, and seeing Edward below in the hall, say, "I don't feel very well. I'm a little lightheaded." I take another step, but my foot is caught in the hem of my gown. I fall. Edward catches me just before I reach the last step.

Two days later, after the doctor has removed the fetus and put a splint on my broken wrist, I lie in bed covered with bruises. A strange woman comes in every few hours and applies ointment to the worst of them. Rebecca has been sent back to her tribe. She is suspected of harming me in some way, but no one can discover how it was done.

I lie there, unable to move very much for the pain. In spite of this, I am much more content than before the accident. I remember now. It is a brief, ancient memory, but it is enough:

I am asleep in my little bed in our London house, when some noise wakens me. It is barely light outside, but I steal out of bed quietly so as not to alert my brothers who are sleeping in the same room. I always want to be the one to waken our father. The floor is cold, but I remember, I do not dare to put on my boots for fear of making a noise.

I tiptoe across the hall, knock quietly, and open the door of my parents' room. Surprisingly, my mother is up and gone downstairs so early. My father is lying on the bed on his back. He is already dressed, but he is sleeping, and the shutters are closed fast. The light from the hallway shows me that he is wearing his best Sunday suit.

I know now what this meant, but I take my four-year-old self through to the end. I go over to the bed and say, "Wake up, Papa! Are we going to church?" There is no reply, no movement, not even the flutter of an eyelid. I shake his shoulder, but it does not move. I touch his hand. It is freezing cold. Why does he not reach out and put his arm around me as he always does?

I try to clasp his fingers to get him to wake up, but they will not move, like the scraping claws of the dragon in my book. I whisper, "Papa?" Then, "You are so cold. Wake up and come down to the fire." I try shaking him, and at that moment my mother, passing by the room where her dead husband's body lies, sees the door open by mistake, and shuts it firmly. I hear the key turn in the lock. She does not notice me.

In the dark he is suddenly not my father, but something else, like a piece of marble wearing my father's clothes. I let go of his hand and start shrieking, "Papa!" But fear of this cold stiff creature beside me grows, so I crawl over to the wall, feeling my way along to the door and begin pounding on it with my fists screaming "Mamma!" over and over until I have no power to cry out and I collapse.

I shiver in my bed, reliving the moments after the door closed. At the time, it had felt like being sealed in a cave with a monster that once had been my father. I thought I would never escape, ever.

What seemed to me like hours later a servant, sent to look for me, heard whimpering sounds behind the locked door. My mother was called to come and open it and found me curled up on the floor. For a long time, weeks, I think, I could not speak. And voices came to me from a long way off. I have a slight memory of her standing over me, a statue in black, sighing wearily and saying over her shoulder to someone, "She is so stubborn. She will not snap out of it. How can she feel it so much, she is only four. It isn't like losing a husband." Once, when I was alone, she came to me and shook me roughly, hoping to hear me cry out, to start the sound of my voice again. When nothing changed, she left the room in exasperation. Finally she ignored me, and eventually I recovered my speech and hearing completely. She must have decided that the whole episode was best forgotten, because she never spoke about it to me or anyone else, as far as I know.

7.

L YING IN BED waiting for my body to heal, I have nothing to do but reflect. Even though the pains continue, I feel a new contentment wrapping me round like a soft fleece, assuring me that all will be well. Something has changed me, for good. Until now, I had guarded a part of myself, never letting anyone know about it, even me. It is what a child does, keeping her secrets, her dark inexpressible fears. Now I know my secret. I shudder when I think of it, the horror of that day, but it has no power over me any more.

Another disquieting shudder moves through me, arising from some hidden place. I wait for it to disclose its source, not wanting to know, because already I suspect what it is. It comes — and I must face it — from the empty space within that once held — "Ohh!" The shudder becomes a moan, as I think of the little unborn one that I have denied life. My child-to-be, lost through my fault, my deluded act. I weep on, quietly now, thinking of what might have been, had I only known what I know now.

But I did not know. I truly thought I was helping the child to live. It was madness of a sort, but it was not a sin. I have lost what I longed for, a child of our own, but I must believe now that it was God's will. I am beginning to understand that something within myself can diagnose and heal me. God has given me that work to do. The sense of reassurance that I felt earlier returns.

Then I think of Edward, and guilt stabs at me. I have been too absorbed in my own pain and recovery to remember his sorrow over the lost child.

We have not spoken of it since. I know I owe it to Edward to explain what happened, but I cannot find the courage to do so. What shall I tell him? That I did not really intend to abort our child, as I was out of my senses, thinking she would die in a cave? He would term me completely insane, even if I assure him that I am recovered now.

So what can I tell him? That I am sorry I fell down and lost the child? That Rebecca gave me something to help me, and it made me lightheaded? Part lie, part truth, but it will revive our marriage. Shall I tell him that my blackouts are over? How could I explain to him about my father, and the cold, and the cave — no, I cannot go that far. It would leave him with too many doubts, which is not fair, as I am sure that all my fear of the dark is over. I shall have to show him that it is true.

Why not do it now? It is almost dark outside. Jenny has been in to light the candles, one beside my bed, the other in the window. I never sleep without two lights — at least I have not been able to before. Soon she will appear with my supper on a tray.

Gingerly I slide over to the edge of the bed and put my feet down. The pain in my stomach erupts. I think I cannot get up. I will. I stand up and force myself to take the few steps to the window. Then, I lean over and blow out the candle. I take myself back to bed. I blow out the other candle, and lie there wondering if this agony is worth it. I blame myself for being such a fool. I could have waited until I felt better but no, I had to prove I could do it now. And it is true: I am no longer afraid of the dark.

I hear Jenny clomping ponylike up the stairs, burdened with the tray. She stops at the closed door, and I visualize her shifting the tray to one arm as she reaches for the handle and opens the door into darkness.

"Aah!" There is the unmistakable sound of crockery smashing on the floor. "Oh no!" She does not move. Poor girl, I feel sorry for her.

From my bed I say, "Don't worry, Jenny. You could not help dropping it."

My voice alarms her even more. "Aah!" and then, timidly, "Are you in there, Mistress?"

"Yes, I am here, and I am just fine. Go and get a taper for these candles and see for yourself."

From below comes the pounding of many feet, and then the glimmer of candles appear as they climb the stairs. It sounds as though the entire household is coming. "What has happened? What is wrong? Is she hurt?" Where is she?"

In all this turmoil, there is not a peep from Jenny. Suddenly, all the candles are in my chamber, and above each one a pair of inquisitive eyes.

I say, "Nothing is wrong at all, good people, except that I will have to wait a little longer for my supper. I expect that Jenny caught her foot on something and the tray went over. At least she did not." I attempt a little laugh, even though it hurts. I must convince them all that I am sane and cheerful.

I watch them look around the room, then at me, and finally at each other. I say, "Thank you all for looking after me so well. I am sure I will be downstairs and bothering you very soon. Now, do please light those two candles, and help Jenny with the bits and pieces. And Cook, I can do with a bit of bread and some broth tonight, to save you more work."

With a manner so affable I can hardly believe it is she, Cook says, "You will have the very best meal I can prepare, Mistress. You will be back on your toes quick as quick, if I have anything to do with it."

At that, they all turn around and make their way below, very quietly. I can just imagine the noise they will make behind the kitchen door. Soon a report will leak out that there has been a miracle at the governor's house. The devils that were attacking the mistress in the dark have departed.

Edward has been away all day at a cattle auction, so he has missed the furor. When he comes home it does not take long for him to hear the story, now so exaggerated that most of the truth has been squeezed out of it. He comes upstairs, where I am dozing after the hearty supper Cook sent up.

"Anne, how are you?"

I smile and hold out my arms to him. He comes to sit on the side of the bed. I can just reach his shoulders with the tips of my fingers. "I have never felt so well, dear. Come closer, do."

He leans forward, bends down and kisses me. My arms go around his shoulders, but a stab of pain forces me to pull back. I say, "As soon as these pains go away, I shall be perfect — perfectly healthy, that is."

"That is wonderful news." Then he pauses. "Jenny says she had some sort of mishap with your supper."

I smile to myself, listening to him approach the subject so delicately. Edward would hardly rush in and say, "I hear you are not being attacked any more," nor do I think he would believe such a story. I say, "Oh, it was nothing. I think she was surprised to find me in the dark. Actually, I am surprised myself, because all of a sudden I am not afraid of it any more. Odd, isn't it?"

He looks puzzled, then his eyes open wide and he smiles. "It is, but thank goodness for it, however it came about. You must be immensely relieved."

"I am." And you must be too, dear longsuffering man. "Now we'll have to find a way to stop the story that devils were seen scooting along Governor's Row and into the river."

He bursts out in a great hearty laugh that says more than any words could, that a gigantic millstone has just been lifted off his chest.

VII
Hartford, 1651

1.

WHEN THIS LETTER was brought to me earlier in the small parlour, I was just about to begin writing to David, telling him that despite the narrow confines of colony life, I was beginning to accept it with a more sanguine attitude. What I could not stomach I would avoid, and I would try to find little jewels of loving kindness in the hard social clay. This was my intention, until David's letter arrived.

Boston, March 21, 1651

Dearest Sister,

I write in haste, as Ursula and I are in the midst of packing our belongings. We have finally decided to return to England, and will leave within the month. As you know, I have been dismayed by the narrow vision of the governor and council of the Bay Colony, and even at times been badly treated. Ever since Governor Winthrop died two years ago, the discrimination against those of us who are not Puritans has grown worse. I see no future for me here.

I have done well as a merchant, so I will not have any difficulties that way. My intention is — this will please you, I am sure — to live for a time at Plâs Grono, before setting up in London. Even after that I will spend as much time there as my business will allow. I want David and Elihu to have the same carefree summers as we had when we were children.

Since Grandfather died, the dear old place has suffered from lack of care. I wish to remedy this quickly, and will make every effort to bring

Plâs Grono back to life. If you and Edward should eventually decide to return, I want you to consider it your home, as much as you would like to make it so.

I am sorry I did not tell you earlier about our decision to leave Boston, but I was afraid to grieve you, and kept putting it off. I fervently hope that we will soon gather across the ocean, where we can all look forward to happier times in London, and in Wales.

Your loving brother,

David Yale

I cannot believe it. It is too much for me to bear. He is going home and leaving me here, David, my firm pillar, the one who never gave up on me, when even Edward wavered. My tears fall, staining my new silk frock, given to me by Edward to celebrate my return to health. The recovery is short-lived.

Edward finds me here a little later, sniffling up my tears and dabbing at my dress.

He is alarmed. "Whatever is wrong?"

I show him the letter. He reads it through and shakes his head glumly. "So he has finally decided to go. I cannot say I blame him. He has not had an easy time in recent years."

He turns to me. "How sad for you, though. And for me, too. David is such a good old friend, as well as my brother-in-law."

I do not dare speak for fear I will start the flood again. I just nod, wipe my eyes, and sit with my head down.

Edward says, "Sometimes I think we should leave too." I raise my head at this. "This colony has changed, and for the worse. The chief problem is that there aren't enough strong, fair-minded people to lead the way and keep control. The conversions are not coming as we had expected, and since Mr. Hooker's death, even some of the recently received saints have fallen away.

"You know I have always believed that all explanations of good and evil come from the Lord, so one should always seek the Lord to know his will.

But lately there have been so many examples of misrule, of revelry run amuck, brutal attitudes on the part of the saints that I am beginning to wonder how the Lord is to be served, by me in particular."

I know he is upset at the hardening of attitude towards those who might appear to be different from the rest of us. For example, last year the Carringtons were found guilty of consorting with the Devil, although no exact evidence was discovered. Edward was a magistrate at the trial, and governor at the time of their execution, which caused him much distress, wondering if they might have been innocent of the charge after all. Then, recently, someone at the council meeting raised the question of what to do about the lunatics roaming their streets. The prison could not accommodate them all, and there was no means of treating them, particularly those who were indigent. Clearly, the town was taking a harsher stand against aberrant behaviour than it had in its earlier days. Edward could not help but ascribe this position to the preaching of Mr. Stone and the attitude of his devoted circle. Privately, I wondered whether the council was indirectly hinting to Edward about me. How that would have angered him.

Trying not to press him too eagerly, for fear that he would think I am losing control of myself again, I say evenly, "You have given twelve good years to Hartford, and served the colony well. Perhaps it is time to let someone else take on the responsibility."

"Perhaps so. I think there is little I can do to change things. I am too old, and I lack the strength I used to have." He pauses a moment.

"As a matter of fact, there is one possibility." I look at him expectantly. "I didn't want to tell you just yet, but with David's announcement, I think I should, even if it is not completely arranged." He is smiling.

"What is it? Please, hurry up and tell me!"

"I have had a letter from Mr. Cromwell offering me the appointment of commissioner of the navy. Evidently he thinks my experience with overseas trade would be useful."

I can hardly believe my ears. "You have? You are? You mean, we will be going home?" I stop suddenly, realizing how selfish this sounds. "Oh Edward, what an important appointment! How proud I am of you!" I throw my arms around him and hug with all my little strength. He laughs and wraps his arms around me too.

"That's better. That's my Anne, full of your old liveliness. Yes indeed, although I have not accepted yet, I do believe I should. Then we will be going home, but not just yet."

I step back, worried.

"You know that I have just been reelected governor for this coming year, so I will have to wait until next summer to take up the position. I will write Mr. Cromwell to tell him so, and I hope he approves. Otherwise, he might want to appoint someone else who could start in earlier. Now, do not be anxious about that. If he decides that I must come right away, then I will resign from the governorship and we shall go."

"Oh hurrah! The sooner the better, I say, but if we must wait, I shall do so with the best appearance I can put on, and think every day gone by is one step closer to home." I hug him again. "I must write David quickly and tell him. He will be so pleased. I will ask him to get Plâs Grono all ready for our return." I start laughing at the thought of it, and go over to my writing table to pick up the pen and paper where I had left them earlier. Edward is writing his letter too. The sun is out. The day is warm. I am alive again.

2.

M Y SECOND LETTER to New Haven brings a doleful reply:

June 9, 1651

My dearest Daughter,

Your letter arriving today brings me mixed satisfaction and sadness. I am so happy for you, to be leaving these bleak and difficult shores for the soft green land that we love so much. It will not be the same as when we left it, but the worst days are over, and your husband in his new position will be able to assure you of a tranquil life.

My sadness comes from the thought of your departure, and David's, as he has written to me too. With only Thomas left to me (Hannah and I are estranged still and Ellis and I were never close), I feel the darkness closing in around me, and wonder when it will all end.

For a brief moment I almost yielded and said yes to the offer from you and your kind husband to take me home with you. How gladly would I have come, had I been able. I would have left the house in a run, bringing nothing with me but a full heart. But I cannot. I must not leave. Theophilus is aging quickly; sometimes he has such severe pain in his legs that he cannot walk unaided. I must stay and look after him now. He has always done what he could for me, keeping me with him after that terrible trial and its consequences, when everyone urged him to banish me.

Ours has not been a loving marriage like yours, but it has been an hon-

361

ourable one. Since he has been less active, he has grown less demanding, easier to please. We have better times together now; you could say that we are friends.

So I will stay in New Haven as long as he lives. Then, if God and time permit, I shall join you. In the meantime, dear Anne, kiss the soil of Plâs Grono for me, and remember me in your prayers

Your loving mother,

Ann Lloyd Eaton

"Amen," I say.

VIII
The Voyage Back, Boston, 1652

1.

OF ALL THE PEOPLE we have spoken to since we arrived in the Bay Colony, not one can remember a hotter summer than this one since the very beginning. Today, with the sun burning through a misty sky, the harbour is almost unbearable. The only visitors to the wharves are the flies attracted to the cargo being loaded onto the ships and the mosquitoes drawn to those doing the loading. The usual groups I had expected to see — of ship owners, traders, and customers — are wisely indoors, probably prostrate on their beds, or vainly trying to alter the temperature with their fans.

As our carriage makes its way into the harbour, we see that at the far end of the Long Wharf the *Susannah* is being readied for her voyage to Portsmouth. Longshoremen are moving back and forth between the quay and the ship loading bales of flax. The English mills are greedy. Tobacco, a risky investment should it get damp, travels in tight wooden casks, the weight of which would bring down any ordinary man. We watch as the last item of the cargo is taken aboard: the prized white pine timber, a hundred feet long, destined to be masts for the largest ocean-going ships. These will be fastened to lie along the deck; there is no other space that can take them.

The driver pulls up the coach beside the *Susannah* for us to get out. I step down gingerly, afraid to lose my footing on the uneven boards of the wharf. Edward takes my arm, as I am still quite frail.

As we approach the gangplank, the ship's captain comes down to meet us. "Welcome aboard, sir," he says to Edward, "and to you, mistress." His dignified tone is meant to indicate that he knows the importance of his passengers, and will attend to us accordingly.

"Thank you," Edward says. Turning to me, he says, "Come, Anne, let us go aboard. The ship will be leaving soon for England."

"Home," I say fervently. "I am going back to Plâs Grono. It will heal me completely. I am sure of it, Edward. Don't worry any more."

I step lightly onto the gangplank.

Historical Notes

ANNE YALE WAS BORN in Chester in 1615 to Ann Lloyd and Thomas Yale, a bookbinder. Her father died when she was four years old, and her mother remarried when she was twelve. In 1636, she married Edward Hopkins (b. 1600) and they left for New England in 1637, where they settled in Hartford in 1639. They had no children. They returned to England in 1652. In 1657, Edward became a member of Cromwell's Parliament, and died the same year. Anne died in 1698, age eighty-three. She is buried in the graveyard of St. Giles Church, Wrexham, not far from Plâs Grono. Of the books she is said to have written, there is no trace of any of them.

Edward Hopkins was magistrate in Hartford in 1639, and governor every alternate year from 1640 to 1654 (even though he lived in England by then), deputy governor for the years in between (at the time, a governor could only serve a one-year term). At his death he left a thousand pounds and a considerable library to the school in Hartford, and five hundred pounds to Harvard.

Ann Lloyd was born c. 1591, the daughter of Bishop George Lloyd of Chester. She married i) in 1612, Thomas Yale, d 1619, by whom she had four children; and ii) in 1627, Theophilus Eaton (d.1658, by whom she had three children, including Hannah). They came to New England in 1637, and moved to New Haven the next year, where Eaton became the first governor. After his death, Ann returned to England in 1658, and died the following year.

David Yale was born in 1613, and came to New Haven with the Eatons in 1637. He and his wife Ursula moved to Boston in 1641. They had three children, Elizabeth, b. 1644, d. two months old; David, b. 1645; Elihu, b. 1649. They returned to London and Wales in 1651. David died in 1690.

After a prosperous career in India, Elihu Yale returned in 1699 to live in London and at Plâs Grono. In St. Giles Church, Wrexham, there is a stone plaque erected by him in memory of his family: his parents, two brothers, and his aunt. The last lines on the memorial are: "Anne Hopkins, spinster, obyt 14th Dec. 1698." Evidently Elihu knew nothing of the story of the wife of the governor of Hartford upon Connecticut.

Acknowledgements

THE IDEA FOR THIS NOVEL did not come out of the blue. I was doing a bit of genealogical research regarding the only ancestor my family ever talked about (I suspect all the others were poor Irish sheep stealers, as my father used to say), the Reverend Peter Bulkeley, founder of Concord, Massachusetts. He was one of the people who was "silenced" by Archbishop Laud, as were the ministers in my book. So he left a good living in England, and brought over a number of his congregation to settle in Concord in 1636, the same year that Thomas Hooker went to Hartford. I started looking through the vast journal written by Governor John Winthrop of the Massachusetts Bay Colony, and while turning pages to find Peter, my eye landed on the entry about Governor Hopkins bringing his wife to Boston to find a cure for her "distractedness," as they called it. As soon as I read that they thought she had lost her wits because she read too much and wrote many books, I knew there was a story there, a retelling that would be much closer to the truth of the matter than Winthrop's.

If you are keen to read further about this interesting time, I can suggest several books that were extremely helpful in my research for this book: Peter N. Carroll, *Puritanism and the Wilderness* (New York: Columbia, 1969); Bruce C. Daniels, *Puritans at Play* (New York: St. Martin's Press, 1995); David H. Flaherty, *Privacy in Colonial New England* (Charlottesville: University Press of Virginia, 1972); Stephen Foster, *Their Solitary Way* (New Haven: Yale, 1971); Stephen Foster, *The Long Argument* (Chapel

Hill: University of North Carolina Press, 1991); Claudia Durst Johnson, *Daily Life in Colonial New England* (Westport, CT: The Greenwood Press, 2002); Michael MacDonald, *Mystical Bedlam: Madness, Anxiety and Healing in Seventeenth-Century England* (Cambridge: Cambridge University Press, 1981); Edmund S. Morgan, *Visible Saints* (Ithaca, NY: Cornell University Press, 1963); Mary Beth Norton, *Founding Mothers and Fathers* (New York: Vintage, 1996) for Ann Lloyd Eaton's story; Frank Shuffelton, *Thomas Hooker, 1586-1647* (Princeton, NJ: Princeton University Press, 1977).

I am delighted to have received permission to have the painting by Nella Marchesini reproduced on the cover, and hope that the owner is pleased with the result.

Several people were kind enough to spend time with some or all of the manuscript, and to give me their honest criticisms and suggestions: Charis Wahl, my go-to editor; Ian Shaw and J. S. Porter, both longtime teachers and lovers of literature.

To my family, "the sibs," and especially my husband Bob, I send everlasting thanks for showing unflagging interest in the project, and encouraging me long after its (or my) best-by date.

Chronologically last, but definitely not least, I am indebted to Luciana Ricciutelli, Editor-in-Chief at Inanna Publications, for her shrewd and insightful skill at making a whole out of some loosely moving parts; and to Inanna Publications for their willingness to bring the story to light.